the Lion's Claw

PETER PADFIELD

THISTLE
PUBLISHING

This edition published in 2014 by:

Thistle Publishing
36 Great Smith Street
London
SW1P 3BU

www.thistlepublishing.co.uk

ISBN-13: 978-1-910198-33-9

EAST
AFRICA
in the
1880's

2°S

Tana River

Osi River

•Witu

Lamu

Kipini

4°S

Mombasa

INDIAN
OCEAN

PEMBA

6°S

•Zanzibar

Chapter One

'Sail on the port beam!'
    The cry floated down from the lookout on the fore cross-trees; below all hands were gathered about the fo'c's'le of Her Majesty's corvette *Dulcinea* shouting a gusty chorus to the wind.

> Round 'is arm 'e 'ad some crep'on
> Cause 'is wife was dead, poor soul,
> Round 'is waist 'e 'ad an apron –

The lookout's cry was no louder than the massed voices, but it had a different timbre, a drawn-out wail such as a drowning man might give, and there was a ripple of movement as faces turned and men stood on gun carriages or bitts to gaze over the rail.

> - cause 'is britches 'ad a nole –

Guy Greville stopped his routine pacing up the weather side of the quarterdeck and moved across to the port side, passing the helmsmen as he went and recalling them to their duty as they tried to peer out past the swelling arc of a staysail. The midshipman of the watch, Buckley, hurried towards him and stared up with a questioning look; he seemed very small against Guy, who made no response; his eyes, tinged with the steel of approaching dusk, swept the horizon. His mouth turned up at the corners, full lower lip and thrusting jaw suggesting a more than usually arrogant mood. The vulturine promontory of his nose, powerful, yet finely formed, was raised as if to scent out the stranger.

'A slaver!' shouted an off-duty youngster, skylarking in the mizzen shrouds above, and immediately there was an excited torrent of conjecture through the rigging. Guy swung on Buckley.

'Up y' jump! See if you can make her out!'

The lad darted forward.

The whole of the western horizon was a vivid, dusty red, which was reflected off the tops of the great seas rolling away in endless procession northwards, streaked with long tails of spume; the horizon was so distinct that the swell could be seen bumping along it. But from the deck there was no trace of the strange sail. Soon it would be dark; night followed rapidly on sunset in these latitudes. The moon would be near full, Guy thought; as yet the only clouds were gossamer threads high up, and low banks of cumulus to the southward.

It was the season for slavers; the south-west monsoons were gathering strength; all along the coastal estuaries from Quillimain and Kilwa, from the mangrove creeks and coral islands of the Mafia and Zanzibar channels, the dhows would be putting out and scudding before the wind towards Cape Guardafui and the Persian Gulf or the Red Sea. A few would be crammed with black human freight brought from the interior, stowed in the heedless Arab fashion amongst the ballast rubble and stores of food on the bottom boards; some would carry just a few slaves virtually indistinguishable from the crew; it would take an experienced man to separate them. Guy had no first-hand experience of the East African coast, but he had heard enough stories of the slave trade in the few weeks since the start of the *Dulcinea's* commission to be able to judge the chances. His anticipation quickened – not the lure of the 'head money' for each slave released, nor the principle of a blow struck in the name of decency, but simple lust for the chase and action.

The men of the fo'c's'le were silent, experiencing the same emotions, he knew, some looking upwards awaiting Buckley's report from the fore t'gallant yard.

'Point afore the port beam!' Buckley's attempt to make his voice carry away to the quarterdeck against the wind made him sound more than usually like a corncrake. 'A two-master – a lateener –'

A spontaneous roar went up from the hands on the fo'c's'le, answered by another outburst from the mizzen rigging.

'– heading nor'-easterly!'

A two-masted lateener; she would be a fair size. Guy calculated an interception course based on the dhow's position and her approximate course and speed by instinct as he turned from the rail and strode towards the binnacle; he dismissed the result almost before he had it. They would need to run straight for her to close the distance quick before darkness came down even though it would mean losing bearing, and in the end a longer pursuit.

He became aware of the captain emerging from his companionway, capless, the great tawny hedge of his side-whiskers and beard spreading across the lapels of a purple velvet smoking jacket; blue serge shore-going trousers and white canvas shoes completed the rig; as ever, the earl of Saxmundham looked immaculate. He had evidently been alerted by the break in the men's singing or the cheers which had greeted Buckley's report, or just by that sixth sense which informed sailing ship commanders, and his gaze swept quickly from Guy at the binnacle through the attitudes of the men on the fo'c's'le, up briefly to the weather leeches of the upper sails; Guy hoped the helmsmen had not allowed the stir of excitement to disturb their concentration, and looked up himself, thankful to see the canvas taut.

He pointed, 'A sail, sir!'

Saxmundham's right brow rose and there was a momentary gleam of humour in his eyes; already in the few weeks of the commission a remarkable sense of trust and fellow-feeling had developed between the older man and the young lieutenant, transcending the normal barriers of rank.

'A slaver! God bless my soul!'

Guy smiled and relaxed his tense position over the binnacle. A number of officers and midshipmen were appearing on the quarterdeck as if they had been summoned; they waited a respectful distance from the great man, drinking in the situation. Guy saw the first lieutenant, Smallpiece, moving towards them with his ambling, rolling gait. Saxmundham glanced at him, then back to the quartering seas, and up at the sails again. As the first lieutenant came up, he said, 'We shall run down and pay her a visit, Mr Smallpiece. All hands to wear ship if you please! And have the stunsails broken out!'

The groups on the quarterdeck and fo'c's'le dissolved in a kaleidoscope of movement as the first lieutenant shouted to the bo'sun, hovering by the mainmast, and the pipe shrilled for all hands. Bare feet pattered over the deck, coils of rope were thrown off the pins, bo'sun's mates chivvied the least rapid movers with hoarse curses which had long since lost their terror through constant use, fowls flapped and squawked in their coops between the gun carriages, and sheep in pens either side of the engine-room skylights described anguished circles and baa-aahed noisily; almost the only still figure was the captain in his customary conning position to weather of the wheel, bracing his legs against the leeward roll, his jacket glowing like the bright western horizon, a centre of calm in the frenzy.

'He'll never mak' use o' ma engines.' Guy found the chief engineer gazing up into his face. 'Saxmundham there –' the chief conveyed a wealth of meaning in the two words. 'He'd no' use the engines if he was chasin' the de'il himsel' – he couldna bring himself to it – he's too much *pride* –' He looked up at Guy, challenging him to dispute his matured conclusions. Guy was intent on the men of the afterguard by the spanker. 'It's a question o' face,' the chief went on, shaking his head. 'It's a terrible pride o' yon Saxmundham –'

'*Ready all!*' The captain's roar cut into the soliloquy. 'Put the helm up!' and after a pause, 'Brail up the spanker! Up mainsail! Let go the after bowlines! Man the weather after braces!'

There was a scurry of men tailing on the braces down the quarterdeck, hauling the yards around as the bows swung to port; the folds of the loose spanker slapped and strained as the wind caught them at a fresh angle from nearly astern.

'Square the head yards!'

Guy thrilled to the perfect timing as the hands in the waist ran away with the forward braces. The great yards stretched their towering expanse of canvas, tinged with a hint of pink from the sky, and swung easily round in the lee of the after sails.

'Helm amidships!' There was a pause as the bows continued to swing off to port, the ship slewing and surging as the seas lifted now under her port quarter. The hands forward were changing over the sheets of the fore sails.

'Steady at that!' The quartermaster repeated the order.

Guy moved quickly to the binnacle, gauging her heading from the swinging compass card.

'Haul aft the head sheets!'

The little ship corkscrewed and heeled to a stronger gust as she settled on her new point of sailing; the bows rose and fell, pressing out a wide lacework of foam as bands of bluejackets, grunting in unison, urged on by the bo'sun's mates, hardened in the sheets and belayed them around the bitts. Saxmundham called out, 'How does she head?'

'Nor'-nor'-west, sir!' They would be pointing just ahead of the dhow; he beckoned to Buckley who had come down from aloft.

'Up to your perch again and sing out how she bears.' The lad hurried away. 'And stay there!'

Buckley reached the fore rigging as Saxmundham boomed out orders for setting the stunsails, and he was almost knocked off the ratlines by a dash of topmen racing up; they swarmed out along the yards to prepare the booms and halliards for the extra canvas. Guy wondered how long they would be able to carry such a spread; the wind had been freshening during his watch, and it was time to think of taking off sail rather than crowding on more; at the same time he was intensely keen to see how the little corvette would respond, intensely anxious not to lose the dhow – stupidly anxious, he told himself; no one would win glory from the release of a few pitiful negroes. Even so, this stirring in the blood would not be reasoned away.

He started forward, the better to hear Buckley's report, which presently grated down, 'Fine on the port bow!' Saxmundham had judged it perfectly, just as he would judge precisely how long to hold on to the stunsails. The admiration Guy always felt during a demonstration of the Old Man's shiphandling flair mixed with exasperation. The thought of the captain rooted to his habitual spot by the wheel instead of being up on the bridge their lordships had provided, feeling the life of his beloved command through the soles of his feet, riding the seas with her like a horseman, sensitive to every movement of every man and group in the rush of activity swirling about him, balancing the pull and set of each sail in the intricate scaffolding of masts and yards was a splendid and at the same time most irritating image; it was a picture of a lifetime's acquired mastery fast becoming valueless. The chief engineer was right, probably more right than he knew: the pride of the sailor challenged by clanking engines that made light of all his skills was a terrible pride. Saxmundham knew it, too. He was not one of the blood and pluck brigade that equated sailing seamanship with the strength and grandeur of the Navy and Empire, but an intelligent man who had made a deliberate choice. He might easily have come to terms with the steam service as others had done, many of far less real ability; with his powerful family 'interest' he might now have command of a first-class battleship in the Mediterranean fleet, well up the narrow ladder to the plums of his profession. But he had made his choice; he was serving out his time in an old corvette on the East Indies station, chasing bug-ridden dhows, bringing British law and Christian standards to warring chiefs and recalcitrant sheikhs – superbly drilling a generation of young officers and seamen in skills that would never be required. And with the wit to know it....

'Hoist away!'

Sheaves squealed as the rolled canvas was run up to the fore topmast yard, now extended by the stunsail boom; the hands on the yard cut the stops, the sail cracked out like a whip and shivered before all until it was brought under control, struggling against the sheet and tack. The t'gallant stunsail and then the lower stunsail followed, juddering and straining against their booms, which looked like broomsticks against the solidity of the yards, and threatened to snap with the pressure of the gusts that tore at them. The *Dulcinea* swooped and heeled and swept on for moments together like a surf boat as seas rolled under, twisting her briefly from the helmsmen's control as they leaned on the spokes of the great treble wheel, then dipped her bows and settled as another sea built up under the counter. The rigging quivered with unearthly sound, and strange groans and jarring noises from below told of the strain the beams and stringers, hull plates and rivets were called on to withstand; overside the water hissed and gurgled and tumbled up the approaching seas.

Guy balanced his way back to the binnacle, sure that adjustments would be needed in the after canvas to damp down some of the little ship's contortions. The captain was silent, watching the helmsmen as they fought her to her course, occasionally staring up at the sails with his head cocked slightly to starboard. The first lieutenant came to the quarterdeck and was told to pipe down the port watch. Not long afterwards the strains of a Christy minstrel rose from the fo'c's'le — 'Now Adam was de fust man an' Eve was de oder' — There was no doubt about what the hands expected to find on the morrow. He walked some paces forward and called up to Buckley for a report on the sail. It was almost right ahead. By the time he came back the captain had made up his mind about the balance of canvas and ripped off a list of instructions. Guy told off the hands for the tasks. Gradually the little ship quietened. She still stormed along with the great spread of forward sail threatening to tear itself from the bolt ropes, and the topmasts and t'gallants and stunsail booms, quivering and bending like alders in a gale, but her leaps and sudden staggers were more predictable, the swing of her stern more controlled.

He called for the quartermaster to heave the log, and stood by with the fourteen-second glass, tapping it against his palm to clear the central aperture; as the piece of white bunting marking the beginning of the measured line ran around the reel and flicked past over the side he turned the glass. The reel unwound at a furious rate and the first leather mark came up in no time, soon followed by the first of the knot markings. He heard the quartermaster suck in his breath.

He held the glass at eye level. The upper cone of sand dwindled to nothing. 'Stop!'

The quartermaster held the reel and seized the line. 'Five was the last 'un, sir!'

They let the reel unwind slowly until the six-knot mark was revealed.

'Two fathoms short of the six,' Guy said. 'Eleven and a half knots.'

'Eleven and an 'arf!' the quartermaster exclaimed. 'They'll want wings, them nigger-stealers!'

Guy walked back to the wheel, calling out, 'Eleven and a half knots!' to the captain's back. He heard the helmsmen exchange oaths. Saxmundham was slapping his hand against his side, muttering invocations to the ship or the wind gods, he couldn't make out the words as they were whipped away by the gusts.

The first lieutenant was on the quarterdeck again, gazing anxiously forward at the stunsails as though expecting them to snap the booms and tear away at any moment. After several minutes of concentrated attention he turned and ambled towards Guy, a worried expression on his broad, dark leather face.

'You'll post extra lookouts.

Guy nodded briefly; the reminder was too obvious.

There was always this tension; a vast gulf in age, experience and background lay between them, and neither was sufficiently forward or communicative to bridge it.

Guy had no idea of Smallpiece's age; he looked and usually moved like an old man, although it was noticeable that when things needed smacking about he could be as active as the best. Certainly the hands respected him as an iron-bound officer who knew the business of a sailing ship better than they did; they worked in awe of his contempt for anyone who failed to measure up to his own rigorous standards of seamanship and duty. Guy knew less about his background than his age. Despite five weeks' close proximity in the wardroom he had never heard a word or a hint about his people; he might have arrived in the world, fully clad in his shapeless serge, by way of the hawsehole of a man-of-war. His accent smacked vaguely of the West Country, but it was difficult to tell if this were a natural dialect watered down by years in the wardroom or whether he had acquired it in modified form from West Country crews. All that was certain was that he lacked gentle upbringing. In this respect he was more out of place than Saxmundham; he was a survivor, one of the few still serving, from an older tradition of officers less socially favoured, who had gained commissions through the now defunct master's branch. It was rumoured that he had won promotion from mate during the Ashantee wars.

Guy had the feeling that there was more to the coolness between them than their different backgrounds; in other ships such differences cemented friendships as often as they created barriers, and he put much of the tension down to his own relationship with the captain, never overstepped on his own part, nor emphasized by the captain, yet the nuances were difficult to disguise. He guessed the first lieutenant's attitude was coloured by jealousy.

'Lower stunsail halliards and tacks'll need hardening in,' Smallpiece said. 'They've shrunk in the locker.'

'I'll see to it,' Guy replied.

They stood in silence. The red was fading from the western sky and the sea had turned several shades darker; the white lines of driven foam stood out starkly. Guy shivered, feeling for the first time the bite in the wind.

'We need another half an hour of light,' Saxmundham shouted over the noises of the weather. Guy hadn't noticed his approach. 'Half an hour – that's all!'

Smallpiece said, 'D'you suppose she's seen us?'

'Scoundrels!' Saxmundham replied.

The wind rose in gusts, howling through the rigging; the ship surged and dipped into the troughs.

Saxmundham turned to them again. 'She's a witch, Mr Smallpiece. God bless my soul –!'

The first lieutenant glanced doubtfully into his face, his gaze lifting to the vast expanse of unreefed main topsail, lingering there. Guy, too, wondered if it were not already too late to shorten sail with safety. At the same time the wildness and fine balance of stresses within the web of canvas and shaking rigging induced a feeling of intense exhilaration.

The captain seemed to sense their doubts. 'The just shall live by faith, Mr Smallpiece,' he roared. 'You and I understand that – and Greville here –? This is the grand point, Greville. You may forget your breaking strains and your seamanship primers – what, Mr Smallpiece!' He laughed hugely.

His shoulders were still heaving as Buckley's voice stretched down from forward. 'Sail is lo-ost!'

Smallpiece started. 'Damn my eyes –!'

Saxmundham put out a restraining hand. 'These fellows take in their sails when it comes on to blow. And at nightfall. I'll wager he's bendin' on a smaller suit – the rascal!'

'If he hasn't seen us.'

'Perhaps the beggar's nothin' on his conscience.' He turned to Guy. 'Find out where they lost him!'

Guy started forward, leaving Smallpiece grumbling that he'd never known an Arab with a conscience, let alone a clear one. The Old Man's bellowing laughter followed him down the deck.

'She was right ahead before she disappeared,' Buckley yelled down in answer to Guy's shout.

'Keep searching!' Guy called up, and turned to the bo'sun who had appeared at his elbow. 'Tell off three smart youngsters and one old hand to the lookout. Make sure they have glasses. She's ahead somewhere. It's my guess they've seen us and taken in sails. They'll set 'em again as soon as it's dark and run down towards the land. The moon won't be up 'till past nine. She has the best part of three hours to throw us off the scent.'

The old sailor nodded slowly, his watery eyes entirely without expression.

'A dollar for the first man to spot her!' Guy said on impulse, wondering immediately why he had said it: to gain esteem? Impress his rank? Was he caught in the grip of the chase?

He leaned back towards the quarterdeck, noting on his way the round form of the chief engineer down on his haunches in the lee of the engine-room skylights, half hidden behind a ventilator, his arm around the neck of a petrified sheep on bent hind legs, talking earnestly.

'– losing vacuum in the condensers. I says to Saxmundham, "I canna keep the main engines goin for nae more'n twelve hour or ye'll ha' nae feed water fr' the boilers." "Nae feed water!" blethers he, "A' th' Indian Seas t'draw 't an ye've nae feed water –!"'

Guy lost the rest of the tale as he passed out of earshot.

'Hold this course 'till we raise the beggar again,' Saxmundham said as he returned. 'If he's seen us he'll make for the beach. He'll lie up in one of the creeks behind the islands off Lamu.' He rubbed his fingers through his beard, looking round at the darkening eastern horizon, now spread with layers of cumulus from the southward. 'The rascals have a strong hand. They'll be in no hurry to close the reefs in the dark though.' He slapped his side. 'By heavens! I'd give something to see their ugly faces when the moon comes up and they spot our jibs close astern!' He chuckled.

Smallpiece pulled his lips into an answering grimace, and as he saw the bo'sun coming down the deck, ambled forward to meet him; soon both men were standing by the mainmast gesticulating aloft at intervals. From beyond came the highpitched quavering plaint of one of the hands rendering an old sea ballad, shortly drowned as the ship's company joined in the chorus.

Guy walked to the side, and jumped up on to a gun carriage. As he stood, listening for a cry from one of the fresh lookouts, the whole midnight blue sky spread with points of light, and as the night closed in and the figures and fittings about the deck merged into shadows from which the men's voices rose with a disembodied quality, the impression of the speed and violence of the ship's progress intensified. He wondered how the dhow was riding the high seas, and how it felt to be chased by a man-of-war. The gap must have closed by three or four miles since she had taken in her sails.

He was aware of the captain balancing towards him; he jumped down to the deck.

'First slave chase, Greville?'

'Yes, sir.'

The Old Man drew a deep breath. 'I've bin after 'em all, my boy.' He started pacing up the deck, and Guy fell into step beside him. 'Elephant, buffalo, lion, tiger, piggy,' he chuckled. 'On my life, Greville, there ain't nothin' to beat a night chase after human game!'

They reached the poop rail and as they turned he glanced up at the sails and the tell-tale of bunting streaming from a mizzen shroud. 'Wind's backed a shade. I fancy she'll blow herself out by mornin'.'

Guy said, 'By my reckoning she'll be twenty miles off the reef when the moon comes up.'

Saxmundham nodded. 'Then we'll see some sport! It's a nice point whether we'll catch the rascal before he goes to ground.' He looked into Guy's face. 'You've had no experience of these fellows.'

'Not yet, sir.'

Saxmundham's eyes were hard. 'You can't be too careful. Give 'em a chance, they'll hack you in a thousand pieces.' He passed his fingers through his beard. 'One dodge they have a particular fancy to if you come up from to leeward. They'll watch as friendly as you please, but just as you're about to board, it's let go the halliards – down comes the sail and you're snared like a rat in a bag. Out with the swords and spears diggin' down through the canvas. On my life!' He gave Guy another hard look. 'Never close without lettin' 'em see you mean business. Never turn your back without you have a platoon of marines behind you. And never pay attention to foreign buntin'.'

He paused as if caught up in another train of thought.

'It was a froggy ensign that saw poor old Charlie Brownrigg off. Charlie was captain of the *London* at Zanzibar. Keen as mustard on the slave patrol. I'm inclined to think 'head money' was the sole object of his existence – that and his family. His wife and his little girl lived with him on board. She was the pet of the whole ship's company. Spoiled I fancy, but a most fetchin' little thing. I was much taken with her. At all events, every once in a while Charlie would put off for the cruising grounds himself in one of the steam pinnaces. "If my men can put up with the inconvenience of boat cruising," he used to say, "so can I!" On my life – the jacks thought the world of Charlie!

'On this occasion he came up with a dhow flying a froggy ensign. His coxswain had a good deal more experience on the cruising grounds, and he begged Charlie to let him open the arms chest. But no – "He's only a French trader," Charlie said, "Let's see what he has to sell!" He sent his coxswain forward to attend to the boat rope while he brought her alongside himself. Of course the Arabs were waitin' behind the bulwarks. Directly they saw the boat alongside and not so much as a man with a pistol drawn, they upped and emptied their muskets into them at point blank. The only one left after the first volley was Charlie himself for those not killed outright jumped straight overboard. Charlie grabbed at a rifle hangin' from the awnin' frame in the sternsheets an' dropped one of the beggars, then turned it end for end and laid into the others with the butt. There were too many for him. In no time his fingers had been sliced clean off the barrel, and another sword split his skull.' He paused. 'I heard it from a fellow who had the good fortune to be rescued from the water. It ain't too pretty what they did subsequently.'

'Pleasant customers!' Guy said.

They continued pacing silently. After a long while, Saxmundham said, 'Make the most of it whilst you have the chance. This coast won't look the same in a few years. Depend on it, the Germans mean business. We'll be obliged to take our share, or let 'em grab all the land from here to Mogadischu, and I fancy even Mr Gladstone would balk at that! On my life – there won't be room for Sultan

Barghash of Zanzibar then, nor the slavers.' He looked at Guy keenly. 'There won't be room for all this,' he swept his arm in a gesture to embrace the pale shapes of canvas and sighing rigging above.

Chapter Two

The *Dulcinea* lay heaving to the swell rolling up less angrily than the night before, sweeping along the side, and away again without fuss. She was pointing east, making virtually no headway under topsails alone, the fore and mizzen pulling, the main braced aback, straining in creased bellies against the mast and shrouds. The wind had dropped as Saxmundham had predicted.

Away on the port quarter the coast of Africa stretched in an indistinct line, sharpened at intervals by outlying coral islands topped with green foliage and fronds of palms; in the distance beyond, the hills rose, blue-grey and remote. There was not a cloud to be seen; the morning was pale and translucent; already there was a stickiness in the breeze betokening torrid heat to come.

The dhow was a long way off to starboard. There had been no sight of her during the night, then at first light she had been spotted – way astern. Evidently she had been lying to or scudding before small canvas while the *Dulcinea* smoked past. All hands had been turned to, the sails taken in and the corvette brought to the wind under her topsails on the starboard tack, and the main yards braced aback. The chief engineer had been summoned and ordered to draw the fires forward and have the picket boats' engines made ready.

'Mak' ready!' he had muttered, leaving Saxmundham's presence. 'And where's a' yer whistlin' wind the noo, Saxmundham –!'

They lay with every glass and telescope in the ship trained on the distant, stumpy masts, for the hull of the craft was barely visible even from the t'gallants, waiting for her move. Saxmundham, in uniform jacket with a shimmering Japanese silk muffler around his neck under his beard and a tall, shining black hat wedged firmly over his brow, paced the starboard side of the quarterdeck in terrible silence, the skin under his normally keen blue eyes puckered and shadowed by the sleepless night on deck.

As the sun rose over the horizon a faint dinning of gongs, followed by a wailing sound, rising and falling on the wind, was borne down to them as the dhow's muezzin called the faithful to prayer.

Smallpiece threw up his arms. 'The heathen devils! It's us should be sayin' our prayers, damn my eyes!'

Lieutenant Heighurst of the marines twisted the end of his moustache. 'I trust that is one will not be answered!'

Smallpiece, if he heard, ignored him. 'She has the weather of us by seven leagues. They'll be ashore and cha- sin' the niggers through the bush before Fat Mac has steam up, may God blast me –!'

Heighurst tut-tutted.

The surgeon came up to Guy and said quietly, 'Have you any notion why we're lying to?'

Guy's brows rose. 'She dead to windward.'

'But why did Old Sax not call for steam before?'

Why indeed! But he knew that Sax could never have brought himself to it. 'Who could have guessed we would raise her astern!'

The surgeon looked at him. 'At all events, she's in no hurry now.'

Presently as they stared out towards her, the white flash of sails rose over the specks of the masts. Saxmundham roared, '*Ready all!*' Guy tensed, and stepped to the binnacle.

'What course does the rascal make?'

There was a pause before one of the midshipmen in the mizzen rigging called, 'Straight for us!'

Muttered oaths rose from the groups on the quarter-deck, and the captain sprang into the mizzen rigging himself, running up as nimbly as a boy, his tall hat and erect bearing lending an incongruous touch to the scene. He stayed in the crosstrees a long while, and by the time he descended it was obvious that the dhow, now perceived as the largest type of buggalow, was heading on a course that would bring her close by the *Dulcinea*. Gradually, as she held her course, the certainty grew that she was not going to alter and make a dash for the coast; with it came the implication that she had nothing to fear from a search by a British man-of-war. There were no slaves aboard. Guy felt strangely cheated; so it seemed did the hands. They went listlessly about their tasks as they were piped to clear up decks, and even the call to breakfast failed to restore their spirits.

The dhow pressed on under full-bellied sails shining in the sun, with a bone in her teeth, and by the time Guy's morning watch ended she was scarcely more than eight miles away. As he began handing over to the navigating lieutenant, Roger Stainton, he noticed her running up a French ensign.

Saxmundham, who had remained on deck, watching her grimly, saw the flag at the same moment. His gaze sharpened. 'False bunting! On my life!' He swung on his heel, calling, 'Smallpiece, Greville, Heighurst!'

As they came up, he snapped, 'Smallpiece, Greville! I'll have the scoundrel! Loose the forty-pounder! Arm the cutter!' He looked at Guy. 'Take the cutter away, Greville! Search him from truck to keel. Examine all hands and every stick of cargo! Bless my soul –!' The prospect of action had put him in better humour. 'Heighurst, take a dozen of your lads to cover the search party! Playin' games with froggy buntin'! The rascal!'

'Hunt the nigger,' Heighurst breathed. His green eyes were flat, the corners of his lips twisted down in habitual cynicism.

'Remember,' Saxmundham went on, 'they're wily rascals. The beggars were sayin' their prayers this mornin'. They'd as soon cut you in pieces for the glory of the Prophet!' His eyes were alight. 'Sharpen up your cutlasses!'

Heighurst snapped a salute. Saxmundham raised his top hat politely, and turned away, calling out to his coxswain, hovering near, that he would take his breakfast now.

Guy, buoyed up at the prospect of a diversion, had the midshipman in charge of the cutter make all ready, and inspected the crew and their arms and ammunition before writing up the log for the watch. Afterwards he went below for breakfast. He heard the hands piped to tack ship, and the familiar pattern of orders and responses, the slap-slap of bare feet on the deck, occasional harder thumps of blocks or coils of rope, the groan of yards as they swung. The motion of the ship changed, and he felt her leaning to her new course. The water chuckled past the side below.

When he arrived on deck again, strapping on his revolver holster, the dhow was only two miles away on the port quarter, her French ensign still blowing out defiantly, the colours glowing in the sunlight. The *Dulcinea* was closing on an interception course under topsails and jib. He saw the chief engineer, his red face and neck streaked with black lines of sweat and soot, standing by Saxmundham at the mainmast, both gazing up at rolls of thick black smoke streaming from the funnel. Guy imagined the pained expression on Old Sax's face, the despair on the chief's; the engines would not be needed after all. His tubby figure made a poignant contrast with Old Sax's elegance.

He looked back at the dhow. She showed no sign of paying any attention to the *Dulcinea* bearing down across her course, although several Arabs in white robes were visible about the poop. The shapely hull was lifting and settling to the following seas like a swan, a delicate roll of foam playing and falling away under her curving bow, her two great lateen sails brilliantly white in the sun and full of wind, bending the yards like giant wings. Closer and closer she came as the *Dulcinea's* converging course narrowed the lateral distance between them; still the Arabs made no move, although more of them could be seen now staring at the man-of-war.

Saxmundham clutched a speaking trumpet, and strode to the quarter, leaping up on a chicken coop so that his head and chest were above the bulwark. 'Ahoy there!' he roared. 'Down sails!' and after a pause, 'Heave to!'

There was no response from the dhow.

He turned and roared at the first lieutenant on the fo'c's'le. 'Stand by to fire!', then again ordered the dhow to heave to, adding, 'Lookee slave!'

A figure on the poop of the dhow moved across and shouted incomprehensibly, waving his arm in circling gestures; soon others with him took up the yelling until a babel of sound rose from the craft, but they made no move towards the gear.

Saxmundham pointed his speaking trumpet at the fo'c's'le. '*Fire!*'

The forty-pounder cracked, grey-white smoke swelled from the muzzle; the first lieutenant's order to sponge and load coincided with a plume of white water rising from the sea some fifty feet ahead of the dhow's stem. There was a moment of silence aboard the craft, then the noise and gesticulations rose again with renewed vigour.

'They are not pleased with us!' Heighurst said.

Saxmundham called to the fo'c's'le, 'Shave his whiskers this time, Mr Smallpiece!'

There was a pause as the first lieutenant made his own interpretation of the instruction, and when Guy looked at the dhow again the sails were spilling, the crew gathering the flogging canvas in.

'Away sea boat!' Saxmundham called, and as the pipe shrilled, '*Ready all!*'

Guy moved across the deck as helm and sail orders followed to bring the *Dulcinea* into the wind. The fourteen men of the cutter's crew were aboard her by the time he arrived, and the midshipman, Bowles, was waiting with a tense, eager expression on his face, fidgeting with his dirk. A line of marines in scarlet with white pipe-clayed bandoliers stood stiffly with rifle butts lined along a deck seam just inboard, their sergeant facing them. Guy turned to Heighurst at his shoulder, 'Your fellows man the boat!'

Heighurst nodded to the sergeant, who shouted instructions, and one by one the marines leaped over the gunwale with a great clatter of boots and bayonet scabbards. As the last two went aboard Guy made Heighurst an elaborate bow.

The marine lieutenant inclined his head. 'Thank'ee kind zir!' and stepped easily aboard.

Guy's eye swept down the boat's falls to the hands ready to cast off the turns, then over to the captain by the wheel. Saxmundham was hurling out an order to round in the main braces to back the topsail. As the bluejackets ran away with the lines and the great yards groaned across, the canvas smacking and flogging, he moved towards Guy and nodded. Guy stepped on to the gunwale of the cutter, his eye passing again over the hands by the boat rope forward and the releasing gear fore and aft, the lifelines coiled freely between the men sitting on the thwarts, the midshipman gazing at him still with that tense expression.

'Plug in, Bowles?' he asked quietly.

The lad started before noticing the glint in his eye. 'Sir!'

He was jumpy. He would settle down once they were under way. 'Ready in the boat!' he called, and turned towards the hands on deck, 'Slip the gripes! Turns for lowering! Lower away!'

His stomach drifted up towards his chest as the bottom boards fell and the boat swayed out from the *Dulcinea's* side, then back again, the fenders squeaking against the pitted black plates and outstanding rivet heads. The seas rolled up to meet them, sparkling blue, intensely deep.

'Handsomely!' he called. The falls unwound more slowly; the sea hissed within two feet of the keel and dropped back again. 'Lower away!' The cutter smacked down in the trough, the Hill & Clark release gear snapping open directly the weight came off the falls. The boat bobbed and rolled, sheering out from the ship's side as Bowles moved to the tiller and threw off the lashing.

'Oars out! Slip the boat rope!' Guy turned to Bowles. 'We'll drop under the stern!' The lad reversed the tiller.

'Back port!' A burst of spray stung his face and neck. 'Give way starboard!' The cutter dipped her side and took a splash of sea water, cold over the gunwale. A marine swore.

'Quiet in the boat!' the sergeant yelped.

'Oars port! Give way together!'

As they cleared the *Dulcinea's* stern, rising on the swell, which seemed so much higher from sea level, the wind caught them and whipped sheets of spray in over the bows. The dhow was about a hundred yards away, her stumpy, forward-raking masts bare save for the offending tricolour and a tangle of hanging lines, her crew spread alone the side gazing impassively at the *Dulcinea,* their former agitation apparently quite spent.

'The johnnies seem remarkably calm!' Heighurst said.

'The first lieutenant should'a aimed closer, sir,' the sergeant growled. "We'd 'a heard a thing or two then!'

Guy gave him a cold look, and he put a hand up to twist one of the fierce upward bristles of his moustache, returning the glance warily.

The hands on the oars leaned their backs to the stroke; spray splashed against the port bow and drove against the gunwale, the bluejackets grinning at each other as they were struck. Guy eyed the heaving side of the dhow; a heavy scent of cloves was borne from her on the wind.

'Zanzibar,' Heighurst said, sniffing. 'We shan't find any concubines, sarn't!'

The sergeant's eyes moved quickly to Guy before he replied. 'What're we a-lookin' for, sir?'

Heighurst turned to Guy.

Guy felt his inexperience showing. 'We'll go round her port side,' he snapped. 'I shall go up first,' he glanced at Heighurst, 'followed by your fellows from the port side of the sternsheets – starboard side and bow men to keep us covered.' Heighurst nodded. Guy turned to Bowles. 'Take charge of the boat directly we come alongside. When the port-side marines have gone up, have the men cover the starboard marines as they follow up. Then shove off. Keep a hold of the bow line and stand off, four men only on the oars, the rest with rifles at the ready. If there's a scrap, don't fire into the brown. Fix cutlasses, haul her alongside and send the men up. And Bowles – stay with the boat!'

Disappointment showed plainly on the midshipman's young face.

'You'll not miss anything,' Guy said. 'It won't come to a scrap.'

'I fear not,' Heighurst agreed.

'And, sarn't,' Guy called.

'Sir!'

'You know about their little game with the sails. They're down now, but if you see any of the beggars by the halliards –'

'I'll know what to do, sir!' the sergeant replied briskly.

Guy turned to Heighurst. 'Have your men at the ready, if you would!'

The lieutenant nodded to the sergeant, who barked a volley of orders. The cutter rocked, then the marines in the bow were sitting with rifles at the shoulder aimed at the dhow's poop; the others were cradling their arms on their knees. The Arabs watched the demonstration without a flicker of emotion.

The men at the oars took the activity as evidence that they were nearing the end of the pull, and swung their weight into the stroke. The rowlocks creaked. Guy saw the intricate carvings around five shuttered windows in the dhow's stern as it opened to view; the deep shadows cast by the sun brought the designs into high relief. As the craft rose to the swell exposing the beautiful curve of the run to the bottom timbers he noticed how clean she was – not a trace of vegetation; she had not been in the water many days since being scraped down and paid.

They began to open the port side and he felt his muscles tense. He resisted an urge to try whether his revolver would leave the holster smoothly. The feeling passed as quickly as it had come on, and as he guided Bowles in the sweeping approach his nerves were as steady as if he were coxing at a fleet regatta.

'Bows!'

The two oarsmen tossed their blades high and shipped them along the thwarts; one stood by with the boathook, the other with a heaving line.

'Way enough!'

The oars came out of the water and the blades twisted horizontal, dripping. The weight of the cutter carried her on towards rough, oiled timbers lined with vertical rows of nails, weeping rust down to the shadowed waves in the vessel's lee. The bulwarks above were lined with faces, some with white turbans, some with short, frizzy hair; the black faces grinned as they stared into the boat. A feeling of unreality swept over him for a moment, as if the dhow and these indolent children of nature, living and sailing as their ancestors had for centuries, were substantial, and the cutter and all its crew mere shadows impinging on the real world. The brilliant scarlet of the marines' uniforms, the points of light darting from their rifle barrels, the twist of Heighurst's lips and the gleam in his pale eyes as he weighed up the scene, Bowles's alert young face as he leaned to the tiller, the glittering gold and stiff white of his own uniform – all strayed from some bizarre other world as remote as Theseus and the Minotaur.

A bowman heaved the line through the air and the disturbing image had gone. Black hands vied to catch and secure it. The boathook grated against the side, fending the bows off as the stern swung in, and another line was falling for them to catch.

'Quite a reception committee,' Heighurst said. 'Sarn't!'

The sergeant cautioned his men as Guy stood and grasped the line with both hands, jerking it hard to ensure that it had been made fast before springing on it and placing his feet against the dhow's timbers. Two heaves and dark arms were reaching over the bulwarks to grasp his shoulders and help him up. The smell of cloves was intense. He clambered over and found himself standing on piled jute bags surrounded by twenty or more men of various shades and variety of loose white or checked garments; the few pure Arabs wore swords at their waist; they stared at him silently with hard black eyes. He wondered which was the nakhoda, when an old man standing aloof on the raised poop decking put a hand to his breast and bowed courteously. Guy bowed in reply and as he heard the first of the marines coming over the side behind, began to pick his way over a tangle of sacks, fibre rope and lumber towards him.

The old man's eyes glinted; Guy was reminded of Saxmundham's warning – 'Give 'em a chance, they'll hack you in pieces!' Deep lines ran down either side of a long, curving nose to thin lips drooping at the corners and partly hidden by a flowing white moustache and beard. A dagger inlaid with silver in haft and scabbard was thrust into the waistband of a flowing white robe, and silver gleamed from a clasp in the centre of the white turban above.

'Lieutenant Greville,' Guy said, 'of Her Britannic Majesty's ship, *Dulcinea.*'

The old man bowed gravely and replied in his own tongue. Guy caught the word '*Allah*'. He responded with compliments from the captain of the *Dulcinea*. The old man glanced towards the ship for a moment, then pointed to the ensign at his own masthead.

'*Furanza!*'

'You have French papers?'

The Arab stared darkly.

'Papers.' Guy raised his left palm and mimicked writing on it with his right forefinger and thumb. 'Your papers!'

The old man shrugged as if to suggest he had no need for useless papers. 'How kaween Vikitorria?'

'Very well,' Guy smiled.

The old man nodded sagely. 'Misiter Giladistow? Puretty well?'

'Very well!' Guy pointed to his own chest. 'I have order,' pointing to the corvette, 'from *bwana Dulcinea,*' pointing to his eyes, 'lookee see papers dees sheep.' And again he mimicked writing on his palm.

The old man swept his arm in a motion to embrace the whole of the dhow. 'No silev – *hapana!*' He made a cutting motion as if the thought of slaves offended him deeply. 'No silave! Tell your kapiteni la! *Hasa, hapana!* No silave on board!'

Guy tried another tack. 'Where – you – go?'

'Go Muskat. *Watumwa* no! No silave!'

'Where – you – from?'

'Unguja.'

Guy recognized the native name for Zanzibar, and turned to Heighurst who had come up and was watching the interview with a flicker of amusement in his eyes. 'I'll take a look below.'

'If there are any slaves they'll be amongst those johnnies. Heighurst gestured towards the mixture of Arabs and native sailors gathered in the waist staring at the line of marines facing them with fixed bayonets. 'At all events,' he went on, 'we'll see you're not disturbed.'

Guy bowed to the old man and indicated by signs that he was going below, then turned and went to the side to call for hands from the boat to help him search the cargo, hearing Heighurst's opening to the nakhoda, 'It's my opinion Gladstone should have sent Lord Wolseley into the Sudan very much earlier –'

He smiled. Leaning over the rail he shouted down to Bowles, then made his way back to the break of the poop and jumped down on to the sacks beneath. Turning and bending low he entered the space between the deck on which Heighurst and the Arab stood, Heighurst still talking seriously. The darkness was intense after the glare on deck; bars of bright light from the shuttered stern windows made the rest of the space seem blacker. The rough beams were excruciatingly low; his senses were assailed by nauseating smells of shark oil, stale fish and evil gases from the bilge.

A rustle of movement from the far end set his pulses racing, and he reached for his revolver, wondering as he drew and pointed in one smooth motion whether he had made the one false move....

Three pairs of eyes were staring at him, motionless. As his pupils adjusted he made out black hoods and yashmaks; his revolver arm dropped and he replaced the weapon in its holster.

There were shapes of pots and bowls and wicker baskets and a brass coffee pot with a curving spout close by where the women were sitting, and what looked like bundles of blankets or rugs and one great wooden chest, carved and studded with brass in the Arab style. Rugs were spread on the deck and hanging from a bulkhead nearby; otherwise the after end of the space was stowed to the deckhead with haphazard piles of boxes, baskets, ropes, nets and lumber. It would take an army to search. He picked his way towards the great chest, very aware of the eyes following him, and tried the lid. It came up easily. There was little inside; white cotton garments heaped indiscriminately with black draperies, but he caught a glimpse of something solid beneath them in a corner, and, uncovering it, found a sextant. He took it out carefully and looked at the women. They returned his gaze, motionless. He put the instrument to his eye and mimicked using it, then pointed to the deckhead above and drew his fingers over his chin to suggest a long beard. The black eyes continued to regard him solemnly. He replaced the sextant, and felt among the cottons, his fingers coming up against more hard objects beneath. Pulling the material aside, he was startled to see an armoury of curved, double-edged swords, daggers, pistols with carved and inlaid butts, an old 'Brown Bess' musket, cases of cartridges and balls. The cotton stuffs were a cover for the old man's private arsenal. He was about to throw the material back when he saw what he was looking for, a sheaf of papers, carelessly folded and tied with a single dark ribbon, crumpled and tucked away in a corner, wedged under the hilt of a sword. He pulled them out. A glance showed him they were in French. Closing the lid, he bent his way back towards the brilliant light on deck, slipping the ribbon off as he went.

It was at once apparent that the papers were cargo manifests ; they were made out in flowing French script, and as he skimmed down the lists he realized he had stumbled on to something very much more interesting than slaves: French 8 mm *Gras* rifles, no less than fourteen chests of them, and a dozen cases of cartridges, two chests of black powder, five boxes of bayonets, several bales of calico and miscellaneous coloured cottons, a chest of naval uniform, an iron bedstead manufactured in Marseilles. They had been shipped from Réunion, the French naval base in the Indian Ocean, and were bound for Witu. Evidently they were direct transhipments from France as the markings on most of the crates were listed as 'Toulon-Réunion'.

Among the manifests was a single-sheet letter, handwritten in French on plain, gilt-edged paper, addressed to the sultan of Witu. He translated as he read.

Most excellent Highness Fumo Akari,
After compliments. Know that we send these gifts as a token of our sincere and cordial friendship with you and your people. As our friendship ripens, so will our understanding and cooperation in the great aims upon which we are embarked. Be assured, before long you shall receive further

consignments. And know this, the lewali of Lamu has never set eyes upon such guns, which will take the eye from a peacock's feather at three hundred paces. Such is the delicacy of our relationship, should you wish to communicate with us, send any messages through Pierre Suleiman in Zanzibar.

His eyes skimmed through the concluding compliments, '*Je prie Hautesse de croire aux sentiments de ma considération la plus élevée ...*' down to the signature, '*Charles Gerharnais, Gouverneur.*'

He read the letter through a second time as the implications clarified. A gift of arms and friendship from the French governor of Réunion to an insignificant but locally powerful chief of a mainland province just inland of the stretch of coastline visible from where he stood, 'the great aims upon which we are embarked' – 'the delicacy of our relationship' indeed!

There was something else about the letter, something about the phraseology. He couldn't quite place what it was –

He made his way back to the poop where Heighurst and the nakhoda were standing, silent now, and held the papers out before the Arab's face.

'Dees sheep come from Réunion!' he said angrily.

The old man eyed him for a moment, then shook his head slowly.

Guy slapped the manifests. 'Paper say Réunion.'

The Arab shrugged, his face expressionless.

Guy held the manifests up again. 'Dees bockass – where you take him?'

'Witu.'

'Ah! Witu! Las' time you say Muskat.'

The Arab's lids drooped as though the whole discussion were pointless. 'From Witu – go Muskat.'

'From Réunion – go Witu!'

'From Unguja go Witu.'

Guy stared at him. 'Dees bockass –' he pointed to his eyes, 'lookee see!'

The old man returned his gaze for a long moment, then poured out a rapid string of instructions to someone in the waist. Guy looked round and saw an Arab beckoning to him. He jumped down, and was led over the folds of the sail and the spar to which it was bent towards the great leaning trunk of the foremast. His guide squatted and started unfastening the lashings of an ancient tarpaulin which was stretched across the top of this section of cargo. When he had a part of it loose, he invited Guy to look beneath. There were wooden crates, solid-looking with thick baulks of timber at the corners and faint painted markings. He bent to examine them.

'Toulon-Réunion.'

Saxmundham smoothed an obstinately upstanding corner of the manifests down on the table for the umpteenth time. 'The bla'guards!'

Guy swayed to the *Dulcinea's* uneasy motion, still trying to puzzle out what it was about the letter.

The captain banged his fist on the papers. 'The froggies are intriguing with Witu!'

Guy nodded.

Saxmundham looked up. 'You doubt it, Greville?'

'The letter, sir. It worries me —'

'The deuce it does! It worries me!' He shuffled the papers until the letter was uppermost. 'The sultan of Witu, Greville, owes allegiance to the sultan of Zanzibar. The lewali of Lamu — whom it appears the sultan of Witu intends over-throwin' — owes a similar allegiance. Under British protection.' He rose to his feet, instinctively ducking his head as it neared the beams. 'Jenkins!'

His coxswain appeared in the doorway from the sleeping cabin, a brass-polishing rag in his hand.

'Chief engineer, Jenkins! Never mind what the scamp looks like, fetch him up here — chop! chop!'

The coxswain hurried out in a waft of Globe polish, tucking the rag in the waistband of his trousers.

'Bla'guards!' Saxmundham shook his great head from side to side. 'They shan't get away with it. They need another sharp lesson, Greville!' His eyes were fierce. He stepped towards Guy and clapped a hand on his shoulder. 'Gun drill every forenoon, and target practice. We have sufficient powder?'

'As yet we've used none of last quarter's allowance, sir.'

'Two aimed rounds in a minute and a half, Greville! I shall instruct the first lieutenant to allow you as many hands as you shall require.'

Greville wondered how Smallpiece would take that.

'How are the sights?' Saxmundham went on.

'The sights, sir?' Guy saw an opportunity and seized it. 'Poorly designed in my opinion.'

The Old Man stared.

'Telescopes are the new thing, sir.'

'Telescopes! You don't say so.'

'We have six pieces sufficiently accurate to do them justice,' Guy hurried on. 'The six Armstrongs.'

'Telescope sights! God bless my soul!' Delight spread over Saxmundham's face. 'A distant engagement! You shall go ashore directly we make Zanzibar, Greville. Purchase six of the very best telescopes to be had.'

'Zanzibar, sir?'

A frown passed across the Old Man's forehead. 'From what you saw of the dhow, d'you imagine she'll tow that far?'

'She seemed sound enough.'

'They break up easy. They look pretty, but they ain't strong. They never sail without they have a soldier's wind –' A knock on the door interrupted him. 'Ah, chief! Come in! Never knock on duty!'

The door opened and the chief engineer leaned in and trotted a few paces with the heel of the ship. His face was still streaked with grey rivulets of sweat and coal dust; his jacket collar was turned up about a muffler that had once been white, but was now smudged grey and black. His pale green eyes were watery, and there was a suspicious aroma of spirits mixed with the smell of engine oil and soot that followed him in.

The animation left the captain's eye, and his lips turned down for a moment. 'Draw the fires forward as soon as you please, chief!'

'Aye!' the engineer replied dully.

'We shall be towin' the dhow to Zanzibar.' The chiefs expression remained blank, and Saxmundham swung his arm in the direction of the coastline. 'Some devilment hatchin', chief!'

The little man shook his head. 'Ye'll be taking her under tow wi' th' engines?' He stared at the captain.

'The monsoon,' Saxmundham replied curtly. 'Zanzibar lies directly upwind, chief.'

The engineer took two steps backward with the *Dulcinea's* motion. 'That would bother ye!'

The Old Man's shoulders jerked. The chief, unaware of the effect he was having, turned to Guy with a conspiring gleam lighting his face, 'What did ah tell ye!' He peered out of the port as if to seek the devilment hatching there, then turned abruptly and made for the door, opening it after one unsuccessful attempt, and leaving without a word.

Saxmundham was silent for a long while after he had gone. 'I trust you'll find some way of handling these fellows, Greville,' he said at last. 'Although how in heaven's name you'll manage when you need to depend on 'em — On my life! It passes all comprehension!'

Chapter Three

Zanzibar shone under a low moon like an image from the 'Thousand Nights and One Night'. The captain's gig, urged on by its crew uniformed in the dark green livery of the Saxmundham house – almost black in the moonlight – cut the water at a fast stroke. Guy looked ahead entranced. It was his first visit to the fabled city. It had a magical aspect. It seemed to be resting on an intermittent line of small fires, glowing like fairy lights at the edge of the water, and reflected in lines of shimmering gold beneath a wall of flat-roofed buildings stretching the length of the harbour front. In the centre, off the port bow of the gig, the sultan's new residence, white as if carved from marble, could be made out through the tracery of a steamship's rigging. It rose through four delicately verandahed storeys topped by a square clock tower with an electric light glimmering uncertainly above. Next to it was the old Portuguese fort, its rough textured walls crumbling in places. A few small trees gleamed silver among the masts of numerous local craft and here and there the trunks and graceful dark fronds of palms broke up the huddle of

close-packed masonry beyond. There was an air of solidity and wealth and mystery. It took Guy straight back to
bedtime stories read by his nanny – of grand viziers and
magicians and exquisite princesses draped on silk cushions
and carpets of Bokhara. He wondered what messages fluttered from those narrow windows past the eunuchs of the
harem to young men waiting under the moorish arches –

The captain's voice cut into his thoughts. 'You know
what Livingstone called the place?' He was sitting opposite
in the sternsheets, wearing a dark tail coat and silk cravat,
his tall top hat gleaming against the night. 'Stinkibar!' he
chuckled. 'Not bad for a Scotsman!'

Smallpiece, sitting beside him, gave a bellow of laughter.

Guy wondered what Livingstone had meant; the heavy
scent of cloves borne across the still water was cloying but
not unpleasant.

The Old Man noticed his lack of response. 'Wait till
you're ashore, my boy!'

Smallpiece snorted. 'Never smelled dead slaves,
Greville!' Guy looked at him coolly.

The first lieutenant bristled. 'Damn my eyes! Dead or
alive, there's nothin' to choose!'

'*Allah kareem!*' Saxmundham said. 'God is merciful!'

'Heathen hypocrites!' Smallpiece exploded; it was evident he would have said more had the captain not been
there. 'God's teeth! A bullet for every man-stealing fol-
lower of the Prophet! That would be a mercy!'

'I'm inclined to agree with you,' the Old Man replied.
'But unfortunately the sultan is our oldest ally in the
Indian Ocean. I doubt we could manage without him. The

Germans would not require a second invitation if we were to drop the rascal. Then where should we be on the coast? Diplomacy makes strange bedfellows, Mr Smallpiece. I fancy we shall have to continue putting a good face on it.'

'We should take the island, sir.' Smallpiece was unusually talkative. 'Set up protected posts inland,' he gestured past the reefs and palm-hung atolls guarding the harbour, towards the coast of Africa. 'Put an end to the filthy commerce at source. We can never stop it by sea, not in a thousand years. We play at it. We annoy the sultan to no purpose. We have the worst of both worlds.'

'The Foreign Office would never sanction it,' Saxmundham replied. 'Far cheaper to use the sultan's friendship! And besides, Gladstone's made sufficient of an ass of himself in Egypt. He'll want no more adventures of that sort.'

'Psalm-singing – hypocrite!' Smallpiece was evidently restraining himself.

The water gurgled under the stern as the blades bit and the crew leaned to the stroke in perfect time. From somewhere among the dark trees beyond the town came the throb of distant drums, rhythmic, insistent. Other, louder drums beat clearly across the water from amongst the maze of masts in the dhow anchorage, and the deep, wailing chant of Arab sailors about their work, the creak of rope through ungreased blocks, groan of timber on timber, shrill orders and imprecations interspersed with calls to Allah.

Smallpiece's mouth turned down in disdain.

To port, the high sides of an old two-decker rose in black and white chequers, the tracery of her rigging sharp against a myriad stars; it was HMS *London,* the Navy's prison ship and base for the anti-slavery patrol.

'Did you ever meet Charlie Brownrigg?' Saxmundham asked, gazing towards her as a cry of 'Boat ahoy!' rang across the water.

'Passing!' the coxswain roared back.

'I never did,' Smallpiece replied.

'It occurred to me,' Guy said in the silence that followed, 'when I visited our friend Ismael in the buggalow – it might not be such a bad idea for the Admiralty to issue a set of instructions for the guidance of officers new to the station.'

'So they do,' Smallpiece said sharply.

'Slave treaties, boundaries of territorial waters,' Guy replied. 'Thou shalt not interfere with the Stars and Stripes lest thou call down the wrath of Uncle Sam – but no advice on what to do when boarding, no vocabulary –'

'Take an interpreter,' Smallpiece growled. 'And your nose.'

'For officers new to the coast,' Guy went on, trying to restrain his voice. He looked at Saxmundham. 'Had it not been for the advice you gave me, sir, I confess I should have been hard put to know what was expected.'

'An encyclopedia of instructions would not have saved Charlie Brownrigg,' Smallpiece cut in. 'As I heard it –'

'Gentlemen!' Saxmundham interrupted. 'Greville is right. If their lordships were serious about this business – but even so, it's not their style. It's not our style, Greville. Imagine, if you can, Nelson thumbing through a volume of Admiralty instructions before throwing the *Captain* so gloriously across the bows of the Spanish Admiral at St Vincent!'

Guy grinned. 'As you put it like that, sir –'

'How else?'

'Nelson took the greatest care to inform his captains what was expected of them.' Guy wondered how far he should venture in argument with the captain, but plunged on. 'His memorandum before Trafalgar was explicit.'

'Memorandum!' Smallpiece exploded.

'No, no, Greville has a point,' Saxmundham said. 'Decidedly. Nelson took his "band of brothers" fully into his confidence. All his officers were fully acquainted with the principles of his tactics, of that there is no doubt.' He turned to Guy. 'Your proposal is that their lordships draw out the experience of officers of long standing on this coast, infuse it with their own peculiar wisdom, and promulgate the results in a handbook for the guidance of officers new to the coast?'

'Exactly!' Guy replied, disarmed.

'They'll never attend to it,' the Old Man continued. 'It's not our way. We meet our difficulties as they arise. I fancy it has a great deal to do with the seafaring mind. We share it with the Arab seafarers.'

'Arabs –!' Smallpiece choked, unable to find words to express his astonishment.

Saxmundham turned to him. 'Have you ever known an Arab who would consider spreading a hatch cover before the rain commenced, or attended to his halliards or his ground tackle a moment before he was required to use 'em? Or even had his chests properly secured against a storm – or his sea boat ready?'

'No, sir!' Smallpiece exclaimed violently. 'And you would not find a British ship in such a condition, on my life –!'

'The Arab has this attitude in more eminent degree –'

'If you will allow me, sir,' Smallpiece pressed on doggedly, 'I do not believe we share this attitude of mind in any degree –'

Guy began to enjoy the exchange, wondering how far Smallpiece would dare, how far the Old Man would allow him.

'In practical matters, perhaps so, but in the higher arts of our profession we make singularly little preparation.'

'The higher arts, sir?'

'Greville has mentioned one. We allow officers fresh to the coast to board local craft knowing nothing of their customs, their manner of life, even their language. They go armed with their instincts as Britons, their ability to sail a cutter, put a horse straight at a fence. Is that sufficient preparation for dealing with the wily followers of the Prophet, d'you suppose, Mr Smallpiece?'

The first lieutenant stared. 'They acquire experience soon enough.'

'If they survive. But the experience is there already, hard won by other officers, and of what use is that to Greville here who can scarcely know *Allah kareem* from a Zanzibar *bebe*.'

Guy raised his brows.

'Young of the fair sex,' the Old Man explained briskly. 'Zanzibar is particularly well favoured – so my interpreter used to inform me at regular intervals – which grew closer

the further we sailed from the place – with the most splendid *bebes* or *bints* to be found outside his own grouse moor.'

Smallpiece's face split into an involuntary half smile;
Guy saw stroke and second stroke grinning unrestrainedly.

'The same with tactics,' Saxmundham continued.
'Officers are not required to learn or even to think about
tactics until they find themselves in command of a fleet. An
astounding state of affairs when you consider it!'

Smallpiece was silent as he considered it. They were
nearing the beach now. Another, heavier launch on an
almost parallel course was slightly ahead of them; Guy
had noticed it earlier, putting out from a British India
steamer ahead of the *London*. The stern of the launch
was filled with chattering passengers of all nationalities,
and the noise struck across the narrowing gap of water
like a babel. Saxmundham turned to glance at them a
moment, facing inboard again with a contemptuous
expression.

'First to the beach, Jenkins!'

'Aye, aye, sir!' the coxswain replied and repeated the
remark quietly to the crew, who had heard it in any case.
Their teeth flashed as they growled responses, and flicking
quick glances over their shoulders, laid back on the oars
with renewed energy. Jenkins leant forward, '*Now!*' They
responded as if for a finishing burst at a regatta, Jenkins urging them on with convulsive movements of face and body.
The thwarts creaked beneath them, the gig surged, rocking
the officers in the sternsheets sideways; sweat broke out on
the men's foreheads, strangely white in the moonlight, and
streamed down their cheeks and noses to their beards; their

legs straightened spasmodically against the stretchers; water boiled at the gig's stem and tugged at the rudder.

The noise from the launch grew less and finally ceased altogether as the passengers watched the gig passing at speed, its erect, top-hatted and uniformed passengers swaying silent, apparently unaware of their existence. Within feet of the beach Jenkins called, 'Oars!' and immediately afterwards, 'Hold water!' The gig swirled to a stop as the keel scraped on sand. The bowmen leaped out with the painter and hauled her up at the run.

Saxmundham nodded to the coxswain. 'Very pretty!'

'Thank you, sir,' Jenkins replied, mightily pleased.

The officers climbed out and followed the captain's tall form up the beach, picking their way over debris and around noisome pools. Guy began to understand Livingstone's comment. The air, still heavy with mixed scents of tropical vegetation and spices contained nauseating pockets of putrescence as if large parts of the beach were awash with decayed refuse.

Smallpiece turned to him. 'You understand why the *bebes* cover their noses when they walk out!'

Guy grinned. He wondered if the first lieutenant were trying to make amends for his rancorous tone in the boat. '*Allah kareem!*'

Saxmundham looked back. 'In this instance His compassion will manifest itself in the form of Colonel Grant Mackenzie's best Havanas!'

They passed one of the small, conical fires that had made such an exquisite effect from a distance. Two men, native Swahili, were squatting, staring into it and singing softly to themselves. Then, skirting barricades of rubble held in place by timbers erected to protect the British Consulate from high tides, they reached the arched entrance to the waterfront building. Two Indian policemen were on duty, evidently expecting their arrival. They snapped to the salute at the first sight of Saxmundham's imposing figure, and led them through a fragrant courtyard to a flight of stone steps up to the first floor, where the *burra sah'b,* Colonel Sir Grant Mackenzie, Her Majesty's Political Agent and Consul General, had his suite of offices.

Mackenzie rose as they entered through a doorless archway, a small, pug-faced man with close-cropped bristly grey hair. 'I can't say how delighted I am!' He thrust his hand out with a quick, decisive gesture.

'Well met again,' Saxmundham replied, looking huge against him, and introduced Smallpiece and Guy. Mackenzie introduced his ADC, Captain Fortescue of the 14th Punjabis, a gaunt man with a luxuriant brown moustache, standing beside a great table which served as Mackenzie's desk.

'Please be seated.' The consul gestured to a half circle of high-backed wicker chairs arranged to face the table, and clapped his hands for a boy, ordering him to serve the guests with brandy and soda and cigars.

'We would adjourn to the roof, gentlemen, but we're in for some rain – eh, so my bones inform me.' He flashed a brief smile as he sat facing them, back and head bolt upright.

A puffed-up little fellow, Guy thought; a little man who liked to sit at an enormous desk in a cavernous office and contemplate the vast importance of his post. He spoke in the clipped, precise tones of the lowland Scot, exchanging ritual civilities about the long rains, the Arab character, shared acquaintance with the Old Man. Fortescue sat some way from him apparently oblivious of everything save his own wreaths of cigar smoke which he followed with his eyes up to the high, beamed ceiling.

Guy relaxed in the haze, feeling the brandy loosening the constraints of shipboard discipline; the rich aroma of tobacco carried him back to his father's snug in the Old Rectory near Godalming, where the family had moved when he was twelve. His passionate, opinionated, grand, generous father rampaging through clouds of cigar smoke like a prophet in a clerical collar –

'- the Navy is the very last profession I should choose for you, my boy. You cannot consider it. These romantic notions you have – what is the reality behind them, hey? What is the truth beneath the febrile inventions of these shilling novels – ? I shall inform you: one hundred and seventy-six post captains kicking their heels in idleness ashore – commanders –' he ticked his fingers '- two hundred and fifty odd – lieutenants – the good Lord alone knows how many lieutenants and midshipmen are eking out a miserable existence on half pay with no prospects of employment in the future and no prospect of promotion whatever. And you wish to swell this Gadarene rush to self-destruction! Whatever put such notions in your head? You have a good head, an excellent – no, I shall not hear of it. You shall attend Winchester. You shall be the good and faithful servant whose talent multiplied five-fold.'

The interview remained with him clearly. It had been the turning point in his young life. The flat rejection had hardened what might have proved a passing fancy into determination. It was strange how selective memory was. He had manipulated his mother afterwards, he could remember her tear-stained face, and he remembered being berated by his nanny for a wicked, wilful, selfish boy –

He saw Saxmundham half rising and tossing the letter he had found aboard the dhow on to the table in front of Mackenzie.

The consul picked it up and screwed his brows as he read. After a while he held it out without comment towards Fortescue, who rose and examined it standing. Before he had a chance to say anything, Mackenzie said, 'It's a hoax, of course. Gerharnais would never write that tomfoolery!'

Saxmundham's brows rose.

'I agree,' Fortescue said. 'I mistrust it.'

Guy saw the Old Man's eyes on him. Evidently he was expected to put the case. He looked at the consul.

'That was my first impression, sir. There are two significant points, however. The first is the cargo which corresponds in all details with the manifests found with the letter. The second is the manner of our coming up with the dhow. By pure chance. I have puzzled over it for hours since. I can think of no way in which a – hoaxer could have anticipated the dhow falling into the hands of a British man-of-war. Besides, it would be an exceedingly elaborate and costly hoax.'

Mackenzie looked up at Fortescue.

Guy went on. 'Nevertheless, I do not believe the letter was written by a Frenchman.'

Mackenzie turned to him again, then to Saxmundham. 'Captain, what is your opinion?'

'Greville is my intelligence officer. I have every confidence in his observations.'

Mackenzie reached up and took the letter from Fortescue, studying it again in silence. At last he said, looking up, 'What d'you suggest?'

'I suggest we submit it to the French consul,' the ADC replied. 'He might be able to inform us whether it was written by –' he paused momentarily, looking at Guy, 'a compatriot.'

Guy felt the blood in his head. 'No Frenchman wrote that letter, sir. Whoever it was learnt the language from a schoolroom primer.'

'In that case it is a hoax,' Mackenzie snapped back.

Guy shrugged.

Mackenzie's face went a shade darker. 'What would you call it, sir?'

'An intrigue, sir!'

'Ah!' Mackenzie leant back in his chair and placed the tips of his fingers together before his chin. 'You are intelligence officer, you say. I don't know how much you may have picked up of the political background.' His tone implied that it was probably little. 'But as you know the entire coastal belt of East Africa from Mozambique northwards and inland to the great lakes is – eh, nominally controlled by independent Arab slave traders who have set themselves up in strongpoints as local sheikhs or sultans, using forces of native askaris – eh, fighting men – to maintain their position, and owing allegiance to the sultan of

Zanzibar. Zanzibar of course has long been the centre of the slave trade. Such was the position until quite recently. The sultan's authority, I may say, was more imagined than real. In the last few years, however, since the creation of the greater German empire under Bismarck –'

Guy listened impatiently; it was common knowledge to any tolerably informed person that Germany had been throwing her weight around since smashing the French at Sedan, and was making a determined effort to catch up with the older colonial powers in the possession of overseas territory. East Africa was wide open – since the British Government's steadfast refusal to annex territory or even acquire formal protectorates, and the Germans were making the most of the opportunities.

'– since the formation last year of the *Gesellschaft für Deutsche Kolonisation*,' Mackenzie's voice continued, 'and their acquisition of enormous tracts of territory in treaties with separate local chiefs – who were persuaded to repudiate their alliance with the sultan of Zanzibar – it became evident that controls would have to be imposed lest the powers become involved in fighting over the activities of their colonizing agents. Accordingly the Kaiser convened a conference at Berlin. I won't go over the details. The main points agreed were: one, a power wishing to annex territory in Africa is bound to give notice of her intention to the other interested powers; two, any territory so annexed should be effectively occupied.'

He paused, and his gaze, which had been wandering in space, fixed on Guy again. 'So you see,' and he brushed the letter on the table before him, 'to treat this seriously

I should expect two conditions to be fulfilled – one, that the French Government had given us due notice of their intention to annex the sultanate of Witu – two, that French nationals were settling the area. On the contrary, gentlemen, we have heard no word from the French, and it is the Germans who are settling there. Our latest intelligence – so far unconfirmed – is that Dr Karl Peters of the DK – the *Deutsche Kolonisation* – will most likely be giving notice of annexation later this year.'

Guy asked, 'Is the sultan of Witu aware of the provisions of the Berlin agreement?'

'The sultan?'

'Of Witu!'

'My dear fellow!'

'He was not a party to the conference,' Guy persisted.

Mackenzie stared at him. 'An extraordinary suggestion!' He glanced at his ADC.

Fortescue said coldly, 'The cables, sir?'

Mackenzie nodded. 'Of course!'

The ADC took a folder from the table and handed it lugubriously to Saxmundham. Guy's blood rose again at the obvious snub.

'You will see, captain,' Mackenzie went on, 'your arrival could scarcely have been better timed.'

There was a long silence as Saxmundham opened the folder and read through copies of cables loose inside, exclaiming once or twice under his breath. Afterwards he passed it to Smallpiece.

'Well, captain?' Mackenzie asked.

'I fancy we shall be paying a call on his Highness!'

The consul nodded. 'I could hardly believe it when you were reported steaming in. I remarked to Fortescue – their lordships must have risen early!'

The ADC permitted a tight smile to flicker over his mouth.

Smallpiece muttered an oath.

'Nasty business!' Mackenzie said.

'Aye!' the first lieutenant replied, shutting the folder sharply and passing it across to Guy. 'In the name of the Prophet!'

Guy glanced at the first cable; it was to Lord Granville, Secretary of State for Foreign Affairs in London, informing him of rumours of the murder of a British missionary, Paul Straker, whose caravan was passing through the sultanate of Witu on the Kipini road. The next cable was a request for details from the British consul at Lamu – and this was followed by one from Lamu with further reports from native survivors of the caravan who had made their way back to the coast; Straker and his wife and small daughter had all been massacred, together with the only other European, the caravan leader, a German named Herr Weismann. Cables informing London and proposing action to summon the sultan of Witu to deliver the murderers for trial in Lamu were followed by further reports of murders of German settlers; no less than five had been killed in or near the town of Witu itself. 'The Germans endeavouring to escape and being pursued by an infuriated rabble, some armed with guns, some with bows and arrows.' A few days later another settler, Karl Schenke, had been murdered in cold blood at Mkonumbi, 'as alleged by direct order of Fumo Akari, the sultan of Witu', and two others had miraculously escaped after their estates had been devastated by wild mobs, and made their way to the coast.

There followed submissions from Mackenzie to the Foreign Office that the sultan himself be summoned to Lamu with the murderers for trial, cables to the commander-in-chief at the Cape, and to and from the Admiralty in London for ships and men to be made available against the probability of a naval expedition against Witu, messages to and from the German and French consulates.

As Guy finished reading, Mackenzie was saying, '- so you see, captain, the commander-in-chief can only make two gunboats immediately available, and one sloop with a detachment of the Royal Welch aboard is being diverted on her way to China. I fancy that leaves you as senior naval officer – at least until Admiral Ralston's demonstration at Delagoa Bay is called off.'

'You are right,' Saxmundham replied.

'I can't say how delighted I am personally,' Mackenzie continued. 'It also means we can prepare our action rather sooner than I had anticipated.'

'What have you in mind?'

'The best course – in my submission – would be to summon the sultan to Lamu for trial. We have to preserve the forms. Besides, it will be two days at least before the gunboats arrive. Meanwhile, captain, we can make all preparations and draw up orders for the expedition that will assuredly be necessary when the sultan defaults.' He paused expectantly. 'If that meets with your approval.'

'Of course!' Saxmundham replied at once. 'Can't let the rascals get away with it.'

Mackenzie nodded. 'Present estimates suggest the sultan may have as many as 9000 fighting men. Expecting us, I dare say.'

'Good!' Saxmundham said briskly. 'The more of the bla'guards to discharge the debt!'

Mackenzie coughed. 'I know you well enough, captain —eh, to know I need not remind you of the danger of underestimating the natives.'

'Lor'!' the Old Man chuckled. 'I may rely on you not to underestimate the Navy, colonel!'

Smallpiece growled, 'We'll see the murderin' savages answer for it – and the little girl.'

'Don't misunderstand me,' the consul said hurriedly, 'I thought you should know, the natives are a branch of the Masai.' He coughed again. 'Enough said! What I propose, captain, is that we draft out a letter to his Highness. We can sign it jointly. Directly I receive approval from Lord Granville – which I expect by the hour –' he looked up at Fortescue, who nodded, 'we can dispatch it with no further delay.'

'Capital!'

Mackenzie clapped his hands, and an orderly in a close-fitting blue uniform and red turban appeared through the arch from the corridor like a diminutive genie of the lamp.

'*Babu!*' Mackenzie said, and the man disappeared as quickly as he had come, leaving an '*Atcha sah'b*' floating behind him.

The Indian clerk arrived shortly, clutching an enormous exercise book, pens and ink bottle, and stood before Mackenzie.

'Letter,' the consul said shortly. The clerk looked wildly at Fortescue, who nodded towards an empty wicker chair in the half circle before the table. As he moved across and arranged himself on the edge of the seat with his bottle of ink at the very edge of Mackenzie's table the consul put his fingers together before his chin and gazed at the ceiling. He began dictating. 'To his Highness – no, to Fumo Akari, sultan of Witu –' his eyes lowered towards Saxmundham, who nodded.

'After compliments, be it known to you that the – eh, news of the *shameful* deeds that have been done in your territory and all the details connected with the treacherous, foul and –'

'Disgraceful,' Saxmundham put in.

'– and disgraceful murder of three British subjects of Her Imperial Majesty Queen Victoria, and of six German subjects of His Imperial Majesty, Emperor Wilhelm of Germany, and the causeless devastation and destruction of the plantations of other German subjects – all these reports – no, all this news has reached us and been made known to our great government. That'll do for the first paragraph.' He paused.

'And now it is necessary that inquiry be made, that the criminals be arrested, and that justice be done. Therefore, we summon and require you, Sultan Fumo Akari, to meet us at Lamu on the – Captain Fortescue will work out the date on their infernal calendar – Fortescue?'

The ADC nodded.

'On the – whatever it is – in order that inquiry be made and justice be done. You are required to bring with you and deliver up for trial, all the *jumbes* and other criminals connected with or implicated in the shameful and –'

'Disgraceful,' Fortescue said.

'– and disgraceful deeds that have been done in Witu, and in the villages. Everyone shall have a fair trial before God, and will receive fair – will receive strict justice. That will do.'

'Property,' Fortescue said.

'Ah, property. A third paragraph.' He composed himself again. 'And reassurance. We don't wish to frighten the beggar. After all he may come to Lamu and save all you gentlemen the trouble of going out to raze his capital!'

'Heaven forbid!' Smallpiece growled.

Mackenzie looked up at the ceiling again. 'Write this! In coming to Lamu neither you yourself, nor anyone else has anything to fear so long as he may be innocent of any knowledge or of any complicity in these fearful –'

'Dreadful –'

'Disgraceful –'

'– in these dreadful crimes. Every innocent man will be allowed to return in safety as he came. Nothing is required by the great government but that justice is done. But we warn you that if you do not present yourself and if you do not deliver up the criminals and make full restitution of the property of the murdered men – and women – by sending it at once to the British Consulate at Lamu, if you do not do all these things as you are ordered you must take the consequences which will be upon your own head.' He jerked his handsdown and looked at Saxmundham. 'How does that strike you, captain?'

'Dare say it'll amuse the rascal!'

'I have your approval?'

'Assuredly.'

'Good!' He looked at them each in turn, as if searching for reactions to his solo performance while the clerk gathered up his pens and bottle and shuffled out.

'And now, gentlemen,' he went on. 'May I suggest that we sleep on it, and meet here again tomorrow forenoon to work out the details of the expedition that will be required?'

'Agreed!' Saxmundham said. 'But haven't we passed over the arms shipment. After what you've just shown us — bless my soul! There's a connection I'll be bound!'

Mackenzie's gaze hardened. 'The French guns. I suggest we sleep on that one, too.'

Guy said, 'There was a name mentioned in the letter. 'Pierre Suleiman. Would it not be an idea to approach him? Unofficially.'

'Unofficially!' Fortescue said sharply.

'Make out we have a message from Witu,' Guy retorted.

The ADC looked at Mackenzie.

The consul put his fingers together and adopted his lecturing tone again. 'Pierre Suleiman is notorious on this coast. A blacker villain you'd travel a long way to find. He may very well be your man. Indeed I'd lay odds he's in this business somewhere up to his neck. But as for tackling him unofficially — a dangerous game.' He paused, then said decisively, 'We'll ask him to call tomorrow.' He put his hand on the letter. 'With this in front of him he'll be obliged to say something.'

To Guy it seemed evident that whatever Suleiman was obliged to say under official questioning need not be the truth. But if someone were to go to him in the guise of an emissary from Witu – the idea grew more promising the longer he considered it.

'– He made his enormous wealth in slaves and ivory,' Mackenzie was saying, describing Suleiman while his eyes explored the top of the far wall again. 'That was in the days when the slave trade was perfectly legal and the island was a clearing house for the whole coast. We closed down the markets – as you know – so he turned his attentions to supplying French plantation owners with indentured labour.' He snorted. '*Engagés!* Humbug! He instructs the wretches to nod their heads when asked – in French if you please, which they've never so much as heard before in their lives – whether they're willing to work for Monsieur So-and-so. Then he gives 'em a dollar or two to make it legal. The poor devils have a worse time of it than any slaves under an Arab master.'

'Pleasant customer!' Fortescue said quietly.

Saxmundham frowned. 'So the fellow's in league with the froggies already!'

'I wouldn't go so far as that, captain.'

Guy put in, 'But he consorts with the French in the islands.'

The consul swung round on him.

'I should like to say –' Smallpiece growled, and all turned with mixed surprise and relief, '– the sultan, he's preparin' for our reception. Greville's scheme –' he groped for words, 'it could be the means of us finding whether the sultan is already possessed of other modern arms, and who's at the back of it all,' he added belligerently.

Guy wondered what had prompted this support; Smallpiece had never struck him as a man who weighed his actions overmuch beforehand – certainly not the man to be deterred by a few modern guns in the hands of savages. He saw Saxmundham gazing at him speculatively.

'What have you in mind, Greville?'

'Simply this, sir. That I go to Suleiman in the guise of an emissary from the sultan of Witu. That is what the letter suggests might very well happen. My message might be – when is the sultan to expect the arms he has been promised? If I manage to convince him that I have indeed come from Witu I may obtain some answers to the questions the first lieutenant has just raised.'

'If you fail to convince him,' Fortescue cut in, 'the crows'll be pickin' over your bones on the mud flats before sundown tomorrow.'

Mackenzie was staring at him as if such an end would be appropriate.

'To convince him, I shall have to find him before news of the dhow's capture gets abroad.'

'I dare say it's all over Zanzibar by now.'

'We came in after dark,' Guy replied. 'The crew are under guard. We've anchored some distance from the dhow harbour. We may have a few hours.

There was a moment's silence, then Mackenzie slapped the arms of his chair with both hands. 'I'll have no part of it, captain. If you're prepared to allow this – young fellow to risk his neck on a damnfool errand – eh, that is your concern. The consequences be on your own head.'

Guy saw a shadow pass over the Old Man's eyes, and knew the game was his. Mackenzie puffed and made soothing noises as if realizing he had overstepped the mark. Saxmundham preserved a terrible silence.

Chapter Four

The alleys were like rift faults through the buildings; some were so narrow Guy could almost have touched the rough walls at both sides with outstretched arms. He had long since lost all sense of direction as he followed behind his youthful guide along their twists and junctions – for all he knew doubling down blind lanes of a maze. Only the different smells and sounds gave the impression of changing localities; in one quarter the aroma of curry and the high cadences of an Indian love song, in another groups of white-clad Swahili swaying grotesquely on bent knees, trance-like to the rhythm of the long drums, texts from the Koran fluttering on paper streamers, Arab clock-makers and jewellers sitting in open shops surrounded by intricate examples of their art shining in oil lamp light like miniature Aladdin's caves, further on a banyan lady in an embroidered sari, a vision of timeless elegance, and everywhere, throbbing on the heavy air, music, tuneless and interminable merged with smells of coffee and spices and rank humanity in the heady ambience of the East.

The boy turned with a flash of teeth, '*M'bali kidogo, bwana!*'

Guy nodded. The lad might have been saying he was lost. But he looked happy enough. He would in any case. Time, distance, urgency meant nothing to him.

He felt conspicuous and dangerously exposed; in the midst of these teeming worlds he was more alone than he could remember. Fortescue's warnings pressed in as they passed signs of the cheapness in which life was held : a dog with protruding ribs and maggots in its empty eye socket lying where it had fallen days since, still bundles of rags in the angle of the walls, emaciated beggars with fly-blown eyes raising their palms, scurries of movement in the shadows, the whisk of rodent tails.

The excitement he had felt at the prospect of the mission had long since been replaced by apprehension; what had seemed so obvious was now clouded with uncertainty. The Lord knew his impetuosity had led him into any number of scrapes; he couldn't remember one which had lost its charm so quickly. At the start it had been splendid as a midshipman's rag stiffened with real and vitalaims; Mackenzie's disapproval had acted as added stimulus, and his purpose had been clear, to assume the guise of a French adventurer, emissary from Witu, contact Pierre Suleiman, and attempt to draw from him the extent and origin of the arms plot on which they had stumbled.

He had changed into a light cotton suit; Fortescue had briefed him on an assumed identity as a French game hunter newly arrived in the British India steamer, and had told him what he knew of the topography of Witu and the character of its belligerent ruler. Mackenzie had given him until sunset on the morrow to accomplish the mission. He had grinned like the overconfident goat he was. Lord, he had thought the time ample! It had begun to stretch before him like a nightmare as doubts surfaced. Did the sultan speak French himself or would the message come through an interpreter? Would it be direct from him or from his vizier or other minister? Was Suleiman a power behind the intrigue or just a courier? His ignorance touched every aspect of the affair; any one of his uncertainties might give him away, and if Suleiman once began to suspect, and question him at all deeply. . . .

The oppressively odorous passages through which he was being led, the close buildings shutting out air and space, his disorientation after their many turns made him feel as though he were passing into a labyrinth from which there was no escape. He had been in danger before, but never so alone. Images of security pressed in: his minute cabin off the ward-room with his sporting gear, the cricket bats and the racquets wedged tightly in the corner, his twelve-bore on the bulk-head by the flowered chintz curtains, the photographs of his parents and his brothers and two younger sisters, the picture of galloping horses done by his favourite little sister, Helen....

His thoughts turned to Saxmundham. Fear would never enter the Old Man's head. He would bestride these pestilential alleys with their filth and dark and greening pools, despising them, as he would despise Suleiman. He would outface the man on his own ground without any weapons save the dignity and awe of the captain of a

British man-of-war. Doubt would never trouble him. It was a reassuring image. And yet it was difficult to imagine Saxmundham taking part in this game; guile was not in his vocabulary.

A momentary weakness seized his stomach as his thoughts came back to Suleiman, according to Fortescue a rogue without morals or scruples. In the beginning his reputation for total ruthlessness had been deliberately engineered as a part of his stock in trade in the slave and ivory business; whole areas of the interior had been terrorized by the sound of his name alone. He had been known as the 'Devastator'. Fumo Akari, now sultan of Witu, who shared his background in the slave trade was known as the 'Lion'. It was his boast that when the 'Lion' roared all the natives to the great lakes and beyond cowered in terror.

The boy had stopped and was gesturing towards an open doorway in an arch, a mindless grin splitting his face. Guy's chest thumped. They had arrived. This was the coffee house where the merchants foregathered – Suleiman amongst them.

He felt in his pocket for coins, his eyes searching the dimly lit interior. It was crowded with Arabs seated on low benches before tables dotted with little porcelain cups and bubbling water pipes. The atmosphere was hung with smoke and the soft hum of a score of conversations. Higher, more urgent tones came from a group of Indians gathered around a central pillar. He saw one draw a green bag from the folds of his robe, untie the neck and cascade a stream of coins on the table before him; the chatter ceased briefly.

He pulled a coin from his own pocket and handed it to his guide, receiving a torrent of Swahili in return. He caught the words, '*bwana mkubwa*' – 'great master'! The next moment the lad had turned and made off. For an instant desperation closed in. But it was too late to turn away. He walked in through the arch.

As he entered the atmosphere of smoke and coffee he became aware of a man staring at him from a corner table to the right. He returned the look – a European with a penetrating green gaze. Beside him was a woman, the only one to be seen; as she noticed the direction of her companion's gaze she too looked up; she had wide cheeks and thick negroid lips which broke into a smile as she saw him.

He walked the few paces towards the two and bowed his head. '*Madame – monsieur – bonsoir!*'

'We speak English!' the man said without responding to the greeting. There was a Scot's lilt to his voice.

'*Bien!*' Guy replied with a flourish, 'I too speak English!'

The woman rose, her ample bosom swaying independently inside a flame-coloured *kanga*. 'You sit – speak Englishi –' she flashed a full smile at the Scot. 'I go –' and she held up a hand coquettishly as if they were about to object. 'Yes, yes!'

The Scot remained seated, watching unconcernedly as she moved away with rolling buttocks. He was young, in his late twenties perhaps. His nose, chin and cheeks were deeply tanned, his forehead white by contrast. His green eyes had lines of strain about them, and the skin was stretched tightly over his cheek bones: not an easy man; a man who drove himself and others. He slapped the bench which the woman had vacated, mimicking her 'Yes, yes!' as he invited Guy to sit. Guy accepted with relief.

'Ye've strayed some distance from the Gymkhana Club!' the Scot began abruptly. There was a resentful edge to his voice.

Guy thrust out his hand. 'Permit me, *monsieur,* to introduce myself. Guy de Longchamps.'

The Scot grinned as he grasped the hand in a hard, calloused grip. 'Alexander Cameron.'

There was silence for a moment. 'It is good to see another white face,' Guy started. 'I do not know the language.'

Cameron regarded him with a curious, direct stare. 'Yer English is good.' He wore a wry smile. Guy had an alarming impression he knew he was no Frenchman.

An Arab boy in a white robe bent towards them. Cameron asked Guy whether he would like sweetmeats; he shook his head and the Scot ordered coffee and sherbet for two. After the boy had gone he patted the pocket of his jacket. 'I have something a wee bit stronger here. D'ye fancy German gin?'

'You know, in France we are not so fond of things German!' Guy shrugged expressively.

The Scot smiled. 'It's only three pence a bottle, and that goes some way to make up for what it lacks in distinction. Ye may say the same of the German trader!' His voice took on the belligerent edge again, and he went on without a pause. 'Ye're new.'

'I come by the British India *pacquet* this afternoon.

Cameron gazed at him quizzically.

'I am come for the sport.'

'Game?'

'Ah!' Guy grinned. 'That is it – the game.'

'Why not Mombasa?'

'In Lamu I meet my good friend who knows the game. He tells me I must go to see Pierre Suleiman in Zanzibar. Suleiman can show me the good shooting – engage the porters –'

'Pierre Suleiman!'

Guy nodded, surprised by the sharp response.

The Scot inclined his head towards the far wall, which was partly obscured by intervening arches across the centre of the room. 'There's yer man.'

Guy knew immediately whom he meant. Even in the dim light one face stood out from the rest in the group of Arabs Cameron had indicated. The man was listening, not talking, but strength of feature and arrogance of bearing marked him out.

Cameron was gazing at him speculatively. 'If ye wish, I'll introduce ye.' He paused. 'Although I think it unlikely he'll bother himself wi' a sportsman.'

'*Au pis aller,*' Guy shrugged. 'My friend say I must talk with him.'

Cameron looked down into his cup, dashing the contents around as he held it between both palms. 'My friend, there's two sub-species of *Homo sapiens* I consider myself an expert on. One is the Masai – an' if ye're after game that's one ye'll need to study. The other –' he paused, 'the English.' He looked up. 'The English *gentleman,* mind.'

Guy's brows rose.

The Scot leaned closer. 'If ye're a Frenchman, I'm a water buffalo!'

The suddenness and certainty of the accusation struck Guy like a blow. There was a fierce, half-humorous light in Cameron's eyes. He was sure enough. He wondered if it mattered; Suleiman was the one he had to convince. Evidently the Scot knew him, and knew his way around here. He would make a good ally; perhaps it was just as well he had been unmasked. He grinned. 'Lord! You smelled me out quick enough!'

'Aye,' Cameron smiled, pleased with himself. 'Perhaps ye'll have noticed, I dinna belong to either one of the species!'

'You're a Scot,' Guy said. 'At a guess –' he added with a grin.

'And no gentleman!' The green eyes bored into his. 'Let's be honest now, would they allow a wild fellow like myself into the Gymkhana Club!'

'I couldn't say.'

'I wouldna bawther.' Cameron's accent became more pronounced as he grew more vehement. 'Ye wish to know how I knew ye were English? It's no' difficult to recognize the lords of the wurrld!'

Guy returned the belligerent gaze.

'A Frenchman doesna stand in the doorway of an Arab coffee house as if he owns it,' Cameron went on fiercely. 'A German, mebbe. But a German will make bloody certain *everyone* knows it. There's just the one species doesna have to bawther. The matter's never in question.' His eyes glinted. Then suddenly he smiled, showing uneven teeth.

'But ye made a good fist of it – aye, ye had me wondering whether I'd not mistaken ye!'

'Will I get past Suleiman's guard, d'you suppose?'

'He's a shrewd man. And a dangerous one to play games with. But I doubt he's made such a study of the species. Aach, but ye *look* too English, man! *Bend* a wee bitty, *give* a wee bitty! And, remember, Suleiman's the master *here!*' He jabbed his finger down at the table. 'Dinna forget that!'

Guy fingered the cup half full of dark, aromatic coffee that had been placed before him while Cameron was talking, and the Scot made a gesture towards the pocket in which he kept his bottle of German gin. Guy shook his head, and raised the cup to his lips. The coffee was strong and bitter.

'Ye'll need all yer wits about ye,' Cameron went on. He sipped his sherbet and gazed at Guy speculatively. 'Not that I know what it is ye're really about.'

'It would take the dickens of a time to tell. Time's not exactly on my side,' he added, thinking of the dhow tied up alongside the *Dulcinea*.

Guy Grinned.

'I heed my marching orders.' Cameron rose. '*Monsieur!*'

Guy swallowed the coffee and stood beside him, noticing for the first time how slight the Scot was. He guessed he was made of steel wire.

'If ye need help –' Cameron said.

'It's very decent of you.'

'Madame Orientale generally knows my whereabouts.'

'*La femme charmante!*' Guy made a Gallic flourish.

Cameron smiled briefly before turning to lead the way towards a central arch that allowed access to the other half of the room. Guy looked across at Suleiman, still a silent listener. He saw that the group about him was spread along divans very much more luxurious than the bare benches on which he and Cameron had been sitting; they glowed with deep hues of carpets and cushions. Suleiman himself was resplendent in white with a cloak of cloth of gold thrown across his shoulders and held loosely across his chest by knotted golden tassels. His white head-cloth was bound with a similar golden rope with tasselled ends; at his waist was a glimpse of crimson silk and the jewelled haft of a dagger. He appeared to take no notice as they approached, although he must have been aware of their presence. Before they reached him, he leaned towards a white-bearded man next to him and began talking, emphasizing points with sweeping gestures of his arm. From up close Guy was struck by his features, a high, broad forehead, widely spaced, light-coloured eyes over a flattened negroid nose, full lips turned down cruelly at the corners, a startling mixture of Arab, European and African. The total effect was extraordinary in its power and rapacious-ness.

Cameron stopped at the edge of the group and when Suleiman looked up, put his hand to his chest and inclined his head in greeting. Guy copied his actions and Suleiman and his companions responded courteously. Suleiman's pale eyes showed neither curiosity nor welcome, but after the ritual catechism of greetings and compliments, he swung his arm with the same flowing action Guy had noticed before, inviting them to a place in the group. Guy wondered if he were expected to sit on the floor, but found on turning that a low, silk-upholstered stool had been placed behind him. He sank down after Cameron had introduced him, speaking in English.

Suleiman replied in English, courtly and sibilant, offering plates of sweetmeats while deprecating the poor hospitality that was all he could offer in the unfortunate house in which he found himself. Guy replied that the surroundings were charming and the sweetmeats delicious. Suleiman inclined his head.

'My friend is a sportsman,' Cameron said.

The Arab nodded with that curious, expressionless gaze.

Guy took the opening, 'At Lamu I am informed that Pierre Suleiman has no equal as leader of the caravan.'

'Your friend is generous,' Suleiman replied.

'Also, he says no one knows so well the *lions* of Witu.'

Suleiman's eyes held Guy's.

'Fumo Akari will not make difficulties for you,' Guy pressed on. He felt a strange elation, as if reaching the crucial move in a planned chess gambit. The thrust of play must now be evident to his opponent.

'But Fumo Akari does not make difficulties,' Suleiman said softly.

Guy shrugged. 'I am informed that for some he makes difficulty, but for you, he has a great regard. You are' – he groped for the word – '*copain*'.

Suleiman's glance flicked towards Cameron, then back again to Guy. 'Your friend is very well informed. It is good to hear news of the "Lion", may God shower mercies on his head. It gives me great pleasure to assist in any way, *monsieur*. It will be an honour if you will accept hospitality under my roof. Travellers are welcome, those who bring words of friends thrice welcome. God's peace be on you.'

Guy bowed his head. 'It shall give me great pleasure.'

Cameron explained something to Suleiman in Swahili, and he nodded then turned back to Guy. 'In the morning we shall talk of safaris and of Witu.'

Guy tried to keep the triumph from his eyes. It had been easier than he had expected, after all. The critical time was before him, but for the moment at any rate, Suleiman appeared to accept his role as messenger.

Cameron threw himself into his part as go-between, establishing that Guy had arrived in the British India steamboat and was well known in Europe as a remarkable hunter; he allowed free reign to his imagination, naming several museums to which Guy had donated specimens of rare beasts. Suleiman nodded appreciatively, but directly the conversation lapsed he took the opportunity to stand and make his farewells. Guy rose with him.

On their way to the door they passed Cameron's half-caste lady friend; he wondered that the Scot had not found himself a less full-blown consort. But perhaps that was the direction his taste lay. It was amusing to think of him, as lean and keen as a whippet, calming his resentment at not being admitted into the Gymkhana Club in her Rubenesque bosom. Cameron was an attractive charac-ter. There was no pretence about him. He had played his part with Suleiman with enormous enthusiasm. He looked back by the doorway and saw him gazing after them with that curiously intense stare of his ; as he raised his hand in farewell he wondered if he would ever see him again.

Outside, they were joined by two negroes – slaves of Suleiman's. One was huge and light-skinned, carrying a dark, rolled parasol with a striped handle, the other was smaller and blacker carrying a long, needle-sharp spear bound with brass, and over his left shoulder a yellowing rhino-hide shield ; both had straight Arab swords and curved daggers thrust into their waistbands. The two appeared silently from the shadows against a doorway opposite and fell in behind as Suleiman turned to the right and led off down the narrow street. The way in which things happened around Suleiman, smoothly and silently and without instructions, was impressive; he thought of the torrent of hurled orders and abuse expected aboard a man-of-war.

'You are young for a sportsman of such fame,' Suleiman said.

'Cameron!' Guy smiled, '*L'imagination!*'

'The gazelle, it was named for you?'

'Assuredly not!' Guy waved his arms as if the idea were preposterous. 'No, no. I tell Cameron I wish to meet you. The stories, that is all his idea.'

'He is a good friend!'

Guy looked round, wondering if he detected a sarcastic bite in the remark. The Arab was staring ahead, little interested it seemed. They walked on in silence. He wondered whether it was the moment to introduce the purpose of his mission, or whether he should leave it to Suleiman to inquire and perhaps give a lead by the nature of the question. Yet it didn't seem that he would; the opportunity had been there with his own denial of Cameron's story;

Suleiman had not taken it; he remained provocatively silent, apparently deep in thought. Perhaps questions were not his style; perhaps he was waiting, confident that he had played his part in bringing about this situation in which they were alone together, leaving the next move to Guy. He cast around for the right approach, the general phrase that would not commit him to anything specific.

There was a screech from the shadows of an alley to his right, and a cat flashed across just in front of them and leaped, clawing up a wooden support to a doorway, crouching, bristling at the top. Suleiman stopped and stared as if transfixed, his hand moving as if by instinct to the handle of his dagger. He looked round at Guy, smiling briefly without humour before walking on, muttering, '*C'est un mauvais augure!*'

Guy glanced at him with new interest, wondering what other omens might affect him in this way. There was no doubt he had been momentarily stricken.

The Arab's stride became longer and more purposeful after the incident, his cloak of silence deeper. The moment to broach a message had passed.

They turned into a wealthier quarter of the town where the roads were limed and rough gutters ran down each side. The great rectangular houses reared like fortresses, each with huge, elaborately carved wooden doors studded with brass to attest the owner's standing. Suleiman soon stopped before one of these, and as it began to open, gestured to Guy to enter.

Beyond a dark entrance hall a courtyard was visible, fringed by trees and shrubs whose foliage was robbed of colour by the night. Verandahs ran along the wall beyond; Guy caught a hint of movement on the lower one but whoever or whatever it was disappeared as he looked. He felt a moment of doubt as he stepped through the doorway, seeing two more armed slaves standing in the shadows. The air was cooler here, and deliciously scented with hibiscus and frangipani from the courtyard.

'You have a fine house,' he said.

Suleiman inclined his head. 'In the name of God the merciful, you are welcome!'

The slave who had opened the door closed it behind them and shot the great bolts. The sound gave a disturbing impression of finality. Guy's uneasiness returned, and he wondered if he had walked straight into a trap. He thrust the idea from his mind. Suleiman could not suspect; nothing had been said yet. But the man's attitude had changed. The twist at the corners of his lips had spread in a curious way up the creases beside his nose; his eyes, shining palely beneath the high brow were as cold as the moonlight. The mask had slipped.

Almost immediately it was up again. 'You would enjoy some refreshment?'

'Thank you, no. You will not think it impolite if I retire?'

'Of course! Nkanda will attend to your needs.' Suleiman clapped his hands, leading the way past two more statuesque slaves identically uniformed and armed with spears, swords and shields, towards a flight of steps within the arches beneath the first-floor verandah. At the bottom of the steps they were greeted by a light-coloured

African of even more enormous proportions than the slave who carried the parasol – evidently Nkanda. He carried a lantern, and his teeth flashed in its light as Suleiman gave him instructions. He had a wide, friendly face with smooth cheeks which puffed out like balloons when he smiled, a frequent occurrence. His voice as he answered was thin and high.

'Now, *monsieur,*' Suleiman said, turning, 'May God bestow all His blessings on your rest. And tomorrow – we shall talk of Witu and you shall tell me of my old friend of many caravans.

Guy felt a shiver of apprehension. 'It is little I have to tell.'

'Little is a feast to one from the desert.'

Guy decided that the moment had arrived. 'Your *confrère,* Fumo Akari, sends felicitations, begging God, the merciful, the compassionate to watch over your house. He sends this message –' He took an impulsive guess, inspired by the affair with the cat, 'It is the time to act. His sooth-sayers have told him, now is the time. He asks when he may expect the guns he is promised. This is his message, *monsieur.*'

Suleiman regarded him steadily. 'It is late and you are tired. We shall speak in the morning. You will remember more.' He nodded his head briefly before turning and striding towards the opposite corner of the courtyard.

Guy's blood chilled. Ever since the bolts had clanged shut, he had sensed a difference in Suleiman's bearing; now it was confirmed. The Arab's words echoed in his mind like a threat '... in the morning. You will remember more.'

'*Shikamu!*' Nkanda said, bowing obsequiously, his cheeks blown out in a grin. He motioned Guy to follow up the flight of narrow steps. '*Fuatana nami, bwana!*'

The room he was led to on the first floor was long and narrow with a high, beamed ceiling making it appear even narrower. It was sparsely furnished with a low bed covered with a rug designed in reds and blues, and there was a similar rug in the centre of the floor, which dipped down towards the right like a warship's deck. In the lower corner was a shallow earthenware basin on a woven coconut fibre mat, and a little distance from it two square stuffed objects like hassocks together with a three-cornered stool with an animal hide stretched across to form the seat. The walls, which were neither straight nor perpendicular, were limed and inset with alcoves and niches of different shapes. Although much of the lime-wash had worn off the impression was of spotless cleanliness. One narrow, shuttered window faced him high on the wall over the bed. He saw a star winking through.

Nkanda waited with his light by the curtain across the doorway.

Guy turned to him. 'You speak Englishi?'

The smile widened; the balloon cheeks twitched. 'Englishi – *ndio bwana, kidogo tu,*' and seeing that Guy did not understand, 'Little, *bwana.*' He made a wavy motion with his hand.

Guy felt suddenly tired as if drained of all energy by the role he had been playing, and he sat on the bed swinging his legs up and letting his head sink into soft cushions beneath the rug. He closed his eyes; the image of Nkanda grinning in the doorway remained behind the lids. He wondered if he were a prisoner. There was little sense in attempting to find out; the interview with Suleiman in the morning would settle questions of that sort. He felt another stab of apprehension as he remembered the Arab's expression in the brief moments when the guard had dropped. He tried to exorcize it by thinking back over the affair from the beginning.

The letter had been explicit: messages should be sent via Pierre Suleiman. This implied that the arrangement was relatively new. Had it been established there would have been no need to mention it. And the whole content – 'token of our trust', 'pledge of our friendship' suggested that the alliance itself was new and untested. 'As our friendship ripens', 'such is the delicacy of our relationship' reinforced the point. If lines of communication had not previously been established, surely no particular emissary could have been expected. Why then should Suleiman suspect the first one?

Perhaps a codeword had been arranged earlier; perhaps the Arab felt there had been insufficient time for the consignment to have reached Witu and a messenger to have travelled back to Zanzibar? Neither was likely. The operation was so delicate that knowledge of it and Suleiman as the courier were likely to be passwords in themselves, while the British India steamer would have made a faster passage from Lamu than the *Dulcinea* with her tow. No, the probable explanation was that he himself was suspect. But he had said little. He could not speak Swahili, but Suleiman didn't know, all their conversation had been in English –

The answer came to him suddenly. From the start he had suspected the language used in the letter; it had been too pedantic; not even a governor would express himself in quite that style. He had been right – and so had Mackenzie and Fortescue. *It was not a French intrigue.* By posing as a Frenchman he had given the game away as surely as if he had announced himself a British naval officer. His stomach felt hollow. He opened his eyes. Nkanda was still waiting by the doorway with his lantern and his wide smile.

He felt certain the man had instructions to prevent him leaving, and he swung his feet to the floor with the intention of finding out when the curtains parted and a young girl holding a pitcher of water appeared, another close behind with towels over her arm. They stared at him, wide-eyed and hesitant until Nkanda beckoned them in. The one with the pitcher made towards the basin in the corner, throwing him glances as she went; she had a round face like a child although he noticed that her breasts were well formed and her hips already large. He rose and walked towards the basin, holding his hands out as she inclined the pitcher. The water was cool and sweet-smelling. He bent and washed his face, and rinsed his mouth, then nodded, and the girl placed the pitcher on the floor as the other came up with towels. She was smiling widely, a coquettish gleam in her eyes. As he took the towel he twisted it suddenly. She jumped back, yelping with fright, then shrilled with laughter; her gums were already dark and her teeth stained. The child-like one started cackling, too, bringing her hands up nervously to her face. He assumed a harsh expression and shooed them out.

Returning to the bed, he saw that a white gown had been laid across it, evidently his night attire. He sat down at the foot and bent wearily to untie the laces. Nkanda took this as a sign to leave, and after placing the lantern in a corner niche, bowed himself out through the curtains with muttered invocations to Allah – '*Rabi el alamina!*'

Guy listened for the sound of footsteps along the corridor, but none came. He was waiting outside. Faithful servant or guard? The morning would tell.

Chapter Five

He awoke to the sound of muezzins calling the faithful to prayer. What he could see of the sky through the chinks of the shuttered window was still dark, touched with a hint of grey. The drums accompanying the prayer-callers far and near reminded him of the night, but there was a different feeling to the rhythm.

Apprehension of the coming interview with Suleiman flooded him like remembrance of a nightmare. Before falling asleep he had gone over the events of the evening time after time, seeking an explanation, preparing different tactics to meet different situations, different attitudes from Suleiman. Now at the nadir of the spirit in the dark before dawn the exercises seemed pointless and unreal. He felt his knowledge so puny that Suleiman would have no difficulty in breaking down his pretence.

He had an image of the mud flats in the harbour and rotting corpses exposed at low water. Nkanda was intoning just outside the curtain. Suleiman would be praying, too.

He knew something of the Mohammedan religion from his father. Suleiman would believe all things predestined, even to the hour and manner of death. He would expect no escape from the all-embracing will of Allah; he would desire no escape, but submit himself to His will at dawn and at regular intervals throughout the day.

Guy had a glimpse of his own destiny woven in the grand design, the day's panel awaiting him in glowing detail as it had since the Creation, a portion of mud flat inscribed in the heavenly mind with his body? Slither of prehistoric reptiles, silt of the earth over living black coral, decayed vegetation, clicking crabs, sea birds wading and dipping, human refuse, husks of coconut and fish bones tipped from the stinking streets of the city stretching back through centuries awaiting his own husk on the numbered day –

Scenes of boyhood superimposed on the repulsive images: the water meadows at Godalming glowed in sheets of buttercup yellow up to white clouds of hawthorn blossom; his two little sisters bent and called out to him as they picked from the rich carpet of flowers – but he was after a brimstone butterfly. He had glimpsed it, then lost it in the thick grass, and he chased in circles, seeking it again. He found a striped caterpillar instead and carried it carefully home to find out what it was. The girls shouted at him for doing always what *he* wished, and Helen pummelled him, knowing that boys were not supposed to retaliate.

The images followed haphazardly in the half-world between sleep and waking – his prep school on the hill – the *Britannia* – his sisters' glowing faces as they were rowed out to the old ship for the Christmas ball. He remembered his father at Prize Day thumping his back after he had gone up to accept the pile of leather-bound prizes from Admiral Sir Henry Keppel – a surprisingly small man the shape of a mooring bollard with a merry eye and a host of unbelievable yarns.

All the care and love and striving extinguished, mud crabs feeding on empty tissues that had been learning and ambition. In the low, half-world of early morning it seemed unthinkably pointless.

He made an effort to shake off the morbid ideas. There was no all-embracing will. God helped those who helped themselves; his father had preached that sermon often enough, and he had proved it himself many a time. He had willed things to happen and used his wits to ensure that they did, going round the end of the wall if he couldn't leap it. 'This boy will make his way', his first *Britannia* report had concluded, 'but whether in Her Majesty's Service or in another field of his own choosing only time will tell.' He remembered his father's puzzled face as he read the sentence through again and again. The term lieutenant had misread his exasperation with the petty regulations that governed every moment aboard the training ship.

He was not a passive puppet in a story already written. Suleiman would believe it though. He would believe it as he had believed in the crossing cat as a bad omen. For whom had the cat appeared, Suleiman or himself? Of course – for Suleiman; only he believed!

He became aware of Nkanda peering at him from around the curtain. The darkness in the room had given way to grey; outlines were forming. The smooth face disappeared as he looked, leaving the curtain twitching momentarily. He threw back thesheets, swung his legs down and walked across to the water pitcher, stumbling slightly as he forgot the slope of the floor; he soused his hands and face and rubbed the sleep from his eyes. With the return of circulation his apprehensions faded. He went to the small window and gazed up at the brightness of dawn spreading almost perceptibly over the patch of sky that was visible; his strength and spirits revived with it. God was in His heaven. He found himself looking forward to meeting Suleiman again, and the battle of wits that must ensue.

He dressed in his underclothes and started the exercises with which he always began the day, ashore or at sea when the weather permitted. Later, in the heat, exertion would be impossible. After loosening up, he stood before the window again and sucked air in, swinging his arms in Indian club motions, then he squatted and jumped his feet back into the press-up position. After twenty-five presses his forehead was beading with perspiration. He paused, then for the sheer exuberance of being on dry land pushed his legs up into a hand-stand and walked on his hands down the slope to the far wall.

He heard a movement and dropped his feet to the floor. Nkanda was standing holding the curtain up with a puzzled expression on his face; next to him was the young slave girl who had brought the pitcher of water the night before. She was holding a bowl piled high with rice and what appeared to be a whole chicken in the centre. Her eyes were childishly round as she stared at him. Behind was the other girl, carrying another two bowls, bending so that she too could see under Nkanda's arm.

The blood pumped in his temples. He performed an exaggerated shooing gesture and they backed away, Nkanda letting the curtain drop before him.

'I dress,' he called. 'You come. After!'

Nkanda muttered something in reply.

He went to his clothes neatly folded at the foot of the bed and dressed quickly but meticulously, dismayed by a faint ring of grime inside his collar, the result of the walk through the steaming alleys to the coffee shop. There was no brush or comb.

'Nkanda!' he called.

The curtain lifted immediately.

'Comb!' he said, miming the actions to suit.

The large man beamed, '*Kitana!*' and said he would bring one in a little time. The girls entered with the dishes.

'Where *bwana* Suleiman?' Guy asked, gesturing to the food. '*Bwana* not eat along me?'

'*Bwana Mkubwa* go.' Nkanda flung his arm wide. 'He come – little time.'

'Where he go?'

The big man shrugged and raised his brows, '*Alitoka tu* –' The girls arranged the dishes on the mat in the centre of the floor, darting glances at him as they did so. When they had gone Nkanda waited, beaming and nodding towards the food. The chicken was cold, but the rice heaped around it was still steaming. There were no knives or forks or spoons, nor were there any with the other bowls which contained little cakes and dates and figs. He patted the bed and indicated that he wished the dish placed on it. The slave complied and Guy sat beside it.

'Nkanda,' he said, wondering how to phrase the question he wished to ask. Suleiman would consult a soothsayer, he was certain. He wanted to see the man first. 'Fetch doctori,' he started. 'Witch doctori –'

The slave frowned.

'Medicine man,' he tried.

The frown deepened.

On an impulse Guy turned to the chicken beside him, and seizing one leg at a time pulled both from the body; they came away easily. He pretended to pull the bird's entrails and spread them on the bed, gazing long and seriously before intoning in a deep voice, 'Chicken say bad day come – much man die –'

The effect of his performance was electric. The slave was moving away white-eyed.

'Fetch man who say dis t'ing,' he said sternly.

Nkanda backed wordlessly through the curtain.

He picked up one of the chicken legs and put it to his mouth; it was deliciously tender. When he had finished both legs and one side of white breast which flaked away in succulent wedges, he replaced the bowl on the carpet and was starting on the dates when the slave girls entered in an aroma of coffee with a conical brass coffee pot, a cup, pitcher of fresh water and towels. Was it his imagination, or was their manner more inhibited than before? He hadn't heard Nkanda saying anything. He went quickly to the curtain and pulled it aside.

A small, wizened creature looked up at him with rheumy eyes rimmed with creases like those of an old monkey. He wore a cloak with red and yellow designs over a light fawn *kanzu* and on his head a red fez. He clutched what appeared to be a slate and a preserving jar close to his stomach with bony fingers. Nkanda, standing beside him like a black giant, introduced him as the mchawi.

'*Jambo, bwana,*' the mchawi said.

'*Bwana* is well?' Nkanda explained.

Guy nodded. 'Ask him if he is well.'

'*Jambo sana,*' the slave said and went through the ritual inquiries, after which Guy gestured to them to enter. He guessed the little man must be the witch doctor – very much sooner than he had expected. The girls left hurriedly as soon as they could, and the mchawi squatted down on the centre mat where the dishes had been, placing his slate before him while Nkanda remained just inside the doorway, watching. The little man shook some fine sand from his jar, moving it deliberately over the slate until a thin layer covered most of the surface. He placed the bottle beside him and looked up at Guy, extending his open hand towards him, nodding towards Guy's right arm. Guy sank to his haunches before him and held his hand out; the old man grasped it and placed it over the sand, muttering something as he released his grip. Guy looked round at Nkanda.

'*Tia kidole, bwana!*' the slave said, and mimed drawing a trace with his finger. 'Speak mchawi which thing bwana like see.'

Guy placed his finger on the slate and drew it through the sand. '*Bwana* Suleiman *friend* along me? Talk along me?' He made a wide gesture with his arms. 'All thing?'

Nkanda translated and the old man gazed into his eyes with a curious, penetrating stare as if seeing through into his mind. Then he drew what appeared to be a coconut fibre or dried leaf stem from somewhere about his person and leaning forward over the slate passed the fibre very rapidly through the sand from right to left in a scribbling motion six times, leaving six roughly parallel marks like crude depictions of wavy seas. Starting at the bottom line he ticked off the waves in twos, clicking his tongue against his teeth as he did so. When he had finished he gazed at the result and started talking in low, sing-song cadences, pointing to the second line once or twice with his fibre.

When his voice ceased Nkanda turned to Guy. 'Not good, *bwana. Hapana kuja sawa.*' He knotted his brow in an effort to interpret. 'Nothing come, *bwana.*'

It seemed a cryptic translation of the monologue. '*Bwana* Suleiman not friend?' Guy gestured to his heart. 'Not talk along me?'

Nkanda's eyes rolled upwards as if he were trying desperately to reconcile the demands of hospitality with the truths he had just learned, and he shook his big head so that the cheeks wobbled. 'Friend – oh, friend *bado kidogo.*'

'No friend now?'

'Not talk with *bwana,*' Nkanda said desperately, shaking his head again.

Guy stared, wondering what he was hiding and why he appeared so agitated. Before he could say anything the mchawi was intoning again, this time pointing occasionally to the top line of his slate. Afterwards Nkanda told him that he, Guy, had a troubled spirit, and after another monologue that the place where he was going was deeply troubled and bad things happened there, very bad things and much blood. After another monologue, which appeared to be an interpretation of the fourth line, Nkanda told him that his hopes would be dashed, or so Guy understood it; the next line revealed that he had no enemies.

'*Bwana* Suleiman no friend,' Guy cut in, 'but no enemy?'

Nkanda seemed as bewildered, but after excited exchanges with the mchawi reiterated more strongly that Guy had no enemies.

The last line was an anticlimax, either because Nkanda's translation was not up to the subtleties of meaning, or there was nothing to reveal. Whichever it was, it didn't come out.

'*Hapana kuona zaidi!*' the mchawi said, staring up at him with his sad monkey eyes.

'Mchawi not see,' Nkanda said.

Guy felt disappointed. Of course, the performance was nothing but a fraud for the gullible – but an impressive one, and he found that despite himself he wanted desperately to hear more. Nkanda's anxiety not to reveal his master's animosity, and the prophecies about his own troubled spirit rang strange bells. The man might, perhaps, have guessed that he was troubled while staring into his eyes at the start of the rigmarole. Yet he had not felt worried then. He had shaken off the morbid half-dreams of dawn; he had been interested, keyed up, confident, eager to gauge the fortune-teller's art and how he might use the man against his master, but not troubled. As for the place to which he was going, Witu was certainly troubled. So indeed were the mud flats.

If the effects on him were so strong, how must it be with believers! He tried to thrust the prophecies aside to concentrate on the more pressing question of how to use what little he had learned. Suleiman might return at any moment.

The mchawi began very painstakingly to sweep the sand with the sides of his palms into the middle of the slate, seemingly trying to ensure that not a single grain escaped his attention. Guy recognized the studied slowness and felt in his pockets for coins, pulling out several, flicking one up on his thumb and catching it. The scraping speeded up and the old man upended the slate over the mouth of the jar so quickly that not much more than half the sand went in, the rest scattering over the mat. He stood and touched his chest. Guy held out the coins and the old man stared in surprise before reaching out for them, repeating his salaams more vigorously, accompanied by fervent blessings of Allah. Then he left, followed by Nkanda.

Guy heard only one set of footsteps shuffling down the passage; he guessed that Nkanda was in his old position just behind the curtain. He wondered if he would tell Suleiman about the soothsaying. It was difficult to assess the effect it might have; the reference to the troubled place Guy was destined for surely fitted Witu – at the least it might sow a seed of doubt. Probably he would consult the mchawi himself. It was for that reason and possible future benefits that he had tipped the old man heavily.

He looked out through the slats of the window, wondering how long he would have to wait. The clear sky of early morning had given way to massed grey cloud; the air was already hot and moist, and as he stood gazing at the ominous scene, he heard the first drops of rain. The patter increased rapidly until the air was filled with the sound of beating water. He wondered if Suleiman were out there somewhere, making his way back. He imagined the parasol held over his head by the slave. It would be small protection in this deluge.

He took off his jacket and lowered himself to the bed, swinging his legs up and placing his hands behind his head.

The morning wore on heavily; the rain gave no sign of easing, the ever-present sound of it damping out all the noises he had grown accustomed to hear from the streets outside. There was nothing but rain and sticky heat and the high, mangrove-beamed ceiling of his room and Nkanda just outside the door – and somewhere, far or near, Suleiman.

He had never taken easily to waiting. As the empty minutes passed into hours his mood changed through shades of increasing irritation to anger. Suleiman was making an ass of him. The man had no intention of talking to him this morning, or any other time; he was keeping him here only until he found a suitable method of disposal.

He would receive a nasty shock when the *Dulcinea's* marines surrounded the house! He thought of the scene aboard; already there would be some anxiety about his nonappearance; preparations would be afoot. Heighurst and possibly Smallpiece himself with a detachment of bluejackets would be planning the assault when the time he had been allowed ran out on the stroke of six. He hoped Suleiman would be back by then to receive them. Perhaps he was back already. Perhaps he had never left. Perhaps this waiting was deliberately contrived to break his nerve before the interview.

Lunch appeared in the same way as breakfast in a haze of curry steam, and was laid out in the same style in great dishes on the mat in the centre of the room. He jumped up and relieved his feelings on Nkanda, cursing him for not remembering that he liked his meals on the bed, and ordering something to eat it with – did he think a white man's fingers made of iron like his own fat head! The slave's eyes rolled whitely.

And where was *bwana* Suleiman! Was it hospitality to leave one's guests for the morning? Were guests like slaves or concubines to wait on the convenience of the master? Was he less than a woman or a slave?

'*Bwana mkubwa* – him come – *bado kidogo* –'

'A little time – you lie! Where *bwana* Suleiman?'

The slave shook his head vigorously and spread his arms, then turned in anguish to the girls, letting out a torrent of orders which sounded like curses. They left hurriedly. He bowed himself out after them.

Guy looked at the meal. The curry was spicy and thick with mutton, but he had no appetite for it, nor for the sweet cakes and fruit to follow. The girl who returned shortly to pour water and dry his fingers was obviously frightened by his expression. How easy, he thought, to become a tyrant if it were expected. Frightened, the girl looked even more childish and he felt a wave of pity for her as she backed uncertainly to the curtains. He smiled and she returned it.

The moist heat built up through the afternoon ; lying down again in his shirtsleeves he was bathed in perspiration. His anger mixed and intensified with feelings of failure. Not only was Suleiman making an ass of him, but Mackenzie and Fortescue would think him one when he returned. They would not say so; their attitude would be sufficient. As for any opinions he might venture after this episode, they would be rendered worthless by the disastrous lack of judgement. He rose from the sticky bed and paced in short turns from wall to wall, wondering whether to demand to see Suleiman. But he knew he would receive the same responses again. Or should he attempt to leave before Heighurst's party was despatched? Which would Suleiman think the more natural behaviour? Would he be allowed to leave? Of course not –

He heard footsteps approaching down the corridor, and voices just outside, then Nkanda's face appeared apprehensively around the curtain. '*Bwana,* come!'

His chest thumped violently, and a hollow spasm gripped lower down. After the hours of waiting, he was suddenly unprepared for the encounter. He stared at the slave and tried to compose himself before turning to put on his jacket; his shirt was uncomfortably sticky against his shoulders.

There was another slave girl outside, one he had not seen before with finer features than his two attendants, and elegant satin trimmings to her white robe; a subtle perfume surrounded her. She studied him curiously as he emerged, then turned and led the way down the corridor past irregular arches looking out to the courtyard. Nkanda came behind. The rain was as heavy as ever; the thick leaves and branches of the shrubs outside bowed, glistening under the onslaught; great beads of water bounced in between the pillars so that the outer part of the corridor glistened with pools and rivulets twisting in the faults of the worn floor. A thousand luxuriant smells of foliage and flowers released by the downpour mixed with the trail of the slave girl's perfume, filling him with a strange restlessness.

They turned along another echoing passage, passing a file of young slave girls with boxes on their heads; they stood aside and gaped or smiled as his guide passed; Guy was impressed by their evident complacency. He noticed one, taller than the rest, with an ivory disc the size of a dollar in her upper lip which protruded hideously.

They arrived shortly in a large hall with several doorways leading off. The perfumed slave girl went to one of these and spoke softly before drawing the curtain aside and beckoning to him to enter. He squared his shoulders and strode towards it with drumming heart, rehearsing expressions of anger at being detained incommunicado – a prisoner.

Entering, he stopped quite still. Instead of Suleiman, a slight girl returned his gaze. The phrases drained from his mind.

Her head was veiled, only her dark eyes showed. She sat cross-legged on a carpet on the floor, a gown of blue silk falling in even folds as if arranged for a portrait. Thick gold necklaces of weird design glowed against it, and the end of a small, bare foot with painted nails poked out from beneath. He saw her through a haze of incense from gold burners arranged nearby, their thin smoke dispersed by a huge, tasselled punkah swinging overhead, the cord pulled somnam-bulistically by a wrinkled old woman cross-legged on the floor some distance away. His mind swam in the combination of colours and perfumed heat as if drugged.

'Peace be on you, Englishman,' she said. Her eyes darted over him, curious and uninhibited as a child's; the lashes were long and black.

She had called him Englishman. For a moment in his stunned condition, he had to think himself back into his role. He bowed, '*Mademoiselle! Enchanté!*'

She held her hand towards him; the fingers glinted with stones. He went forward and touched his lips to her perfumed skin; the scent was heady as champagne. She motioned him to sit, her eyes still darting over him with unrestrained curiosity.

'My husban', God be merciful, tell me of his guest. Is dangerous, my husban' say. Is one tall Englishman who say he is Firranch!' She laughed.

'Your husband is mistaken, *madame.*'

'Nkanda say one tall Englishman make reverential bow at dawn with feet to heaven.' She laughed again. 'Oh, I know dis t'ing. Nkanda say Englishman eat with two han' – I know dis,' she nodded her head sagely. 'Englishman make spell with fowl.'

Guy smiled, captivated by the mixed curiosity and amusement in her dark eyes.

'Mchawi say one big man come from land long long way,' she went on, 'an' concubine live one, two day from Master's house an' dog is sacred an' dog is give coat of fine skin and fur and rich food an' him belly scrapes groun'. Oh, I know dis is Englan'.'

'England without doubt, *madame*. I come from a civilized country. The dog is treated with the scorn he deserves.'

'An' concubine?'

'The concubine is given coats of finest skins and furs and lives on rich food in elegant houses.'

'Mchawi is wrong?' She evidently disbelieved him.

'He is mistaken.'

'Las' night my husban' come to me. Every night my husban' come to me. Mos' of all his wife he like me – my husban' tell me dis t'ing, Oh, I know dis.' She was gazing into his face like a child to gauge the impression her tale was making. Satisfied with his rapt expression, she went on, 'My father one big merchan' in Lamu – oh, very very rich – very stric'. Two hun'red silave. My dowry one hun'red frassilahs ivory, one hun'red silave, one bed steel spring from Birmin'am, I come to my husban' in *Sambuk* from Lamu. One hun'red silave on oars. My husban' call me his little Sambuk. Is me he like mos' of all his wife. Oh, soun' of conch shells and drums when little Sambuk sails up harbour – never is such noise before – not for Sayid Barghash, not such great noise –'

Guy was becoming confused at the breathless sequence of her tale, and she paused, perhaps sensing his amusement. Her eyes held his, large with naive curiosity, lustrous as a young doe's, deep as the centuries, and his pulse beat faster.

Satisfied again that she had his attention, she went on, 'Las' night my husban' go out to speak of tall Englishman.' She paused, staring into his eyes. 'He is not come back.'

Her voice took on a sharper note. 'Still he is not come back.'

'He was to speak with me this morning. Of Fumo Akari,' Guy added.

'Fumo Akari?' Her eyes questioned him. 'Is business? My husban' not speak me no business.' She swept her arm as if it were of no consequence. 'You tell me, why is my husban' not come back?'

'Where did your husband go?'

Her voice took on a stronger note. 'Mchawi say to me, ask Englishman. Englishman make my husban' go. Make him come back.'

'Mchawi is wise.'

'Las' night my husban' is angry.'

'Whom did he go to see?'

'Oh —' She raised her hands as if despairing of him. Then her voice lowered. 'Mchawi say Englishmen hear of little Sambuk. Englishman make my husban' go away so he come to little Sambuk.'

'Mchawi sees much.'

'Arabs say lovers has no conscience.'

His pulses raced away again at the expression in her eyes, and he made an effort to think, wondering if this were some subtle game of Suleiman's; he dismissed the idea at once. There were simpler ways of gauging whether or not he was genuine. One thing was certain : so far as his own mission was concerned the interview was taking the wrong course, one which promised to become exceedingly dangerous. Other tactics were necessary.

He said briskly, 'Mchawi is right. My great government has power over your husband. I have been sent to summon him. It is best you tell me where he has gone and who are his friends.'

Her eyes opened with surprise turning in a flash to anger, and she shook inside her bangles as though the passion was too fierce to be contained. 'I *spit* on Englishman!' For a wild moment he thought she was about to suit the action to the words. 'Englishman is snake! Englishman say my husban' is bad keepin' silave – Englishman sen' ship, warship takin' my husban' ship, takin' silave – my husban' tell me dis t'ing.' She waved her hand furiously. 'How do Englishmen make safari? Oh – oh – one t'ousan' silave, two t'ousan'? Speke, Captain Burton, Sitaniley – all Englishmen take silave carry food, tent, gun. Oh, Englishman tell my husban' fin' me porter –*porter!*' she spat the word out, 'is silave. Englishman have two tongue, one tongue for English people, one tongue for Arab people. Firranch say "*Perfide Albion*". Is right –'

She rose with a sinuous movement, and went quickly towards the curtained doorway, her gown rustling and flicking past his face, leaving a mixture of sensations tumbling in his brain – heightened awareness of her physical presence, a keen desire to know whether her face matched her eyes and voice and artless egotism, sudden unease about why she had risen and whom she was about to summon. Again he wondered if Suleiman had arranged the interview, and again dismissed the thought. At the same time he had a curious feeling that he was observing the scene from a long way off, noting the absurdities almost as his sisters would. He imagined Helen's scorn for this painted, preposterous creature with her veils and overpowering perfumes and extraordinary satisfaction with her charms for her 'husban''. And telling! He imagined their giggling scorn for *him,* sitting at the creature's feet, drinking in its lustrous eyes, feeling weak at its so obvious charms.

Why had she passed so close as to leave the intoxicating imprint on his senses? Artless but calculating, innocent of the world outside, but infinitely worldly-wise, she had not done it by chance. The thought of it left him weak. She had come back from the door, and was standing, looking down at him, one leg forward so that the thrust of her knee was outlined in the silk. He realized that he should have been standing too, but she had moved so suddenly and he had been so stunned by her performance he had been left stranded.

'You have fine eyes, Englishman.' Her voice had softened. 'Your eyes are clear like dawn after rain. I see storm too. It'ink you soldier, yes I like my son havin' eyes like dis – oh, I like my son *great* fighter.'

Was this a general observation, he wondered, or a specific wish to be fulfilled? He felt out of his depth. What outlandish customs did she expect him to conform to? His heart thumped painfully.

She called to the slave girl who was waiting, and gave her instructions; they were evidently to remove her veil, for she had soon been divested of it, and stood before him, head tilted to one side, eyes burning quizzically from a delicate, pale oval face. He rose.

'*Madame* – What should he say to her? She had a freshness and youthful bloom he had not seen since leaving England, a veritable blossom in an oriental garden.

She looked pleased with the admiration in his eyes. 'You will return.' It was statement more than question.

He bowed his head. 'How could I stay away?'

'Come back, Englishman! Tell me of my husban'. I like to hear dis t'ing from you.' Her eyes gave the words added meaning. Then she called, 'Nkanda!' and when the slave appeared in the doorway, gazing round-eyed from her unveiled face to Guy and back again, she gave him a string of instructions. He stood to one side inviting Guy through the curtains.

He turned to her. 'Good-bye!'

'Peace go with you.' There was a curious expression in her eyes. He wondered if he had disappointed her. What had she expected? 'God be with you tall Englishman! Like the storm, may you return!'

He walked the few steps to the door. Nkanda held the curtain and he passed through quickly without a backward glance, then followed the slave through the hall to the verandah around the rain-splashed courtyard. He puzzled over her insistence that he should return: return to her room? Or was she letting him know in a devious way that he was free to go and find her husband – returning afterwards himself? If the latter Nkanda didn't seem to know about it; he was being led straight back to the room in which he had been held before.

Be hanged if he was going to be incarcerated a moment longer!

'Nkanda!' he said softly.

The slave stopped and turned.

He pointed towards the front entrance in the court-yard one storey down. 'I go now.'

Nkanda's brows rose; it was evidently an unexpected development. Guy looked past him, measuring the distance he would need to run if he swung himself to the ground from a frangipani that had thrust its branches through an arch to his right. He might surprise the guards, but the great door would be locked and bolted. He would need to put both men out of action to give himself time to find the keys about their persons. It was a tall order; their spears were needle-sharp, and he had no arms of any kind. He was gauging the distance, wondering how he might create a diversion, when he heard voices and looking round saw the elegant girl who had taken him to the little Sambuk's room leading a file of young slaves towards the steps down to the courtyard. She flashed him a long glance as he turned, then he lost sight of her behind a pillar. Was it imagination or had there been a message in that deep look. Lord! Had the little Sambuk unbalanced him completely!

Nkanda was waiting for him. To gain time, he pointed to the front entrance hall again, repeating his earlier remark. The slave laughed.

Guy looked down again. The girl, sheltered from the beating rain by a parasol held by one of her diminutive followers, was making towards the front entrance, the straggle of young slaves crowding behind, hunched against the downpour, their loin cloths clinging to the contours of their shivering bodies. He saw the guards move non-chalantly from their leaning positions under the arch of the front hall; she harangued them and they looked at one another, half annoyed, half amused at being shouted at by a girl, then turned and disappeared from view under the arch. The meaning in her eyes as she had passed flashed upon him. Assuredly the moment had come!

He looked round at the slave and said quietly, 'I am extremely sorry, Nkanda. Forgive me!'

As the man's brows drew down in an effort to understand, he launched his right fist straight at the side of the heavy jaw. The blow was perfectly judged; he felt it from the spring in his toes through every sinew in his body to the knuckles at the point of impact in an instant of savage satisfaction. Nkanda rocked backwards, astonishment transforming his face and toppled half sideways, ramming the top of his head into the wall and falling to the floor without a sound, his arms still by his sides.

Guy turned and leaped for the frangipani he had marked out, feeling a sharp pain through his right hand as he swung himself to the ground from the wet foliage, which bent and tore under his weight; he landed in a pool of brown water, stumbled and struck his knee against a coral flagstone. The last of the young slaves was passing through the arch into the front hall, but he was too near the wall of the courtyard to be able to see the guards inside. He raced the few yards to the side of the arch and peered round. The great door was open, the party of slaves passing out into the street; he noticed the guard who held the door had left his spear and shield leaning against a pillar. He darted forward and grabbed both, feeling again the sharp pain through his hand; he wondered if he had broken a bone on Nkanda's jaw. Covering his body with the shield, he charged the second guard, standing with a loose grin on his face, his hand around the neck of one of the slave girls who was pretending fright. The smile dropped away; the eyes protruded in alarm as the man took an involuntary half-step back. Guy swerved past.

He was outside! It happened so quickly and easily it was difficult to comprehend. He looked back. Both guards and all the slaves in a wet huddle were looking at him dumbly. He saw little Sambuk's servant gazing with an inscrutable expression from under her parasol. He bowed his head to her, then looking at the guards again, waved his spear menacingly. They stared as if he were an apparition. The silence was extraordinary. He heard the rain beating on the beaten lime roadway and a musical gurgle from rivers rushing down either gutter. His clothes were soaked, clinging to him.

He turned and started running through the downpour along the deserted street, splashing in pools between the magnificent, brass-studded doors and high, blind walls above.

He thought of her eyes : 'Like the storm, may you return –'

He turned a corner and slowed to a walk, realizing that he was not being followed; his mind whirled with mixed relief at the escape and sickness at his failure – despair at his gaucheness with little Sambuk. He wanted desperately to see her again.

Chapter Six

The first face to catch his eye as he entered the consul's office was Saxmundham. The Old Man was sitting, half facing the doorway at the far side of a circle of chairs before Mackenzie's great table. His brows lifted and he moved in his seat as though an impulse to rise had been damped at once by rank.

'God bless my soul!' His voice was unusually hoarse. 'Greville!'

'The hunter returns,' Heighurst said; Guy saw him looking back over his shoulder, one eyebrow raised quizzically, as he gazed at the spear Guy was still gripping. 'That's what the froggies use nowadays!' He turned back to the assembled company. 'Sportsmen, indeed!'

'Small arms on the table outside,' Mackenzie said crisply across the laughter. He was staring at him from behind his enormous table. Fortescue was standing beside him in much the same position as the day before. Had it been one day only? Smallpiece was sitting back to the door, his broad face twisted towards him, frowning; next to him was an older man with ruby cheeks whom Guy had not seen before, and on the other side – Cameron! There was a strange look in the Scot's eyes.

He turned to stand his spear against the wall behind him. 'A small trophy.'

They were all moving and talking. Heighurst jumped up and came across, clapping him on the arm. 'By Jupiter! We'd given you up!'

Guy put a hand up to his chest. 'The mercy of Allah!'

'Young fella!' Mackenzie said crossly, 'We've done next to nothin' all day but make preparations for your release. Devil we have!'

'Dashed inconsiderate,' Heighurst said quietly. 'You might have waited another couple of hours – we should have been on our way!'

'Well –!' Fortescue's eyes gleamed belligerently.

The ADC's manner and his own sense of failure brought the blood to Guy's head. 'It's fearfully wet. You don't happen to have some dry duds?'

'Duds!' Mackenzie's fist crashed to the table. 'Where've you *bin* all this time?'

'This is the young fella – ?' The old, ruby-faced man leant towards the consul. He had a pleasant, deliberate voice.

'Yes, yes,' Mackenzie said fussily. 'Lieutenant Greville – Sir Francis de Wansey –'

Guy had heard of Sir Francis, the British traders' answer to Dr Karl Peters of the *Gesellschaft für Deutsche Kolonisation*. The elderly man rose and came over, his hand outstretched. 'I am pleased to meet you Greville. We've talked much of your gallant undertaking.' He smiled and shook Guy's hand warmly. 'I must say, I admire your pluck. Wild horses would not have dragged me into Suleiman's parlour –'

Cameron must have told them.

'Exceeding kind of you, sir.'

Smallpiece turned to Saxmundham. 'We should send word to the ship – call off the landing. The boats will be putting off–'

'Quite right,' the Old Man replied, looking at Mackenzie, who grunted and clapped his hands for the orderly.

While making out the necessary chits signed by the captain, and sending the orderly on his way, the consul motioned Guy to a chair and had a large brandy brought for him. He took a gulp of liquor, feeling it bite the back of his throat and glow. They were all looking at him.

'The brute made off,' he said.

Fortescue frowned. 'Where?'

'No one seemed to know.'

Saxmundham leaned forward. 'Learn anything from the beggar before he went?'

'I'm not sure, sir. In a negative sense I believe I did. You see, he cottoned on to me right away –'

'The devil he did!' Mackenzie barked.

'I hadn't let on a word about why I was there or any-thing of that sort, so it rather suggested we were on the wrong track –' Seeing Mackenzie's puzzled look, he went on, 'We assumed it was a French plot.'

'As I recall, you assumed that,' Fortescue said drily.

'Everything pointed to a French involvement.' He stared at the AD C. 'But directly a French courier appears – he's in the wrong box!'

Cameron interrupted, 'If only ye'd told me what it was ye were about, man!'

They looked at him.

'It's the Germans – *never* the French!'

Mackenzie nodded.

'Aye,' Cameron went on more vehemently. 'A pity Akari didna chase the lot of them out.' He thrust forward in his seat, addressing the consul. 'Because if we don't watch out they'll take the whole of the sultan's dominions from here to Lake Nyasa and beyond.'

'We should've taken over years ago,' Smallpiece said fiercely. 'There'd be no man-stealing by now.'

They turned, momentarily startled by the change of tack. Sir Francis nodded. 'Quite right! I was talking to a fella the other day. Just in from Kilwa. It was eighteen days' march, so he informed me, before he came to a village with a living community. The road – stank with corpses! He found his way by the smell. Of course we all know that used to go on, but what a disgrace that it does so still! What a disgrace to our fine talk! By George, unless we put a stop to it the whole area will be depopulated within a few years.'

'Bla'guards!' Saxmundham growled. 'I confess I look forward to placing a halter round this scoundrel Akari's neck.'

'But it's the Germans behind him,' Cameron started again.

'Gentlemen!' Mackenzie said sharply. He went on in a quieter tone, 'Now that we have Greville back with us, we can turn our minds to the – eh, the main object.'

He reached over his desk and picked up a cable form. 'As you know, captain, authorization has arrived from Lord Granville to summon Fumo Akari to Lamu for trial, and for preparations to be put in hand against the likelihood of his – eh, noncompliance.'

'Cast-iron certainty,' Fortescue put in. 'Latest intelligence is that he's still gathering the clans and making prodigious efforts to throw up fortifications.'

'Excellent!' Sir Francis said. 'It is of the very first importance in this form of warfare to obtain the most accurate information. I have always found it pays to establish an intelligence department whose duty it is to obtain the fullest possible information as to the numbers, arms and fighting capacity of the tribes to be attacked –'

'A branch of the Masai,' Mackenzie put in drily, and before the old man could go on, 'There is however one complication. Lord Granville's instructions are explicit, we must liaise with the Germans. On no account must we undertake the expedition without, at the least, a token force from the German squadron –'

'On my life!' Saxmundham exploded.

'They're behind it all –!' Cameron was almost out of his seat.

'That may be so. The figures are against us, I regret,' Mackenzie replied. 'They have six dead against our three.'

Heighurst turned to Guy. 'We can thank our stars it ain't the froggies. I shouldn't fancy monsoor at my back when it comes to a rough and tumble.'

'Nor I!' Smallpiece said with feeling.

Mackenzie pressed on, 'The Germans are decent enough fellows. They work hard enough, hanged if they don't.'

'Very likely,' Cameron said. 'They're making their preparations,' he explained darkly. 'It's the French and the Russians just now, but mind it's the Germans who'll challenge us next. That's the real struggle of the future. It's us or them without a shadow of doubt.'

'They've no ships,' Smallpiece said shortly. 'None to speak of

'Not yet,' the Scot replied.

'Gentlemen!' Mackenzie cut in again. 'So far as the arms shipment is concerned, we've had – eh, discussions with the French authorities naturally. Naturally they deny all responsibility. The letter's a forgery. They even implied the thing emanated from this office, a calumny which I need hardly say did not assist towards a cordial exchange. However, it transpires that an arms shipment was expected in Réunion some weeks ago. The brig carrying it was driven on a reef in the Mafia Channel – although what she was doing so far off course is something of a mystery –'

Smallpiece brayed. Mackenzie looked at him.

'My apologies! It's not the first Frenchie never knew where he was!'

Mackenzie went on. 'They only received word of the wreck a couple of days ago. But apparently the brig had been stripped down completely. So far as the boarding party could make out there was nothing left in her at all.'

'Plundered!' Saxmundham exclaimed.

'So it appears.'

Fortescue put in, 'It will be some time before they can check copies of the manifests we supplied them with the home authorities, but there can be little doubt that the shipment you intercepted, sir,' he turned to Saxmundham, 'came from the wreck.'

Guy said, 'Whoever it was plundered her decided to use the arms to stir up mischief in Witu. And Lamu as well if the letter is anything to go by. It could have been anyone.'

Mackenzie nodded.

Sir Francis came in, 'I've bin listening carefully to all you gentlemen have bin saying. If you'd allow me —'

Mackenzie thrust his palms towards him. 'Please continue.'

'I believe you need to approach this business from the other end. Go to Witu. Find the sultan and his vizier. Get *them* to tell you who's behind it all.'

'I agree,' Saxmundham said.

'The dhow and the arms are in the harbour,' Sir Francis went on. 'The French consul knows all about it, Pierre Suleiman's run for cover. By George, you'll not make much headway here!'

'Speed is essential,' Saxmundham agreed.

'Decidedly.' Sir Francis leant forward. 'In my experience the native expects his punishment swift. Delay and he forgets. Wonders what it's all about.' He leaned back again. 'He doesn't reason as we do.'

'The letter has gone off to Fumo Akari,' Mackenzie said drily.

'I don't mean to suggest everything is not being done, but the first essential is to get up to Witu. Go in at once.

And once you're in, stay for a day or two. Nothing demoralizes the natives more. Send scouting parties out along the roads and if you find there are other villages nearby, destroy them. You should not leave the district until you have thoroughly demoralized the whole tribe. Do not destroy Witu itself until you leave. Then blow it up.' He turned to Saxmundham. 'Guncotton is best.'

Fortescue said, 'In this case it is important to capture the sultan and his ministers alive. If possible.'

'I agree. But don't forget, the success of the expedition will turn on the number of porters you can engage – and keep.'

Mackenzie nodded towards Cameron. 'Mr Cameron has kindly undertaken to assist in that department.'

'You'll need four hundred at the least,' Sir Francis said.

'No trouble,' Cameron replied shortly.

Mackenzie and Fortescue stared at him.

Saxmundham said, 'We've arranged to take on seedies for use as additional porters.'

The talk circled on the numbers available from different sources, and moved from there to the detachment of Indian Police and Zanzibar and Lamu irregulars that would be needed to supplement the naval force. Guy's attention wandered. Suleiman filled his mind. He wondered where the Arab was and what he hoped to gain from the trouble in Witu. Perhaps his ambition had grown; in return for helping Fumo Akari to throw out the Germans and march on Lamu, perhaps he hoped to establish himself in the lewali's place. An ordinary palace revolution with none of the great powers involved. Suleiman was ruthless enough.

He was also shrewd enough to know it could not succeed against European arms. But why had the man not bothered to question him? Why had he not returned home – ?

His pulse throbbed at the thought of the little Sambuk. Why had she summoned him? 'Arabs say lovers has no conscience.' What would she have done if he had responded to the promise in her eyes – or had it been curiosity? He would go back – and hang them all!

Chairs were scraping back. The meeting was breaking up. He stood, breathing in a waft of wet suiting and feeling his feet suddenly very cold as he moved. To his surprise he saw Cameron coming over, his hand thrust out. He smiled and grasped it.

They were silent for a moment, then both started at the the same instant. Guy grinned and backed down.

'My, but I'm glad, to see ye!' Cameron said.

'I lost your friend, I regret.'

The Scot's gaze bored into his. 'I felt responsible –'

'Of course not!' He saw the Old Man, Smallpiece and Heighurst looking at him from beside the doorway. 'I must be away!' He raised his hand briefly, then turned and made his farewells to Mackenzie, Fortescue and Sir Francis, before moving towards the door and handing his glass to the orderly. He found Cameron beside him again.

'Ye'll have to tell me how it was ye found ye're way out.'

'I'm not absolutely certain myself,' he smiled, thinking of the startled look on the guard's face as he charged past. He moved across to recover his spear.

Cameron followed him. 'Ye should have let me know what it was ye were about.'

'I'm rather glad I didn't,' he said, thinking of the little Sambuk.

'Greville!' Saxmundham's roar jerked him round. 'On my life-!'

He waved the spear at the Scot and moved quickly out.

Chapter Seven

Guy leant back in his chair and stared up at the reflections from the water playing on the deck-head beam. Knobs of white paint stood out like warts; the flickering light over the ridges and hollows was strangely mesmeric.

He wrenched himself back to the sheet of writing paper with the embossed ship's crest at the head. He had got as far as the date 'at Zanzibar'. He dipped his pen in the ink again and forced himself to concentrate.

Dearest mama and papa,

As you see we have put into Zanzibar unexpectedly. There is a British India steamer lying not far away and I hope to get this off by her so have not time for much. I expect to be thoroughly well occupied for the remainder of our stay here, what with my duties as intelligence officer which I cannot say I will enjoy as the ADC whom I am supposed to liaise with is a dry stick. You know I never was good at turning the other cheek, papa, but I believe I shall have many opportunities for practice in the course of the next few weeks. I may *amaze* you when I come home!! We are off to a queer place called Witu to punish some old boy who don't care for missionaries or Germans. I mention this so you don't worry mama if you see something in the papers. Everyone here is looking forward to it like anything but you must not worry, the natives are armed only with bows and arrows and shields made of rhino hide. I already have one of their spears! and have hopes of bagging other trophies on our way. The heat and bugs will be our worst enemy, it's like some awfully fierce Turkish bath here during the day and at night the flies and cockroaches *swarm.* You never saw such amazing dragonflies. I have hopes of bagging some rare butterflies as all the bugs here are *twice* as big as anywhere else. I've told my man that if he forgets to pack my nets and killing jars I'll put *his* head in! It would not make the slightest difference, he's a *leatherneck.* Duff is his name. He is known as Figgy from one of the ambrosial dishes they produce on the mess deck! He's a thorough good fellow at heart –

He leant back. Only another paragraph and he would have done the necessary. He glanced at his favourite photograph of his two sisters together in the sternsheets of a skiff on the river. Helen's face smiled back, impish as ever. He must write and tell her – but first.

Zanzibar itself looks a capital place from the harbour, but ashore you never saw such beastliness as there is in the streets. I'll not spoil your breakfast with the details. The houses *look* very fine, in particular the front doors which are works of art. I was told they were always the first part of the house to be put up! They are carved with lotus leaf, fish, pineapple and all manner of queer designs and studded with great brass bosses and spikes – No admittance until the week after next! There ain't a lick of paint on the walls though. Once he's built his house Jimmy Arab don't believe in spending another penny on it. The truth is he's a queer customer and I've a mind to study more of his habits if I get the time, in particular his *religion,* papa, which is meat and drink to him. Quite puts us to shame!

We are to attend a ball tonight got up at short notice in our honour by the Gymkhana Club! I trust it don't rain like yesterday or we shall need dancing p*umps* indeed!! My fond love to all.

Yr affect^e, Guy

He lodged the pen in its rest and stood to ease his legs, cramped from the awkward position forced by his minute cabin. There was a knock on the door, which opened to reveal Duff, cradling in his arms the light cotton suit of yesterday. The creases in the trousers stood out knife-sharp. He nodded his approval. 'A1!'

The marine came in and laid the suit carefully on the bed until he could prepare a more permanent home for it.

'I shall be needin' ball dress this evenin',' Guy said.

'I knows that, sir.'

'I shall surprise you one of these days, Figgy.'

'You did an' all, sir. Yesterday!'

Guy turned back to his desk. He had been ribbed sufficiently about his escapade.

'I reckon they're fanciful meself,' the marine pressed on. 'The yarns that's being put about. I says to the sarge when 'e quizzed me I says, there's one thing I'm main sure of – all of 'em can't be right!'

Guy ignored him, and settling in his chair again took out a fresh sheet of writing paper. He heard Duff moving behind him as he looked at the imp-face of his sister in the photograph frame.

Dearest Trojan –

Duff squeezed past his chair back and out of the door, closing it gently behind him.

The very queerest thing happened yesterday. I can't believe it yet, as if it were a dream, one of the *colourful* ones you get when you sit after dinner and nod off! I'll tell you the best part first, I'm in love, furiously!!! I'm certain of it. You wouldn't take to her in the least, she is astoundingly conceited!! She has a husband!!! And he has a number of wives and concubines as is the custom out here. I dare say you've guessed? Remember the colour plate of the Princess –

A gun had sounded. He paused, about to recharge his pen, and listened. Another! Saluting guns by the sound and intervals. Perhaps the gunboats had arrived. Yet they had been ordered to Lamu direct. He replaced the pen, rising, and went out and down the wardroom towards the companionway.

The quarterdeck was bright from the wash it had received earlier, the awning above damp and tight from the rain of the night. He saw the master-at-arms and two of the ship's police with the usual line of bleary-eyed defaulters. The captain was at the side, standing on his favourite hen coop, looking out over the hammock nettings with a telescope. Most of the other officers were also up on guns or pens to stare out over the starboard quarter. He joined them.

'Five of the beggars!' the surgeon exclaimed.

They were coming in under steam in line ahead in perfect station, their upper sails furled harbour stow, courses clewed up to the yards, the Imperial German ensigns with black crosses flying out crisply above thick reels of smoke from yellow funnels glancing darts of sunlight. It was a thrilling sight. Four were gunboats, but a sizeable corvette flying the flag of a rear-admiral was leading ship. As he watched, a puff of white smoke burst from her side, followed immediately by the report of the gun.

'They mean business!' he said, astonished at the size of the squadron.

They watched as the corvette completed her 21-gun salute to the sultan and turned to make her anchoring approach; the second ship, then the third followed round in precisely similar arcs.

'What d'you suppose Old Sax will make of it?' the surgeon asked.

'He won't care for the admiral's flag,' Guy replied. It would make it extremely difficult for him to assume command of the joint operation. The unusually strong squadron with its high-ranking commander seemed to lend conviction to Cameron's belief that the Germans were behind the business at Witu; at the least they intended winning capital from it.

He heard Saxmundham's voice raised in anger. Looking round he saw he had returned to the deck to face the first defaulter.

'You miserable little rat,' he thundered. 'Bring disgrace on the *Dulcinea* — *your* ship — *our* ship. Aren't you man enough to steer clear of those lousy drink shops!' His great beard quivered. 'Rich!'

'Sir!' the master-at-arms snapped.

'Category for leave?'

'Special, sir!'

Saxmundham turned back to the bluejacket. 'You have disgraced your privilege and you have disgraced your ship. What do you have to say? Speak up!'

'It were the liquor, sir. It weren't no or'nery liquor —'

'Leave stopped. Rich!'

'Sir!'

'Shore leave stopped for six months. And see to it the scamp stands on the quarterdeck three hours after duty each day for a fortnight, repeating, "I was drunk and a disgrace to my ship," at each bell.'

'Sir!' the master-at-arms snapped, and to the offender, On *cap!*'

'Sir – it were like this 'ere –'

'That will do,' Saxmundham growled.

'Me raggy'll swear the same, your Grace.'

'Take him below!' Saxmundham roared, then with a quick glance towards the spars of the German squadron, turned and strode towards his companionway, calling angrily to Smallpiece to see to the defaulters.

Before going down he paused, 'And I'll thank you to ensure the drunken curs pay for their bestial behaviour!' Turning, he barked, 'Greville!'

Guy jumped to the deck and stepped across to follow him down the ladder; below, he stood silently just inside the door of the fore cabin as the Old Man placed his cap carefully on the table and threw himself on the settee.

The blue eyes stared up.

Guy guessed quickly. 'A sizeable force, sir!'

'Why did their consulate not inform us as to the extent of their interest?' Saxmundham banged his fist on the table so that the cap jumped. 'And what's to do about it? Be hanged if they won't desire command.'

Guy thought of the British ships which had been ordered to attach themselves to the Old Man's broad pennant in Lamu, and received sudden inspiration. 'We might submit that overall command should go to the senior military officer.'

The captain stared up for a moment. 'The Royal Welch! Bless my soul, Greville! On my word, I'll speak to Mackenzie!' His eyes danced. 'The Royal Welch! I'll

wager there's a lieutenant-colonel at the least. I'll speak to
Mackenzie. I'll go now. As you leave, Greville, be so good as
to have the officer of the watch call away my gig.'

'What d'you like to shoot, young man?'

Her voice was piercingly English. Guy saw her through
his third glass of champagne; she had a wide face with
dark wrinkles beneath her eyes and a turned-up nose that
reminded him of a sow.

'That depends, ma'am.' Lord! He couldn't lecture her
on the English seasons. His heart was not in it. His heart
was in Suleiman's house; the eyes of Suleiman's girl-wife
glowed brighter with each burst of bubbles teasing the
back of his throat.

'Depends?' she repeated.

The champagne induced the truth. 'I'd sooner catch
butterflies.'

She looked at him doubtfully.

He stole a glance around, seeking a familiar face in
the chiefly male press around them, but he had become
separated from the other officers. 'I have a collection at
home,' he added.

'Oh, where is home?'

Now she was back on familiar ground; her eyes lost
their puzzled look. He wondered what she was doing in
such an exotic setting as Zanzibar. He imagined her exasperation with the Swahili house boys she would employ,
her shrill complaints about their stupidity and dishonesty
to the other memsah'bs drinking tea from Spode china
in facsimiles of English drawing rooms – with moorish

arches for windows, and the spiced air and the drums outside....

He simply had to return to Suleiman's house. He took another gulp of champagne. His blood ran high.

'Home?' he said. 'Surrey – Godalming –' He had a vision of Suleiman's girl-wife at the Rectory; 'Father, I should like you to meet Mrs Little Sambuk.' He smiled, 'Oh, my husban' like me – mos' of all his wife he like me. My husban' tell me dis t'ing – Oh, I know it –'

She was gazing in puzzled disapproval of his abstracted look. He went on quickly, 'And you?'

Her mouth turned down. 'Unfortunately, we appear to have taken root in this place.' She said it as if it had a nasty smell.

'I envy you,' he said with a smile. 'By Jove, I like it here! Amazingly!'

She flapped her fan and bent him another disapproving look. 'If I'd a mind I could tell you stories would make you *blench!*'

He grinned. 'Them's the kind I like best.'

She looked confused and somehow flattered. The orchestra began to play and she lowered her fan and opened her programme. Noticing it briefly he was struck by the number of unengaged dances. Although the ladies were greatly outnumbered the card was half empty. He saw her looking at him.

'Are you engaged?' he asked. It was a way of ending the pointless conversation.

She made a show of looking again at her programme. 'Why, no!'

'May I have the honour?' He raised his arm.

On the way through the moving press to the floor, he saw a group of young officers in ball dress similar to his own but subtly different; the Germans had been invited! He wondered if it were some tortuous scheme of Mackenzie's. Yet it was the obvious thing, since they would be marching together. One of the Germans returned his glance and held it a moment. He was strikingly good-looking in a flaxen-haired, light-blue-eyed way; his mouth was wide and firm, puckered upwards at the corners. Guy felt a brief surge of belligerence, then he was past and bowing his partner into her line. It was a Roger de Coverley. She looked flushed and pleased as he bobbed to the music. He had a feeling that he had made her evening.

He heard a familiar voice at his side and looking round saw Saxmundham, his brow beaded with perspiration, his eyes alight. 'Greville! A word with you directly after!'

He nodded, and then it was his turn to jig between the lines. He twirled, willing his partner to change into the little Sambuk.

By the end of the dance, his shirt was soaking and his neck chafed by the starched collar. He escorted his partner off towards the great arches which served as windows from floor to ceiling along one side of the first floor hall, bowed and made his apologies. She smiled wanly as he left.

It was not difficult to spot the captain; his commanding height made him visible above the crowd. He was standing by one of the open side arches beneath an enormous garland of casuarina, his gilt-tasselled epaulettes gleaming splendidly against the night outside. Approaching, Guy saw that Smallpiece was next to him. The first lieutenant's face was dark, his brown eyes intense. He was holding a champagne glass out for a white-robed servant to fill, and as Guy came up, he turned, jerking his arm so that the wine spilled on the floor.

'Damn you!' he roared at the servant, and to Saxmundham, 'Damn my eyes! The nigger's bin at the bottle!' He lunged after the man, spilling more of his champagne, and tugged at the loose garments. The Swahili's eyes widened in alarm. Smallpiece wrenched the magnum from his grasp, puffing heavily, and held it up to stare at the level of liquid.

Saxmundham placed a restraining hand on his shoulder. 'It's a mercy your defaulters ain't here to see you, Mr Smallpiece!'

Guy had a vision of the first lieutenant standing on the quarterdeck bellowing after each bell, 'I was drunk and a disgrace to my ship!'

'Ah, Greville!' Saxmundham said, noticing him. 'See what you make of this – you and Mr Smallpiece – Smallpiece?'

The first lieutenant straightened and lowered his magnum. Satisfied with his attention, the captain went on, 'This is what I propose. You've seen these Germans? Their admiral is here somewhere. Von Pullitz. I've had words with the fellow. I fancy he's a sportsman of sorts and straight enough so far as these fellows go, so I propose to challenge him to a race.' He gazed at each of them in turn with a pleased expression. 'Sail, naturally.'

Smallpiece jerked his head as if to clear his brain. 'Where shall we race?'

'What in heaven's name've you bin drinkin', Mr Small-piece! On my life! We'll race the fellow to Lamu. We're bound that way, ain't we!'

The first lieutenant turned to Guy with bleary eyes.

'What is the prize to be, sir?' Guy asked.

'You've rumbled it, Greville! One hundred guineas!' Sax-mundham's great face was alight with anticipation of approval.

Smallpiece said slowly, 'The reason I inquired, sir, we'll need to keep 'em in sight. You follow me?'

'Hanged if I do!'

Smallpiece screwed his brows in concentration. 'They don't have our notions, sir.'

'Notions! Bless my soul, Smallpiece, you're speakin' in riddles.'

'They'll not play fair, not if they can steal an extra knot after dark with their screws down.'

The Old Man started rumbling with laughter. 'On my life, Mr Smallpiece, it don't matter! It don't matter what the rascals get up to. Not that I share your opinion of von Pullitz.' He jabbed his finger into the first lieutenant's white waistcoat. 'They can't rig the *start*. Once they accept the challenge they have to wait for us. We can keep 'em here until we're ready –' He glanced at Guy. 'Until the *Rutland* with the Royal Welch makes Lamu.'

Guy looked doubtful. 'I wonder, sir. If they believe they can secure an advantage by sailing first, will they not take it? A hundred guineas ain't much against a sultanate. If that's what they're after.'

Saxmundham's keen expression faded. 'I never thought to hear it – not from you Greville. On my life!' His eyes were cold and distant. 'Spoken like a tradesman, sir!'

Guy felt a flush darkening his face.

Saxmundham stared at each in turn. 'Thank you for your opinions, gentlemen.' He turned away ostentatiously. 'Resume dancin'!'

Guy looked at him for a moment, then made away, hearing Smallpiece muttering behind. After a few paces he felt a tap on his elbow, and saw the first lieutenant staring at him. Together they skirted a laughing group, Smallpiece swinging the magnum angrily by his side. They came upon Heighurst, his face flushed; he nodded towards the champagne. 'I congratulate you on your choice of partner!'

'Go to the devil!' Guy snapped.

Heighurst's right brow rose fractionally.

On impulse Guy said, 'D'you fancy a venture outside?' He went on quickly, 'We've some unfinished business, if you remember.'

Heighurst looked at him, puzzled.

'Pierre Suleiman.'

Heighurst said quietly, 'Go to the devil yourself!'

'You're not game?'

'Game!' The marine's lips drooped as he probed Guy's expression. 'You're mad!'

'I have a particular reason.'

Heighurst's eyes opened slightly. 'A very particular reason?'

'You might say so.'

'D'you suppose there are other – particular reasons?' Heighurst smoothed the tip of his moustache.

Guy grinned. 'One is exceedingly particular.'

'How much force shall you require?'

'Damn my eyes!' Smallpiece growled. 'Damn you and your riddles! Damn both of you!'

Two ladies nearby turned to stare ostentatiously.

Smallpiece looked down.

'He's appropriated a magnum,' one of them said in a loud voice.

Heighurst bowed to them. 'Our apologies! You will appreciate, it is necessary on board ship for the first lieutenant to be heard from the quarterdeck to the fore royal truck against a gale of wind. It is not easy to adapt such virtuosity.'

They smiled at him, charmed. He clicked his heels and returned the smile, then turned back to Guy. 'I'm game.'

'I'll send a man for our revolvers.'

'A platoon of my fellows, too?'

Smallpiece thrust himself between them, glanced over his shoulder in the direction of the two ladies, and growled, 'Revolvers?'

'With your permission, sir,' Guy said, 'I should like to have a shot at surprising Suleiman at his home. He must have returned by now' – he invented an excuse – 'if he is following his normal routine.' The thought of the Arab entering the little Sambuk's bedchamber tightened his jaw muscles.

The first lieutenant swayed as he digested the idea. 'You're right!' he said at last, and swung the magnum by his side as if about to make a cast with the hand lead, then leaned towards Heighurst. 'I never was privileged to attend dancin' instruction.'

The marine turned to Guy. 'You know the house. Will three be sufficient to turn the defences?'

Guy looked at Smallpiece, wondering if he would inform the captain. The implications of the sudden impulse began to come home: suppose they were to fail. Smallpiece would bear the responsibility; suppose someone were captured; it could mean the end of his career – absenting himself without leave on an unauthorized mission exposing those under his command to undue risk, bringing opprobrium on Her Majesty's flag with a clandestine, insufficiently planned operation. The man was in no state to take a decision, let alone one of such gravity.

'It might be better sir, if Lieutenant Heighurst and myself were to go in alone –'

Even that involved risking Heighurst's career in what was nothing more than his own desperate desire to see Suleiman's girl-wife again. That was the real issue: 'Come back, tall Englishman – like the storm, may you return –'

Smallpiece was staring at him malignantly. 'Seekin' the credit for yourself, Greville!' His eyes were heavy with drink. 'A limelight man! God blast my eyes, I knew it! You're a limelight man, sir!'

Guy stiffened. The sparkle of the early evening had gone. Looking at Smallpiece's livid face and chunky jaw thrust forward above the points of his stiff collar, he knew that his first task was to get the man back to his cabin aboard.

'May I suggest – if we are resolved on the mission, we should return to the ship first, and change into suitable rig?' He glanced down at his own immaculate waistcoat, and knife-edged dark trousers.

Smallpiece considered the idea, then nodded his approval.

'You gentlemen not fancy the gallop?' It was Mackenzie, resplendent in scarlet, blue and gold, his close-cropped grey head held very high to make up for his small stature. 'I'll introduce you to von Pullitz's officers. Know your ally! I should think so!' He noticed the magnum waving in Smallpiece's clutch, and his manner changed. He turned to the first lieutenant, 'These Germans are first-rate fellows and most anxious to do the right thing.' He leaned closer. 'I fancy they make you chaps their model. It's important we don't – eh, do anything to impair that relationship, don't you think. I fancy it's our biggest asset just now.'

'Greville here could give 'em dancin' lessons,' Smallpiece said loudly. 'They learn it, colonel, in the *Britannia.*'

Mackenzie frowned at the slur in his speech.

'Fancy gen'lemen –' Smallpiece went on.

Mackenzie was looking around outside their group. 'D'you know Mr Smallpiece, I've the devil of an appetite.' He put a hand on the first lieutenant's arm. 'I happen to know they have two gross of fowls prepared for supper – eh, what d'you say to splitting one between us – ?'

Smallpiece looked puzzled, but was saved from the need to reply by the sudden appearance of the midshipman, Bowles, who came up to him flushed and breathless.

'Captain's compliments, sir. He wishes to see you, most urgent. He's outside, sir.'

Smallpiece's jaw thrust forward and his eyes took on a determined expression. He handed his magnum to the lad, nodded briefly to Mackenzie, and moved away, fending off a wicker chair in his path, and walking crabwise around a table with a number of glasses unattended on its shining surface.

Mackenzie motioned to Guy to go after him.

He turned and followed, seeing him diverted by his avoiding action away from the direct route to the end of the hall, and towards the great open arches along the side. He was stopped briefly by the surgeon with some pleasantry, then he moved on more quickly, turning directly towards one of the arches. Before Guy realized what he was about, he had marched straight through. The surgeon stared after him. Guy started to run. When he reached the scene, the surgeon and several others were clustered in the arch, gazing over the edge of the floor into the night.

Guy peered down. The branches and leaves of a fig tree immediately adjacent shone in the light from the hall behind him. There wasn't a sound – only the cicadas and a croaking frog, and in the distance the drums and throb of Indian music.

They all moved at the same time, hastening towards the entrance arch at the end of the hall, people turning and staring as they passed; some caught by the urgency of the stampede, joining them.

'What's up?'

'Fella walked out of a window –'

'The deuce –!'

'Not a word.'

As they clattered down the steps outside Guy pressed to the front, and at the bottom broke into a run, almost impaling himself on a bush which reared up across his path before his pupils adjusted to the darkness. A figure banged into him and cursed. He started off again more cautiously, but slapped his foot in a pool of water left by the rains; he felt cold soak through his socks. Then he was at the tree. He parted the branches, for the first time hearing Smallpiece growling faintly, and seeing his dark shape against the glow through the leaves.

'Are you hurt?' he called up.

There was a pause in the growl, then a querulous voice, 'Where are you, damn you?'

'We've come to get you down.'

'Down! God blast me, Greville! I wish to get *up!*'

Guy pressed into the foliage until he could reach out and touch the hanging legs. He could see now. The light from above was diffused prettily through the leaves and branches. The sound of a minuet floated about him.

'It would be easier for you to come down.'

'Is that you, Greville?' the voice sounded puzzled. 'How in hell did you get below there?'

'You are up a tree.'

There was a short silence.

'Shock!' the surgeon said. 'Better go up and get him.'

'I'll jump up on your back, Guy replied, 'if you'd be good enough to bend –'

'Allow me to remove my jacket first – *monkey* jacket – ha! ha!'

They heard the crack of a branch, an oath from Smallpiece, rustle of leaves and small twigs, thud of a body to the ground, and Smallpiece was sitting, staring up palely into their faces. The surgeon pushed towards him and knelt to feel his leg. Smallpiece stared at him.

'You too, sawbones!' He shook the leg free and made to stand up, muttering an oath, and catching hold of a branch as he sat on the ground again.

'Easy!' the surgeon cautioned.

'Can I help?' a voice came from behind. It had a foreign ring. Looking round, Guy made out the blond German lieutenant who had caught his eye earlier in the evening.

'Yes,' he replied. 'I fancy we shall have to carry him out.'

'Very good!' the German said, bending and scrambling in under the branches. 'This is good sport, yes?'

'Take him under the left shoulder. I'll take his starboard side.'

They moved round Smallpiece as he struggled upright again.

'Is this a bet, I am thinking?' the German asked as he bent towards the first lieutenant's shoulder. 'You have won, yes?'

Smallpiece grimaced with pain.

They half lifted, half dragged him out from beneath the branches, then raised him slowly between them until he was standing on his right leg, his arms about their shoulders. His waistcoat was torn open and dark stains stretched across the starched shirt front.

'Is that you, Mr Smallpiece?' It was Saxmundham's voice. The light from the windows above shone on his epaulettes and made a ribbon of gold down the sides of his tight dark trousers.

'An accident,' Guy said.

'I can see that!' the captain turned to him. 'Look here, Greville, you'll have to go instead. Leave Mr Smallpiece with the quack here.'

As the surgeon changed places with him, the captain went on, 'The privilege leave men if you please, havin' a crack at our German allies. I've sent off young Heighurst for an armed guard. See what you make of it!'

'I will go too,' the German said.

Saxmundham turned to him.

'Lieutenant Mann, *Kapitän,*' he said, clicking his heels, 'His Imperial Majesty's Ship, *Meteor.*'

Smallpiece grunted with pain.

'*Gut!*' Saxmundham rasped. '*Gehen Sie schnell!*'

'Where, sir?' Guy asked as the German lieutenant handed his side of Smallpiece to one of the civilian spectators.

'Down by the grog shops. Oh, that cursed drink! The sultan's askaris have rumbled it. They have muskets of sorts and I fancy they like hearin' 'em go off!'

As Guy and Lieutenant Mann started off at a brisk pace, two men appeared from the shadows behind the captain and followed. He recognized one as the captain's coxswain, Jenkins.

A shot rang out; instinctively they broke into a run, Guy and Mann side by side. Another shot sounded, and after it a ragged volley, accompanied by what sounded like cheering. It was difficult to tell where the sounds came from as they had entered one of the narrow streets and the houses pressed close, baffling analysis of direction.

Guy wondered what they would find. Drink-maddened bluejackets locked in brawls with their German opposite numbers, surrounded by the sultan's undisciplined irregulars firing indiscriminately into the brown was not a business he would expect to be unscrambled by two lieutenants in ball dress. Heighurst would not even have reached the ship yet.

Mann was cracking on at a tremendous pace, evidently in the pink of condition despite the champagne. As they went, the firing grew spasmodic, but the cheering increased in volume, and then quite suddenly it was upon them. The noise swelled, and as they turned a corner burst on their ears like a hurricane; a mass of figures was moving towards them, an avalanche of fluttering pale robes and limbs filling the narrow alley, eyes wide, mouths open, yelling it seemed with terror.

'Into a doorway!' Guy snapped.

He saw Jenkins jump smartly into a shallow doorway to the right and he and Mann leaped two stone steps into the next one, flattening themselves against the timber as the rabble approached. The other sailor made to follow but hesitated, then darted across the street and squeezed himself into an opposite opening. He was just in time. The leading figures stormed past, olive, brown, black faces staring and mouthing, bare feet leaping the steps leading to the doors, flowing cottons brushing the officers' uniforms as they passed, powerful odours of body and sweat.

'It is good we are not so fat,' Mann breathed.

As the torrent began to thin, they became aware of the cheering they had heard earlier, and leaning out to peer down the alley saw a dark mass of bluejackets pressing after the rout, some waving muskets or carbines over their heads, others with knives glinting.

'Ye gods!' Guy exclaimed. Evidently the rabble that was passing was the sultan's force of askaris, disarmed by the bluejackets and fleeing before them. He made out German and British uniforms among the leaders. 'Our lads have joined forces already!'

The German smiled. 'It is good!'

'Fancy stoppin' them?'

Mann stared, then said, 'Of course!'

Guy wished the German were not with him. By himself he would have regarded discretion as the better part. As it was, neither of them could very well remain where they were, skulking in the doorway.

'Here goes then!'

They stepped out into the street at the same time as the last struggling natives ran past. Jenkins and the other sailor, seeing them, also emerged. Guy beckoned them behind him; the officers' uniforms were more likely to have an effect on the men. He crossed his arms over his chest and stood foursquare to the stampede, swept by a wave of fear at the prospect of being flattened by the men; with the German lieutenant beside him there was little room for anyone to get past, only over.

Surprise contorted the faces of the leading bluejackets as they saw the small party emerge ; they tried to slow their pace, but were pressed on by those behind. The noise dropped a little, though, and Guy opened his lungs.

'*Dulcineas! Halt!*'

The quarterdeck yell, higher than the deep-throated roars of the men, echoed back from the houses. Mann followed immediately with a similar order to the Germans.

The charge was now in disarray; those in front, seeing their way barred by the two officers shoulder to shoulder, stiff white shirts and waistcoats and gold epaulettes gleaming very close before them, leant back against those behind, but try as they would it seemed there was no way of stopping the tide funnelling up the alley. The thought of them pressing on, touching, jostling, defiling the Queen's uniform brought the blood to Guy's head.

'Damn you! *Halt!*' he roared.

Almost simultaneously from somewhere in the middle of the seething mass came the crack of a musket, and a scream of pain. Whether it was his yell or the musket shot was not clear, but the pressure on the leaders eased, and they were able to bring the struggling mass to a halt just in front of the officers. Guy could have reached out and touched the nearest without stretching. They stood face to face, bewildered and uncertain. In place of the former cheers and growls, mixed questions and oaths in English and German rose from their back. The smell of spirits was overpowering.

It was necessary to take the initiative now and turn them right around before their own leaders took matters into their own hands again. He turned to the sailor behind him, 'On the knee! Quick!'

The man looked startled, but did as he was bid, and Guy looked at the coxswain, 'Jump up on his back! We'll hang on to you. Order them to turn back and make for the beach!'

Jenkins swayed up, one hand in Guy's, the other in Mann's, and twisted a shoulder so that his chief petty officer's badges were in full view before he roared out the order.

There was a shout from the crowd. 'Nobby's shot 'isself!'

'All the more reason for them to move back and let us get to him,' Guy called up.

'Sooner you clears a path, the sooner the officer can 'elp 'im!' Jenkins roared.

The crowd started moving.

'Shake it up!' Jenkins bellowed. 'It ain't a funeral – not yet! Let the officer get to 'im! Give 'im a chance lads –!'

His efforts had the required effect; the movement back down the alley gathered momentum. They helped Jenkins down.

'Good man!' Guy clapped him across the shoulders.

'Oh, Jesus! Oh, my holy grandmother's landlady's Siamese perishin' tom –!' the coxswain croaked. 'I don't want to see nothin' like that never again – no, sir, an' that's a fact!'

Guy smiled with relief. 'I felt rather like Canute,' he said to Mann, realizing as he said it that the German was unlikely to know the English legend.

'Horatius!' Mann beamed, and thrust out his hand. 'We four – we held the bridge!'

They shook hands on it. Guy felt the power behind the German's grip. He was a magnificent specimen. He thought of Cameron's remark about the coming struggle with Germany. He would much rather have Lieutenant Mann as a friend.

Chapter Eight

Weighurst cascaded the pack easily from hand to hand. 'Penny a point?'

Guy shook his head. The evening air was oppressive, the idea of whist and chaff repugnant; all ideas repelled. His mind soaked in despair. Cards would not deaden the feeling, nor did he wish that. He would savour it to the full without an opiate, keep the ache sharp and take a savage satisfaction from the punishment. He turned for the companionway; on deck he might find space to brood alone.

They were to sail at dawn; it was all he could think of, that and the waste of so many days; they had slipped away: liaising with the consulate and with Cameron as he strove to engage and keep sufficient porters, taking over from the injured Smallpiece the engagement of extra native seamen, 'seedies' as they were called, together with his own responsibilities as gunnery officer for drilling the bluejackets in their role ashore, had left him no time for himself. In any case Saxmundham had been in such a sulk over the reception of his grand idea for a race he had scarcely passed a civil word; to have suggested another attempt to trace

Suleiman would have been impossible. The Arab's disappearance remained a mystery, his favourite wife a mystery within a mystery; both mingled into this desperate sense of failure and lost opportunity. It hurt to fail; to miss a prize within his grasp left a void in his self-respect.

He reached the deck. Saxmundham and Mackenzie were pacing the starboard side together; to port was a straggle of gunroom officers, evidently in high spirits. Forward both sides and all the boats and hatchways and skylights between were crowded with dusky, white-robed porters and seedies, some squatting, some curled on their sides, others shuffling between and over them, chanting in time to different groups of musicians ; the repetitive conflicting beat and wail was confined and intensified by awnings stretched overhead. The air was as warm and close as it had been below, throbbing but scarcely moving, heavy with the musky scent of the natives, close-packed.

'Greville!'

His heart sank.

'Well, Greville!' Both great men had halted, facing him. Saxmundham's extreme height made the consul appear almost absurdly small, something of which Mackenzie was obviously aware, and trying to overcome by rocking on his heels and puffing out his cheeks.

'Well, Greville! The rascals sailed yet?'

Guy glanced quickly to port and saw beneath the awning the distant silhouettes of the German masts and rigging against the night.

'No, sir.'

The blue eyes regarded him quizzically. 'Breakfast tomorrow – after weighing?'

'Thank you, sir.'

'Good!' The eyes glinted as merrily as before the sulk had descended. 'We'll give 'em a run for their money.'

'I know we shall, sir.'

Saxmundham turned to the consul. 'You'd not believe the preparations they've bin makin', colonel. They've shifted all the guns from the corvette and distributed them amongst the gunboats. A prodigious quantity of ammunition and water besides. And all the extra hands.'

The consul looked up sharply. 'I trust you've made a protest.'

The captain's eyes glinted fiercely. 'Won't be the first time the Saxmundham colours carried extra weight, colonel!'

Mackenzie gestured forward towards the crowd of porters and seedies. 'Good heavens –'

'Movable ballast! We'll trim her within an inch of her life. Then we shall see! Greville?'

'We'll give 'em a run for it, sir!'

'Indeed we shall!'

The consul gestured forward again. 'Would it not be possible to transfer our extra hands – I mean to say, the sultan's steamer, the *Star.*'

'The *Star's* loaded down to the gunwales already,' Saxmundham replied shortly, and turned to Guy.

'Over three hundred porters, two hundred Balochs and other irregulars and all the extra stores,' Guy said.

'So you see –' Saxmundham turned back to Mackenzie. He looked into his face for a moment and started chuckling. 'Colonel! On my life! You've plunged!'

Mackenzie looked startled.

'God bless my soul!' Saxmundham's sides shook. 'You're in deep, sir!'

'Nothing too much,' Mackenzie replied, annoyed.

Saxmundham turned to Guy, eyes alight with amusement. 'There's more at stake than we imagined –'

'Think nothing of it, captain,' Mackenzie said sharply. 'It's not my principle – eh, playing high.' He paused. 'I must confess on this occasion I ventured – eh, in the belief that Herr Ebermann could not be apprised of your reputation in the Service.'

The Old Man nodded acknowledgement of the compliment.

Guy said, 'There's not a man in the ship's company hasn't got his shirt on us.' He thought of his own arrangement with Lieutenant Mann: five German crowns for every hour between the ships at Lamu. If they lost it would swell his debts to a level he didn't like to contempate.

Mackenzie rocked back on his heels. 'I'm pleased to hear it–'

Of course!' Saxmundham put a reassuring hand on his shoulders. 'Now, colonel, won't you do me the honour of sampling my port – I have a '47 laid by for just such an occasion.'

They turned towards the companionway; Guy started walking towards the stern, becoming aware as he did so of heightened commotion to port; midshipmen were dropping to the deck from the mizzen rigging, one after the other, greeted with catcalls and cheers from others watching. The cheers and screams reached a crescendo as the last one in shirtsleeves emerged beneath the awning and half jumped, half fell in his haste, landing asprawl near the slide of the lashed sixty-four-pounder. As the others crowded in to help him to his feet, Guy realized with a start that it was Cameron. He was laughing and blowing, half bent, rubbing his middle as if winded while the youngsters crowded about him.

It was a side of the Scot Guy had not seen before. He had spent much time with him over the past few days and had come to admire his professional competence and the *rapport* he was able to establish with the Swahili he engaged as porters; they quickly became laughing, gambolling children under his mixed jokes and insults. Now that all were safely embarked, it seemed he was relaxing.

The Scot looked up and caught sight of him. He turned away and continued aft, pretending he had not noticed, but soon heard footsteps closing from behind, and felt a hand in the small of his back. He knew it was Cameron before he spoke.

'Dinna like to leave the delights of the shore!' The Scot's forehead and cheeks were beaded with perspiration, his lips parted in a smile, his shirt collar and tie uncharacteristically loose.

'Delights!' Guy replied wryly.

'Aw – come!' Cameron's smile widened. Guy had the same startling feeling he had experienced when meeting him first in the coffee shop that his mind was being read. His thoughts dwelled on that first meeting, and shifted to Suleiman. He had never asked the Scot about his acquaintance with the Arab ; there had never been a quiet moment.

'Tell me,' he said. 'How was it, d'you suppose, I was allowed to get away so easily from your friend Suleiman's house?'

Cameron thought for a moment. 'Ye were very fortunate!'

'I had reached that conclusion.'

The Scot's expression changed at the irony in his tone. 'Exceedingly fortunate. And dinna think Suleiman was a friend of mine!' He looked round, his former exuberance vanished. 'Why d'ye suppose I offered my services on this jolly jaunt?'

Guy was taken aback by his vehemence. 'Tell me.'

The Scot's pace increased, and his slight figure seemed to quiver. 'I imagine ye've heard the squealing of pigs that's being castrated.' He looked round. 'Think of it wi' little boys if ye can. Boys that's been marched half across Africa by swine like Suleiman with scarce enough victuals to keep body and soul together – just the whip to keep them on their feet. Imagine them left to crawl in the street after, entrails hanging out as like as not, and the flies settling and the dust.' His eyes blazed and he jabbed his finger at the air. 'That's why I'm here. Aye – but to ye it's a game. An' promotion if ye're fortunate.' He jerked his head round. 'Then mebbe ye don't need so much good fortune – ye've the pull in any event. Although why ye should volunteer for that damn fool errand –'

'I've no family interest,' Guy cut in sharply.

'Saxmundham has plenty where it matters.'

'I dare say.'

They reached the stern once more and turned in silence, Cameron gazing straight before him. Apparently regretting his outburst, he went on in a calmer tone, 'I have a queer feeling tonight.' He seemed to choose his words carefully. 'Have ye ever had the feeling at a particular moment, as though all yer previous life had been a preparation, as though the moment were predestined?' He looked round into Guy's face and went on without waiting for a reply, 'I see my course clearly through the past as directed by an unseen agency. There is a purpose marked out for all of us. I have always known mine. I have early recollections – listen! "The many skeletons we have seen amongst the rocks and woods, by the pools and along the paths of the wilderness all testify to the awful sacrifice of human life which must be attributed to this trade of hell." D'ye know when I first read that? I was eight. I remember it as clearly as if it were yesterday.'

'Dr Livingstone?'

'That's correct.' Cameron looked round, surprised. 'From that time I felt my course was directed in his footsteps, to carry on his great work.'

Guy was puzzled. 'Does the slave trade pass through Witu, then?'

'Now ye're thinking like the shopkeepers at the Foreign Office! A raid here, a raid there, it'll never stop the trade any more than yer cruisers at sea. Cut off one route and another opens, mebbe more distressful for the slaves, mebbe raising the prices in the market, stimulating the slavers to larger profits. No – ask yeself the question, what is the *origin* of the trade?' Without giving Guy a chance to reply, he went on, 'Is it not, at bottom, there are some who are strong, others who are weak?'

Guy wondered if it were so simple.

'From biblical times,' Cameron went on, 'from the Queen of Sheba and before. But now for the furrst time there is a new force, a strong people, the strongest on earth – with this difference from all the conquerors of the past, they view the capture and enslavement of their fellow men with repugnance as a crime against God, the maker of all men. This is the hope gleaming through Africa. We are the chosen people. It is upon us that the Africans' hopes for liberty and progress depend, and we cannot escape the charge.' He paused to note Guy's reaction.

'And Witu?'

'Just the first step on the way. A staging post to the interior. The furrst bloody rotten apple to fall! By God, we're about to start shaking the bough,' he sucked in through his teeth. As they reached the stern again, Guy noticed his eyes gleaming in the light from the lantern. 'This is surely the grandest moment of my life!'

Guy smiled at his enthusiasm. 'Capital!'

'But ye dinna feel it.'

The ache which had been temporarily forgotten, flooded back. He gestured towards the twinkling lights of Zanzibar. 'You were right first time.' He smiled to hide his feelings, aware that Cameron was not deceived. The Scot put an arm over his shoulder as they paced, then suddenly started declaiming.

'Live I, so live I –' The dim light from behind them emphasized the tight-drawn skin over his cheek and long jaw-line, 'to my Lord heartily – to my Prince faithfully –'

Guy joined in, 'To my neighbour honestly. Die I – so die I!'

They laughed together.

Guy awoke with an image of the mchawi seated cross-legged on the Persian carpet in his father's snug. He wanted to ask him about the lion – which lion was not clear, but it was very important to know. He could hear the call of the muezzins, nasal and urgent, very close; he had to find the mchawi again before the old man started his evening devotions. Even as he searched the vanishing images he knew it was a dream. He tried to hold the knowledge at bay. The sounds of the morning filtered through; hens clucked and scraped in their coops. The mchawi escaped.

The deck pressed up hard against his right hip; he ached horribly. His right arm, bent beneath his head, was afflicted with different, sharper pains and his fingers were numb. As he moved to ease these tortures he discovered others and felt the copious sweat of the night cold against his body. He levered himself into a sitting position.

Near at hand scores of other forms lay about the grey morning deck in or half out of sheets, some shifting uncomfortably or snoring, one struggling to its feet. He recognized Smallpiece, evidently willing himself to stand without the aid of the stick he had been using since the accident. He had to admire the man's spirit. Against all the surgeon's remonstrations Smallpiece had been hobbling the decks, up and down ladders with his splinted and bandaged leg thrust out before him, yet refusing to give up any of his duties. Prickly heat and ulcers had developed beneath the bandages and spread around his thigh; still he had refused to give in.

Watching sleepily, Guy saw him stumble and scramble to regain his balance, in the process bringing his splinted leg down on one of the recumbent forms nearby. A cry from the sleeper was followed by a bellow of pain from Smallpiece as his leg was clasped, and he fell. The air filled with oaths.

Guy jumped up, and pulling his sheet around him, made towards the scene. He found Smallpiece propped on an elbow, scowling at the chief engineer, who was kneeling, grunting with inexpressible rage. The sheet had slipped from his white and podgy body which was quite naked. Guy placed a hand on his shoulder, and he looked up.

'There's nae man calls me wi' a foot!'

'Greville!' Smallpiece growled, his face contorting with pain. 'I'll thank you to leave us.'

'No' Saxmundham himsel',' the chief went on, brandishing his free arm, 'Nae man calls me wi' a foot in th' fork –' He turned back to Smallpiece, his voice quavering, 'If it's steam ye're wanting, take y'rsel' doon t' th' furnaces –'

The first lieutenant manoeuvred himself into a sitting position, and glared up at Guy, oblivious of the chief's harangue. 'Damn you, Greville!'

'Prepare y'rsel',' the chief thundered, 'it's where ye'll be gaun –'

Guy looked from one shaking form to the other, nodded with exaggerated courtesy, and, hitching his sheet, moved off. He met the quartermaster of the watch coming

towards the scene. 'Assistance not required,' he snapped.
'Give my man a shake. Tell him I require a bath.'

The quartermaster hesitated, staring past him at the
first lieutenant now hauling himself to his feet by a gun-
slide. Guy said angrily, 'Move then!'

The man turned and made his way forward. Most
of the sleepers were awake long since, propped up on an
elbow or sitting, staring towards the dispute. Guy lost interest and walked wearily towards the companionway.

Forward and in the waist and fo'c's'le the deck and
boats were astir with white-robed figures in different stages
of their ablutions before prayers; some, perched atop the
bulwarks, were drawing up water in canvas buckets, others
squatted before minute bowls cleaning their mouths out
with the index finger of their right hand, others gargled,
others bent, washing their noses and ears, while a few who
had started earlier stood looking towards the pale glow in
the eastern sky, preparing their minds in silence. It was an
oddly humbling scene.

Descending the companionway, he was met by a rising
stench of close-packed humanity. None of the hands had
been able to sleep on deck because of the porters and seedies; their hammocks were packed together from end to end
of the berth deck in an atmosphere that was almost visible.
He hurried on, turning with relief into the comparative
purity of the wardroom and his own cabin.

Presently there was a knock on the door, and Duff
entered with a jug of steaming water. He was surprised to
see the marine fully dressed.

'Quick work, Figgy!'

Duff raised the mahogany flap that served as desk top and washstand cover and placed the jug carefully in the enamel bowl beneath. 'I didn't need no shake, sir.'

'I don't wonder,' Guy replied, thinking of the foul air forward. 'Tell me, Figgy, d'you have dreams at all?'

Duff shot him an appraising glance. 'Not as 'ow I'd like, sir. The sarge now, 'e 'as dreams. 'E 'as this 'areem – 'e carries it in 'is mind.'

'Most convenient.'

Encouraged, Duff went on, 'After pipe down 'e says, "Which one's it to be tonight, lads?"' He paused, still gauging Guy's tolerance as he reached up to unfasten the knots about the shallow tin bath lashed to the deckhead. Satisfied, he went on, '"How about the Ottentot?" we says. "That bint you purchased last week with them pendelem ears?" "I've sold 'er," 'e says, "I don't go for them pendelem ears no more, but I'll tell you what, I sees this one in the market with scars – ten dollar she were an' scars all over. Cicatrix they calls 'em. I 'ad to make sure they was all over," 'e says. "You 'orrible beast!" we says. "I believe I'll wrastle with 'er tonight, I fancy them scars," 'e says. Well, in the mornin', "How was she, sarge?" Then 'e tells us. I won't particularize sir. Somethin' shockin', the bobbery them nigger women get up to, sir!'

'I'm surprised,' Guy said, thinking of the marine sergeant's stolid red face and belligerent moustaches. 'I had no idea the sarn't was blessed with imagination.'

'Oh, no, sir. It comes to 'im in 'is sleep.'

'I see. The best place for the harem, perhaps.'

Duff glanced at him suspiciously as he lowered the bathtub to the deck. 'Funny you should say that, sir. I was only speakin' of that to this gen'leman –' He picked the sponge and soap tray from the washstand and placed them carefully inside the oval bath at the end.

'Gentleman?'

'Not a proper gent – if you know my meanin' –'

Guy's mind flashed to Cameron. 'He'd like to be?'

Duff nodded.

'A Scot?'

'A proper 'aggis – 'specially when 'e lost 'is rag –'

'Cameron! You were speaking with him?'

'Last night. The rats it were – nibblin' me toes an' I couldn't get no sleep so I goes up on deck makin' out as 'ow I was goin' to the 'ead an' I gets talkin' with the QM. "There's this passenger," 'e says, pointin' up to the main top – " 'e's bin up there the best part o' the watch. Now, you're a reasonin' man, Figgy, why don't you jes' run an' see what 'e's up to?"

'"Why don't you?" I says.

'"You know what'd 'appen to me if I was to leave me post o' duty," 'e says –'

Scenting a long story, Guy eased himself from the bed, pulled off his nightshirt, and stepped into the bath; sitting down, he took the soap tray out and placed it on the deck.

'Since you're here, Figgy, you may do the honours.'

Duff moved to collect the jug of hot water.

'What did Cameron say when you got up there?'

''E were prayin', sir.'

'Praying!'

Duff held the jug above Guy's shoulders and tipped it so that the water flowed over his shoulders and down his back in a steady stream. As it flooded the bottom of the bath, Guy charged the sponge and brought it up quickly to rinse his forehead and eyes. He began to feel more human.

"E stops directly 'e sees me,' Duff went on. 'Makes out as 'eow 'ee's up there for 'is 'ealth. "Come an' join me, my man," 'e says, "We shall 'ave a yarn or two far above the cares of this wicked ol' world.""

'What was he praying about?'

'Askin' to be forgiven – some terrible thing 'e done –'

Guy looked up quickly. The marine's eyes were serious.

'After a while we got to talkin' of relijun, an' these Mooslims an' all. I says to 'im, "If it's the same God they worship, 'ow is it 'e gives 'em diff rent orders? Take these slaves," I says, "Is 'e a-tellin' them Mooslims they can ketch niggers an' keep 'em like we might keep cattle or donkeys? An' this same God is 'e a-tellin' us it's a mortal sin to keep niggers what 'e's made in 'is own image – ?"' Duff paused. 'I gets puzzled at times, sir – if God made everyone in 'is own image like we're told, 'ow is it there's blacks an' whites an' coffee-coloured an' all, an' them savages that's eight feet 'igh –'

Guy smiled. 'He tends to take the form most admired by the worshipper,' which wasn't really an answer.

'That's what I says, sir –'

'Some other time, Figgy. What did Cameron say?'

Duff frowned as he poured another stream of deliriously warm water. 'Well – 'e says, "Strange you should mention that my man, 'cause I've 'ad many an argiment concernin' exactly that. Now the Mooslim slave dealer, 'e says, Yes, all men are God's chil'ren, but them niggers they don't acknowledge it. They don't hold with no God, they 'ave spirits an' suchlike they worship, so God 'as lost in'erest in 'em, an' they're fair game for ketchin' and keepin' an' teachin' concernin' God."

"'Well," I says, "I knows chil'ren ain't regarded much by some folk an' they lose in'erest in 'em soon enough without so much as askin' if they're acknowledged

There was a bitter edge to his voice, and Guy realized suddenly he knew nothing of the marine's background. He looked up, and saw the scar which a musket ball had ploughed through his cheek, twitching.

'But you wouldn't call them folks Christian,' the marine went on. "'Anyway," I says, "what about the Prodigal son?" 'E looks at me as much as to say, "I didn't allow you'd be preachin' parables at me my man," an' I says, "Do they 'ave that story in their Koran?"

'An' 'e looks at me again, "You've caught me there, you've properly caught me – "'

'Capital!' Guy said, genuinely delighted. 'You spotted the flaw!'

'Thank you, sir,' Duff said with a pleased look.

Guy heard the pipe for 'Clear up decks' sounding, and he nodded at the marine to indicate that he could go. Then, suddenly remembering Saxmundham's invitation, he said, 'I shall be breakfasting with the owner.'

'Number ones!'

He nodded. The marine replaced the jug in the wash-basin and made to leave, pausing with the door open.

'What d'you rate our chances, sir?'

'I'd back Old Sax.'

'That's what I says.'

He knocked the deck beside the bath. 'And she ain't too bad!'

'Right an' all, sir!' Duff grinned broadly as he left.

Chapter Nine

The ship was still and so quiet that the small wavelets of the harbour could be heard distinctly lapping the plates below. The deck was clear from end to end, the porters having been sent down to the orlop to be out of the way and the seedies to the main deck to help turn the capstan. The awnings and awning stanchions had been struck and the planks either side of the central skylights and ventilators presented a clean sweep, broken only by the lashed guns, glistening in the early sunlight. The bluejackets in clean white frocks and trousers, straw hats tilted rakishly, were gathered in tense groups, midshipmen in attendance, the topmen in the lee of the bulwarks by the shrouds at each mast, every attitude expressing nervous tension. Right forward were the fo'c's'lemen with Smallpiece slightly apart from them, perched on the slide of the Armstrong bow chaser, peering over the side at the cable which had been shortened in to little more than the depth of water; his splinted leg was angled out sideways. Elsewhere small parties of the afterguard, interspersed with marines in plain grey working rig and watched over by petty officers, stood by to cast off halliards, tacks and sheets from the bitts and pins. The marine band, perspiring in the deep green, brass-bound Saxmundham livery and straw boaters banded with the earl's green and yellow racing colours, stood just abaft the foremast, eyes screwed against dazzling shafts of light from their instruments.

On the quarterdeck the officers waited in groups, engineers dressed within an inch of their lives to ape the military branch, with white gloves and swords uncomfort-ably jangling, the surgeon and the old paymaster together, the schoolmaster by himself, and Heighurst with flat shoulders and stiff spine, smoothing his moustaches beside Mackenzie and Fortescue. Cameron was aloof and alone at the stern. They stood in constrained silence as if the small-est move might disturb the actors. The navigating lieuten-ant, Geoffrey Stainton, stood with Guy beside the binnacle; nearby were the quartermaster and bluejackets who would take the wheel, their attention concentrated on a group of signalmen with the fourth lieutenant and a midshipman by the entrance port, glasses and telescopes trained on the German flagship quarter of a mile away. The only moving figure was Saxmundham; he paced the deck with a show of nonchalance, up and down past his retinue of aides and messengers, his speaking trumpet clasped behind his back, his face expressionless, a scarlet cravat lending a touch of colour to his long blue, gold-encrusted coat. The steady click-click of his leather heels against the deck imprinted itself on the scene like the tick of a clock in a hot, still room.

Overhead a huge white ensign floated out against the pale blue of morning; vivid yellow masts and wide yards, each crowned with tightly rolled white canvas struck right angles against the taut steel and hemp tresses of the rigging, shining black blocks glanced changing angles of light as the ship moved to slight shifts in the breeze.

Guy's attention wandered shorewards.

Somewhere beyond the national ensigns fluttering over the flat roofs of the consulates, and the palm fronds along the shore, among the buildings which looked so much fairer at this distance with the low sun brightening their white or yellow walls, in a scented room, surrounded by a retinue of household slaves, she was starting another day, quite unaware of his thoughts for her – a brilliant butterfly caught in Suleiman's web of luxury – seen for a moment – and lost.

He wondered, as he had so many times, whether Suleiman had returned to her, or whether perhaps he had taken a dhow and sailed north to warn the 'Lion' of Witu. Not that he needed warning after Mackenzie's letter.

He heard a shout from the yeoman of signals; looking quickly towards the German flagship, he saw the small, striped pennant at her main descending rapidly. Even before the cry, 'Away aloft!' rang over the deck the topmen were springing into the shrouds, racing up hand over hand, shaking the ratlines in a frenzy of bare feet – up over the futtocks, the lower yard-men running straight out along the yards and dropping to the footropes while the upper yard-men continued their headlong dash up the topmast shrouds. Shortly afterwards a few were swarming up the t'gallants. One missed his footing, hung for a moment like an eagle outstretched, then plummeted, caught hold of a halliard and swung like a circus artist for a wild moment before climbing again.

Guy was caught up in the delirium; he found himself pacing to no purpose, gazing up and willing the hands on as they lay out and loosed the sails, while others in the tops overhauled the bowlines, lifts and trusses.

'Topsail sheets!' Saxmundham roared, and after a pause while the outermost yard-men worked their way in clear of the blocks, 'Haul taut! Let fall! Sheet home!'

The parties down the deck ran away with the sheets as the great expanse of courses and topsails tumbled down, ballooning and folding against the shrouds and lower masts. As the courses were sheeted home, other lines of men ran away with the halliards for the topsail yards, which squealed up the masts, stretching the sunlit canvas into familiar deep shapes. In quick succession afterwards the t'gallants and then the royals were set, and the hands on deck manned the braces to swing the yards for casting to port.

Guy glanced over at the Germans and saw the corvette in much the same position as themselves, nearly all plain sail set. Most of the gunboats were not so quick. He heard Saxmundham's order to heave round the capstan and saw him signal to the bandmaster.

'Hearts of oak are our ships,' the rousing notes blared brassily; the big drum thumped a beat to lift the hands straining at the capstan bars below.

Presently he saw Smallpiece signalling with his arm; the anchor cable was 'up and down'. A midshipman scudded along the deck towards the Old Man, who nodded at the message and strode towards the starboard side where the quartermaster in the chains waited with the lead line hanging vertically. Guy checked that the wheel was amidships. Turning, he saw the Old Man walking back from the side; evidently the quartermaster had reported sternway; the anchor had broken out cleanly. The bows began swinging to port. He saw Smallpiece gesturing to the hands on the fo'c's'le, and guessing the jibs were about to be set, turned to see that the hands aft were manning the spanker outhaul. She fell off faster, the head canvas braced for the port tack bellying back against the shrouds, the main and mizzen sails braced hard up for the starboard tack shivering and slapping.

'Head braces and spanker outhaul!' Saxmundham's roar sounded over the buoyant notes of the band, and as she swung further off to port and the after sails began to lift and swell, 'Brace round the head yards!' The hands on the port forward braces charged aft; the sails on the foremast swung, slapped, shivered, lifted, winged gracefully.

Guy glanced to check the spanker, then over towards the German squadron, seeing with a thrill that the corvette was not yet round, while the gunboats were heading all angles at different stages of the evolution. The *Dulcinea* had taken the first points.

As if aware of her advantage, the little ship leaned and surged to a stronger gust. The green ranks of bandsmen swayed to starboard. Saxmundham strode towards the wheel, pocketing the gold hunter with which he had timed the evolution, eyes alight with triumph at the performance; it had been a faultless display, worthy of a crack Mediterranean ship at the end of her commission.

'Extra tot for all hands this evenin'!' he said as he passed.

They gathered way over the smooth water, heading almost straight for the German flagship which was now round on the same tack with all sails pulling. Starting from further out she would beat them to the pass through the reefs guarding the harbour – but not by very much. The *Dulcinea's* fractionally better performance in getting under way meant that she was moving faster; the gap between them would narrow for a few minutes yet.

As he watched Guy became aware that one of the German gunboats was in difficulties. Her head had not paid off, all her sails were flat aback, and she was gathering sternway, her anchor cable leading forward; to his astonishment he saw the links moving down from the hawse hole.

'Hell's delight!' Saxmundham exploded.

There was little doubt that if she continued paying out her cable and dropping astern at her present rate she would fall across the *Dulcinea's* course.

'Bla'guards!' Saxmundham raged in a lower tone, as if unable to believe his eyes, then snapped to the quartermaster, 'Keep her at that!' He strode forward faster than Guy had seen him move for a natural emergency, his midshipman aide and messengers stretching their legs behind. Guy followed. Stopping in the starboard entrance port, the Old Man gazed at the gunboat for a moment, gauging her stern rate, then turned to the mishipman, 'Have Mr Stainton tell off a party to attend the spanker brails and outhaul!' As the lad darted off he looked up the quarterdeck and called to Heighurst.

'Sentries to the starboard bow!' he snapped as the marine came up. 'Rifles at the ready! A volley across her starn!'

Heighurst's salute was as crisp as the order. He ran for the companionway, yelling, 'Sarn't!'

'I trust he'll not be too particular as to aim!' Saxmundham muttered and raising his speaking trumpet called out to the forward parties to stand by the jib sheets. He turned back to gaze at the gunboat and the narrowing stretch of blue water between them. Her sails were still cracking and slapping back against the masts, men running wildly about her decks, officers shouting, yards being braced round in confusion, and her anchor cable still veering out. The contrast with the smart and silent manner in which the German flagship had got under way was glaring. Saxmundham raised his speaking trumpet and shook it angrily, then put it to his mouth. 'Cowardly cheats!' He turned to Guy, 'What's that in their beastly lingo?'

Guy searched a blank memory.

Mackenzie bustled up with Fortescue close behind. 'What's to do, captain!'

'Let the weakest fend off!' Saxmundham growled without turning.

The consul stared at the gunboat. The *Dulcinea* was moving at a good seven knots, leaning nicely to a strengthening breeze, the tip of her jib-boom pointing somewhere above a whale-boat suspended from the davits over the gunboat's stern. The distance between them was shrinking dangerously. Unless the *Dulcinea* payed off it looked a certain collision.

'What's the matter with the fellow?' the consul said querulously.

Out of the corner of his eye Guy saw three figures in scarlet racing forward with rifles.

'Fancies he'll place us in balk,' Saxmundham replied. He turned to Guy. 'Well – ?' His eyes were hard.

'*Das ist nicht cricket!*' It was all he could think of. '*Nicht richtiges cricket!*'

A gleam of amusement lit the Old Man's face, and he raised his speaking trumpet again, delivering the message in stentorian tones and repeating it twice. Guy could see the German commander, a young lieutenant, staring from his poop at the *Dulcineas* bow cleaving straight for him. He saw Heighurst waving, and called Saxmundham's attention to it. Two marines were steadying their rifles on the rolled hammocks in the nettings; Heighurst had drawn his sword for greater effect. Beyond them, Smallpiece was shaking his fist at the German quarterdeck, now less than fifty feet from him; his words were inaudible beneath the band, still rendering 'Hearts of Oak'.

Saxmundham pointed his speaking trumpet at the bow. '*Fire!*'

Heighurst brandished his sword. Two shots cracked, puffs of smoke trailed from the rifle barrels.

'Ye gods!' Mackenzie exclaimed. 'Captain –!'

The Germans stood their ground; the young lieutenant raised a trumpet to his lips and bellowed something Guy couldn't catch.

'The brute!' Saxmundham growled. Then, seeing the *Dulcinea's* jib-boom falling downwind away from the

German, he rounded angrily on the men at the wheel, 'Keep her up, damn you!'

The bluejackets' eyes were as wide as Mackenzie's as they heaved at the spokes, staring at the German masts almost aboard.

Guy looked at Saxmundham again, and realized that he was enjoying the situation hugely. He had the speaking trumpet to his lips and was shouting, 'Fenders out!' to the German lieutenant, who was now thoroughly alarmed. Guy noticed that the gunboat's sternway had been checked; the cable was no longer veering out from her bows, and the yards had been braced sharp up in a desperate attempt to swing the head off the wind and move her stern fractionally forward, away from the *Dulcinea's* advancing stem. Together with the unauthorized slight easing of the *Dulcinea's* helm and the leeway they were making it might be enough.

He saw their flying jib-boom sweep past and above the gunboat's stern with some fifteen feet of lateral separation, just sufficient to prevent the vessels touching if the Old Man played it right; the whaler hanging from her stern was a different matter. He glanced at Saxmundham; he was leaning outboard, speaking trumpet by his chest, the brilliant cravat rippling in the breeze, eyes alight with the excitement of hazard and nice judgement. Guy wondered whether he would have eased the wheel if the helmsmen had not taken it upon themselves.

They were sliding towards the German like an express. The whole sweep of her deck opened out below, the sparkling brasswork of the binnacle, burnished bars over the open skylights, yellow funnel, monstrous black Krupp breechloader abaft the foremast with the arcs of its bright brass training racers curving on the deck like tracks in a marshalling yard, sheets and braces trailed in apparent confusion, the expressions of the officers and hands alow and aloft caught for an agonized instant like posing figures in an extraordinarily sharp photograph, white gaze fixed on the impending point of impact, etched in the sunlight.

There was a splintering crash and the scene exploded in running figures, gesticulating and crying out. The German davits juddered and bowed. The *Dulcinea's* jibs, fore course and fore topsails spilled and slapped, blanketed by the gunboat's canvas, and an instant later the mainsails were aback and the ship was coming upright, still surging at a terrifying rate past the small gunboat which was rolling slightly apart from them, shifted by the impact or by the pressure of water under the *Dulcinea's* shoulder. The whaler which had been at the German's stern was nowhere to be seen, only the broken falls trailing in the water from davits bent like crazed old men, and white planks floating beneath.

A spontaneous s roar went up from the *Dulcinea,* ringing around decks and rigging like a blood cry from the Roman Colosseum.

'Silence!' Saxmundham bellowed, and raising his speaking trumpet again, 'Let fly the jib sheets!' He turned to his midshipman. 'My compliments to the first lieutenant. Report on damage!'

The lad scampered forward ; the captain turned and strode back to the wheel.

With the pressure off the head sails the *Dulcinea* rounded up to the wind, throwing her stern away from the gunboat as she swept past. As the fore and mainsails filled once more, Saxmundham ordered the jib sheets hauled aft, and the ship leaned away, leaving the German in confusion astern. Two hundred yards ahead the German flagship was leaning away at a similar angle, sun glinting off the panes of her stern gallery; way above, the great black cross on her ensign stood out starkly against the piled, sunlit canvas. Guy turned from her to look for the other gunboats ; two were under way, the third hove to off the bows of the ship they had shaved past; he wondered if she had been in the plot as well, an additional hazard for Saxmundham if he had contrived to luff up and pass ahead of the other. Or had the whole thing been simply poor seamanship, or the result of one of those natural hitches which bedevilled anchor work?

He saw Heighurst striding towards him from forward, his normally sardonic expression changed with a smile of genuine enjoyment.

'Smartest work it's been my pleasure to witness!' he said as he came up. 'Did you ever see a fellow so sick as their captain when he saw his little game was rumbled?'

Mackenzie stepped up to him anxiously. 'Where did we hit?'

'We never touched,' Heighurst replied. 'The anchor it was hooked their beastly jolly boat, ripped it away from the davits like you or I might snatch a jug from a drunk and held it out on the fluke as if we was thumbin' our noses at the blighters! It was the prettiest thing I ever hope to see!

Old Smallpiece hopped about so delighted he damn near broke the other leg.'

'Never touched?'

'Not so much as a whisker.'

Fortescue nodded ahead at the German flagship. 'Let's hope he don't try it again!'

They laughed.

Guy moved back to the binnacle, where Saxmundham was gazing out at the German flagship, talking to Stainton. 'I wonder which one of the rascals it was cooked that one up!'

'They'll not attempt it again, sir!'

The Old Man rumbled with laughter, turning to Guy as he approached. 'The gallant colonel recovered his colour yet?'

'He hopes you'll show the flagship more respect.'

Saxmundham's shoulders heaved.

Forward parties of bluejackets and carpenters' mates had hauled up the remains of the German whaler to the level of the bulwarks and were rigging lines and tackles from the rigging to sway it inboard. Guy wondered that Smallpiece thought it worth preserving. Beyond them he saw the German flagship entering the greening, white-flecked water of the pass through the reefs. She would be bearing away any moment, and setting her stunsails; the race would be truly on.

They watched her without speaking, and presently saw her broadside begin to open. Her yards squared; one by one the stunsails broke out, restrained by the sheets to set in tight curves up her fore and main. Plumes of foam rose under her bow and played down the dark side; the great, black-crossed ensigns and von Pullitz's flag cracked stiffly forward, then she passed from view as she crossed ahead of the *Dulcinea's* canvas.

As they neared the reef themselves, Saxmundham sent word for the band to pipe down and for Smallpiece to attend to the stunsails. The wreck of the German whaler was on deck now, and the hands, assisted by the seedies from below, were working furiously to get the anchors catted. As the music stopped, they heard the belly-grunting as they heaved in unison, and from the chains the sing-song tones of the leadsman.

'Ease her a shade!' Saxmundham said to the quartermaster, and to Stainton, 'To the fo'c's'le if you please, and signal the instant we're clear to bear away. Don't cut it too fine, mind!'

Stainton grinned and strode off. Guy looked astern. The four German gunboats were following in a straggling group, the nearest almost a hundred yards behind. Two outrigger fishing canoes with lateens like white wings were flying over the bright water between them, men balancing on each windward outrigger holding the sheets. He envied them their exhilaration and the simplicity of their life. Already the heat was making the shirt stick to his back beneath his high-collared white tunic.

Beyond were more fishing boats, some with square matting sails, and a dhow was putting out from the shore with a great dinning of gongs and beating drums and chanting voices carrying clearly on the breeze, laden as always with the scent of cloves. The castellated fort and the crowded city shimmered behind the masts and rigging of anchored vessels. Dissatisfaction crept up on him again. He turned to shut out the thoughts.

Stainton, perched up to peer over the fo'c's'le nettings, raised his hand.

'Up with the helm!' Saxmundham said, then with a roar, 'Weather after braces!'

Guy forgot the city as the hands rushed to trim the yards and check the sheets while the bows swung to port and the wind drew away on the quarter. They were hardly round, feeling the new motion before Saxmundham was hurling out orders for setting the stunsails, and the hands, waiting aloft with the booms out, cut the stops. The helmsmen leant their weight to the spokes as the ship felt the pull of the new canvas increasing minute by minute with each sail loosed and sheeted home. Saxmundham leant on flexed knees, weighing the balance of forces straining in the taut rigging above, glancing occasionally at the wheel, sometimes at the tell-tale bunting from the shrouds.

'God bless my soul!' he muttered to himself. 'Now we shall see!'

The savoury aroma as Guy entered the captain's fore cabin reminded him of England. The round, green baize-topped table had been covered with a spanking white cloth, against which silver settings and china side plates, gilt-ringed and emblazoned with the Saxmundham arms, mirrored reflections from skylights and ports. Only two places had been laid. Another crisp white cloth covered a cabinet against the bulkhead to his right, and this was agleam with larger plates of the same pattern and covered silver serving dishes, the source of the delightful aroma.

'Ah, my boy!' Saxmundham was evidently delighted; Guy found it difficult to imagine the black looks and ostentatious 'cuts' he had been subjected to during the last days in Zanzibar. He was standing with a file of papers in his hands, his back to the blue chintz settee along the side; he held the file up for a moment, then dropped it deliberately to the cushions as if signifying the end of nonsense of that sort while they enjoyed the meal. He waved Guy towards the cabinet.

Guy took a plate; it was warm. Lifting the lids of each of the five dishes in turn he found heaped braised kidneys in the first, eggs poached and running in butter in the next, cold tongue in the third, then curry with meat swimming in deep, oily brown liquid steaming with heady spices, and in the last, delicate portions of a small fowl.

'Now then, my boy,' Saxmundham called, 'What's it to be, tea or sham?'

He looked round surprised at the choice. The steward had come in to the cabin and was standing by the door leading to the pantry.

'Champagne I'd say, sir!'

'So would I!' the Old Man beamed and nodded to the steward, who left as silently as he had appeared on rope-soled slippers. 'It ain't the mornin' for tea! On my life!'

Guy turned to the curry, heaping it onto his plate, as much as he dared. 'If there was ever a smarter evolution I should like to have witnessed it!' It sounded disgustingly sycophantic, but it was the truth. The images of the crisp and perfect departure, the precise timing of the orders, and the instant anticipated responses as the ship cast to port under all her shaking canvas still crackled in his mind.

Saxmundham looked pleased. He eyed Guy's plate for an instant longer than he might have done, but made no remark, waving him to a chair as he came across to the serving cabinet himself. 'I own it was well done.' He helped himself to kidneys, and as if the few words had been quite inadequate to express what was in his mind, added, 'There's *life* in it! Bless my soul –!' He evidently wished to say more, but couldn't find the words, and shook his great head instead.

The steward came in and placed two champagne glasses on the table. Guy took his as the ship gave a deeper lurch than usual. The drum-shaped chintz and tasselled lamp-shade above swung. Saxmundham leaned, his expression suddenly keen. As she settled to her former heel, he came and sat down opposite. 'It'll blow up later I shouldn't wonder.' His eyes were alive with zest. 'A stormy night, I fancy!'

'We shall be ahead by then.'

The Old Man chuckled, thrusting a kidney into his mouth. The steward came in with a champagne bottle protruding from a silver bucket; it was misty and beaded with moisture, and there were chinks of ice as the man lifted the bottle to pour half an inch for the captain to taste. Saxmundham took his glass and sipped.

'I wonder if von Pullitz is enjoyin' his brekker!' He had such a conspiratorial glint in his eye Guy had to restrain an outright laugh. 'I thank heavens I was born in time,' he went on, as the steward filled both glasses and placed the bucket by his right hand. 'Know why I challenged the beggars, Greville?'

'You did tell us –'

'The real reason? To stymie Mac!' He gazed at Guy expectantly.

Guy grinned.

Saxmundham nodded his delight. 'The scamp has no excuse to pester me on this little run!' He raised his glass. 'The best ship!'

'Best ship!' Guy repeated, and drank. The champagne was curiously flat and tasteless with the curry burning his tongue. He'd been an idiot.

The Old Man leant towards him. 'Did you see 'em on deck this mornin' with their beastly collars? I'm a charitable man, but there's something I cannot abide, and one of 'em's a fellow pretends what he ain't.'

'I don't believe Mac has any pretensions, sir.'

'The young 'uns. Have you noticed 'em recently? Have you seen how cocky they've become since they messed in the wardroom?'

Guy made no reply, thankful that his mouth was full. Saxmundham went on, 'You'll learn, it's a fixed rule of life, my boy, the more you give 'em, the more they want. They're no different to any other class of person in that respect. First uniform,' he ticked the engineers' successive demands off on his fingers, 'an equality with the military branch – messing in the wardroom – there'll be no end to it. Make no mistake, my boy,' he leaned over the table, 'they mean to take over the Service. I thank heavens I'll not live to see it.' He thrust a forkful of kidneys fiercely between his teeth. 'Unfortunately I cannot say the same for you, my boy.'

Guy tried to square the prediction with naval engineers as he knew them. A more humbled class would be hard to find. There were exceptions who made no bones about their resentment at being treated as third-class officers, but most accepted the gulf in station between themselves and the fighting branch, gave themselves no airs, and were usually sound good fellows, whom he rubbed along with better than many of his own class.

'I hadn't given it much thought,' he began carefully. He was about to say that he expected they would be so busy looking after the increasing amount of auxiliary machinery being built into the new warships they would have little time to extend their skills to seamanship and the military arts, but he was cut short.

'I detest 'em!'

He busied himself with his curry.

Saxmundham rose and went across to peer through the forward port, whose gleaming brass scuttle hung horizontally inboard. Returning, he seized the champagne bottle and twisted it in the ice, seeming amused by Guy's questioning look. 'It's the last furlong that counts, my boy! Besides we have something up our sleeve.' He re-charged the glasses. 'I'm not of a philosophical turn of mind, but I fancy we may learn something from the salmon, Greville.'

Guy adjusted to the new tack; images of a holiday spent standing in the rapids of the Mora rose to mind, the leaps of the splendid fish aglow with changing colour. ...

'The stronger the current, the more he likes it,' Saxmundham went on, the more he fights it. He don't know why any more than you nor I. He hurls himself on as if his life depends on it. What a grand time he has! On my life, Greville! If I was of a literary turn I'd write an ode to a salmon –' He glanced up. 'It ain't been done?'

'Not that I've heard of, sir.'

'No more do I know why I can't abide the new navy and their beastly steam kettles.' He frowned as if trying to find words to express his mind. 'D'you fancy they ever stop to think where it's all leadin'? Where's it to end? D'you fancy they ever consider that?'

'In my opinion, that's the excitement of it. No one can tell.'

'I want no part of it.'

The Old Man emptied his glass. 'There's no golden age, Greville. Never was, never will be. Mackenzie said to me last night, "Ain't it marvellous, captain; I've received instructions from Lord Granville dictated in London not twelve hours since!" I replied, "They're the same damnfool instructions whether you received 'em in twelve hours or three months as formerly!" He didn't like it! Help yourself to some more!'

Guy glanced up, sensing sarcasm, but there was no hint of it in the blue eyes, and he rose and took his plate to the cabinet. The ship was heeling at a steady angle; there was little swell in the lee of the land. He felt none of the usual queasiness on first putting to sea.

Saxmundham was silent as he returned to the table, breaking pieces of dry toast on his side plate and popping them into his mouth absent-mindedly. After a while he said, 'There's a matter I wish to discuss.'

Guy's heart sank.

'I make it a rule not to poke my nose in my officers' affairs —unless they request it — their private affairs you understand —' His eyes had lost their former zest. 'On this occasion I feel obliged to say something.' He looked down, pausing a long while before he went on, 'It would be fair to say there is ill-feeling between the first lieutenant and yourself?' He looked up.

'It's none of my making, sir.'

'None of your conscious making.' His eyes were serious. 'I've known Smallpiece a long time. I requested him for my first lieutenant.' He leant forward. 'I sometimes think promise the most damnable thing, Greville. There was real promise in young Smallpiece. I knew him first as a mate in the old *Agincourt.* My first voyage to sea. Not one of your passed-over old mates — a bright lad, keen as mustard on anything appertainin' to the ship, helpful to a degree to anyone who cared to request it. I fancy he taught me more than most.'

Guy returned his gaze, trying to fit these startling new images of Smallpiece into the pattern he had acquired in the *Dulcinea.*

'He was an orphan as I understood it. Sir James Darcy took a fancy to him and signed him on as a first-class volunteer —none of your Admiralty meddlin' in those days! While Darcy had command Smallpiece was sittin' pretty because Darcy thought the world of him – and quite right, too. He was the smartest fellow you ever saw. Quiet and studiously inclined as well. He never looked at a bottle in those days —all his thoughts were for the Service.' He paused. 'If Darcy had lived he'd have taken Smallpiece with him as lieutenant. But Darcy died of the fever in the West Indies – he caught it from a slaver he'd taken near the end of her run.' He thrust a piece of toast into his mouth, and crunched it. 'Young Smallpiece didn't find another appointment for twenty years.' His eyes were hard. 'Can you imagine that, young fellow?'

Guy shook his head. It was near enough his lifetime.

'Had it been any of his fault,' Saxmundham went on, 'had he not always given of his best – had he not known he was a smarter hand than most with the "interest" to obtain a com-mision – perhaps it might have been easier. As it was – on my life! His only mistake was old Sir James pegged out on him.'

Guy thought of Smallpiece's aggressive competence in the *Dulcinea*.

'I'll say this, it never broke his spirit,' Saxmundham went on. 'He shipped out in the merchant service so as not to forget his business, and he never gave up hopes of finding his way back into the Service. On my first obtaining a post command he wrote to me, and I was glad to take him. By the time I received his application I had a full complement of lieutenants and it was as mate he came to me. It didn't incommode him. "Just so long as I have another chance," he used to say. When we lost the fourth lieutenant in the Ashantee campaign I had no hesitation in promoting Smallpiece, and their lordships confirmed the appointment in their own good time.'

'He was never made up to commander.'

'It was too late by then, my boy. There were any number of smart lieutenants under half his age – and with scientific backgrounds. Besides, the ill-fortune that started with Darcy's death dogged him.' The Old Man lifted the champagne bottle and, seeing it empty, called to the steward. 'Promise is the very devil! I know of nothin' like it for breakin' a man's heart. I believe I've learnt to value it for what it is.' He glanced up. 'Not for what it may become in the course of time.'

'Present mirth hath present laughter,' Guy thought, his mind flying for some reason to the fishermen on their outriggers that morning.

'Bless my soul, Greville!' The Old Man's expression relaxed. 'Did you ever have such a philosophical brekker! I never did. On my life!'

'An agreeable change,' Guy smiled, and meant it. 'I confess to having been curious about Mr Smallpiece.'

Saxmundham left the table and lowered himself to the settee, gesturing to the steward to fill the glasses as he came in with a fresh bottle.

'I'm not clear what it is you expect of me,' Guy said when the man had left.

'That is the difficulty! Well, now – you've heard something of Smallpiece's history. Let us examine yours –'

Guy smiled at his air of conspiracy. 'There's little enough of it.'

'As the kitchen maid said of her baby! But from Small-piece's point of view that is an important consideration. You have little behind you.' He searched Guy's eyes. Guy was puzzled. 'Much ahead,' he finished.

'With luck!'

'Assuredly! But then you have the advantage of a sci-entific education in the *Britannia* and the *Excellent* and the Royal Naval College. It is common knowledge you acquired a reputation for a larger share of brains than is usually considered healthy for anyone aspiring to become a practical seaman.'

Guy grinned.

'Fortunately for your career, you also acquired a repu-tation as a sportsman. You played for the United Services –' Guy nodded.

'Cricket for the Navy whilst a midshipman in the Channel Squadron – almost unheard of. And it's noised there's not a man in the Service can touch you in the rac-quets court.'

'I've not heard that, sir.'

'Devil I care! Smallpiece has for a certainty. These things get about. The Navy is the most intimate club. Now consider – Smallpiece has enjoyed none of these advan-tages, and I may say nor could have done. None of us have, nor could have. In our day, Greville, professional attain-ments were measured by the handling of a sailing ship ; they began and they ended there, and by heavens, a good sailor was a good officer and there was an end of it. As for sport, we had little enough time or need for it. Shootin' was the thing, shootin' and huntin' and polo for them with a long purse. So you see –' He paused.

Guy nodded. 'I believe so, sir.'

'No, sir!' Saxmundham's voice rose. 'You do not see, sir!' Guy looked at him in surprise.

'You do not see, Greville. You cannot see. I may tell you but you will not see until you have grown very much older and have looked on the generation of young officers following you and found they know very much more than you do and what you have learnt is out-dated and you have not the advantages of the youngsters. Then you will *see*, my boy!'

Guy remained silent.

After a while the Old Man said, 'That is the way we learn.'

'The first lieutenant is jealous of my advantages, sir,' Guy pressed on determinedly.

'Look at yourself' Saxmundham replied. 'Did you ever make it easy for him? Your arrogance in your own capacities, my boy –' he searched for words. 'It's astoundin'.'

Guy felt himself flushing. It was unjustified.

'There you are,' the Old Man gestured, 'the *beau idéal* of the young Englishman, trim, faultlessly turned out. Eyes like a nor'-easier. A reputation as a sportsman second to none in the Service, a cool way of expressin' yourself without ever so much as a damn my eyes! On my life, Greville! Put yourself in *his* boots!' His eyes were almost pleading.

Guy felt himself at a loss.

The Old Man rose and lifted the fresh bottle from the bucket. 'No need to look so down, my boy. I should indeed be sorry if my officers were not arrogant young puppies.

I could wish they all had as good reason to be.' He filled Guy's glass, then his own.

'In practice, sir – ?'

'There you go again. My dear boy, these things cannot just be made straight. It's only in mathematics and gunnery the answers come out. I'll tell you what disturbs me.' He paused, choosing his words. 'He's become bitter. You may say he has every reason. He never did before.'

'I put it down to his leg.'

'It was quick, I grant you. He's drinkin' more than is good for him.'

Guy felt the blue eyes probing. 'You don't suggest I am the cause of it, sir.'

'The cause of it goes very much deeper than this commission.' He was silent for a long while, his face grave. Guy tried to imagine the youthful, studious Smallpiece, and thought of the wasted years, the best years sliced out of the middle of his career by the blind fates and a perverse system – 'And you wish to swell this Gadarene rush to self-destruction!' His father's tones returned –

'I don't like to see a good man go this way,' the Old Man's voice cut into his thoughts. 'Besides he was a sea daddy to me. I looked up to him like anything. It makes a difference when you get to be my age.'

There was a knock on the door and a midshipman entered holding a narrow brass plate. 'First lieutenant's compliments, sir,' the lad began, 'and he wonders if you might care to keep this, sir.'

The Old Man took the plate, glanced at it and started shaking with laughter. Then he passed it to Guy. It was the name-plate from the German whaler.

'Please thank Mr Smallpiece. It shall be my most prized trophy!'

The midshipman smiled and hurried out.

'Von Pullitz's Challenge Plate!' Guy said, handing it back.

Saxmundham called for the steward and gave it to him with instructions to polish it well.

'And now, my boy –'

Guy rose. 'Thank you for the breakfast, sir.'

'Philosophy!' the Old Man exclaimed, rising too and clapping him on the arm. 'It don't do in our profession. Especially it don't do at breakfast!'

'I enjoy a change, sir!'

Saxmundham laughed as he walked with him towards the door. 'There's one thing. This fellow, Cameron. You've seen something of him –?'

'Rather a lot, sir.'

'What d'you make of him?'

'I like him. He knows his business. He's a wizard with the natives. And marvellous keen.'

'Keen – ah! Mackenzie said that. As a matter of fact Mackenzie's a trifle concerned about his keenness. Fancies the fellow's up to something.' He paused. 'Makin' a name for himself – something of that sort.'

Guy's mind returned to his conversation with the Scot the night before.

'You've heard of Thomson, I expect,' Saxmundham went on. 'The fellow that took a caravan through the Masai country near Mount Kenya last year. No white man had ever ventured to do such a thing before – not that Thomson stayed long!' He chuckled. 'It's Mackenzie's belief this fellow Cameron has some idea of penetrating the Masai country from the other direction. From Witu. Virgin country –unexplored. He'd gain great kudos. Make his name. Mackenzie fancies the fellow wishes to try it with a detachment of our bluejackets.'

'Our jacks!'

'It was something Cameron said to him about goin' after the 'Lion'. He don't seem to think he will stay in Witu to be taken by us. I'm inclined to agree with him, and he made some suggestion that we should give him a small party to get after the rascal and hunt him down.'

'That agrees with what he told me, sir.'

'He's talked with you about it?'

'He has an idea we should take over all the land from the coast to the great lakes.'

'The devil he has!' Saxmundham pulled his great beard. 'I fancy Mackenzie will be interested to hear that!' Then, suddenly remembering more pressing matters he made over to the port and peered out again. When he turned back his eyes were alight. 'Be good enough to ask Mr Smallpiece to have the porters sent up from below, Greville!'

Guy repeated his thanks for an enjoyable breakfast and left.

PETER PADFIELD

'Almighty God, who alone workest great marvels,'
Saxmundham sang out as if addressing a recalcitrant hand
in the main top, 'grant unto the officers and all the company of this ship the knowledge of Thy heavenly grace,
that trusting in Thee, they may triumph over all adver-
saries. Most especially we beseech Thee to grant them
strength in this hour of trial to overcome the advantage
unfairly wrought by their competitor, *Meteor,* that in the
end they may vanquish and overcome her and leave her
utterly astarn, for Thy name's sake – through Jesus Christ,
our Lord –'

The chorused 'Amen!' carried deep conviction, and
there was a ripple of movement along the bowed, bare
heads like wind over grass as each man attempted a stealthy
glance over the bow.

'Eyes *down!* Damn you!' Smallpiece's brazen whisper
carried clearly over the quarterdeck.

The Old Man glanced at him; Guy thought he detected
a compassionate gleam in his eye.

'A prayer for the Queen's majesty. O Lord, our heavenly Father . . .'

Guy allowed the familiar words to pass over him
as he studied Smallpiece from under lowered lids. The
pace of deterioration had increased. His weathered face
was blotched like a patchwork, the skin around his eyes
puffy and dark, his jowls heavy, his expression a mask of
pain and anger. His injured leg, swollen by the bandages
was thrust out in front of him, and he continually shifted
his position as if the ulcers and prickly heat gave him
no mercy. The blue serge frock coat he wore on formal

184

occasions whatever the weather looked as if it had been drawn through a mangle; he was kneading his cap in his hands. He seemed to sense Guy's scrutiny, and looked towards him; his eyes were suffused with pink veins. Guy looked down.

Only the man's spirit was keeping him going, and that had turned into black, unrestrained belligerence. He tried again to imagine the years rolled back – 'the smartest fellow you ever saw'.

'On – *caps!*'

There was a pause while the Roman Catholics doubled aft to take their places in the divisions; when all was still again Saxmundham addressed the company, 'Dulcineas! I have every confidence that you will do your duty, and no doubts whatever but that we shall beat these German scoundrels.'

A low growl of approval rose from the ranks.

'There is one circumstance, however, which might prevent such a satisfactory conclusion –' He paused, aware that he had their whole attention. 'I mean the falling of a man from aloft.' He raised his voice. 'You all know what it is. There is so much show in it, so much of swagger about the top coming first in the evolutions –' He cast his eyes along the divisions. 'We cannot afford an accident during the race. To haul round to fetch a man from the sea –' he left the sentence unfinished. 'I intend instructin' my officers to have any man they consider is behavin' dangerously sent down from aloft, and removed from all duties aloft.' He allowed the threat to sink in. 'Any man that falls overboard will have his leave stopped.'

A stunned silence greeted the threat.

'For the remainder of the commission,' he ended, then tucking his prayer book under his arm, rapping his white gloves against the side of his frock coat, he strode abruptly away towards his companionway to leave Smallpiece to tell off the men for their duties. The click of his heels on the deck was magnified in the silence.

When he had gone, Guy strolled up to Smallpiece. The first lieutenant eyed him balefully and, anticipating a request for men, growled, 'All hands are required for the ship, Greville.' He blinked with pain as he shifted position.

'We have the ammunition to prepare,' Guy said as pleasantly as he could. 'It will be a lengthy business.'

Smallpiece glowered at him, then without a word turned to the bo'sun on his other hand, and started giving him instructions to rig martingales for the stunsail booms. Blood rose to Guy's head. If Saxmundham expected him to offer the olive branch in the face of such gratuitous hostility –

As he looked at the first lieutenant's thick figure and crumpled uniform his anger cooled to pity. He walked away, his mind turning to the immediate problem of how to get the ammunition boxed up for the expedition – there would be little enough time in all probability once they reached Lamu. He looked around for Cameron, thinking the porters themselves might be used, but caught sight of the surgeon instead; he was bustling forward towards the sick bay. It reminded him of Smallpiece's condition, and he stepped out after him, catching him as he manoeuvred through the throng of seedies in the waist.

The surgeon raised his brows. 'Guns! Some trouble?'

'Not myself I'm thankful to say. But look here, do you not think Smallpiece – can you not make him quit his duties?'

'D'you imagine I haven't tried! I've drawn Old Sax's attention to it on three separate occasions. I've pressed very strong.'

'He'll not do anything?'

'He considers it would be more injurious to restrain him forcibly – and he'll not give up voluntarily.' He stared at Guy as if wondering whether to say all that was in his mind. 'It had its beginnings some while ago. I've been treating him for pains in the head for weeks. For all I know he was afflicted before he came aboard.' There was a meaning look in his eye. 'I cannot disclose confidences.'

'I see.' He wondered if he did. All manner of possibilities were opened up by the half hint.

'He is quite determined,' the surgeon added, as he turned to resume his progress forward.

Guy made his way back to the quarterdeck. There was a great deal more activity among the seedies than there had been, and he noticed porters mixed among them, being harried by their headmen. Cameron was standing by the main bitts looking on, and slightly apart from him Smallpiece and Saxmundham intent on the activity, which evidently had to do with water. There were an amazing number of buckets on deck. He saw more porters grouped by the mizen and seedies ascending the shrouds. By the time he came abreast of the captain and first lieutenant the pattern was beginning to emerge; the pumps were being manned, buckets filled, lines of men stretched to whips rove from the tops, and seedies spread along the footropes above. A human chain was being formed to pass buckets aloft and out along the yards in a continuous cycle to wet the canvas, drawing the fibres closer to hold more wind.

He went to the side, and jumping on a gun-slide, stretched to look out over the bow; the German flagship had drawn very slightly further ahead. On this point of sailing, and in her lightened condition, the *Meteor was* evidently a fraction of a knot the better ship. He imagined Lieutenant Mann with his fellows looking astern from their quarter-deck, crowing. He looked astern; the four gunboats were straggling after them, the furthest a long way behind. Their canvas flashed in the sun, the rolls of foam at their bows sparkled against the deep blue, white-ribbed sea. Numerous snow-white lateen sails of canoes and two large dhows shone between them and an ethereal Zanzibar of colonnades and arches, floating banners and gigantic palm fronds which rose above a colourless plane of heat on the horizon. He stared at the mirage for a moment, entranced.

He was drawn back to the activity on deck by the porters chanting as they began to pass the buckets. They were enjoying the work hugely. One of the chain at the mizzen detached himself as chant leader, and began to stamp and hop along the line, calling out in a high falsetto, to which the gang responded with the chorus, moving their bodies with a rhythmic, swaying motion, grinning and clapping or even breaking out to do a little shuffle in the intervals between buckets. Similar scenes were being enacted all the way up the deck, and he saw the first splashes of water darkening the taut opacity of the canvas above. "Way above that a bluejacket at the royal truck was rigging a spar from which to set one of the moonrakers that had been stitched in Zanzibar. He wondered if its tiny area would have any effect.

He found the gunner beside him. He too was gazing up, glass eye glinting dully; the scatter of pockmarks left by a blank which had blasted his left cheek was dark against his sunlit front face and beard. For some reason he had his deaf side towards Guy. Disapproval or absent-mindedness? Perhaps he, too, was lifted by the grand scene, the taut curves of canvas with shadows of rigging arched across, the slant of the masts and the rush and shake as the *Dulcinea* pressed in chase. Guy tapped his shoulder and pointed to his ear. Reluctantly the gunner turned to face him.

'I've not managed to get hold of any hands, Jason. You'll have to work with porters, I fear.'

Jason's good eye fixed him belligerently. 'Not niggers! Not Swahilis – not in the magazines – sir.' He gestured disgustedly towards the chanting lines of porters.

Guy's brows rose. They were going to have another tussle about the 'right an' proper manner' of going about things. He heard footsteps and the Old Man's voice from behind.

"What about it, Greville!'

He turned. 'Capital, sir!'

'I don't care a straw for your progress! God bless my soul!'

It was an expression of the supreme fitness of the scene. 'What d'you say Jason?'

The gunner, who had been eyeing the porters by the mainmast and had only caught his name as he turned, raised his hand to his cap. Saxmundham responded courteously.

'Mac's in a furious sulk,' he went on to Guy. 'Sent word he had a swollen groin and can't leave his bed.' He chuckled delightedly. 'Don't wish to come up and see how pleasin' it is without his poisonous effusions I should say!'

'Indeed, sir!'

'Make the most of it, my boy – while you can!'

The thought of the idle engines and the stricken chief gave Guy an idea. As Saxmundham strode off forward, he clapped a hand on the gunner's arm. "Nil *desperandum*, Jason! I've a notion I may find you black men who'll prove white enough!" He made off quickly towards the companionway.

Knocking on the polished surround to the chief's door, he heard the clink of glass; some while afterwards there was a wail, which he took as an invitation to enter. The engineer was lying on his bunk beneath a bulkhead scarcely visible beneath photographs of groups in dark suits and hats, staring lugubriously from black frames, of children, little girls lost in frills, boys in kilts posed and caught in a moment of unnatural solemnity against painted backgrounds of opulence they had never known. He had not been in the engineer's cabin before; the ranks of pictures took him by surprise, adding a new dimension to his image of the chief – a sad old Roman in an alien land stretched out beneath his *lares* and *penates*.

He was lying on top of the sheets, wearing nothing but his long drawers, his middle rounded up like risen dough, his chest, arms and neck white by contrast with the florid hues of his face, and little beads and runs of sweat glistening. He gazed up with a studiously unconcerned wide-eyed, guilty look; from the smell of spirits Guy knew he had tucked a bottle away somewhere. He felt sorry: the bottle and the photographs told their own story.

'I've tol' Saxmundham I'm no' fit today.'

'I know, chief

'De'il he'd care!' The engineer twisted his shoulders to have a better look at Guy, and his face lit in recognition. 'Ye saw it a'!' He put a hand gingerly to his groin. 'Ye saw tha' nobbut Jimmy –'

Guy nodded sympathetically, 'Indeed I did!'

'He'll no' get awa' wi' 't. I'll put tha' much reek and soot over his decks, he'll no' recognize this vauntie jad!'

'I came to see you about the first lieutenant actually, chief

The engineer's brows drew down suspiciously.

'He'll not allow me any hands to box the ammunition.'

The frown deepened. 'Aye – they're the same, the both of them. They'd prefer to fight wi' bows an' arrows.' He winked heavily. 'Powder's wurrse 'n soot for makin' a dibble in th' decks.'

'I wondered, chief, whether I might have a loan of some of your hands?'

The engineer stared, then suddenly waved his arm. 'Tak' 'em a'! I've nae use for any of 'em. Ye c'ld eat yer dinner frae th' cylinder head – aye, an' drink the feed wa'er, so help me!'

'Twenty good hands, chief –'

'Tak' 'em a'! I'm pleased tae help ye!'

Guy thought for an awful moment the old chief was going to weep, but he managed a ghastly smile instead. Guy thanked him hurriedly and left.

Chapter Ten

*B*y the time he went on watch at noon the race was alight. During the morning the *Dulcinea* with her porters and seedies working one hour on, one hour off like the moving parts of three immense chain pumps spilling water across the towering spread of sail, had held her own; she had even crept up a little on the *Meteor* as the two ships leaned over the comparatively calm sea in the lee of the land. Reaching the green island of Tumbatu off the north-western corner of Zanzibar their tracks had diverged slightly, Saxmundham keeping a tighter course towards the reefs skirting Pemba Island. He had gambled on the strength of the current through the opening between Zanzibar and Pemba, anticipating a sufficient northwest-erly set to allow him to hold the course, yet clear the reefs. His estimate had proved correct; no alteration had been needed so far; the wake stretched back in a smooth line over the blue swell.

Far astern Tumbatu and the northern tip of Zanzibar could still be seen, plantations of clove trees making geo-metrical patterns amidst the denser green of the forest, fringed by isolated palms apparently rising straight from the sea. Sails of the gunboats and dhows sparkled a long way behind.

Close on the starboard hand lay the reef girdling Pemba; the seas broke over it and filled the air with a continuous rolling din. Beyond, stretching away on bow and quarter were a myriad small islands among greening channels and lagoons mirroring a thousand different hues of sky and cloud and foliage, blazing white sand beach or coral cliff. And over and between the islands the forested slopes of Pemba rose in a variety of the freshest greens, lit and shadowed by the overhead sun; the wind was spiced with tangy scents.

On the port side the scene was entirely different: the sea rolled away, white-capped and deep blue to a clear, bright ring around the horizon; beyond the distant hills of Africa could be seen under massy clouds. But the sight which held all eyes in the *Dulcinea* was the German flagship, something under a mile away, right abeam – neck and neck so far as anyone could tell, stretching before the following swell under every piece of canvas that could be found a spar or stay to spread it, the sun brightening the canvas and yellow funnel, the sparkling paint of her quarterboat at the davits. The sight was so grand, the race so much in balance that many of the hands who had been on watch during the morning had remained on deck to gaze at her and speculate on which if either had the advantage.

Guy stood close to the wheel as the new helmsmen worked themselves in. The ship was strangely quiet; even the porters were feeling the effects of the sun striking down almost vertically, liquefying the deck seams, reflecting from brass or metal or water spilled from the pumps with a glare that hurt the eyes; gone was their enthusiasm of early morning; they worked silently like automatons, arms and faces glistening. The officers and passengers had gone below to escape the heat; only Saxmundham remained on deck, swaying to the heel over an etched shadow scarcely larger than his feet. Way forward on either bow two quartermasters scanned the water for any tell-tale change of colour over a reef; extra lookouts in the foremast were at the same task.

The wind was rising. Every now and again a gust laid the ship over further, humming in the shrouds, snatching at the stunsails and moonraker high aloft so that their thin spars and the t'gallant masts themselves bent like palms. He guessed they were in for something. The race would be decided by the captain with the nerve to hold on the longest without shortening down, or the skill to take in sail before he lost his spars – the good fortune to judge it right.

His gaze returned to the deck, and he saw Smallpiece jerking his leg over the coaming of the companionway. The man's face was dark with the effort, his eyes burning. He made his way towards the wheel and not bothering to call Guy out of earshot of the hands, growled, 'You had no business to use the black gang, sir.'

Guy stiffened. 'You gave me little alternative, sir.'

'Dismiss them!' Smallpiece's lips worked involuntarily.

Guy made an effort to calm his flaring temper. 'Who shall pack the powder?'

'Damn you, sir!' Smallpiece's lips were shaking. 'Dismiss them!'

Guy glanced over towards Saxmundham, within earshot but deliberately paying no attention. He would receive no help from that quarter.

'Aye, aye!'

Smallpiece seemed a little surprised by the mild tone; he stared for a moment, then turned and made his painful way back to the companionway. Guy glanced at the quartermaster; his expression was as wooden as the wheel. He walked forward, calling out angrily to Buckley to fetch the gunner. When he returned Saxmundham was still giving no indication he had heard. His forehead under the brim of his tall hat was beaded with perspiration, his face shadowed, only his out-thrust beard caught the sun as he stared up at the stunsails.

Guy glanced to port. The *Meteor* had not changed her relative position at all. He went to the binnacle, and waiting until the card was steady, leant to take a bearing. She was right abeam.

By two o'clock the wind increase was very apparent, the gusts pressing the ship down and jerking the sheets, lifts, martingales like bolting horses. The foam along the crests of the seas spread in lengthening streaks; above, layers of high opaque cloud filtered the sun; the atmosphere was heavy with the threat of storm.

Saxmundham called off the bucket gang, and Guy immediately drafted a score of porters with a headman to assist the gunner, quelling Jason's incipient mutiny by

telling him to address any complaints to the first lieutenant. The man backed down with ill-grace, disclaiming all
responsibility for the explosions that were sure to follow,
which would set them all before the judgement seat.

'Make your confession,' Guy snapped. 'Be sure I shall
prepare myself with prayer.'

As the gusts increased in strength and duration
Saxmundham studied the *Meteor* more frequendy. Guy
imagined the German captain gazing towards the
Dulcinea with similar thoughts. Probably the heaviest
burden lay on Saxmundham, for the *Dulcinea* liked the
stronger gusts better and was running appreciably ahead;
there was little discernible change of bearing, only a
study of the compass card revealed the German's dete-
riorating position.

Saxmundham hardly moved; when he did, it was to
walk to the side to gaze over the quarter into the eye of the
wind, then up at the clouds which had gathered, darkening
over the whole sky, leaving only the smallest patches and
confused streaks of blue high up. He was in this position
as the bells sounded for the end of the watch; simultaneously there was a sharp report from aloft, and looking
up he saw the spar holding the moonraker on the main
hanging broken; the sail and all its gear were blowing out
forward in confusion. Three sailors from the watch being
relieved were already darting across the deck and up into
the weather shrouds before any order could be given.

As he went below, after turning over the watch he
heard Saxmundham calling out orders for the lower stunsail
tripping lines and topmast and t'gallant stunsail downhauls

to be manned; he wondered if the Germans would follow suit when they saw the *Dulcinea* shortening down.

When he came on deck again before dinner, Pemba and its sheltering reefs had been left astern and the ship was feeling the long swell coming in from the open sea, plunging and pushing out swathes of foam which glowed with a pale phosphorescence in the twilight. The sky was heavy with cloud. To port, lightning played over the far hills; thunder crackled. The wind was still rising; the spanker had been furled to ease the steering, the flying jib taken in, and the sheets of the royals and t'gallants eased. The sea boiled past the side, the deck quivering with the complex strains transmitted from masts, rigging and hull plates through the beams and planking.

The *Meteor* was by now well behind on the port quarter; she was pitching to the heavy swell, showing all her stem down to the keel one moment the next dipping to her cathead in a flurry of spray. He noticed she had not taken in any jibs, nor her spanker. A few lights about her deck glowed dimly.

He heard Cameron's voice behind, 'Enjoyin' yer sport!'

He turned. 'I fancy we have her licked in this weather.'

The Scot had a cynical expression. 'The Germans dinna play games.'

'It ain't a game!'

Cameron snorted. They left the side and took a turn towards the waist where the porters were squatting, strangely quiet, some in acute discomfort at the ship's motion, a few retching where they lay. Forward the hands were enjoying the extra tot earned by their performance that morning. A stout Welsh AB was standing on the fore bitts throwing his fervent tenor to the clouds.

Let Britain to herself be true, to France defiance hurled; Give peace America with you, and WAR with all the world –

The chorus roared in,

And a cruising we will go, oho! oho! oho! –

Guy joined in too, 'and a cruising we will go, oho! oho! oho!'

Cameron shook his head. As they turned towards the stern, he caught sight of Saxmundham, and gestured towards him, 'He sent word he wished to speak with me earlier, directly he came down. The old devil's been up here since!'

'He'll not go below 'till we've thrashed von Pullitz.' Guy wondered why Saxmundham wanted the Scot, and his thoughts turned to their conversation after breakfast that morning. 'Tell me,' he said. 'What are these Masai fellows like?'

Cameron shot him a quick glance.

'We might be seeing something of them,' he added.

'I doubt that. They're a branch of the Masai at Witu, I'll grant ye – but much inferior, interbred with the coastal peoples. Yer real Masai occupies the high plateaus up-country. He's very different, an aristocrat ye might say.'

'They're held in some awe as warriors, I gather.'

'They're raised as warriors.' Cameron's voice warmed to the subject. 'Magnificent specimens. Ye'll not as a rule find one under six feet. There's nothing gross about them though – more of yer Apollo type. They have a smoothness and a curious languid stoop ye might even call effeminate. I suspect it has to do with their diet – it consists solely of blood which they take directly from a vein in the neck of their cattle – that and milk. Although every now and again carnivorous longings overcome them, and they retire to the bush away from the kraals – they live in kraals with none but other young warriors and young unmarried women, ye see, in a truly remarkable state of promiscuity.' Cameron grinned as he looked round. 'Ye might describe it as a colony of free lovers. though few conceptions occur as they practise a method of separation before coitus – but that's not what ye wish to hear –'

'Go on!' Guy grinned. 'I've an amazing fascination for savage customs!'

'The Masai's no savage. I'll mebbe qualify that – he has savage proclivities, but he occupies a very much higher posi-tion in the scale of humanity than other natives of central and southern Africa. His cranial development, fineness of bone, his features, the straighter nose, thinner lips – aye, were it not for his colour and a tendency for his hair to be frizzy he might pass for a European. He's a golden, chocolate colour. When he's oiled for war he shines like bronze – ye know, he's most likely descended from the ancient Egyptians. Philologists profess to have discovered his language belongs to the Hamitic family, like the languages spoken by the tribes of the Nile basin.'

Cameron stopped abruptly and looked around as if he felt he had been talking too long. 'Aye – but it's the Germans who interest me just now. There's a curious sub-species for ye!'

Guy tried to steer him back, but he refused to be drawn. 'Do ye not consider it curious they should have a squadron of five ships of war appear in the same month – almost to the week – as the disturbances in Witu?'

'Coincidence probably. I find it difficult to believe they would instigate the murder of their own countrymen.'

'Ye have no great knowledge of the German! Listen, I've studied the Wa-deutschi, too. But in any event, have ye considered the murders were never intended?'

'It's you who insists on a German plot!'

'Aye – but might they not plan for just the one execution, say. Then it all gets out of hand. Once ye've aroused the natives it's mebbe not easy to hold them. And ye'll remember it started with the killing of a *British* missionary. Then again,' he added, 'mebbe no murders were intended. Mebbe the arms were for use against Lamu.'

'As suggested in the letter.'

Cameron nodded.

'You connect the letter with the Germans?'

'Of course! We know they have settled the area. We know Karl Peters intends claiming it as a protectorate under the Berlin agreement. They have five ships of war here to back the claim. Just now. Just at the right time. Who else would wish to write such a letter?'

'Pierre Suleiman?'

Cameron glanced at him quickly. 'Against us and the Germans?'

Mackenzie and Fortescue paced past in the opposite direction, the consul giving Cameron a look as if he had caught something of what he had been saying.

'A party man!' Cameron said disgustedly, not waiting for them to move out of earshot. 'Sits on his backside waiting for cables to give him instructions!' He grinned suddenly. 'If I could get meself into that cable office!'

Guy smiled at the thought of Mackenzie's face if he received the kind of instruction Cameron might compose.

It was time to go below for dinner. As they turned for the companionway, Cameron adopted a mock-English accent. 'You really should have explained the rules of the club, Greville. How was a poor bloody Scot to know that ladies' names were not fit to be mentioned at the wardroom table?'

'You'll allow the Masai their tribal customs,' Guy retorted.

'There ye go again – putting me in the wrong box, damn you!'

Guy rested his arm across the Scot's shoulder. 'Stick to chaff and banter. If you tell a story exaggerate it. Argue to the death on trivial subjects. Treat serious subjects with contempt. Never talk shop. If you have facts, withhold them. If you have prejudices, air them.'

The Scot's tense expression eased. 'Aye, but it's the putting of it into practice!'

'Try it! And after, you may treat your Masai friends to a description of the singular rituals of a wardroom in the Royal Navy.'

'I believe ye may have more brains than most Englishmen.'

'You must not insult me.'

As they started down the companionway, the ship heeled to a stronger gust and Guy looked over the port quarter for a glimpse of the *Meteor;* her sails were grey shadows against the night, her green sidelight glowed dimly above the brighter lights from the ports, which were reflected in the tumbling black water, then the *Dulcineas* side rose to shut out the view.

Cameron sat beside him at dinner. He was silent; Guy could almost feel him holding himself in as comments about the race and chaff about individual's performances passed up and down the table. Mackenzie sat almost opposite, another reason for his silence. The general mood was buoyant as if the *Dulcinea* had won already. Only Smallpiece at the head of the table was as quiet as the Scot, distanced by his own private mantle of pain. Guy noticed the surgeon glancing at him from time to time.

Talk of the race and the prospect of winning led to discussion of the part played by the native bucket gangs, and from there in seemingly logical progression to slavery, and the inevitable stories from the older hands of chases and hunting slaving ships down by night, 'using only the information supplied by our noses!'

Mackenzie, who had been led by the earlier talk to count the stake Herr Ebermann had laid down as practically in his pocket, was in expansive mood. 'That may very well be so, indeed one has heard of such cases.' He paused and leant back, 'But I am by no means prepared to assert that the effluvium from a body of slaves is more sickening than that from a body of the lower class of labourers in Europe.' He looked around as if expecting a challenge. 'My distinct impression is that the European effluvium is the worse of the two.'

Guy glanced at Cameron's tight face and kicked his shin. The Scot looked round angrily.

The old paymaster said, 'Since you raise the matter of comparison, colonel, I have to oppose you. The odour of the negro – I think you will agree – has a particular musk-like quality. Wa-Swahili for instance have a rank fetor reminding one of the ammoniacal smell exhaled by low caste Hindus –'

'No!' Fortescue cut in, 'The beastly smell of the pariah is caused by external application – aided I grant you by a certain want of personal cleanliness –'

'That's as may be,' the paymaster persisted. 'But I doubt that cleanliness has much to do with it. I have often heard it remarked that negroes who bathe are no less nauseous than those who do not.'

'I had heard that,' Fortescue admitted.

'Indeed, the fact is that after bodily exercise or during mental emotion the negro exudes a foetid sweat, oily as orange peel – very much more powerful than the per- spiration of a European. As an instance I well remember some bobbery in the old *Cormorant* – a porter carrying the commander's gun case had left two perfectly hemispherical marks of his palms upon the oak.' He paused for effect. 'No amount of scrubbing would remove them.'

Fortescue nodded. 'A black man's feet will stain a mat.'

Encouraged, the paymaster looked up the table again at Mackenzie. 'Allowing this particular difference, colonel, imagine it confined in the hold of a slave ship –'

The surgeon cut in, 'Perhaps we could continue this discussion after the plates have been cleared away.' Amid the laughter, he went on, 'The nose and the palate are connected somewhat intimately –'

Mackenzie looked towards the paymaster. 'Leaving aside the question of bodily exhalations – of which I've no doubt the surgeon will be able to instruct us more scientifically when we come to savour the bouquet of the ship's number one port – leaving that aside for the moment, I may say I have found a general misconception regarding the East African slave trade – born I've no doubt of the very different circumstances of the West Coast trade, and the sufferings of the plantation negroes in the Americas. Out here it is quite different. Indeed I would go so far as to compare the lot of the slave in the household of a Zanzibar Arab very favourably indeed with that of, for example, a free Irish peasant.' He glanced down the silent table, evidently determined on controversy. 'If – God forbid I had to choose between the two states for my reincarnation I should unhesitatingly settle for slavery.'

The silence greeting the remark was profound. Guy tried to imagine the arrogant little soldier as one of Suleiman's slaves, but found it impossible. He noticed the marine servants behind the chairs exchanging glances. At the head of the table Smallpiece was mouthing, but no sounds were coming out.

'Perhaps, colonel, you would like to be taken from your village in a raid,' Cameron's voice was ominously low, 'and driven half across Africa with a halter round yer neck and an elephant tusk on yer head to reach that happy state –'

Mackenzie stared at him. Guy aimed another kick at the Scot's shins.

'I'll thank ye to leave my ankles alone, Greville! Now, colonel – I've no doubt but I'll be blackballed – but it's not my habit to listen to such nonsense.' He turned to the table at large. 'Unlike the colonel, who's only seen the effects of the trade from over his desk in Zanzibar, I've had the misfortune to witness it at source. If I may I'll attempt to help ye to a proper understanding of its evils.' He looked down the expressionless faces. The ship gave a sudden lurch. Guy heard the drum of rain against the sides and deck above.

'I well remember my first experience of the trade. We were two weeks' march inland from Bagamoyo when we came upon the annual caravan. We were somewhat weary I'll agree. Weary or not it is impossible to describe the impression the sight of it made upon my mind. They had walked from the upper Congo – over a thousand miles distant, and if I ask ye to imagine beings who have passed beyond despair – the living without life, an endless file of inhuman degradation and misery –' He shook his head despairingly. 'No words can express the effect of it. Many were chained by the neck, others had their necks fastened into the forks of long poles supported on the shoulders of the ones in front. All had tusks of ivory or some other burden on their head. Women were as numerous as men and many had babies on their backs in addition to the tusks. Their eyes were fearful, their bodies wasted by starvation, matted with filth, scarred by the cut of the hide *chikotes* the headmen used to enforce obedience. Their feet, legs, arms, shoulders were a mass of open, suppurating sores upon which the flies swarmed.'

He paused. The quiet in which the officers and servants were listening was of a different order to the stunned silence which had greeted his outburst against Mackenzie.

'I asked one of the headmen, a villainous half-caste with a rifle, spear, knife and *chikote,* what he did with the slaves who became too ill to walk. "Spear them at once," was his immediate reply, and he grinned like a fiend from the inferno. "If we did not kill them, all the others would pretend they were ill in order to avoid carrying their loads." I asked him what happened when women became too weak to carry their baby and the ivory. "We spear the child and make her burden lighter!" The matter-of-fact way in which he made these replies – I can only describe it as chilling the blood. "Ivory first, baby after!" he said. I had not been long from my home. I had been conditioned by my reading of Livingstone's works, but I could scarcely believe my eyes or my senses. When I came to myself and recognized the cruel gleam in his eye for what it was, I had to take a hold of myself to prevent myself striking him down. But what could I do? What could we do – two Europeans against Tippu Tib's armed caravan?' He paused. 'They went their way. We went our way – the way they had come – following our noses. Corpse after corpse – lying in the bush by the side of the track for the hyenas –'

No one spoke as his voice died away. The servants moved quietly to take the dessert plates from their officers.

PETER PADFIELD

After grace, as the fruit plates and port glasses were set before them, and the decanters began to circulate, they remained silent. Smallpiece's voice came as a relief, 'Mr Vice –the Queen!'

The fourth lieutenant raised his glass, 'Gentlemen! The Queen!'

'The Queen!' The response was unusually heartfelt.

Chairs were eased back and cigars or pipes lit, only Mackenzie and Cameron remained quite still, staring at each other like gladiators.

'I am prepared to concede the horrors of the trade itself,' the consul said at last. He ran his fingers around the base of his glass. 'The point I was attempting to make was that the lot of the ordinary slave in Zanzibar, and I believe in the Muslim world, is not as might popularly be supposed from the pamphlets of the mission societies and from the general ideas pertaining to the treatment of negroes on the plantations of the West Indies and elsewhere. To tell the truth, there is some doubt in my mind as to whether the slave in Zanzibar is a slave in anything but name. Of course you will be aware that there is no distinction made between a slave and a servant – the same word is used for both.'

'What's in a name?' Cameron snapped. 'It's the *system* that creates the demand for the trade, and it is the trade which induces men to use their fellows in a manner they would never employ with the lowest animals – out of considerations of economy if for no other reason.'

'That may be so. You will be aware though that the system of slavery is not only sanctioned by Muslim law but is an integral part of their social and religious system.'

'The system must be changed,' Cameron retorted. 'In our system the principle of slavery is abhorrent. And our God is more powerful, I think ye'll agree, colonel!'

Mackenzie nodded. 'I think it may be you who have become confused by names. Let us consider cases. Let us consider the case of a free negro labourer on a British plantation on an island in the Indian Ocean. Let us consider the case that he has completed his term of service and is advancing in years – as plantation workers go – and that his employer does not wish to contract for his further employment. What is he to do? He has no means of subsistence, no property, no savings, he belongs to no one, his former employer bears no responsibility towards him. What is he to do? I can tell you what he will do. He will become a destitute, dependent on the charity of neighbours. Now compare his pitiful case with that of a slave belonging to an Arab master. The Arab – and I may say the Arab is far too indolent to be cruel in the manner of many a European master – the Arab will take his labour for five days of the week. In return he will give him his food and lodging and as much land as he can cultivate on the remaining two days. The relationship between them will be that between – eh, a feudal chief and his dependant. The slave will have all the protection and all the care in his advancing years that we understand by the feudal relationship. He will belong.' His eyes puckered. 'Given these two cases, Cameron, and the far harder work expected on the European plantation, if unfortunately I was obliged to make the choice, I would have no hesitation in deciding which state I should prefer for myself. I may say,' he went on, 'the Arab slave, if once he proves himself to be a person of intelligence and trust will generally be freed to serve as overseer or suchlike. He will then assume Arab dress and associate with his master on the footing of an Arab of inferior family.'

Guy found his attitude to the consul undergoing a change during the homily. Beneath the little man's cock-sparrow manner a sympathetic intelligence was at work, and a resilience of character that had allowed him to withstand Cameron's emotional onslaught. He had misjudged him.

Smallpiece was scraping his chair back, breathing heavily as he manoeuvred his stick to take his weight. His servant hurried up and grasped his arm ; he shook him off angrily.

Cameron said, 'Had ye seen the slave caravans, colonel, ye could never say the Arab is too indolent for cruelty. When I see a tusk of ivory placed higher in the order of things than a human baby I consider the man that exhibits such a scale of values to be capable of the utmost depravity and inhumanity. Beyond anything imaginable.'

Mackenzie bowed his head. 'I have already conceded on the question of the trade and the manner in which it is carried on. I hope you will allow me some small knowl-edge of the system as it affects everyday life in Zanzibar.'

Heighurst struck up brightly, 'Honours even, I'd say! Perhaps a small story of mine might assist –'

The faces turned towards him gratefully.

'It was this way, you see, we was out hackin' on some ponies from the sultan's stables –'

Guy swallowed the remainder of his port and pushed his chair back. Cameron glanced round with a curious

210

look like a boy who knew he'd been naughty and was not in the least bit sorry.

He grinned. 'You held 'em spellbound.' He put his head closer as he rose. 'It's the exception proves the rule. Your membership's not in doubt now! I have to go on watch.'

The rain was torrential when he arrived on deck. Saxmundham was a dark, oilskinned figure, glistening faintly in the light escaping the binnacle shade. The helmsmen moved stiffly away as they were relieved and leaned forward towards the glow from the main hatch; odd segments of lower rigging and the paintwork of the boats were caught in the light. Beyond the lee bulwarks as the ship lay over, the pale froth of the waves, flattened by the rain, could be seen moving out towards the enclosing darkness.

He jumped up on a coop and stared over the port quarter. A faint green light was just discernible, blotted out every now and again by thicker patches of rain, or the swell perhaps, as the German ship dipped her head. She had not fallen back much since he had been on deck before. Contrary to the mood below, the race was still wide open.

'Can't seem to shake the blighters off,' Stainton said.

Guy glanced up at the set of the canvas. 'I'll see what I can do!'

They went to the binnacle to study the course, and shortly afterwards Stainton moved off. Guy walked forward to look over the hands huddled for what shelter they could obtain in the lee of the steam pinnace in the waist, returning past Buckley who was pacing, pretending the angled rain made no difference.

'Watch the bearing of his sidelight,' he said to give the lad something to occupy him.

They both lost their balance and half ran down to the lee bulwark, clutching at the pin rail as a stronger gust laid the ship right over. The water surged past very close. Looking round, he saw Saxmundham leaning at an incredible angle as if glued to the deck; the men at the wheel were heaving up at the spokes. Then she righted. He looked aft. The German's lights winked back through the rain.

As he moved back towards the wheel he saw a figure appear from the companionway and go up to Saxmundham, holding the flapping tails of a light coat; he recognized the Old Man's steward. After a few words he hurried back the way he had come. Saxmundham gave a long glance aloft, then turned and leaned his way towards Guy.

'Goin' below, Greville. Ten minutes.'

'Aye aye, sir!'

The Old Man stared at him. 'I fancy the scoundrels have a line fast.'

'They're amazing obstinate.'

'So am I, my boy!' There was a hint of his former exhilaration in his eyes. 'Don't generally blow up so bad at this time of year. We'll catch him napping yet! Don't hesitate to call me!' He made off, stopping at the entrance to his companion-way and searching the spread of canvas again as if reluctant to leave the deck even for a moment. At last he went down.

Guy made his way to the weather side, clambering up on a hen coop and glancing out over the quarter into the eye of the wind and lashing rain. The swell seemed higher than ever, the rain driving across it diagonally, flattening the spume in lace trails which mingled with the boiling flux of their own progress. He was about to jump to the deck when the ship came up slightly, and the pressure against his oilskin shoulders and hat eased. There was a distinct lull. The sounds were less, the surface of the swell less chased with spume; the ship seemed to hurtle through a vacuum in which all noise had been strangely muted. He searched the darkness beyond range of visibility for any sign of the gust he felt must strike to restore normality. The rain was less than before. He had a sense that something was about to happen. It was the silence perhaps, or the shape of a rogue swell building up on the beam, or a premonition; he was certain that a climax had been reached. Instinctively he called out to the quartermaster to stand by, and to the hands in the waist to attend the jib sheets and forward braces.

The next instant it hit them. He saw it on the water off the starboard bow fractionally beforehand and shouted to the helmsmen, '*Helm up! Hard over!*' The words were whipped from his mouth as the squall struck from the bow on the forward sides of the sails, slapping them back against the masts and rigging with a thunderous tattoo. The ship staggered, giving the barest swing upright before heeling right over in the trough to leeward. He circled a shroud with his arms and locked his hands. A rumble arose from the decks below as chests and stores broke loose, and a tinkle of broken crockery from the officers' pantry. A sheet of spray, hard and cold, struck his face, blinding him for a moment and leaving trickles running down inside his oilskins. He tasted salt on his tongue. An unholy wail rose from scores of voices in the waist, high above the roar of the wind and slapping sails and clatter and jangle of blocks aloft.

As the ship began to come upright again, he found he could see. The helmsmen were at all angles against the wheel. He hoped they had managed to get it up some way before being forced to look out for themselves. He could see no one else on the quarterdeck. He heard the hens raising a terrified squawking, beating their wings against the coops, and in the waist saw a pale frenzy boiling up by the lee bulwarks —cotton garments and dark arms threshing.

'Trim sails!' he roared. 'Lee head braces!' wondering if his voice would be heard above the cacophony from the hysterical porters. He yelled at the helmsmen, '*Hard up! Look alive now!*'

He released his hold around the shroud and half jumped, half fell to the deck, leaning, sliding down and forward towards the mainmast, wondering where everyone had gone. The cries of the porters rose in pitch, mingled with British oaths. He saw a giant Irish bo'sun's mate laying into the Swahili with a rope's end to clear a path for the hands tailing on the head braces. The terrified natives scrambled clear, falling and screaming before this new terror in the night.

'*Haul taut!*' he bellowed, screwing his eyes towards the pin rail to make sure the weather gear was being attended.

From the corner of his eye, he saw the Swahili escaping the rope's end towards the quarterdecks, and he ran and slid towards them, aware that Buckley had appeared from somewhere beside him. 'Good lad!' His voice broke with relief. A porter leaped at him, a white shape with staring eyes, arms around his neck and warm breath reeking of betel nut. He brought his fist up in a short jab to the pit of his stomach, and felt the wind expelled in a grunting scream. The arms went limp. He grasped the body under the knees and shoulders and, swinging it towards the advancing hordes, pushed it towards them with all his weight. He heard English voices beside him —several of the hands had worked their way aft from somewhere or other. He released the body and stepped back to give himself space to use his fists on the rabble still pressing on. Buckley had gone down beneath two of them. He grasped the loose cottons of their tunics and heaved. The material split. He caught hold of their hair, slippery wet in the rain, and heaved again. A fearful shriek greeted his effort and suddenly, easily they were on their knees before him. At the same time the pressure eased. Bluejackets were rushing from either side and the porters fell back before them.

He looked up and saw the head yards swinging, the canvas beating wildly as it neared the wind. The bow was falling off fast; the helmsmen had done their job! As he stared up, the sails shivered and filled again. As he turned and shouted to the quartermaster to steady at that he caught sight of Saxmundham at the entrance to his companionway. He called to the men in the waist to belay the fore braces, and walked aft.

'Thank you, Greville!' Saxmundham nodded as he approached, and walked towards the wheel to take over. Looking forward again, Guy saw with a surge of pride that there was little left to do: the ship was steadying nicely to the new course, the fore sails pulling well, and the hands were already racing to trim the shaking main and mizzen canvas.

When all the yards had been trimmed and the ship was leaning away on the new course, Buckley came up and reported that the lights of the *Meteor* had disappeared. He had forgotten her.

'Gone!' he exclaimed in disbelief, swinging over to the lee bulwark. If she had come round on the same course as themselves she ought to be slightly abaft the port beam. He searched the darkness, but there was nothing. The rain, heavier than before, lashed a lumping cross swell. He stared aft, then went across to the other side and narrowed his eyes against the stinging gusts as he peered over the quarter. There was only the night and the rain and the tossing sea.

'Slipped the tow-rope, has she!' Saxmundham said when he reported it. He seemed unconcerned. Yet as the watch wore on and there was still no sign of her lights, he spent longer periods gazing astern.

'That's a deuced odd thing, Greville.'

'Perhaps she took out too much ballast, sir?'

The Old Man gazed at him. 'At what d'you estimate the visibility?'

Guy peered into the swirls of rain. 'Three miles? Probably less.'

'She might have lost a yard. Or a mast. We were fortunate.'

Guy nodded, hearing again the blast as the squall hit. He knew what Saxmundham was thinking. It had been like sailing in company with the German. There was a sense of loss, even a presumption that they should go back and find out whether she needed assistance. He couldn't imagine that the sudden backing of the wind would have turned her right over. For all that, there was an unsatisfactory feeling of running away and leaving a consort to her fate. He was glad he didn't have to make the decision.

'We would have seen her rockets,' Saxmundham said after a while, and after another long pause. 'The gunboats will pass her close.'

The decision had been made.

The Old Man was silent for a long while, then he said, 'Smart piece of work, Greville!'

He felt again the swing of the bow in response to his orders, and the little shudder she had given as the head canvas filled and lifted.

Chapter Eleven

'What d'you make of her?' Heighurst asked.

The squalls had passed; the morning was bright, the decks white and dry except in the shade. The stunsails on fore and main, set while it was still dark, stretched either side over the clean blue of the following seas. The horizon was a sharp line with Africa rising above it in the distance to port, the hills hanging like clouds. Way astern, the small upper sails of the *Meteor* showed like a white fleck on the rim, von Pullitz's flag a minute spot through the long glass. The sight which claimed Heighurst's attention and that of the other officers pacing the quarterdeck was the triangular sail of a dhow on the port beam. They had raised her half an hour ago. The Old Man had left the deck to have a bath and breakfast, but he had given strict instructions to the lookouts to watch her and report her movements.

Guy shrugged. 'I trust she holds her course.'

Heighurst glanced into his face.

Mackenzie and Fortescue paced past briskly, the consul very chipper at the turn the race had taken. He called out a genial 'Good morning!' then stopped and turned back. 'I understand it was in your watch, Greville.'

'A change of wind, sir. Caught us both aback. It's my guess she sprung a yard and lost ground while she fished it.'

'Don't understand a word of what you say.' The consul turned to his ADC. 'She fished a yard, Fortescue.'

'Capital!' Fortescue replied, surprisingly friendly, too.

'Eh – let 'em fish as long as they please,' the consul went on.

'And we'll give 'em a *pasting!*' Heighurst added.

Fortescue groaned.

Mackenzie turned to Guy. 'And when d'you suppose we'll make Lamu?'

Guy was looking out at the dhow again, alerted by the sight of Saxmundham emerging from his companionway. Evidently he had been roused from his bath, for he wore nothing but a violently striped bath robe and his tall hat for dignity.

'I hardly know.'

Something in his tone made the consul follow his gaze out to the port beam. Guy glanced at Saxmundham striding towards the wheel. The consul looked from the dhow to Saxmundham and back to Guy, an incredulous look in his eyes. 'You don't mean to say – ?'

'I'm not certain.'

'Damnit!' Mackenzie stretched up on his heels and puffed his cheeks out.

Smallpiece had joined the captain and the fourth lieutenant and midshipman by the wheel; he was supporting himself between his stick and the binnacle.

'No, no, no!' Mackenzie exploded, gesturing astern in the direction of the *Meteor.* 'Fortescue!'

The ADC looked at him.

'Madness, Fortescue! What's to be done?'

'It is of course the captain's sole responsibility −' The ADC saw the approaching storm in the consul's eyes. 'Nevertheless, he is required to take full cognizance of the advice of Her Majesty's accredited representative −'

'So he shall!' Mackenzie snapped.

Guy noticed the midshipman of the watch hurrying towards them. 'Captain's compliments!' the lad said as he came up. 'Would you gentlemen be kind enough to join him?

Mackenzie was off before he finished speaking, and Fortescue stretched his long legs behind. Guy followed.

'Gentlemen!' Saxmundham began as they gathered; the skin beneath his eyes was puckered and dark from his night on deck, but otherwise he gave no sign of the long vigil since leaving Zanzibar. His voice was as crisp as ever. 'A new situation has unfortunately arisen. As you are aware, we raised a dhow some while back. I instructed the lookouts to ascertain her course and any alterations she might make −'

'What has this to do with us, captain?' Mackenzie interrupted, his jaw thrust out.

'Just this, colonel. When we raised him he was steerin' a parallel course nor'-nor'-easterly. Now he's showin' us his starn.'

'So!'

A brief gleam of amusement lit Saxmundham's tired eyes. 'We have our duty, colonel.'

'Our duty, captain, is to sail express for Lamu to join our squadron and dispatch a force to Witu.'

'We have a duty to suppress the slave trade by sea.'

'We do not know she has slaves aboard.'

'Why is she runnin'?'

'Making for Mombasa perhaps – one of the small rivers. What can it signify?'

'We passed Mombasa some while since, colonel.'

'You and I know, captain, one slaver more or less – and I have not conceded her a slaver mind – one slaver the less cannot make the smallest difference to the volume of the trade. Whereas if the murders in Witu are not avenged,' he puffed out his cheeks, 'no European's life on this coast will be safe.'

Saxmundham turned to Smallpiece. 'What is your opinion?'

The first lieutenant cast a lowered brow at the consul. 'We've time and to spare to cut out the dhow and make Lamu before the Germans.'

Mackenzie glared at him, then swung round on his AD C. 'Fortescue!'

The soldier chose his words carefully. 'I was taught the importance of the aim, sir. I believe our present aim is to march on Witu. Other operations, however desirable under ordinary circumstances, ought not to be allowed to interfere with the aim, that is my opinion.'

Saxmundham gazed at him for a moment. 'I confess I never did believe in councils of war. To my regret, gentlemen, I must take the decision which it appears to me in the circumstances most consistent with my duties as captain of one of Her Majesty's ships of war. I must chase her.'

Mackenzie's red face mottled. 'You cannot, captain!'

'It is unfortunate, colonel. My duty as a British officer compels it.'

'Your duty, captain —' Mackenzie glanced quickly around their faces, then went on in lowered tone, 'If I might have a word —'

'Of course, colonel!' Saxmundham turned to Smallpiece. 'See the port stunsails taken in Mr Smallpiece. Bring her round on a course to fetch the rascal!'

Mackenzie puffed himself out like a bullfrog.

Saxmundham nodded. 'If you would care to accompany me, colonel.'

Saxmundham made few appearances on deck during Guy's forenoon watch as they drove westerly towards the cloud-capped hills of the mainland. When he did come up, he said hardly a word, but glanced silently at the compass and the set of the sails or stood staring ahead at the sparkling white cotton lateen of the dhow. He never looked astern. What could be seen of his cheeks beneath the luxuriant whiskers seemed drawn; his eyes were hard. Guy wondered what had passed between him and Mackenzie. The consul himself seldom left the deck, but paced with his ADC, and on one occasion with Cameron, whose anger and astonishment at the captain's decision had equalled his own, drawing the two into an uncomfortable alliance. Both glanced astern continually to watch the progress of the *Meteor* as she passed from the port side across to the starboard quarter, hull down most of the time.

Guy wondered what the German officers would make of it – an error of navigation or some mysterious quirk of the British cult of sportsmanship which they would never be able to fathom? He searched the horizon behind for any sign of the gunboats, but could find nothing. They had been left far astern.

When he went among the hands about their tasks it was apparent the atmosphere had changed completely; they moved listlessly and spoke little and that usually in surly tones. The petty officers whose duty it was to keep them on their toes pretended not to notice; they too avoided Guy's eye and made none of the little observations that normally oiled the business of the watch. When Smallpiece struggled by with his brows drawn down in pain they tried to avoid him. Guy wondered if he sensed their mood, or whether he was living entirely in his own enclosed world of ulcers and prickly heat and duty.

By eleven o'clock they had narrowed the distance to the dhow to some seven miles. Accurate bearings of the land were impossible to obtain as there were no recognizable marks, but Guy estimated that they were within ten miles or so of the reef which guarded the coast. He told Buckley to slip aloft to look out for it, and the lad soon reported a line of white breakers a mile ahead of the Arab. Knowing the deceptive effect of distance over water, Guy doubled it and sent him down to report to Saxmundham.

The Old Man came on deck. He was in his uniform frock coat and cap with a black silk cravat and scarcely a trace of his usual colour save for a crimson silk handkerchief flowing from his left sleeve. He touched his peak in response to Guy's salute. 'Greville!'

Guy nodded in the direction of the dhow. 'It's my guess, sir, unless he chances on a channel through the reef, he must haul round to the nor'ard shortly.'

'We might come round to head him off.' His tone was dull.

Guy made a rapid check of his assumptions. 'That's my belief, sir.'

'Very well then! Bring her round!' The Old Man walked forward to the quarterdeck rail and stood gazing ahead as Guy called the watch on deck to man the braces and told off the topmen for the stunsails.

'Down helm!'

As the bows came round, and the controlled pandemonium of trimming the yards commenced, he wondered if the hands would have jumped to it half so smartly if the Old Man had not been looking on. When they were round and headed on the new course with the wind right aft, he asked Saxmundham whether he should set the stunsails. The Old Man nodded without looking at him.

He wondered whether Saxmundham's decision had been the right and rational one, or a streak of perversity. There was little danger in the exercise unless the wind swung into the east again – surely unlikely at this time of year – nor was there much doubt that they had time to bring the dhow to and still make Lamu before the last of the German gunboats. The lurking doubt was whether it was right to go haring off on an unimportant diversion when the real object was to land an expeditionary force for Witu.

Buckley came up. 'The dhow's coming round, sir.'

Looking at her, he saw her hull opening as she altered. He glanced towards Saxmundham and saw that he had noticed the change. There was little doubt now about the result of the chase. The dhow was rolling wildly to the following sea, the foot of her mainsail a deeper colour from splashes and spray, flapping in huge bellies as the vessel leaned and careered back. The crew had set another piece of canvas which flapped above it, and another small lateen from what looked like a broomstick on the poop. These would have little effect; he guessed the *Dulcinea* was making between three and four knots more under the double spread of stunsails. It was time to alter towards her.

Saxmundham thought so too, for he came aft and, gazing into the binnacle, told the quartermaster to come a point to port. He looked up with lacklustre eyes. 'Have the engineers light up the fires in the pinnace, Greville! And arm her!'

When Guy returned after giving the necessary orders he was pacing by himself. He stopped at a cry from one of the lookouts; it sounded like a garbled 'Man overboard!' Guy seized his glasses and ran to the side, jumping on a gun slide to look over the rail. He found Buckley beside him.

'They're throwing the niggers overboard, sir!'

Guy focused his glasses: a crowd was massed along the side of the dhow, and as he watched a figure separated and fell into the sea, followed by another and then another. At this distance they looked like thin black dolls, arms and legs splayed, quite naked.

Saxmundham was training a long glass on them; his jaded air had vanished. 'Give her the bow chaser, Greville!'

Guy started forward, calling out to Buckley to have the gunner send up common shell and charges for the Armstrong, and to the stand-by quartermaster to follow. A feeling of revulsion flooded him, and he broke into a run. Seeing two ABs staring out over the hammock nettings he called to them, and they ran after him, their earlier morose mood dropping away. He set them to unlash the gun and the quartermaster to prepare the sponge and water buckets. More bluejackets appeared, cursing the slavers, and he stationed some on the side tackles, others in a chain to the hatch to pass the shell and charges. Going to the little cabinet he had had constructed, he unlocked it and took out the sights and firing tube and lanyard; he screwed the tube into the breech of the gun and hooked the lanyard on.

Recognizing one of his gun captains, Purkiss, he beckoned the man over to stand by the breech while he slipped the sight into its socket and set the deflection and range. Afterwards he motioned to the tackle parties to train the piece on an approximate line to the dhow, and to Purkiss to open the breech. The black forms were still being dropped from the dhow's side.

"Angin's too good for they bastards!' Purkiss growled.

'They'll answer for it!' he replied grimly.

The first of the shells was passed from hand to hand along the ammunition chain and rammed home in the breech, and shortly after it the silk sausage holding the charge. Purkiss swung the breech to and turned the locking handle. Guy took the firing lanyard and stepped back to its fullest extent, looked up at the quarterdeck and raised his arm.

Saxmundham's order to fire followed immediately.

He bent and stared along the sights, motioning to the men on the side tackles until they had the gun trained to a point just ahead of the dhow still rolling drunkenly to the long, following seas. He felt the *Dulcinea* heel to port. As she came up again she yawed, throwing the sights back along the dhow's side and past her stern. He waited. The ship came back, the sights drew ahead again. The deck was level and steady. He jerked the lanyard. The black breech charged towards him with the familiar roar; white smoke rolled from the muzzle, thinned out forward in the wind. He saw the shell mounting on its path, growing smaller in the sky above the dhow. It began to fall, a black spot against the clouds over the mainland, and entered the sea in line with the dhow's stem, some distance short, bursting as it touched and throwing up a column of white water.

'Sponge!'

His eyes remained fixed on the dhow as he heard the breech thrown open, and the sizzle as the sponge hit the metal. Another black doll, arms akimbo, fell from the Arab's side into the sea, then another. The shot had had no effect, unless to spur the slavers in their devil's work....

'Cease fire!' Saxmundham's order carried forward clearly. He had concluded that at such a range the warning shots were ineffective.

227

Guy left the quartermaster in charge of the gun and returned aft, finding Smallpiece and the captain together gazing over the hammock nettings. Two more bodies dropped from the side of the dhow together.

'Another twenty dollars' worth,' Smallpiece muttered. His face looked clear of pain for the first time for days.

'The ship is worth more than the cargo to her nakhoda,' Saxmundham said quietly. 'The bla'guards know we cannot haul up to rescue the poor devils without the risk of losing him.

Smallpiece stared a few moments longer, then lowered his leg painfully to the deck and humped away towards the party preparing the steam pinnace.

Saxmundham turned to Guy. 'It's a most unsatisfactory reflection, Greville. The plight of those poor devils in the water is entirely due to our presence.'

There was no answer to it.

'It is a curious thing,' he went on, 'how frequently our efforts to do what is right appear to have the opposite effect.'

One of his father's aphorisms flashed into Guy's mind. 'Who shall conceive what the Lord willeth?' he said.

Saxmundham's brows rose.

'The wisdom of Solomon!'

'Ah! Indeed!' The Old Man nodded. 'I have always found it to be so. You know, Greville, it is the great strength of our Service that it is founded upon duty. I never yet knew a man went wrong through doin' his duty. God or man, it comes to the same thing. You know, Greville, I feel no hatred towards those bla'guards. I'd shoot them down like the dogs they are if I had to, but I cannot find it in me to hate them as Smallpiece does.'

Guy was saved from the need to reply by the arrival of Mackenzie. The little consul's face was grim, his step unnaturally brisk. He eyed Guy for a moment, then thrust his hand out towards Saxmundham. 'You did your duty, captam.'

'Thank you, colonel,' the Old Man nodded unsmilingly as he took the hand.

Mackenzie flexed himself on his shoes. 'One has of course heard of these things –'

Saxmundham looked back towards the dhow.

'The seeing of it,' the consul went on, 'creates a different impression.' Mackenzie looked at him, then at Guy, and turned suddenly to stride off again.

Saxmundham said, 'Curious. I must confess I thought –perhaps on this occasion duty played me false.' The blue eyes regarded him quizzically.

'No, sir. We must bring her to justice!'

'Justice, Greville? Or vengeance?'

They looked towards the dhow again. She had none of the grace of the buggalow Guy had boarded; her stern, which came to a point at the rudder post, was uncarved ; her gunwales were hardly sheered, the timbers of her hull looked grey and crude and even from this distance weak as if they might be opening and closing as she dipped and strained. The sparkling rollers lifted her like a cork and swung her wildly as they dropped her; flurries of spray were whipped over the side and into the huge, white billowing lateen, while the smaller sails filled and shook as erratically as the wings of white butterflies. Still the negroes were being dropped overboard. Guy wondered how many could possibly have been packed into the frail hull.

They were diverted by smoke issuing suddenly from the brass funnel of the steam pinnace in the waist; it thickened quickly, rolling out oily black and whirring in the lee of the mainsail. Saxmundham's eyes hardened. 'See what the sweeps are up to, Greville!'

When he had checked the worst of the effusions, and returned, the captain was pacing by himself

The reef was very apparent now, marked by a line of broken white water beyond the dhow and stretching without interruption as far as he could see, dividing the blue of the ocean from calmer, greening shades the other side; the growl of the breakers was loud. Beyond it, the shore off the bow was close enough to distinguish individual palm fronds and grotesquely twisted baobabs lining a long stretch of white sand beach, burning in the sun. He glanced back to the dhow and saw another body falling from her side. His mind slipped back to the little Sambuk and her scented slaves; how remote she seemed among her cushions and incense from the crude reality of the trade; yet she was a part of the hideous system.

As he watched, he saw a dark line extend from the foot of the dhow's mainsail upwards, and a mass of agitated figures gathering beneath; suddenly the line lengthened and widened; he realized the sail had split a seam. Another seam started to go, and in a moment one section of the canvas was blowing out from the yard like a huge sheet on a wash line, the other, larger sections ballooning uncontrollably.

He turned quickly and found Saxmundham already beside him.

'I guessed he'd not stay the distance,' the Old Man muttered, then called to the helmsmen to steer straight for her. 'Have the sea boat's crew piped, Greville, and all hands. Stand by the Armstrong again. I doubt I'll need you, but we may wish to frighten the beggars.' He turned to Buckley who had come up to report the split sail. 'Tell Mr Stainton I desire him to take the sea boat away. Have Mr Heighurst parade his men!'

The midshipman hurried off. Guy passed the word to the bo'sun's mate and told the quartermaster to find two smart hands for the gun's crew. He started forward as the pipe began to shrill.

By the time the quartermaster and his men had cleared away the Armstrong again, the dhow's yard was down and her crew were gathering in the flogging canvas. The quartermaster gazed at the craft in disgust.

'Not even sailors, sir!'

Guy adjusted the gun's sights down to five hundred yards ; it would not be long now before they reached that range. He heard the sergeant bawling orders and saw the marines running to line up along the bulwarks in the waist, resting their rifles on the hammock covers over the nettings. Another group of marines was clambering into the cutter, Stainton and Heighurst looking on. The quarterdeck was crowded with figures who had come up to witness the final act. Both watches and the seedies were also on deck grouped about the pin rails and bitts, the bo'sun's mates curiously silent as they looked out towards the dhow with set faces. He saw Smallpiece making his way towards the fo'c's'le. It was curious, the change that had come over him since they had begun the chase; he still walked with difficulty, his face drawn with concentration, but his eyes had lost their shadowed look; he gazed out instead of in towards his private pain. He stumped past Guy without a word or flicker of recognition, and levered himself on top of a mooring bitt in the bows.

The *Dulcinea* was now within a mile of the dhow, bobbing over the swell right ahead, and Saxmundham called for the stunsails to be taken in. The ship awoke to frantic life, the hands determined to put on a show of superlative seamanship for the Arabs whom they despised for their defective gear and passivity as much as for their inhumanity. The deck resounded to the stamp of bare feet, the shouts of the bo'sun's mates, the smooth rumble and squeal of rope through sheaves, slap of hemp against teak, clack and rattle of blocks and slap of loose canvas. In no time they were reduced to plain sail – still booming on with a scarcely noticeable reduction in speed, but a kindlier lift and surge. Saxmundham hurled out orders for the royals, t'gallants and flying jibs to be taken in.

Guy looked at the dhow again, trying to catch a glimpse inside as she pitched and rolled. She was a desolate sight, scarcely a man visible now, except for two figures in white sitting on benches on the poop, hunched, not bothering to look astern at their approaching fate. All was in the hand of Allah. The small lateen on the poop had been lowered and lay flapping where it had fallen; the mainyard had been hauled into a diagonal position from bow to quarter, the after end resting on the poop rail with the canvas caught loosely in folds and bights which moved with a life of their own as the wind funnelled underneath. The tackles of rough coir from the head of the raked stump mast swung in confused bights; more rope was tumbled on the short triangle of decking at her bow. The stem timber rose above the gunwales, a short spar fixed to it and a piece of canvas set to keep her before the wind. A loose rope trailed in the sea.

The whole of the craft, from the short fo'c's'le aft to the poop was undecked, the timbers to port lit fiercely by the sun where they could be seen beneath the ballooning folds of the mainsail. He thought of the horrors below and shivered involuntarily. There was a fascination about the beastly little tub – a fascination rendered more horrible by contrast with the playful sparkle of the sea lifting beneath her. Yet she looked so nondescript, old and hopeless.

He went to the breech of the gun, adjusting the sights again as they neared, and depressing the barrel as far as it would go. Even now that they were almost upon her, the white-robed figures on the poop made no move. In the shadows of the hold, he thought he glimpsed the flash of eyes and moving figures.

Saxmundham shouted orders to brail up the fore and main courses and man the lee braces. The wheel was put over and Guy lost sight of the Arabs as the ship turned and brought the small craft under her starboard bow. Shortly afterwards the wheel was put hard over the other way, the jib sheets let fly, and as she came to starboard, slewing across the beam swell, the yards were braced up; the topsails shivered and slapped aback. Simultaneously the davit falls rumbled as the cutter was dropped. By the time she hit the water the fore topsail had been braced to the wind, and the *Dulcinea* was lying quietly hove to with the dhow less than a hundred yards off her quarter. The marines in the waist pointed their rifles as the cutter's oars slapped down into the rowlocks. The crew stretched forward to begin the stroke.

Telling the quartermaster to secure the gun, Guy walked aft to the quarterdeck and jumped up to watch the boat as it pulled across the smooth in their lee. Its brilliant white paintwork lined with a green band just below the gunwales, the scarlet and white of the marines, the white jumpers of the sailors made a striking contrast to the greying hulk beyond; it rose to the swell and swooped down, oars out like wings glistening in the sun for an instant before they dipped.

'I trust his Grace is satisfied!' Cameron was beside him; there was a bitter edge to his voice.

'I doubt it.'

'Worthy the grand traditions of the Royal Navy!' Guy's mouth tightened.

Cameron was undeterred. 'And how much head money will ye all see from this day's work!'

'Less than we shall lose on the race.'

The Scot snorted. 'That's mebbe why they made the poor creatures swim for it. If they canna get their head money, they'll at least prevent ye makin' yer's!'

'Rot!'

The Scot smiled cynically. 'The waste of it all!'

'Stainton will measure the dhow before he leaves it,' Guy said in an even tone. "We shall make four pounds ten shillings a ton in lieu of the blacks thrown out.'

'And who will check yer measurements?'

Guy swung on him. 'Perhaps you would care to.'

The Scot snorted. 'Ye've little enough time left and ye continue to waste it in this senseless manner!'

Guy turned back to the dhow. The cutter had reached her and secured to the trailing line. He heard the headman porter whom Stainton had taken as interpreter calling out to the nakhoda, who was paying not the slightest attention.

'Ye could say ye're all in this together,' Cameron pressed on. 'Saxmundham there, and the poor ignorant dhow-masters, all of ye makin' yer head money from the trade – aye, and what jolly sport!'

Guy turned wearily. 'You saw them. Someone has to make a stand.'

'Ye're only playing at it.'

Guy watched the marines clambering up the worn sides. However ineffective it might be, someone had to make a stand on behalf of the human race as a whole; it was a gesture as much for the Arab slaver as for his slaves. The lives it claimed, Charlie Brownrigg one amongst a countless number killed by Arab swords or coastal fevers, were lives given for mankind, a pledge, signed in blood, that there was a higher law and a stronger people prepared to uphold it. Redemption! The thought of it gave him a momentary surge of pride so strong it brought the tears to his eyes. To hell with the Scot's clever cynicism!

The marines were herding the crew on to the poop at the points of their bayonets. Some bluejackets had disappeared into the hold, others had begun passing negroes with spindle limbs over the side in bowlines. The cutter's crew stretched their arms up to receive them. One after another they were passed down. Guy marvelled at the number there must have been originally; they must have been lying on top of one another like sardines in an open tin. He saw Stainton on the poop stride to the stern rail with a sounding line to take the length of the craft. No one would make anything from her; fifty tons at the most. By the time the agents and the commander-in-chief on the station had taken their cut he would be lucky to get a few shillings. Even Saxmundham, who was entitled to the lion's share, would not make a fifth part of what he would lose in his wager with von Pullitz. Not that the money would matter to him.

He saw a woman being lowered into the boat, naked, clutching a child to her shoulder. Like the men, she was a mere skeleton stretched with dark skin. He felt sick. More women followed, some with babies, and were found a place in the sternsheets of the cutter, now very low in the water. Occasional bursts of spray shot up between it and the dhow and drenched the occupants; when she rolled the water swept high along the gunwale, threatening to swamp her. Saxmundham told off the senior midshipman to take the second cutter away. Guy was relieved it was not him. Another wave of nausea racked his stomach, and he clutched the rail, praying he would not be physically sick. He was sure it was sunstroke, but it would appear as though the sights had been too much for him. He swallowed hard. The feeling persisted. The rail began to revolve; bright green and violet shapes chased across behind his lids as he closed his eyes. There was only one thing for it: he leaned down the deck to Saxmundham to ask permission to go below for a few minutes. The Old Man took one look and sent him to his cabin.

There was a different motion to the ship and a different sound to the sea along the side below; as he opened his eyes he saw the wind blowing the curtain out from the port. He remembered the slaver, and swung his legs off the bunk. The sick feeling had passed, thank the Lord! He stood and made for the door.

Reaching the deck, he saw the ship was moving along under topsails and jib. The reef foamed loud to port; the dhow, apparently deserted, was rolling beam on to the swell some two hundred yards off the port bow. He saw one of his gun captains named MacCorquodale, crouched over the firing lanyard of the Armstrong, taking aim at her. As he watched the man fired. The faces on deck turned ; the familiar column of water stood up from the blue sea beyond the dhow; the vessel itself rolled untouched. Guy started walking forward as the gun's crew began the sponge and loading drill; by the time he reached them MacCorquodale was crouching again, peering over the sights.

The man's arm jerked, the gun cracked again, white smoke rising and the dark cylinder of the projectile flying up. Again it passed some way over the Arab. As the crew sponged the breech Guy found MacCorquodale staring at him.

'Take your time,' he said encouragingly.

The man bent again, waiting long seconds as a gust heeled the ship and the sounds from the bow wave intensified. As she leaned back he fired. The shell passed close by the port side of the dhow, entering the water past her stern. The man glanced round at Guy anxiously.

'You'll blow her to blazes next time!' he said, resolved to take the firing lanyard himself if he didn't.

The next shot missed to starboard. As the column of water rose clear, Saxmundham hurled out orders for the main topsail to be backed. Guy turned to MacCorquodale. 'I'll give you a spell!'

The man looked relieved.

Guy moved the deflection leaf on the sight bar to zero. As the breech was slammed shut and locked, he stepped back with the lanyard and bent, closing one eye to line the bead foresight in the 'V' of the backsight and gestured to the side tackle men. The greying timbers of the dhow came in line. 'Enough!' He waited as the deck levelled. The foresight rose above the projecting stem of the craft – a devilish small target she made from this angle! No wonder MacCorquodale had missed. It would be pure chance if he succeeded. He wished he had purchased at least one telescope at Zanzibar, but Saxmundham had lost interest after the French had been ruled out, and he had no money of his own. The ship started swinging to starboard and the sights veered off target. He waited; he would fire on the swing back. As she started to come back a swell lifted under the quarter and the sights dipped into the waves tossing against the dhow's waterline.

Despite the small target she presented, he had a sudden premoniton that he would hit her. There was an extraordinary hush around him. His legs ached from the unnatural position. He rested his left hand on his knee and blinked his eyes. She was coming back now, the sights swinging towards the Arab's bow between waterline and gunwale. He saw her very distinctly, the stem perfectly in line with both sights as he pulled the lanyard.

His concentration was so deep the gun seemed to fire and recoil in a vacuum from which all sound was exhausted. His gaze locked on the shell diminishing towards the target and right in line. He saw a gap open in the dhow's timbers by the stem post, and a moment afterwards the whole of the port side disintegrated in flying wrack and smoke, above which he saw the top of the mast and its depending ropes hanging for a second before toppling. Sound flooded in —deep, growling roars from the throats of the hands on deck. Straw hats were flying in the air, several caught on the wind, sailed over the side and into the sea. He saw Saxmundham on the quarterdeck waving his own cap above his head round and round like a boy. The stem of the dhow leant at some forty degrees as the smoke blew clear, then it started to rise slowly like the curved breast of a dying sea monster, showing a greening, weed-streaked bottom beneath. As it leant further and began to settle Saxmundham shouted orders for the main yards to be braced up to the wind and the courses and spanker set.

He patted the breech of the Armstrong, removed the sights and firing lanyard, locked them away, and called to Mac-Corquodale to secure the piece.

As he walked aft he saw a small group of Arab and half-caste Swahili whom he had not noticed before. Some stood, others squatted in silence by the funnel casing; one, smaller and slighter than the others, stood up on the casing itself, staring out towards the debris that had been the dhow. His eyes were bright and black like a bird's under dark brows; sharp lines were etched in the sallow skin of his cheeks. Instinctively Guy knew it was the nakhoda taking a last look at what had been his. He stared at the face, trying to penetrate the mask to glimpse the nature of evil. The man sensed his gaze and looked round. To his astonishment he saw the dark eyes were moist with tears. The face was of the type he had seen many times among Arab sailors while searching for porters and seedies in Zanzibar – nervous and somewhat hawk-like, small-boned, undernourished on this occasion, but proud and fierce with a firm jaw emphasized by the drawn skin of the cheeks – not an ordinary face, but neither in any way extraordinary. Its expression had been resigned; it turned to hatred as he looked. He passed on, thankful the monster had been relieved of his knife.

If he were a monster, how many others had he seen?

The slaves were on the other side of the deck, huddled together, and almost completely surrounded by bluejackets, some of whom held children in their arms, all heads and eyes like unfledged chicks, and rocked them gently. What extraordinary characters these jacks were; they had a spontaneity and generosity his own class could never attain. He reminded himself as on many previous occasions never to despise them for their ignorance; they were the salt of the earth, and of the sea. ,

Saxmundham beamed as he came up. 'God bless my soul!'

Guy smiled with pleasure at the thought of the shot through the dhow's timbers. He saw Stainton hovering, and realized he had not yet turned over the watch; he joined him and walked to the binnacle.

'How was it?'

Stainton grimaced. 'You may think yourself exceeding fortunate.'

Guy couldn't rid his mind of the expression on the nakhoda's face. 'And Jimmy Arab?'

'They took it well enough – after the sarn't had tickled a few! No, the niggers it was proved bothersome. They'd been told we was after 'em for the pot! They believed it! Bin Mahomed told 'em they wasn't plump enough for our taste though! Poor devils!' He shook his head sadly.

Guy thought of the trail of bodies drifting astern. Glancing down the deck he saw the nakhoda still standing in the same position; there was no hint of contrition in his bearing, no remorse in the deep lines of his face, only hatred for those who had deprived him of his only property. He thought of Duff's account of the Arab justification of slavery, and found his mind somersaulting, searching for justification for depriving a man of a livelihood which was sanctioned by all his social and religious beliefs. It was a moment only, then his certainties returned.

After handing over the watch and writing up the log in some detail he crossed the deck to take a closer look at the rescued slaves. The sight was more than he had bargained for. The figures were even more wasted than they had appeared from a distance, mere huddled bone and cartilage with discoloured, blotchy skin drawn tight across it; their faces were shrunk, the eyeballs a dirty yellow colour left hideously prominent by the retraction of the surrounding flesh. Few could support themselves even in a sitting position, but had to be propped up with their fellows. Their chests appeared caved in, the breasts of the women loose folds of skin, their arms hollow between unnaturally swollen, knotted joints, their legs and feet open, suppurating sores. But it was their expressions which touched him most. They showed nothing, neither despair, nor relief, nor gratitude, nor feeling; they were passive with a mindlessness he had never imagined.

They had been hosed down to clean them, and a party of bluejackets was swabbing the deck around; they seemed not to care, scarcely even to notice. Other bluejackets were lifting and carrying them tenderly when they had to be moved out of the way. He saw a quartermaster holding a woman, wrapped around the waist in a clean length of some white materials they had found for her, propping her head against his broad chest.

He became aware of Smallpiece coming towards him, his stick banging the deck as he jerked along. The man said nothing as he came up, but looked at him, then at the slaves with an expression the nearest to pleasure Guy had seen him exhibit. They stood in silence.

'Not a pleasing sight,' Guy said at last.

'It'll put Mackenzie off his lunch!' Smallpiece's tone was surprisingly friendly.

Guy smiled. 'I dare say.'

'It proved too much for your stomach, I saw!'

'Sunstroke!'

Smallpiece grunted cynically. There was another long silence. This time Smallpiece broke it. 'Mackenzie will not enjoy his lunch today!'

Guy looked round, wondering suddenly if his mind had been affected by his sufferings. Again he noticed the curiously pleased look on his face, as if the negroes' wretchedness acted as a cathartic for his own problems.

'It's impossible to understand,' Guy waved his arm, 'the nature of the men who could do this –'

'Men!'

'They take that form,' Guy said thinking of the little nakhoda.

Smallpiece lapsed into silence again. Guy was about to move off when he said, 'Greville! You have the captain's ear.' His tone was urgent.

Guy turned in surprise.

Smallpiece's gaze was fixed on a point somewhere beyond the slaves and surrounding bluejackets. 'I never sought friends. I never felt the need of it. No one shoved an oar for me at the Admiralty, I never poured warm water down anyone's back. Damn me if ever I do!' He looked at Guy suddenly with pained eyes. 'It took me forty years to learn it, Greville. Attention to duty is not sufficient. It took me forty years. I had too much pride – too much pride – and I didn't know how –'

The jerky flow was interrupted by the arrival of the surgeon, his pink face as jolly as ever as he glanced from the natives to the two of them. Smallpiece turned and glared. His smile dropped away.

'Gentlemen!' he began hesitantly. Smallpiece continued to stare at him belligerently, and he looked at Guy. 'Gives rise to some curious reflections on the theories of Charles Darwin, don't you think?'

'Sawbones —' Smallpiece muttered thickly. 'In God's name!' He gave Guy an anguished glance before heaving himself away on his stick, muttering.

The surgeon blinked 'D'you suppose that was intended as a contribution to discussion?'

Guy looked after the hobbling figure. 'On the whole I wish you had not joined us. Just then,' he added.

The surgeon followed his gaze. 'The poor fellow!'

Chapter Twelve

Dearest Trojan,

This is turning out the queerest business. "We got here yesterday evening after the most desperate sailing I ever witnessed. I fancy Sax used only his nose and ears – the former to smell his way towards the beach which is more beastly even than Zanzibar being a mud flat at low water onto which the whole sweepings of the town is deposited, the latter to hear the reefs which beset the approaches hissing like the hair of Cerberus. Not all the reefs can be heard, of course, and I suspect Divine intervention! Which reminds me, you must intercede with papa on my behalf. I have written him for an *immediate* loan to cover my *expenses* over this race, which I may say we was all set to win thanks to the extraordinary exertions of yours truly at the time of a squall catching us all aback in the dark of the night – I have no one here to puff myself to! We was all set to win and the Germans'

hull down astern when what should come up on
the horizon but a beastly slaver!!! Everyone was
for letting him go his rascally way on account of
which old Sax determines to give chase!! A capital
chase it turned out until he blew out his mainsail.
Now, say nothing to papa about the cause of my
debt which for your ears was a wager, but describe
the *pitiful* condition of the slaves we rescued and
the risk we ran to set the poor creatures upon the
path of freedom and morality – the former they
shall assuredly have here, although the latter is
unknown as I've been made aware by one of our
passengers, a caravan leader, a Scot amazing keen
I have come to like him very much. Now I must
tell you concerning the little Sambuk I wrote of in
my last, Cameron – that's the Scot has told me that
the rich Arab wives hereabouts are much given to
love affairs!! and that far from being the favourite
as the trollop informed me Suleiman was heartily
sick of her for one reason and another!! Although
how Cameron knows it, I haven't a notion. He
appears to know all that goes on. He also told me
that favouritism among wives is thought quite
improper anyway, and age counts for far more so I
dare say the little Sambuk is the very least of them
all! I can't seem to get her out of my head. I wish
you could meet her.

At all events we arrived here all shaking to
find the Germans crowing but we soon disabused
them of their supposed 'victory' by showing them

the slaves we had stopped to pick up by the way-side. Also at anchor here the *Kingfisher* and *Egret* gunboats, but no sloop with the Royal Welch as we had been led to expect. No one knows what's become of her. It was a blow for us as Old Sax was banking on gaining command of the expedition to Witu via the Welch CO! Now here's the queer part of it, von Pullitz waived his claims to com-mand of the expedition in any case, says he has the fever and Old Sax shall command it with their flag captain as chief-of-staff. Directly Cameron heard of it he suspected von Pullitz was up to something – he believes the Germans are behind the whole business – and off he flies to the *Meteor* to make arrangements about the porters the Germans have engaged, but really to enquire into the health of their admiral! And what d'you think no one he spoke with had heard of the admiral's fever! Curiouser and curiouser! Cameron believes he is staying back deliberately to hatch some treachery against the lewali of Lamu who is very favour-able to us – you might almost say he is under our protection as he is a direct dependant of the sultan of Zanzibar. Don't it just begin to sound like a shilling novel! I shall d.v. find out more tomorrow as I'm off ashore with Old Sax to interview our agent here, a ruffian named Bull-Driver he's fat as a toad and has been drunk since our arrival! Overcome by the unnatural activity it seems. In any case my being intelligence officer enables me to hear everything tho' I confess we are all pretty much in the dark about who is behind the bobbery at Witu –

He paused. How he wished she were here and he could listen to her illogical chatter and the sharp observations she distilled from her own singular viewpoint. He wondered what she would make of it; he could almost hear her, 'But isn't it *obvious* –!' Probably it was if only he could shift his own viewpoint. A drop of sweat fell from his forehead. He tried to blot the blur it made on the letter, then put his pen down and leant back. He was tired. He would finish it tomorrow.

Saxmundham pulled the gold hunter from inside his frock coat and glanced heavily around the company assembled in wicker chairs on the flat roof of Bull-Driver's residence, Mackenzie, Fortescue, Smallpiece, Guy. He studied the time ostentatiously.

'How long's the beggar bin gone?'

'Patience, captain!' Mackenzie said soothingly.

The Old Man turned on him. 'First time the fellow's drunk. Now he ain't here. What sort of a reception is that!' He shifted in his chair breathing heavily. The air was sultry despite the evening breeze over the parapet and beads of perspiration stood out on his forehead above the angry red ring left by his hatband; the deep hues of the sunset blazed in his beard.

Fortescue said, 'Can we not begin without him?'

Saxmundham stared at him coldly. He had missed the point.

Mackenzie coughed. 'Eh – we have received a second communication from the sultan.' He glanced at Fortescue, who leant forward and opened a leather despatch case at his feet.

'Be damned to his communications!' Saxmundham rapped. 'There's only one way to deal with these fellows!'

Smallpiece yelped his approval.

Mackenzie nodded. 'I'll grant you it's quite as unsatisfactory as his first.'

The Old Man took a scarlet handkerchief from, his pocket and wiped his forehead. 'First time the fellow's drunk. This time he's disappeared.'

Fortescue stood with a sheet of paper in his hand and came towards him. Saxmundham waved him away with the handkerchief. 'Confound him and his communications! Show it to Greville there if you must!'

Fortescue stepped across and handed the sheet to Guy; it was a letter in a painstaking hand, sinuous with flourishes.

To the honoured Captain Lord Saxmundham and Colonel Lord Mackenzie, in the name of God the merciful, a salutation more gentle than the air of morning, sweeter than a shower received by the meadows ...

His eye flew over the compliments, '. . . perfumed minds . . . abundant blessings . . . rarities of the times . . .' until he came to the first substantive sentence.

. . . received your honoured letter and understands fully that you wish him to come to Lamu, but this is a very delicate matter to him, and he must beg of you to excuse him. And about the criminals who killed the Europeans, he does not know them, and cannot say that such and such a man has done such and such because there was war and the Europeans it was began the fight, consequently my people did the same. And we are much annoyed that this should happen and we did not commence to do bad but this has happened by the will of God, and the Europeans began it, and if anyone goes to another person's place and beats and kills people is it not your custom and law to punish the wrongdoers? Please let us know so that we can learn. Or is it only you want to come against us for nothing? And we have received letters from the German admiral, but I told you in my first letter and I told him that I looked after all Germans thoroughly and when I saw they intended to behave badly I took their arms in order to keep them quiet until I informed their government. If anything is going to happen from you or from the German admiral please let me know....

The final, exotic compliments began. Guy looked up. Fortescue had resumed his seat and was gazing seawards, cigar smoke blowing from his lips, but he found Mackenzie's eyes on him.

'What does he mean by taking arms from the Germans when he saw they intended behaving badly?' he asked.

The consul nodded. 'He mentioned something of the sort before.'

'The bla'guard's not prepared to come down and answer for it in a court of law,' Saxmundham said dismissively. He added after a pause, 'In my experience communications with Arabs are mere wastepaper.'

Guy looked at the letter again. The omissions were as significant as what was said; there was nothing about the French arms, nothing about how the sultan had found out the Germans intended behaving badly, nothing about any steps he might have taken to apprehend the criminals. It was as if the man knew it would come to a fight and was simply spinning out time in the traditions of Eastern diplomacy.

His thoughts were cut short by a pandemonium of voices from the house below, an English roar loud over the rest. They glanced at each other. Saxmundham pulled out his watch again. Smallpiece leered. 'Drunk first time and drunk second time! Damn my eyes!' The idea seemed to please him.

Mackenzie's straight back stiffened perceptibly, and Fortescue's lips turned up briefly in a sardonic smile that was not lost on Smallpiece; his expression darkened.

They waited in silence as a slow tread sounded on the steps leading to the roof, accompanied by the rasp and whistle of breath drawn in and expelled with difficulty. Presently Bull-Driver's huge head and shoulders appeared, followed after a pause by the rest of his figure draped in a linen suit of vast proportions. His face was fiery in the last light of the sunset, and glistening with trickles of perspiration. His eyes, surrounded by folds of flesh beneath almost colourless brows, fixed on Saxmundham looking down at the timepiece in his hand.

'Gentlemen,' he began, 'my deepest apologies' – his voice, though breathless, was not slurred – 'for not being present to receive you.' He stood firm on trunk-like legs, seeming to gather himself after his ascent before moving towards Saxmundham and putting out his hand. 'Best *salaams,* captain!'

Saxmundham pocketed his hunter slowly before standing to take the hand.

Bull-Driver paused as if to say something, but moved instead to an empty chair beside Mackenzie and lowered himself in. 'At all events – I trust my boys have seen to your needs.' He nodded at their brandy glasses.

'Indeed!' Mackenzie said sharply.

The agent, for the first time, seemed to sense their disapproval. His expression became keener and his voice between the rasping breaths brisker. 'It's Saood bin Mahomed,' he looked at Saxmundham, 'the local lewali.'

'I'm obliged,' the Old Man replied with heavy sarcasm.

Bull-Driver appeared not to notice. 'I received a visitation from Abdullah – his general factotum and jack-of-all-trades – shortly before you gentlemen were due to arrive. Saood wished me to go to him most urgent.' He spread his arms. 'I had no choice. I could tell something was up. Well,' he looked at Mackenzie, 'it turns out there is disaffection amongst Saood's troops. He believes it preliminary to an attempt on his life.'

'The devil he does!' The consul stared. 'Whom does he suspect?'

'Several candidates present themselves.'

'Any favourites?'

'His brother, Selim.'

'D'you suppose there's anything in it?'

'Saood believes it. I'll vouch for that.'

Saxmundham said, 'Have you considered, the cause of it may be our presence?'

Mackenzie turned to him.

'You know I have never myself believed,' he went on, 'that either the Zanzibari or Lamu troops – nor for the matter of that the Balochs and Kirobotos that we brought with us in the *Star* – could be trusted to take part against their coreligionists at Witu.'

They looked at Bull-Driver, who shrugged. 'That is a possibility.'

'Indeed it is.' Mackenzie turned to Fortescue. 'Any signs of the Zanzibaris not wishing to fight?'

'None that have come to my notice.'

They were silent. Guy's mind had flown back to the letter he had found on the dhow, and the French arms intended for use against Lamu; he thought of Cameron's conviction that the Germans were behind the plot and the Scot's suspicion of von Pullitz's supposed fever, and a pattern began to emerge. He turned to Saxmundham to voice the ideas, then checked at the thought of Mackenzie and Fortescue; they would consider it as fanciful as his exploit in Zanzibar. To his surprise, he saw the Old Man looking at him, a quizzical glint in his eye.

'Out with it then!'

He wondered how to put it. 'Do we know where Selim's sympathies lie?' he said at last, looking at Mackenzie.

The consul seemed puzzled.

'Might he favour the Germans?'

'Ah!' Mackenzie's eyes brightened. 'Selim's sympathies will lie with whoever is willing to aid him – eh, in assassinating his brother and usurping his position.'

'An Arab tradition of long standing,' Fortescue said drily.

Smallpiece growled his approval.

As Guy had feared a smile was flickering over the consul's lips. 'A German intrigue this time?'

'Would it not be useful for the Germans to have a client ruler in Lamu once they acquire Witu? As you say they will.'

'I grant you that.'

'Suppositions!' Saxmundham exclaimed. 'Bless my soul! This is what I propose. We send back for young Heighurst and a file of marines to set these fellows at the palace to rights – Greville to accompany them and nose out what he can. How does that strike you, gentlemen?'

Mackenzie nodded.

Bull-Driver said, 'Saood would sleep more soundly tonight, be sure of that.'

'There's nothin' to equal a file of marines for sortin' out disputes of this nature,' Saxmundham went on cheerily. He turned to Guy. 'That suit you, young fellow!'

'Very well indeed!'

'Good! Mr Bull-Driver here can supply you with a reliable interpreter, I'll be bound!'

The agent nodded ponderously, and pointed to a hand-bell behind the circle of chairs. 'Be good enough to shake the ding-aling!'

'One thing –' Saxmundham held up a restraining hand. Guy paused.

'No stalkin' on your own this time!'

Mackenzie laughed.

He felt foolish as he strode across to the bell.

Guy patted his holster as he waited with Heighurst and the interpreter while the marine sergeant mustered his party by the entrance port. Looking up, he saw Cameron approaching : the Scot's lean figure seemed more than usually charged with emotion; his gaze as he came up darted from one to the other.

'I've some news.' They waited.

'I'm informed there is a movement among the Zanzibari troops to refuse duty.'

'The Balochs and Kirobotos, too?'

'So I believe.'

'On what grounds?' Heighurst asked.

'They say they have no desire to take arms against their co-religionists.'

'You do not believe it?'

'Aach! They dinna fancy going against the "Lion's" men. But I suspect there mebbe more to it than that.'

'Von Pullitz?' Guy said.

Cameron looked at him sharply. 'It had occurred to me that in the event of us leavin' them behind – on account of their unreliability – they would provide a useful force for anyone wishing to overthrow Saood bin Mahomed.'

'And Saood's own men?'

Cameron smiled briefly. 'I regret I have no informants amongst them – as yet!'

The sergeant stepped up and reported his party correct. Heighurst nodded down towards the jolly boat, and he barked out orders for the men to embark.

Guy looked at Cameron; he would be a useful man to have with him, and he thought of Saxmundham's injunction not to stalk alone; it provided an excuse for exceeding his orders. 'Care to accompany us?' He added, 'We've an invitation from Saood.'

The Scot's expression changed through surprise to evident delight; he nodded at Guy's holster. 'I noticed ye had a social engagement.'

Guy motioned the interpreter towards the entrance port after the last of the marines, and held his arm out for Cameron to follow; he and Heighurst turned behind them.

'I trust Old Sax don't get to hear of this,' the marine said.

Guy hoped he would; it was a satisfaction to hoist the Old Man on his own needless order.

They were silent as the boat pulled away from the *Dulcineas* side. The water was black and still, the air clammily oppressive. Lightning flickered in the distance; the crackle of thunder provided a continuous background to the drums and other night sounds that rose from the trees surrounding the water on all hands. Guy wondered when the storm would break and his thoughts turned to the deluge in Zanzibar and his flight through the streets with her voice tinkling in his memory, 'Like the storm may you return. . . .'

She had come from Lamu. 'My father one big merchan' in Lamu – very rich, very stric'.' He smiled, wondering if that were another of her tall stories. Yet probably not. A man like Suleiman would choose his wives from the highest echelons in society. The thought of Suleiman brought him up with a jolt, and another piece dropped into the pattern –Suleiman's disappearance, disaffection amongst the Lamu troops, the German involvement all linked together. If his own muffed visit to Suleiman had warned the Arab that the plot was discovered and time was running short, might he not have taken ship to Lamu immediately, might he not be here already, the cause of the disaffection amongst Saood's men? And if he were acting with or for the Germans might that not explain the tortuous scheme with the French arms? The Arab was familiar with the French in the islands, and it might seem an obvious gambit: intrigue was second nature to an Arab – so everyone had been at pains to inform him.

He looked at Cameron. 'I wonder if he's here?'

The Scot's head turned.

'Suleiman.'

A puzzled expression passed across Cameron's face, then he laughed shortly. 'What gives ye that idea?'

'We know he was involved with the arms for Witu. We know the arms were intended for use against the lewali here, so he might very well be here instigating the disaffection. We know he is not in Zanzibar.'

'How d'ye know that?' Cameron's mouth was twisted cynically.

Guy had seen the missing links in his chain as he uttered the words. He grinned. 'A speculation.'

'You notice he must needs bring this particular Arab into his speculations,' Heighurst said with an exaggerated look at Cameron.

'Aye, well —' Cameron grinned. 'Mebbe he has something.'

'Assuredly, the Arab has something indeed!'

'But ye can rest assured she willna be here,' Cameron put in.

Heighurst smoothed his moustaches. 'Damn! Another forlorn hope!'

'Curious,' Guy said, 'how you misjudge my interest in the Arab.'

Cameron laughed drily.

The town loomed close ahead; Guy recognized the arches of Bull-Driver's waterside residence to starboard and saw light peeping from a narrow upstairs window. They felt the bows scrape and shortly afterwards the boat embedded and shivered to an abrupt stop. The sergeant yelled and the marines leaped out, splashing noisily. Lightened, the boat danced about again and the bowmen hauled her up until the officers could jump onto more or less dry mud. The familiar putrescent smell wafted over them.

Once clear of the nauseating shoreline Guy started knocking his boots against a boulder to clear them of mud when he felt Cameron grip his arm.

'Look!'

Following the direction of the Scot's gaze, he saw two figures walking across the narrow road between the houses about fifty feet from them; one was a native youth, the other a larger man, a European with a fair sheen to his hair.

He couldn't see the features as both were walking away, but he recognized the cut of the shoulders and the athletic swing to the walk – Lieutenant Mann – unquestionably. Then they were shut from view by the walls.

He swung round on the interpreter. 'After them, Ahmed! Watch where they go!' and turning to Heighurst made a mock bow. 'We may see you at the palace.'

The marine shook his head. 'How long shall we allow you on this occasion?'

'If Old Sax enquires – I have company!' He beckoned to Cameron, and leaving the marine's party they padded as quietly as they could up the beaten roadway after the interpreter, stopping before they came to the corner of the house around which Mann had disappeared. Ahmed beckoned them on. They went up to him and he pointed down the crossroad to an imposing building with one of the great studded doors familiar from Zanzibar. It was closed. The walls of the house about it were blank, the alley itself a dark chasm, the only sign of life a dog with a pale, mottled coat shifting its head uneasily at the disturbance.

Guy looked at the interpreter. 'Who live dis house?'

Ahmed cast his eyes skywards before answering, 'Oh, Abdullah bin Moussa lib dism house, *bwana.*' It was evident from his expression that he expected them to be in some awe at the name. When he realized they had not heard it, he went on, 'One big merchan' – oh, werry much big ship, werry much silave, I t'ink so, one numberone fellow!'

Guy's mind winged to the little Sambuk, to Suleiman and to Mann, flag lieutenant to von Pullitz. The circle closed.

'Him girl marry Pierre Suleiman?' he asked.

Ahmed's teeth bared and he clucked like a hen. 'I t'ink so indeed! Numberone gal – oh, all right. He marry it to Suleiman, werry big man – pilenty silave –' he clucked again.

Guy turned to Cameron, eyes alight. 'There you are! What more d'you require?'

The Scot's expression was hidden by the night. He shrugged. 'I believe I told ye a while back, it was the Germans behind it.'

Guy looked at the door and the grey walls of the house, solid as a keep. They would not be able to enter without making themselves known; in any event, what purpose would be served? They knew already that Mann was inside; they were unlikely to be able to work their way close enough to hear what was being said. Wait, perhaps until he came out again? Follow him to the next conspirator? It seemed the best bet. He turned to Cameron.

'There's little chance of getting inside.'

Cameron's teeth showed for an instant. 'She's in Zanzibar now!'

'Can you not forget her!' He pretended irritation as his heart gave a little leap at the reminder. 'Each time I mention Suleiman you must talk of her!'

'I've mebbe caught the disease somewhere. But no, we'll not get inside easily.'

'I propose we wait until he comes out.'

'Mebbe discover his next port o' call.'

They looked about for a place of concealment that would allow them to keep the great doorway in view, finding one eventually in another alley some way beyond Abdullah's house. They had scarcely gained it and flattened themselves against the rough walls when they heard a metallic creak from the direction of the great doorway and a pencil of light appeared across the road. It widened as the door swung back, and shortly afterwards Mann appeared, alone this time. He turned right, in the direction from which they had come, and swung briskly away without a backward glance, skirting the dog which seemed too weary or weak to do more than cower. They watched until he turned down the road to the beach, then emerged quickly and followed, Guy sending Ahmed ahead again.

Ahmed waited for them at the crossroads, gazing down towards the beach. He turned as they approached. 'Him go for boat.'

Guy felt a surge of disappointment. 'Sure?'

The native waved his arms as though he could think of no other reason for anyone to walk that way.

They waited, leaving Ahmed to watch. Two Arabs appeared from a side alley and came towards them, passing close, almost brushing them with their dingy robes but betraying no interest; they might have been as commonplace a sight as the dog, now curled up in sleep. Guy stared after them.

Cameron, catching his look, said softly, 'Make no mistake, those two could describe every item of our apparel.' He added, 'The Arab is one of nature's gentlemen.' There was a bite in his tone. Guy smiled at the implication.

'I'd agree with that,' he said.

Cameron looked at him suspiciously.

Presently they heard the sound of oars and brief orders shouted in German, then silence for a minute followed by a hail and Mann's answer. More orders followed and they heard the splash and squeak of oars once more. Guy knew what Ahmed was going to say as he turned.

'Him go!'

They relaxed and came from around the corner of the house to look – whirls of phosphorescence trailed in the wake of the boat and behind the oars as they left the water. There was only one figure beside the midshipman in the stern-sheets; even at this distance Mann's blond hair was recognizable against the night. Guy felt ripples of the failure he had experienced in Zanzibar.

Cameron looked at him, questioning.

Returning the glance, he knew he had to go back to Abdullah's house. There was no reason; it was a sudden compulsion stronger than reason. Irritation, failure were mixed with it, and curiosity, but above everything was a sense that something was about to happen.

'I shall reconnoitre the house,' he said.

Cameron seemed about to say something, but thought better of it.

Guy turned and set off, not bothering to go quietly; his footsteps echoed between the close walls on either hand. The dog started from slumber and clawed the dust with its hind legs, trying to rise, but apparently too weak. Anger seized him as it always did at the sight of suffering creatures, and he wondered briefly about taking it aboard and keeping it as a pet; it had a keen face. The impulse was forgotten as he neared the doorway and his eyes were drawn to the intricate patterns of shadow. It appeared solid and immovable as ever.

'Englishman –!'

He swung towards the voice. A small figure robed in a cloak had emerged from the blackness of an entrance to his right; it wore a fez, and as he stared at its old, crease-rimmed eyes he started with recognition : it was the mchawi.

The old man studied him for a moment, then motioned him to follow, and moved towards the great door. They had scarcely reached it when the same startling squeal they had heard before made him jump and it began to swing back; light spread across the beaten lime road and picked out red and yellow designs on the mchawi's cloak. Guy was reminded of the entrance to Suleiman's house. He had to steel himself, comforted by the feel of the revolver against his hip, and the thought of Cameron watching from behind as he stepped in under the portal. A negro slave with a long head and scarred cheeks grinned widely. The fragrance from the courtyard was a pleasant change from the dusty odours outside. He followed the mchawi between flowering shrubs, hearing the creak of the door swinging behind, and the squeal of a bolt rammed home. His momentary fear had passed, in its place anticipation. If the mchawi were here surely Suleiman must be. How or when they had recognized him was a mystery, but he felt certain he was being led into the presence of the Arab. This time it would be evident from the uniform exactly who he was. Perhaps that was the reason for the summons; perhaps, realizing that the plot had been discovered, Suleiman hoped to prepare a double deal with the English.

They climbed a flight of worn stone steps, and then another to the top storey of the house, and entered a passage at the end of which was a plain timber door. The mchawi padded towards it, wheezing painfully from the climb. Guy's boots sounded like an army behind him. Just before the old man reached it, the door swung open and a girl appeared. Guy's heart skipped a beat as he recognized the little Sambuk's servant and a shiver passed down his legs, suddenly weak. She gazed at him, then moved out and stood aside to allow him to enter. Her perfume carried him straight back to Suleiman's house; as he stepped forward he was flooded with a chaos of sensations.

He had visualized this moment so many times, and here she was, her pale face uncovered and that inquisitive, dark, darting look taking in every detail of his uniform and person from head to mud-stained boots. He stood with the blood drumming in his ears, smiling as if in a dream, and heard his own distant voice saying '*Salaamalik!*'

'*Aleikum es Salaam!*' she replied softly. 'Mchawi say Englishman will come back.'

He wondered suddenly about the strange compulsion that had brought him to her door. 'Did you wish it?' The remark was amazingly clumsy, but he had to know: had the mchawi told her what he knew she wanted to hear, or – the alternative was incredible.

She looked down. 'Mr Mann? Is frien'?'

He smiled at the innocent tone. 'I suspect he is my enemy.'

'Is nice,' she replied firmly. 'Oh, I like Deutscher.' She looked up eyes glistening, and her voice rose. 'Deutsch ship not take silave out of Arab ship, no! Oh – *English* ship –' Her gaze rolled upwards with such an exaggerated expression of horror that Guy was forced to laugh.

Her face froze, and he sensed she was making an effort at control. She was half lying on a mass of coloured cushions disposed on a bed draped with a blue silk coverlet, the edges chased with designs in white. Her shimmering gown was a deeper shade of blue, her neck, breast, wrists and fingers were encrusted with the heavy golden bangles and charms of bizarre design he remembered so vividly from the previous meeting. Her bare feet poked out over the edge of the bed, the nails painted to match her dress, or so it seemed to him.

Suddenly her face relaxed, and she clapped her hands. He heard the door behind him swing open – he had not realized it had been closed – and the girl servant stood in the entrance. She was given brief instructions and departed as silently as she had come.

As he turned back to Sambuk she pointed to a stool against the wall on the opposite side of the room to the bed on which she was reclining, inviting him to be seated. The austerity of the hide-covered stool compared with her sumptuous cushions, and its distance from her brought a smile to his lips. She was used to her own way. Indeed he had made no impact whatever on the interview so far. She ignored questions she didn't like, if he laughed at her play-acting she froze and banished him to the outermost distances!

'How did you come here?' he asked as he sat on the stool and leaned his back against the wall.

She paused before replying, '*Haraka haina baraka!*' and gazing at his set expression, smiled. 'Arabs say, haste has not blessing.'

'And lovers has not conscience,' he countered, irritated.

Her eyes widened for an instant. He went on quickly, 'Aboard the *Meteor* with your husband I dare say.'

She laughed, but he sensed that the accusation had caught her off guard, and guessed by her manner that the wild shot had gone home. He pressed on, 'Your husband is here, too.'

Her hands flew up, quivering. 'Oh –!' She seemed to struggle for words and her eyes darted venomous shafts into his. 'You know where is my husban'.'

'I assure you I have absolutely no idea. That is to say,' he corrected himself, 'I believe he is here with you.'

The anger in her look subsided to speculation. 'Mchawi say Englishman take my husban'.'

'No!'

"Why Englishman not take him?'

The question scarcely seemed to make sense; why in any case should she be so concerned about her husband if, as Cameron alleged, they were on distinctly chilly terms? He felt that she was genuinely puzzled none the less.

The door opened and her servant stood waiting just inside as two slaves brought in a conical pot of coffee, cups and dishes of cakes. They placed them on a circular mat in the centre of the floor and departed; after a glance at her mistress the girl departed too, closing the door behind her.

The little Sambuk uncoiled from the bed with a rustle of silk and, alighting on the rug, took up the coffee pot. The small, handleless cups beside it were of exquisite white porcelain, paper thin. She poured until each was half full, then replaced the pot, looking up at him. The puzzle of Suleiman's whereabouts seemed suddenly less important. He rose and went across to the mat, sinking down near her. She offered him one of the cups, her fingers glittering gold and coloured stones; her perfumes at such close range made his head swim again. He stretched and kissed her fingers. Afterwards, as he took the cup, he saw her eyes alight with amusement; he had seen such devilish expressions many times in Helen's eyes, and they boded ill.

'How Englishmen love?' she asked innocently. 'I t'ink you like woman be so good – oh, not do no bad t'ing –' She assumed an ethereal expression, swaying from side to side. 'Englishwoman is like spirit,' she gazed upwards devoutly. 'Is for make you feel good too, perhaps you not too bad if woman never do no wrong t'ing?'

Guy grinned at her. 'And Arabs?'

'*Arab!*' She made a face. "Woman get plenty son for Arab is good. Oh, my husban' come to me, one t'ing he want, I know dis. An after – pshww – he go! I do not like talk of my husban'. My husban' is snake!' She made another disdainful face.

Guy gazed at her, wondering if this dissatisfaction were just another of her roles.

'I like talk of Englishman,' she said. 'I like go to Englan'!'

'I should like to show you England.' He meant it as much as he had ever meant anything, but he knew at the same time it was impossible.

'Oh – no!' She waved her hand. 'You go in ship, war-ship is right?'

She knew it was impossible, too. 'I go in warship,' he grinned. 'Catch slave!' The dialect was infectious.

She tossed her head. 'You tell me of Englan'. I like hear dis t'ing from you. How you live? Big house – pilenty room?' The glint came in her eyes again. 'How you keep big house cilean? No silave? Oh, but what you call it silave? You give it little money perhaps? Like Firranch *engagé* so you not call it silave. Oh, I know.' She took up the coffee pot and replenished his cup, halfway again. Was it imagina-tion, or had she shifted fractionally closer as she set the pot down?

She fixed him with her inquisitive gaze. 'In Englan' when boy become man – is much joy?'

His heart thumped as he held her eye and the implica-tions of the question flooded him, sending uncontrollable shivers down his limbs. He tried to set his face in a smile. 'In England it is a continuous process.' He went on quickly at her puzzled expression, 'A boy goes to school –'

She nodded.

'He lives in the school, away from his home. Bigger boys make him slave for them –' he smiled as her eyes widened. 'Sometimes bigger boys hit him if he does not do what they wish.' He clenched his fist and made a mock punch at his own jaw. 'He has to stand up for himself He made a show of fighting off the bigger boys. 'Perhaps they hold his head under water or kick him or beat him. He has to show he will not flinch. The masters – who teach him at the school – beat him if he breaks the laws of the school. A big cane. He bends over a chair and they beat him. He hears the footsteps of the master running at him and he hears the swish of the cane through the air, then he feels the great pain. The master walks back for another stroke. He does not flinch or cry out as he hears the footsteps coming at him again. He is taking it like a man.'

She stared round-eyed. 'Is how Englishboy become man?'

He nodded, smiling, and thinking of many other trials and tortures.

'There is no joy?' she asked.

Images of sunlight on cricket pitches and the smell of fresh-cut grass, and little yellow and orange flowers and butterflies fluttering in the outfield, the sweet sensation of the ball flying low and true between the fieldsmen to the cover boundary flashed into his mind. 'There is much joy, too.'

There was no doubting it now; in some mysterious way she had come closer. There was no mistaking the expression in her eyes. He leant across and touched her lips with his. She eased her head away teasingly. He moved towards her, taking the slight shoulders in his hands, feeling a shiver through the silk as he pulled her towards him, aware of her small breasts firm against his chest, and the pressure of her fingers at his back as she sighed deeply, 'Englishman –'

He eased her shoulders to the floor. She lay unresisting, her eyes no longer teasing, but soft with a warmth he had not seen in her before. He was reminded of the Song of Songs, 'thou has ravished my heart my sister, *my* bride. . .' She was an exotic fruit which had reached a perfection of ripeness.

'Sambuk,' he breathed, touching her cheek with his finger, letting it meander down to the exquisite line of her neck, 'Little Sambuk –!'

'Is long time,' she whispered. 'Love me – Englishman. I not like worship –'

The beating on the door drummed into his waking consciousness; there was an urgency about it – he was late on watch – an emergency. He started up as memory flooded in –the little Sambuk was moving next to him.

'Englishi! Englishi!' the voice outside was urgent.

She was sitting beside him, calling out a question. The voice outside replied rapidly.

'Your soldiers!' she said. 'They search for you!'

He had guessed it before she spoke and was already tumbling from the bed. 'A light –!'

'No, no, no –!' She caught his arm. 'Here you stay. I talk wit' soldiers.'

He felt her brush past him and heard her gathering his clothes from the floor, the revolver holster thumping on the rug before she swept them together and threw them on the bed. 'You, too!' She pushed him, and caught off balance, he fell back. He felt her hands shoving at him, and started laughing softly. Stark naked on a scented couch as the sergeant of marines burst in! He felt a cushion land on him. 'By wall!' she whispered urgently, trying to shove again.

'Heaven's sake!' he choked, standing again. 'Find a light, will you.' He had to get something on. There was a din of English and Swahili voices from below and, even as he spoke, he heard heavy boots pounding upstairs.

There was only one thing for it. He jumped back onto the bed and shoving the scrambled clothes away, tried to draw the cover up. He heard the little Sambuk running across the floor. Boots were thudding up the passage; he heard them stopping, but other sets pressed up to the door, which was beaten open unceremoniously. The little Sambuk uttered a cry as it caught her on the arm; light flooded the room.

He blinked. Heighurst stood in the entrance with revolver pointed, a private close behind, fixed bayonet glinting; they stared at him. The little Sambuk had hidden herself from their eyes behind the door.

'Forgive the intrusion!' Heighurst's voice was icy.

'Give me two minutes.'

Heighurst gazed at him. 'We shall wait for you below.' He turned, nodding to the private and others who had come up behind as he swung away.

The little Sambuk pushed the door shut. 'Go!' she hissed, vibrant with anger.

He heard her moving towards him. What could he say?

'My father's house! You shame me, shame my father —shame my house! Oh, *Englishi* —!' She fell on the bed in a paroxysm of sobbing and hammered him with her fists.

He took her wrists to restrain her. 'I love you.'

'Love — oh, you say love —' the sobs choked her. 'You love me an' you go. Oh — you talk of love —'

'I love you,' he repeated firmly, and pulling her towards him, breathed, 'Thou fairest among women.' He kissed her, and she sank down crying wildly. He looked at her for a moment, then started feeling for his clothes and putting them on. By the time he was fully dressed she was quieter although her breath still came in long, racking periods. He wanted to kiss her again; all he could make out in the darkness was her hair; her face was buried in the cover.

'Little Sambuk —'

'You will not come back.'

'If it is the last thing I do.' The words came up into his throat as he thought of her as she had been that night.

'Good-bye, Englishman.' There was a despairing finality in the cry.

He hesitated then walked to the door, opened it and passed through, torn by desperate feelings of repugnance at his own behaviour in leaving her. What else could he do? He had overstepped his time, disregarded his instructions. Heighurst was waiting for him. What else could he do? They were all excuses. Was it his duty to abandon a lady at the sight of a marine detachment? Yet he had his instructions; he owed his first loyalty to the Service and the country, and the little Sambuk had told him much of importance that must be reported.

Heighurst's look was stony. He hesitated, wondering whether he should say that he was staying until dawn. Even so, what could he do? He could never comfort her if he stayed a month, nor begin to atone for the disgrace of clumsy English boots desecrating her father's house and her name. It would be a useless gesture compounding the original infamy. He nodded and walked out; Heighurst gestured to the sergeant; the sergeant's china-blue eyes were expressionless.

Saxmundham glared at him, beard thrust out, lips tight. Guy noticed the shadowed, wrinkled skin beneath his eyes.

'Jenkins!' he barked at last, and as the coxswain appeared, 'Clear out!'

The man looked up quickly at Guy as he hurried to the door. Guy felt the awful numbness he had known before the headmaster's study at prep school.

'Be good enough to explain yourself, sir!' Saxmundham said directly they were alone. His voice was ominously quiet. It was no ordinary display of annoyance, Guy knew, but the far more terrible anger that came of broken trust; the next few minutes would be critical; if he failed to convince, he would be broken and on a steamer bound for home within the week – perhaps he would never find employment in the Service again. His tongue was dry as he answered.

'I have discovered the extent of the German intrigue – in Lamu itself, that is, sir.'

The blue eyes held his, unblinking.

'Suleiman's wife it was who told me. She took passage to Lamu in the *Meteor* in the guise of a boy. At the insistence of von Pullitz. How she came to know von Pullitz I am not certain since she insists that her husband never discussed business –' his thoughts flitted uncomfortably to Mann, as they had several times since she had told him, wondering what part he might have played. He shut them out. 'Suleiman himself has disappeared and the Germans needed her as go-between.'

Saxmundham frowned in disbelief.

'She was to liaise for them with Selim,' he went on desperately, 'who is to be the German vassal here when Saood is overthrown. I gather that she was also to take a part in the *coup*. Saood is partial to beauty and she was to work her way into his favour, but exactly what her part was after that, I could not discover since she would not respond to questioning. I had to allow her to tell me what she would when she wished to do so.'

'Under what circumstances did you speak with her?'

'Somewhat intimate circumstances, sir.'

The blue eyes bored into his. He held the gaze steadily, and after a moment the ice cracked. 'On my life! You young rascal! What more did you discover? Where has her bla'-guard husband gone?'

Guy felt as if a great weight had been lifted from his mind. 'She believes we have taken him – she is convinced of it. To my way of thinking it lends credence to her story for why should we take him unless we believed him implicated with the Germans in a plot against our dependant here?'

'And what of Witu?'

'She said not a word of Witu. It was all of the business with Saood that she spoke and particularly of her part in it. I believe she was anxious about her role. She may believe that by informing us she will not have to go through with it – if the plot is discovered she may think the Germans will not go through with it.'

Saxmundham stared at him.

'Unless,' he hesitated, 'she appeared not to care much for her husband.'

'Getting her own back on the scamp!'

'Perhaps.'

'How far advanced are their preparations?'

'The Germans intend transferring a large body of men to one of their gunboats before we depart. They will keep her here on the pretext of repairs to the engines, and directly we have sailed Selim will strike. They will be on hand to ensure he succeeds.'

'The bla'guards!' Saxmundham's brows drew down. 'We've little enough dependable force for Witu as it is – unless the Royal Welch show up.' He looked up, beard thrust out. 'But we'll need to match the rascals!'

'Assuredly, sir!'

'It explains von Pullitz's illness I dare say,' Saxmundham went on. 'Try if you can discover the force he intends leavin' behind.'

Guy was beset by sudden doubts. He had succeeded in convincing Saxmundham, but he wondered if he had convinced himself; little Sambuk contradicted herself so often and talked so much for effect, it was difficult to know what was truth and what her perverse imagination. He kept the doubts from his face as he took his leave.

Cameron was in the wardroom as he entered. Guy had the impression he had been waiting for him; the Scot called out, 'How did ye get on?'

'Fair,' he replied, making towards his cabin.

Cameron came across to him. 'He wasna angry?'

'I believe he was at the start.'

'Aye – well, I couldna think what had happened to ye-'

'You did the right thing.' He paused with his fingers on the door handle. 'What really bothers me – what will they do to her?'

Cameron gazed at him. 'Under the Koranic law – oh, aye! Infidelity?'

'I believe they have somewhat – barbaric customs –' Guy refused to admit the word and its tawdry implications. It had not been like that.

'It is exceedingly final,' Cameron began, but seeing the look on his face, went on quickly, 'Have no fear. They'll not deal with her in that way. For the one thing she'll most likely spin a pretty yarn about an English naval officer *creeping* in past the guard and surprising her – and all her struggles to no avail!' He grinned. 'For another thing she has no husband to accuse her.'

'No husband?'

A shadow flitted across the Scot's eyes. 'Did ye see him?'

'He must be somewhere.' Cameron shrugged.

'And once he knows about it,' Guy went on. 'She'll come to no harm.'

There was a certainty about the Scot's tone that fed Guy's curiosity. 'It's my guess he's in Witu,' he said.

Cameron grinned. 'In that event, no doubt we'll capture him,' he assumed his English accent, 'and bring the brute to the justice he richly deserves, what! Well,' he grasped Guy's arm briefly. 'I'm glad ye managed to turn away the wrath. I feel a wee bitty easier about being the cause of the – interruption. But ye had time enough to learn the secrets of her intrigue –'

'Be damned to you!'

The Scot laughed softly as he made away.

'I've called you together before our – allies are due to arrive,' Saxmundham started, 'since there are one or two things I wish to communicate first. As you know the beggars are never late!' He pulled the gold hunter with a habitual gesture from inside his frock coat and studied it.

The silence in the after cabin was intense. Guy glanced around the faces, 'Tubby' Harris, commander of the *Egret,* sitting next to him at the long dining table was looking down at his hands, avoiding Smallpiece's livid eye just opposite. Beside the first lieutenant Cameron sat, apparently relaxed, but Guy saw his knuckles taut above the polished mahogany top as he clenched his fingers on the edge. The old paymaster sat next to him arranging piles of duplicated papers, his thin-rimmed spectacles reflecting light from the ports. Fortescue sat beside him, and at the far end Mackenzie next to a chair reserved for the German flag captain. Other places for the German officers had been left along the table at Guy's side.

Saxmundham pocketed his timepiece. 'Firstly, I must apprise you of the delicate situation that has arisen with regard to our – allies.' He gave the word exaggerated emphasis. 'There is little doubt that once we have sailed – as you all know we shall sail for Kipini to begin the march on Witu – our allies intend replacin' the lewali, Saood, with a usurper of their own choosin'.'

Harris looked visibly startled.

Mackenzie said, 'That is by no means certain, captain. It rests on little more than a story,' his eyes met Guy's, 'extracted from – eh, a female under decidedly unusual circumstances.'

Guy looked at Saxmundham and thought he detected a gleam of amusement in the blue eyes. 'The story as you call it tallies with everything that has occurred since our arrival. And this morning,' he looked down the table, pausing for effect, 'the mutiny of the Zanzibaris, Balochs and Kirobotos that we brought with us.'

'Mutiny!' Fortescue exclaimed.

'They refuse to embark for Kipini. I'd call that mutiny.'

"We've known that's been in the wind for some days,' Mackenzie said. 'It's susceptible of a very simple explanation.'

'No desire to fight their co-religionists,' Fortescue added matter-of-factly.

'And von Pullitz's fever?' Cameron asked.

'These fellows recognize our experience,' Mackenzie replied. 'It could very well be an excuse for him to retire gracefully –'

'Gentlemen!' Saxmundham cut the argument short. 'So far as the Balochs and Kirobotos are concerned, I'm not displeased they've shown themselves in their true colours before we start. I never did count on their loyalty. I propose we split 'em up – a hundred or so for porters,' he glanced at Cameron, 'and let the rest do garrison duty at base camp. Pull out the trouble-makers.'

'I'll know how to deal with them!' Smallpiece growled.

'As to the business with Saood,' Saxmundham went on, 'I propose – whether or not we obtain proof of the German intentions – to leave a detachment at Lamu to ensure the lewali's safety.' He looked at Mackenzie.

The consul nodded. 'I agree.'

'It remains to decide the size and composition of the force.' He turned to Harris. 'Commander, the palace guard, if you please!'

Harris's face showed his extreme disappointment. 'Of course, sir,' he said, adding, 'I was rather looking forward to the safari.'

'Can't be helped,' Saxmundham went on briskly. 'Now, there's one other point before our – allies arrive.' He turned to Cameron. 'I share your opinion that the "Lion" will not wait to be taken in his capital when it falls, and in view of the questions raised by the arms shipment and the possibility of German involvement I believe we should make every endeavour to go after the rascal and catch him.'

Cameron's face expressed surprise and pleasure.

Mackenzie nodded slowly. 'Mind, I'm not hopeful of the prospect. It's unexplored country and not the easiest.'

'A small flying column, consul.'

'Aye!' Cameron cut in eagerly. 'The very thing!'

Mackenzie looked at him quickly.

Saxmundham turned to Guy.'I am placin' you in command of the column Greville, with Mr Cameron here as your guide.You shall have Lieutenant Heighurst and a half-company of marines. And travel light.'

Guy felt his face colour with pleasure. 'Aye aye, sir!'

'It'll be no picnic!' the Old Man snapped.

'Hardly more dangerous than your previous clandestine missions,' Fortescue put in with a wry look. Guy guessed he would have liked to lead the party himself.

'Naturally the Germans must not get wind of it,' the Old Man continued, 'and you must choose your men and make all preparations before Kipini. Once we have entered Witu you must be prepared to leave in search of the "Lion" without orders, on your own initiative.'

'I understand.'

'Inform no one of your purpose – excepting Lieutenant Heighurst.'

There was a knock at the door, which swung open to reveal a midshipman. 'The German pinnace is on the way, sir.'

'Ah!' Saxmundham nodded to Smallpiece, who had already started to lever himself from his chair, then seeing a spasm of Pain cross his face, he rose. 'Be seated, Mr Smallpiece, I'll meet the beggars myself

Smallpiece continued levering himself up, muttering as he twisted towards the door. The midshipman came towards him, but he waved his free arm, 'Clear off, damn you!' The lad hesitated, then turned and left.

Saxmundham came up and took the first lieutenant's arm, and together they made towards the door.

The silence after they left was broken by Harris. 'Do I understand von Pullitz is suspected of some duplicity?'

'We know the Germans are determined on taking Witu into their sphere,' Mackenzie replied briskly. 'That is all we know. The rest – I rather think is – eh, speculation.'

'Aye,' Cameron said sourly, 'And so it will remain –speculation! Until they have Witu and Lamu and then no doubt we'll speculate on whether or no they wish to take over the whole area!' He waved his arm in the direction of the mainland.

The rising and falling cadences of the pipe saluting the German flag captain sounded clearly through the open skylight.

Mackenzie said, 'You have no cause to complain, Cameron. It seems your wish has been granted.' His tone suggested that the Scot would not have been guiding the flying column if the decision had been his.

Cameron made no reply, but sank back in his chair, turning an angry gaze on Guy.

There was an embarrassed silence until the door opened; Saxmundham gestured the German flag captain, Herder, inside, and they rose to greet him. Behind, Guy saw Mann. The light blue eyes lit in recognition. Guy wondered again whether the little Sambuk had drawn him into her sensuous web and felt his jaw muscles tighten. Mann's expression changed. Behind were three other officers, a commander and two lieutenants – the gunboat captains, he thought, wondering why there were only three.

After the introductions Saxmundham took his place at the head of the table, clapping his hands for the steward and calling for champagne.

'To your taste?' he asked Herder.

'We shall be very happy,' the German replied; he was a small, dark man with a strangely pinkish tinge to his brown pupils.

'I trust so,' Saxmundham rumbled. 'I'll drink to that!'

Herder laughed, showing stained yellow teeth, and the others joined in.

The steward entered from the pantry with a silver tray agleam with a dozen champagne glasses and placed it on the table. The Germans looked impressed by the splendour of the reception. Presently the man returned with a magnum of champagne, clinking in a silver ice bucket; the sound was music in the oppressively sultry cabin.

'We shall have more councils, captain?' Mann said with a smile.

They laughed.

After pouring the champagne the steward came round the table with the full glasses.

Smallpiece rasped, 'They'll attack through the elephant grass.'

They glanced at him in surprise. He was gazing at Saxmundham, who recovered quickly, and nodded, 'On my life!' He explained to the Germans. 'Mr Smallpiece and I was in the Ashantee war together.'

Herder's brows rose in polite interest.

'King Cofi!' Saxmundham went on. 'A bloody business, captain!'

'There will be so much blood this time?'

'I trust it shall be theirs!' In the ensuing laughter, Saxmundham raised his glass. 'Allies!'

'Allies!' they repeated, clinking with the nearest ally. Smallpiece did not respond, whether from perversity or because he was immersed in his own dark thoughts was impossible to tell.

Herder raised his glass again. 'Witu!'

'Witu!' they repeated and drank.

'Same as fightin' in the dark,' Smallpiece said, 'through the long grass.'

Saxmundham nodded benevolently. 'Impossible to see the rascals!' He looked down the table at Herder. 'Before we discuss details, captain, I have some disquietin' news. Our Zanzibari and Lamu troops are refusin' duty.'

Guy watched Mann's expression; it reflected what appeared genuine surprise, and he glanced towards the German flag captain; he also looked as if the news were unexpected.

'Why so?'

'They have no desire to fight their co-religionists.' Saxmundham stared at him. 'So they say.'

Mackenzie came in quickly. 'Very natural!'

'I don't care to compel them,' Saxmundham went on, 'and I propose we use the best of 'em as porters and on garrison duty, and in order not to weaken the main force, we call off the proposed diversionary attack on Mkonumbi.'

Herder nodded. 'We concentrate the blow. But there is no news of your ship with the military?'

Saxmundham shook his head. 'Now, as to your numbers –?' He looked questioningly at Herder, who turned to Mann.

'Unfortunately, captain,' Mann said, 'there is much fever in our men, and there will not be so many as we wished –'

'Fever!' Smallpiece exclaimed. 'You allow your men ashore!'

Before Mann could reply, Saxmundham said, 'We must send our doctor over, captain.'

'No, it is not necessary,' Herder replied quickly.

'Thank you, we have doctors,' Mann smiled. 'We shall move the sick men to a ship which shall stay here.'

'You intend leavin' a ship behind?' Saxmundham's stare was very innocent.

'Unfortunately the engines are broken,' Mann replied.

'I see.' The Old Man's eyes were suddenly fierce, and he nodded at Harris, 'We shall be leavin' a gunboat too and a strong detachment of marines.'

Mackenzie shot him a hard look in the ensuing silence.

After a moment Herder said, 'That is necessary, captain – ?'

'The lewali has fears as to his safety.'

'We shall have men –

'He is under our protection.'

Mackenzie said quietly to the German, 'He has requested our protection, captain.'

'Yes, naturally!' Herder's expression was inscrutable, but Guy thought he seemed less relaxed.

Saxmundham broke the short silence, 'As you know the *Kingfisher* has already sailed for Kipini to establish an advanced base and water depot. As to the main column I propose to leave the details to be worked out by Greville and Mann later, and for the moment to discuss tactics suitable to the country and the native mode of warfare.' He looked at Herder. 'I fancy it is not too much to say that the success of the expedition will hinge on the proper understandin' of each man as to his duty in the event of attack whilst the columns are in the bush or the long grass.'

Herder nodded with a tight mouth.

'We was firing on the Black Watch outside Amoafo,' Smallpiece said, 'and they on us, damn my eyes!'

Saxmundham nodded. 'Never witnessed such amazin' confusion as there was. Once the Ashantee got inside our lines no one knew at whom he was firin'!' He added, 'They lay doggo in the bush, allowin' our front to push past 'em, and attacked inside the flankin' columns. It's a favourite dodge with natives. Now, we've drafted a set of instructions, Mr Smallpiece and myself, and Pay here has duplicated 'em and he'll hand 'em out,' he nodded at the paymaster, 'for your officers to communicate to the men under their charge. It is most important to remember in this form of warfare that not only will the men be unable to see the enemy, they will be unable to see their own people – apart from the few immediately adjacent – a disability that naturally extends to the officers. It follows there will be no grand deployments as in a set battle and few if any tactical orders issuing from the staff. I may say, in connection with the staff, that Saood has kindly loaned us some hunters from his stables.' He grimaced, and there was a ripple of laughter from the British officers.

'At all events,' he continued with a sharp look at Herder, 'each section will be on its own, each man relyin' on his immediate fellows and his officer. Consequently the tactical unit should be as small as possible – we suggest half-companies of some twenty-four men each commanded by an officer. Once these half-companies have been detailed off they should not be broken up for any reason other than a large number of casualties.' He looked at Herder again.

'It is good sense,' the German agreed shortly.

'Our latest reports indicate some eight thousand or more warriors gatherin' in defence of Witu – more than ten to one I need hardly remind you. It will allow the rascals ample scope for their favourite dodge of outflankin' and encirclin' from the rear, consequently we propose advancin' in the square formation wherever practicable.' He paused as the officers took up the duplicated sheets the paymaster placed before them. 'And now, gentlemen, if you would be good enough to read through, and if there are any questions –' He left the question unfinished as he took hold of the magnum, turned it once or twice in the bucket, then passed it to Smallpiece. 'Perhaps this may assist.'

Herder smiled thinly. 'You think of everything, captain!'
Saxmundham returned a hard look. 'I trust so, captain!'
Guy started reading.

The advance will be made by companies in columns, fours, file or single file according to the practicability of the country. In the event of a general attack, or should an attack be expected, the force will be halted and formed in a hollow square. Officers are warned that such deployments from file should be made along a line perpendicular to the line of advance, the compass bearing of which should be known at all times. Whenever the nature of the country permits, however, the advance will be made in the square formation.

If the leading sections of a force advancing in file discover the enemy, or expect an ambush, they are to halt and kneel, the front rank turning to the right front, the rear rank to the left front. Two volleys are then to be fired by order, searching all places where an enemy might be . . .

He had a sensation that he was being watched and, looking up, he caught Mann staring at him from the far end of the table. The German dropped his eyes to his papers immediately.

Guy was on the quarterdeck in the cool of the evening, snatching a moment of relaxation before Mann was due to arrive to coordinate the details of the march when Saxmundham appeared and called him over.

'How d'you find the first lieutenant, Greville?' There was a worried look in his eyes. Seeing Guy's startled expression, he went on, 'If only the ass would give in. Sawbones has informed me on a number of occasions of the diabolical pain and discomfort the poor fellow must be sufferin'.' His tone was fierce. 'The beggar will not lie down!'

Guy fell into step as he started pacing.

'I've humoured him to the limit. On my life! I've allowed him command of base camp. You know the goat wished to go to Witu?'

'He was most anxious not to be left out.'

'Practically fell on his knees – except he wouldn't have got up again! On my life! It gives me no pleasure to see a man reduced to that state.'

'The work of the ship has not suffered, sir.'

'Nor will until such time as he drops.'

'The bo'sun told me the jacks will do anything for him in his present condition.'

Saxmundham appeared not to have heard. 'You know the chief came up to see me. The beggar kicked him, he said. He said you saw it all.' The blue eyes were pained. 'He was asleep on deck and Smallpiece kicked him in his parts. It was so as to tell him what he already knew, viz., the engines would not be required.'

'That was several days back –

'You saw it?' A shadow passed across Saxmundham's face.

'Not as he has reported it. He stumbled and fell on him. It was pure accident.'

'You are certain?'

'Absolutely. He was attempting to rise without his stick.'

'The chief invented the rigmarole about the engines, d'you suppose?'

'He is somewhat obsessed –

'You've noticed it! The black scamp!'

'It's strange he should wait so long before telling you.'

'I've ceased wonderin' what prompts his actions, Greville. I find the beggar incomprehensible, I don't mind tellin' you. At all events – he found my champagne to his taste – the scamp! Bless my soul! He has a wife did you know?'

Guy thought of the picture gallery on the engineer's bulkhead. 'A numerous clan as well!'

'You don't say so! His wife is partial to gin and water!'

Guy heard a boat hailed from the gangway and an answer floating back in accented English. 'Our visitor!'

They turned and started walking towards the entrance port. 'You know,' Saxmundham said, 'I find it surprisin' these Germans allowin' us to decide the arrangements. D'you find it surprisin', Greville?'

'I confess I do, sir.'

'I'll grant you, they haven't a tenth part of our experience. All the same – I fancy they're up to something.'

'Decidedly!' Guy thought of the speculative look he had caught on Mann's face in the after cabin.

They stopped by the entrance port where Stainton and the quartermaster were standing. 'As regards the lewali's safety,' Saxmundham went on, 'I fancy we've shown our hand plainly enough.'

Guy grinned. 'I doubt they can have any misconceptions there, sir.'

'Harris don't like it, but he'll have to put up with it. If the Royal Welch ever do show up, he can come on after us and leave them to guard duty.'

'We'll need all the force we can muster.'

'We've a sufficiency, Greville.' The blue eyes had cleared again. 'The golden rule, my boy. You'll never obtain all that you require. Be thankful for a sufficiency!'

Mann appeared at the entrance port, and they turned towards him. He stepped up smartly, a broad smile on his face, and banged his hand up in salute, 'Captain!'

Saxmundham lifted his hat. 'Lieutenant Mann. And very prompt I'll be bound!'

'We Germans make good clocks, captain!'

'You do indeed!' The Old Man laughed. 'Your guns are as good?'

'Our guns are better than our clocks!'

'I trust we shall make excellent *time* to Witu!'

They laughed, the suspicions of the previous meeting put aside for the moment.

Chapter Thirteen

The *Kingfisher* lay at anchor some four miles from the beach in water shading a pale, milky blue reminiscent of Cornish china-clay pits. Off her starboard bow a square fort and a few houses above a dazzling sand spit were all that could be seen of the little town of Kipini. Beyond, dark green mangrove foliage stretched around the estuary of the Ozi River, whose mud was the cause of the peculiar colour in the coastal water. Stretching north of the town towards the *Kingfisher,* white sand dunes were interspersed with low scrub and scattered palm clumps and occasional isolated baobabs behind a shining beach.

The quartermaster in the chains sang out reducing depths as the *Dulcinea* sounded in towards the gunboat under topsails and jib. The *Meteor* followed close astern, and the three German gunboats after her. A cloud of black smoke miles in the offing was all that could be seen of the sultan of Zanzibar's *Star.*

They brought to in the late morning abreast of the *Kingfisher* and a quarter of a mile to seaward, the *Meteors* anchor splashing into the water fractionally after their own, while the gunboats diverged to form a second line in the shallows near the *Kingfisher.* Directly the cables had been secured the hands were piped to dinner and the seedies set to lowering the boats and rigging awnings and windsails over fo'c's'le and poop. Guy, as beach officer, snatched a hurried bite; afterwards he had a cutter brought alongside and embarked with Cameron, two headman porters, Buckley and two other midshipmen armed with a score of flags bent to staffs to mark out the rallying points for the different companies, their provisions and equipment.

As they shoved off, a small white stallion which they had carried from Lamu was being hoisted over the hammock nettings, whinnying screams. The hands were in carnival mood after the midday grog and with the prospect of action stretching ahead like a holiday spiced with violence, and jests and shouts rose as the creature was swung overside and down towards a waiting launch. They heard the bellowing of bo'sun's mates above the din, which suddenly stilled. Guy smiled.

The single dipping lug of the cutter was run up, and as she leant to the wind, he moved the crew to trim her ; she burbled along, dipping the lee gunwale to the water's edge as the breeze gusted. It was a long run to the beach, but pleasant. Overside through the shallowing water a sparkling scene was enacted; the shadow of the boat moved along the sand bottom, rippling over ridges, up on shoals, down into grottoes of coral, pink, mauve, amber, grey, green, white pods of lace and convoluted stems and branches; among it all fantastic fish waved, darted, hung like impossible images in green crystal. Guy was carried back to midshipman's picnics and seining parties in the tropics; however many times he witnessed it, the brilliant display could never lose its fascination.

By the time they reached broken water on the run in to the beach the whole stretch of sea astern and on either quarter was alive with the sails of scores of boats, British and German, some laden with marines, others with braying donkeys, horses, porters, stores; here and there amongst them the brass-bound funnel of a steamboat gleamed beneath rolls of oily smoke, thinning downwind. With the ships at anchor in the background, ensigns flying out stiffly against a blue sky dotted with the whitest puffs of trade wind cumulus the scene was as lively as a fleet regatta, heightened in every mind, Guy knew as he looked at the faces in his own boat, by anticipation of novelty and danger.

He called for an oar to be passed aft, and had the tiller unshipped as he thrust the blade out over the quarter to steer the craft through the breakers. The stern lifted, spray blew cold against his cheek; he levered the blade to starboard, fighting the swing of the stern as the bow plunged. The wave swept beneath, lifting and hurling them onwards for wild moments before the stern sank again. He looked out towards the next approaching breaker.

By the time they reached the calmer shallows he was soaked with sweat and spray. The bowmen, with rolled up trousers, leaped out and seized the gunwales, soon joined by the rest of the crew, hauling the boat rapidly on the long approach to the beach, which was pitted with dazzling pools before the stretch of white sand up to and beyond the high water line. The glare was painful.

As they neared the pools whole colonies of small birds which had been feeding, rose up and whirled, filling the air with startled cries. Guy recognized the spotted breasts and rapier beaks of sandpipers among them, and the distinctive black bellies of plover, but it was too bright to stare. Two solitary grey herons turned their bent necks for a moment, then resumed the search for food, dipping meticulously like old men at the water's edge. They lacked the proper fear of men their European counterparts had learnt. Way to the southward, a line of dark-plumaged storks, touched with pink on their heads, strutted like drill sergeants, great pale beaks at the ready.

The boat grounded and he jumped out, water soaking over his boots and gaiters. He was up to his calves in a pool of waving violet weed. Small white and black striped fish shot away like a shower of arrows. He lent a hand to run the boat up, noticing a large German cutter being hauled up to their left. Mann walked behind, lifting his feet high. Orders rang out from all sides as other boats beached.

When they got to the dry sand the grains were so sharp they squeaked underfoot. He walked up to the high-water line of wood, stopping and shading his eyes against the violent light with his hand as he surveyed the extent of the beach. Despite the sea wind the heat was reflected from the sand as if from an open oven, draining his energy.

Mann and a German midshipman holding a bundle of flagstaffs approached, squeaking on the sand. Their uniforms and cork helmets were dazzling white; had it not been for damp marks up their trousers they might have been dressed for divisions. He glanced down at his own uniform stained with a witch's brew of coffee water and other ingredients Duff had refused to specify, and as they came up made a show of shielding his eyes from the dazzle.

Mann smiled. 'But your face is clean!'

'An oversight!' He gestured towards the grassed dunes behind. 'Let's look for the track the advance party took!'

They stepped up towards the bank, the *Dulcineas* midshipmen hastening to join them. Guy turned to Mann, 'How is your admiral?'

The German's expression closed in. 'Always you ask about our admiral.'

'We are concerned.'

'He was taken ashore in Lamu,' Mann said shortly. 'That is all I know.'

They climbed a dune, hauling themselves up with the coarse grass. Guy wondered for a moment if they would be greeted by shots as they reached the skyline. There had been no sign of life so far, and yet –

A butterfly flew up before him; Guy caught a glimpse of a pattern of white spots on black wings beautifully marked in cream and ochre. A Danaide, he thought and thrust his hand out quickly to still the party.

Mann dropped to his knee, unflapping his revolver holster in the same motion. '*Wo?*' he hissed, as he withdrew the gun. The midshipmen behind were also on the knee looking up at Guy, wondering why he had not dropped, too.

He smiled, leaning towards Mann. 'It was stupid. I'm sorry. A butterfly!' He pointed.

Mann's eyes widened.

'A Danaide, if I'm not mistaken.'

Mann pulled himself up, brushing sand from his knees and thrust the revolver back in its holster; his eyes were puzzled and angry.

'I collect them,' Guy explained.

Mann stared, then threw back his head in a full-blooded laugh. 'You like butterflies! That is good. They are beautiful.' He scrambled further up the dune. 'My friend, I, too, like beautiful things.' He flung his arm wide in an operatic stance and roared out a few bars of an aria. 'You know *Siegfried?*'

'Wagner!' Guy shook his head.

'Forging the sword!' Mann said dramatically.

They had reached the top of the bank; there was not a sight nor sound of life, only desiccated, greyish thorn scrub and a few doum palms with long trunks curved delicately outwards with forked tufts high up. He saw what appeared to be an opening in the scrub to their right and started towards it.

'I must teach you about Wagner,' Mann said. 'He is *torment!* I sweat all over when I hear him. He is German, all German! But I shall teach you, that shall be my task. You will understand us.'

'You wish us to?'

Mann roared with laughter again. 'You do not trust us.' He clapped an arm briefly across Guy's shoulder. 'But we shall see!'

As they approached the opening in the scrub Guy saw deep ruts left by the wheels of gun carriages and a wide band of trodden sand and grass. 'The track!' he pointed.

'That is the track,' Mann agreed, then on a suddenly sharper note. '*Halt!*', and crouching, whipped out, '*Sehen Sie?*'

Guy crouched, too, peering through the spiky grass.

Mann was staring to his left towards a dense thorn thicket. He said softly, '*In jenem busche!*'

Guy stared as he pointed his revolver, but he could see nothing.

'*Ein vogel,*' Mann said suddenly, '*Ein grosser Sperling, ich denke!*'

Guy straightened, aiming a mock blow at the German's helmet as he rose. Mann ducked away roaring with laughter. 'Now we are the same, yes?'

Time burned down through the shoulders of Guy's tunic; sand and metal ached in his eyes; his ears rang to hoarse commands, shouts of porters, cries of men on the drag ropes of the field pieces, the startled bray of donkeys, squeak, squeak of the sand underfoot, and the continuous roar of the breakers. The piles of paraffin tins fitted as water containers, biscuit tins packed with rations, kit bundled into sixty-pound loads, pioneers' spades and axes, had grown high as the boats ran in and discharged and the porters toiled.

He saw Saxmundham in his tall hat astride a grey pony barely taller than himself.

'Tried your mount, Greville?'

Guy shaded his eyes. 'Not yet, sir.'

'I advise you to do so, my boy!' The Old Man leant from his saddle. 'I believe that rascally lewali intended sabotagin' the expedition! At all events, this fellow don't know his helm orders. Bless my soul! We've saved 'em from the knackers if you ask my opinion! Everythin' all right?'

'Going on famously, sir. May the hands bathe when we have everything ashore?'

The captain looked out to sea, green shading to blue from this angle with the rollers sweeping in and the spume of the breakers rising, whisked away by the wind. 'Barracuda!'

'In the shallows, sir.'

'Very good. Make certain our jacks understand the danger.' He added with a glint in his eye. 'The Germans can fend for themselves!'

Guy laughed. 'I believe they will, sir.'

'So do I, Greville. All Europeans to sleep aboard tonight. Let the guard consist of the Indians and the sultan's regulars —split 'em up – all the sultan's men to have Sikhs or P'thans on either hand. If the Wa-Deutschi wish to post a company of their own, it's up to them.'

'I'll inform Mann.'

The captain gazed down. 'The night miasmas from the swamp are a good deal more deadly than the barracuda, Greville. Depend on it, we'll lose more men to fever than to the sultan's guns.' He stopped as the grey swung its head towards his leg, teeth bared. He kicked it in the flank, and it danced round in a half-circle. 'All aboard by dusk,' he called out over his shoulder. 'Bear away, you brute!'

The afternoon wore on in a continuum of heat and movement and faces, Buckley, Cameron, Heighurst, Mann, the gunner. . . .

At last, with the sun in the palm fronds and no more boats riding in through the breakers, the pressures eased. He gave permission to bathe, and watched as the hands flung off their jumpers and trousers where they stood and plunged into the water, rollicking and splashing and fighting like boys released from school; but their bodies, marked in segments of harsh, red-brown and white, were firm and taut like no boy's ; corded muscle stood out, highlighted in the slanting rays of the sun. By contrast, the porters appeared almost flaccid. 'Look out, Witu!' he breathed.

'Knowin' you'd fancy a swim, sir –' Duff was standing at his side with a striped towel.

'Lor! Figgy!'

The marine wrinkled his glistening brow. 'Watch out for stone fish! I saw a sojer that put 'is foot on one. I shouldn't want to 'ear nothin' like that niver again.' The bullet scar through the marine's cheek twitched. "E killed 'isself. Wanted me to chop 'is foot off first – 'e meant it an' all, but I couldn't git near to suck the pisin out. All of a sudden up 'e jumps an' e's in the water and off like a threshin' machine. That's the last anyone seed of 'im.'

Mann came running up, singing operatically. He stopped beside them, glancing at the towel and nodding admiringly. 'You think of everything!'

'*Naturlich!*'

'We shall see who can swim out furthest?' The blue eyes were very clear.

'I'll allow you best!'

Mann roared with laughter.

Beyond him, Guy caught sight of Smallpiece, stump-
ing through the sand on his own, his face twisted with the
effort. He had a sudden feeling that the first lieutenant, like
the soldier Duff had described, wished only for release in
death. He wondered if the strange conversation watching
the slaves had been a call for help. No one could help a man
who thought he had failed in the only thing he knew or
cared about. He thought of Smallpiece's anguished attempts
to gain a place in the column marching on Witu – perhaps
he would have tried to enlist his own support if they had
not been interrupted : 'You have the captain's ear Greville –'

Mann was looking at him curiously.

He unbuckled his ammunition belt and handed it to
Duff, unfastened the clips at the neck of his tunic, then the
buttons. His spine pad was wet against his back. He pulled
the tunic off and handed it to Duff, then his soaking cholera belt, feeling the breeze cool against his bare shoulders
as he bent to untie his laces.

Mann was undressed fractionally before him and running down the sand the muscles of his calves and upper
legs bulging as powerfully as the rest of his splendid frame.
He increased his pace as he heard Guy's feet squeaking
behind, and they entered the pools at a sprint, kicking the
water into showers before them and running on through
the tepid spray, shouting. As the sand began to fall away,
Guy plunged in. The warmth and relaxation, the hint of
the gentle evening sun on his back combined deliciously.

Trojan, luxury is only found in contrast. To appreciate fully our bathe this evening it was necessary,

I am certain, to have spent the day grilling within an inch of our lives under a vertical sun on a burning white sand beach!

Mann is a capital fellow we get along famously despite the rascally way his side is going on, but I fancy Old Sax has the measure of them! And tomorrow, we march!! Be sure the 'Lion's' *pride* will fall before our Gardner guns!!

The beach was a pale grey thread between the black sky and the sea as the boats filled with men and left the ships. As they sailed towards the sheen of the lines of breakers iridescent green shapes moved beneath the surface. Guy wondered what manner of creature they were and what purpose the eerie glow served. His imagination filled the water about them with razor-toothed killers; the possibility of the boat capsizing did not bear thinking about. He wondered how many of the bluejackets sitting quietly on the thwarts, shivering as the spray whipped over the low gunwales, had similar thoughts. Their bearded faces were stolid as timber. He thought of the marine sergeant's night fantasy world, and studied them again.

They reached broken water, and he began to fight the boat through with a steering oar; the visions vanished.

Grey light began to creep up from the seaward horizon; gradually the details of the ranks of waves began to clarify, and by the time they reached the shallows the day had begun; the bases of banked cumulus astern were touched with a brilliant golden glow. Towards the beach a low mist hung above the sand obscuring the grassy dunes and all but the upper parts of the trees beyond. The men's spirits began to return with the light and, as the keel grounded, they leaped out eagerly, their patchily stained bell-bottoms rolled to the knees, boots slung around their necks, rifles held high. They were a motley crew, stained hat covers of every shade from deep cocoa to the palest fawns, cutlasses at their belts.

Guy jumped out after them, reaching inside again for the rolled Union flag he had been careful to carry with him, then waved to the midshipman who was to take the boat back. Higher up the beach, he saw Cameron in the midst of a chattering crowd of porters, making almost as much noise as they as he attempted to regulate their scramble for the softest or lightest loads. To their right a detachment of German sailors stood in line at ease, their arms stacked in a neat circle around the flagstaff denoting their number. The few British detachments, partly hidden in the mist further up the beach were more active, shifting restlessly, trying on their unaccustomed boots, taking them off again, scraping the edges of their cutlasses with coral, adjusting cartridge belts, whittling wood.

He saw Saxmundham in blue frock coat and top hat shadowy in the mist beyond, leading his grey on a short rein; reminded, he made his way towards where the other horses had been tethered under the shelter of the dunes. The native boys whom the lewali had loaned as grooms were squatting, chattering by the animals, and he shouted to them, pointing to the mare he had chosen previously. She was a mottled silver-white with pinkish shoulders and a pathetic expression; unpromising to look at, she had proved more biddable than the others. He had christened her Rosinante; she reminded him of Don Quixote's poor old charger. He patted her neck as the boy ran up with the tackle. After she had been saddled up, he lashed the rolled Union flag to the pommel and mounted.

'Bless us, if it ain't St George!' Heighurst gazed up at him.

Guy pulled gently on the reins. 'See how she steers!' He slapped her on the flank with his palm and made off easily. He knew he had chosen well. He called back, 'See you in Witu!' and patted his rolled flag.

He saw Smallpiece moving clumsily up the beach from the water, his stick digging deep in the wet sand, his stiff leg soaked to knee level and scraping arcs like the track of some tailed animal. Looking at the man in the early morning light, Guy felt he had been wrong about him the day before. Pained and struggling he might be, but fiercely alive and determined; death was as far from his pugnacious features as any intention of giving in to his disabilities.

He turned Rosinante's head and cantered towards him, coming to a halt and swinging himself out of the saddle across his path.

Smallpiece stopped and stared.

Guy gestured up. 'Would you care to ride? I could hump you up.'

The first lieutenant's eyes widened, bulging. His lower lids were reddened, the dark leather of his face blotched with fiery veins. His thick lips opened wordlessly for a moment as he drew his stick from the sand and he almost overbalanced as he fought for words. Guy thought for a moment he was about to collapse. Instead, he dug the stick in fiercely before him and hauled himself after it, changing direction so as to give Rosinante a wide berth. His brows were drawn straight, deep vertical lines intersecting them; sounds of effort choked up from his chest.

Guy looked after him, wondering if he had been so wrong after all. The man seemed scarcely to have recognized him, regarding him only as a hostile obstruction to be negotiated. He jumped into the saddle and started Rosinante in the direction he had last seen Saxmundham. The beach was crowded with men now, some on the move, most gathered by their rallying flags; the mood was subtly different from yesterday's carnival atmosphere; there was a tension and quiet that had been lacking then – no lack of eagerness and confidence, but a deeper look in the eyes as if all knew it was no picnic party they were embarked on. He made out Saxmundham, very upright on his grey, a huge cigar between his lips, calling encouragement to a party of bluejackets on the drag ropes of a twelve-pounder. He dug his heels into Rosinante.

Saxmundham raised his tall hat as he saluted. His eyes were alight with anticipation. 'First class!' he beamed. 'I never saw a disembarkation better managed!'

Guy felt himself flushing with pleasure. 'Our allies are amazing thorough.'

'Stuff! I don't give a straw for thoroughness! It's the spirit counts.'

Guy wondered how to put his suspicions about Smallpiece. 'If I might venture –'

Saxmundham raised his brows.

'About the first lieutenant.'

A shadow passed across the Old Man's eyes.

'His condition—' How was he to continue without implying criticism of the Old Man's judgement? 'In my submission, sir, the controlling of the sultan's men in their present state, and the Indians, will be no easy task. I have come away from the first lieutenant just this minute and his condition is not such as would give me confidence —'

'His condition, sir!' Saxmundham's eyes were icy.

'Not entirely his health – his state of mind —'

'What can you know of his mind!'

Guy held the gaze steadily. 'He is a desperate man, sir.'

'By thunder!' Saxmundham roared with a suddenness that made him jump. 'You overreach yourself, sir!'

Guy stiffened. 'I believe it my duty, sir.'

'Your duty, sir, is to see to it the men are mustered with dispatch. That is your duty, sir!'

Guy felt the blood pounding in his head. He made an effort to control his voice. 'The first lieutenant seeks his own destruction, sir, and that is not the man I should place in charge of troops.' He knew he had gone too far. What had possessed him? It was irrecoverable.

Saxmundham's face had paled beneath the weathering. He made no move, uttered no sound, but stared at Guy with a ferocity that froze his blood. His eyes and the physical animosity he radiated filled all Guy's perceptions and a despairing emptiness crept up from his stomach.

'Be about your duties, sir!' The words were clipped and cold.

He saluted, receiving the merest hint of a response, and pulled Rosinante around. Moving away, despair turned to anger. It had been his duty –

Someone had cantered up and come to a swirling stop before him; he focused his eyes and recognized Mann on a large bay with fine shoulders and muscular quarters. There was a broad grin on the German's face, and he was patting a rolled flag, white and black, lashed to his saddle.

'We have the same idea!'

'But different flags!' Guy snapped.

Mann's smile fell away. He said stiffly, 'I have to inform you, our divisions are ready.'

Guy nodded back to Saxmundham. 'My apologies! Look out when you report it!'

Mann glanced across, then back to Guy and nodded, raising his hand as he dug his heels into his mount and directed it towards Saxmundham.

Guy continued towards a party of bluejackets who were jogging towards their muster flag. They were the last ones. There were no more boats coming in; most were returning to the ships under sail, the steamboats and a few smaller cutters lying to an anchor just off-shore. The beach was quiet with expectation. He waited while the midshipman in command checked the men and inspected their arms, then kicked Rosinante into a trot back towards Saxmundham, now in the midst of a group of officers. They sat a strange variety of mounts, Herder stiff and uncomfortable on a beast almost as bony as himself, Mann on the powerful but wild-looking bay, the first lieutenant of the *Meteor* on a small white stallion with an equally wild look, and the surgeon with his medical case stuck astride a fat-flanked, iron-grey pony with a back that seemed to sag under the weight.

Guy saluted as he came up. 'We are ready to move off, sir.'

Saxmundham's face was expressionless. He glanced at the Germans. 'Let us proceed!'

They pulled their horses round. Guy made over to the *Dulcineas* bugler, whom he ordered to sound the advance, then to the group of native guides and askaris who were to lead in skirmishing order. He cautioned them through the interpreter not to proceed too fast. They shook their carbines and grinned their understanding as they started off towards the track through the thorn scrub, their bare, splay-toed feet squeaking on the sand.

The beach was in an uproar of bugle calls and shouted orders, and the throb of the great drum as Saxmundham's band struck up the inevitable 'Hearts of Oak'. The bandsmen were in green livery, their only concession to bush warfare straw hats with tea-stained covers in place of the peaked caps they wore on board. The first section of German bluejackets swung towards the track after the askaris, rifles at the shoulder, a sub-lieutenant in the lead, an expression of pride and innocence on his young face. Another German half-company followed, led by a lieutenant, and after them two half-companies of Dulcineas; he smiled at the bluejackets shambling gait and uncouth appearance, their obvious dislike for the squeaking boots they had been forced to wear. They would have blisters before the day was over. After them the Germans who were to form the left flanking column looked like soldiers with their stiff step and exact spacing. They had silent faces.

The machine-gun companies came next, and after them the Indians and Zanzibaris, the latter strolling with ostentatious lack of enthusiasm behind villainous-looking officers. When they had passed it was the band's turn, and immediately behind, Saxmundham and the headquarter's staff. The great man passed at a walk, magisterial in his high hat and blue and gold encrusted frock coat with his cigar and great beard thrust out. Despite the air of confidence he radiated, Guy detected the shadow still behind his eyes. Herder rode next to him, shrunk by the weight of his presence, and after them the German first lieutenant, with German and British midshipmen and aides walking importantly behind. The old paymaster walked beside the surgeon's pony, one hand on the bridle, 'and after smelling Kilwa I may say I didn't wonder the cholera had killed off half the settlement within the past two years. . . .'

The field-gun parties strained behind, grunting on the drag ropes of the seven-pounders and their limbers. The gunner scowled, his glass eye bright in the low rays of the sun as he growled encouragement. 'Only an 'undred an' one more little ant 'ills to go. . . .' After the *Dulcineas* guns came the German Krupp pieces with their distinctive long breech extensions. Mann joined him as his men toiled them up the incline.

'The captain is in bad form?'

'I'd say I was,' Guy replied. 'I criticized his dispositions.'

The German stared. 'This is permitted in the British Navy?'

'*No:*

Mann clapped a hand on his shoulder. 'It will be forgotten. You will fight like Siegfried and we shall march into Witu. It is nothing.'

'Let's hope you are right!'

'I know these things. It is the morning stomach. We Germans – always we have the morning torment!'

The rocket parties followed the guns, and after them Smallpiece struggling alone up the incline, leaving that odd, broken-arced track with his stiff leg, and a line of splayed holes where his stick had bitten in. He grunted with effort, appearing not to notice them as he heaved himself past, shoulders hunched and head down, followed shortly by 'B' Company of Dulcineas. Mann looked round with a surprised expression.

'He is marching, your first lieutenant?'

Guy nodded.

The German stared after him.

Following the Dulcineas came a small half-company taken from the *Egret,* and after them the donkeys with the officers' tents and comforts on their backs, led by their grinning Swahili owners. The track was just wide enough for them to walk in twos. Behind them Cameron, with a soft felt hat at a jaunty angle and a double-barrelled Express rifle from a sling across his open-necked shirt, stalked ahead of the first group of porters. The rest straggled three or four deep half a mile or more down the beach. They carried their loads of tins or boxes on their heads as if they were the lightest down, grinning and chattering or chanting in chorus. Cameron swept his hat off in an exaggerated salute as he passed. One of the headmen strode after him, a small white fez on his crinkly hair, curved sword hanging from a cartridge-studded belt. He too carried a double-barrelled rifle over his shoulder, and in his other hand a rhino-hide whip.

Guy had a vision of little Sambuk – 'how do Englishmen make safari? Englishmen tell my husban' fin' me porter – fin' me *silave* –' His mind flew to the night in Lamu, and he was attacked again by the desperate remorse he had felt at his part in her disgrace; the dark thoughts slipped to his gaffe with Saxmundham earlier. His stomach felt hollow. It had been unforgivable. He looked round for Mann, but found he was moving on up the track to catch up with his gunners.

The porters jogged past in seemingly endless succession to be swallowed by the scrub, only their arms and boxes swaying in a long line above the parched foliage. He jerked Rosinante's head round towards the beach and dug his heels in, urging her into a gallop, sand spraying from her hooves. The breeze soothed his face. He steered her to the firmer sand below the tide mark and turned parallel to the edge of the water, exulting in the speed. Cheering rose from the side; looking round, he saw the rearguard of *Dulcinea's* marines watching as they waited to go behind the porters. He wheeled and cantered to them.

Heighurst looked up. 'All the others are going that way!'

Guy grinned, envying him his detachment and control.

Chapter Fourteen

Saxmundham gazed at the skewed, axle-deep gun carriage as cheerily as if about to propose the toast at a
wedding. Only the increasing tempo of his cigar puffs told
of the strain and irritation Guy knew he was feeling.

It was difficult to estimate how far they had come
since leaving Smallpiece and his native garrison at the
zariba the Kingfishers had constructed, but he doubted if
it were more than six or seven miles. With luck they might
make another one or even two before the necessity of
making a secure camp for the night put a halt to the day's
march. It would still leave between three and five miles
to cover on the morrow. Saxmundham had hoped to get
further so that the men would not have to march before
the final assault.

The men not helping the gunner to rig tackles to
heave the piece out of the mud had sunk to the ground –
thoroughly done up Guy thought looking at their expressionless faces; they were only too grateful for the spell. The
white rig they had taken such pains to stain with tea was
plastered with a far darker mixture of mud and burnt grass,

and their arms and faces were splashed and streaked with black sweat.

The headquarters party looked on in silence. How many times had they waited under the merciless sun during similar incidents with the guns or donkeys? Guy had lost count. Each change in the terrain had brought its different problems. After the sand and dense bush of the first mile or so from the beach they had passed to a low plain forming a marsh at high water; the track, already pitted with holes of rhinoceros and hippo had deteriorated under their feet into a morass of dark grey mud; by the time the gunners came to it, the holes had been impossible to detect beneath the glutinous surface and the wheels had sunk deep ; the efforts to heave them out had extended the holes into craters lined with clay, filled with mud; they might have been created expressly as donkey traps.

From the swamp, the path had risen to higher ground where the Kingfishers had constructed the advance water depot. The canvas tank had been erected under the gnarled branches of a magnificent baobab whose shade had provided the officers with their first real respite from the rays of the climbing sun. A drink – sixty minutes pause – a change of garrison – and they had started out again to the strains of the band – 'Fare thee well but I must leave thee'. Guy had a picture of Smallpiece waving his helmet round and round, his face black with heat and dust, an oddly triumphant look in his red-rimmed eyes as he watched them go.

'Is the fellow desirous of adding sunstroke to his other ailments?'

He had wondered suddenly if he would see the man again. And yet he looked in better spirits than he had for weeks.

They had descended again to a dry river course along a track trampled and torn by large animals. And again the wheels of the gun carriages had fallen into invisible pits.

The sky was a colourless glare. There was no shade; no breeze reached them. The heat pressed Guy between his helmet and his saddle, squeezing all vitality out. His spine pad was a tepid sponge, his legs sticky, his tunic limp. Blinking the sweat from his eyes, he saw a figure which had once been green-liveried moving towards them. It came on slowly, stumbled, fell, picked itself up again with a new coating of mud, wiped its brow, smearing it to the semblance of a native mask. The headquarters staff waited, expressionless.

At last the figure stood before the captain, raising a dark hand to its hat. Saxmundham blew out a cloud of cigar smoke as he raised his own.

'The drummer's fallen down, your Grace.'

The Old Man beamed encouragingly. 'That don't surprise me. Not in the least!'

'We can't shift 'im.'

Saxmundham turned to the surgeon, who kicked his pony wearily. The beast jumped, but refused to move. The surgeon dismounted with a sliding roll, clutching at the reins as he lost balance and landing on his knees.

'I never asked for a horse,' he said looking up accusingly.

'Nor got one!' Saxmundham replied.

The midshipmen laughed dutifully, and one helped the surgeon to his feet. Guy recognized Buckley under the grime.

'The poor chap!' Mann said in his precise accent; it was not clear whether he referred to the surgeon or the drummer.

'Ready lads!' The gunner's roar cut through the quiet. As the hands clambered to their feet to tail on the system of tackles from sheer legs and a withered acacia, Guy saw Cameron approaching from the rear. Stopping before Saxmundham and shielding his eyes as he looked up, he said, 'I have bad news, captain.'

The Old Man beamed.

Cameron hesitated a moment. 'A good many of our porters, I have discovered, have let the water out of their tins to lighten their load.'

The Old Man began to puff furiously at his cigar. 'Started the water, have they! How many of'em?'

'Mebbe two or three score. I havena checked every one. I've set someone to examine the rest.'

'Why did no one discover the rascals?'

'The headman of the section unfortunately collapsed.'

Saxmundham looked at Guy and nodded his head in the direction of the porters. After the momentary show of annoyance, his face had resumed its cheery expression.

Guy pulled Rosinante round and patted her rump, inviting Cameron to jump up, then started back past the other guns and their resting crews.

'I'll flay him alive!' Cameron hissed in his ear.

'For collapsing!'

Cameron snorted. 'For drinking, man! He reeks like a French whore, the serpent!'

Guy was about to ask him about the drinking habits of French whores when he heard a burst of small-arms fire from behind them. He felt Cameron twist round, and reined Rosinante in, looking back quickly over his shoulder. As he did so there was another burst, a sharper disciplined volley this time, probably from the front of the column he thought, the skirmishers replying to the attack. As the rattle of shots continued there was no doubt about the different sounds of the guns. He turned to Cameron. 'I shall have to leave you.'

The Scot jumped down. 'So long!'

He grinned at the sailor's idiom, as he pulled Rosinante round and dug his heels into her flanks. She responded gallantly, and he was back with the headquarters staff in short time. He noticed the German first lieutenant spurring away up the path towards the firing, mud spattering the already black legs of his mount; the rest of the staff gazed at Saxmundham expectantly. He heard *Dulcinea's* '*A*' Company bugle call from somewhere beyond a reed bed on the right flank. They were well hidden. After the bugle came a volley of rifle fire, followed by a rattle from a miscellaneous variety of weapons. Saxmundham turned towards the new sounds. The enemy were on the flank as well as ahead. A large colony of baboons, alarmed by the noise, leaped away up a slope beyond, bounding on all fours and barking incongruously, their rear quarters shifting blobs of bright colour. A myriad of birds rose chattering before them.

'Greville,' the captain said, 'Scout towards the rear. Use your judgement if there's any point needs reinforcin'!'

He acknowledged and turned Rosinante again, dodging the gun parties, now on their feet, as he made his way back. The enemy had had plenty of time to get around their position; the danger point was the long straggle of porters stretched out behind on the confining path through the high grass which the rest of the column had left. Between the rear of the right flanking column, and Heighurst's marines bringing up the rear of the main column there could be a sizeable gap —unless Cameron had kept the porters well closed up.

He saw the Scot jogging ahead of him to get back to his charges, and coming up with him, reined in and patted Rosinante's rump again. Cameron grinned as he climbed up.

'Welcome aboard!'

He saw Stainton gesturing his half-section of 'B' Company to the side of the path and reined in as he approached, holding out the whistle around his neck. '"B"'s if we need you, pilot!'

Stainton nodded.

Guy returned the salutes of the grinning Dulcineas as he passed. 'Looking out for some employment for you lads!'

They growled their approval.

The next half-company of Dulcineas was led by the senior midshipman, Aimes, and Guy repeated the message. The young man nodded cheerily as he made off and the bluejackets called out requests to follow.

The path climbed a rock outcrop, and for a moment he thought Rosinante was going to slip under the weight she had up, but she jerked and pulled herself over the smooth surfaces to the stones beyond. He patted her neck. She was a tryer. He was coming to like her a great deal.

The thorn scrub and dwarf trees on the rise gave way to high grass, and turning a sharp bend they came on the leading Swahili, squatting, completely blocking the narrow path with their legs and loads for as far as he could see. He yelled and flapped his legs against Rosinante's side; the nearest ones rose in alarm and the panic spread back. As Rosinante picked her way through the pungent smell of bodies and sweat rose in waves about them. He scanned both sides over the top of the burnt grass tops, wondering just how far the flanking parties extended to the rear, or whether he had already passed beyond them, open to any enemy who might have worked his way this far. The porters stretched interminably.

A shot sounded from the left very close; as he turned, he saw through the grass the heads and shoulders of warriors with narrow, shaved skulls; the sun gleamed on patterns of white paint, bone ornaments, wide spearheads, the metal of gun barrels; they were scarcely over a hundred yards away; it flashed upon him that they were either abnormally tall or standing on a hillock. A fusillade of shots followed the first report. He felt the air humming with slugs. Instinctively he drew his revolver and dug his heels into Rosinante's flanks. She bounded on. Something slammed into his helmet. He took the reins with his revolver hand and with the other, whipped the whistle into his mouth. There was a report by his left ear, deafening him – Cameron's Express – his ear rang with sound. He blew a long and three short blasts for the *Dulcinea's* B Company and was about to repeat it when he saw the path coming up to meet him. In the same instant he glimpsed another, more extensive group of dark and painted faces, spears, feathers, long ear ornaments in the grass to the left of the first group and rather nearer.

He landed on the writhing limbs of a porter. The man was screaming – or was it Rosinante? The horse was jerking her head frantically and trying to scrabble to her feet again. He smelled her moist breath and her fear. Impossible to tell if she were hurt or in a panic, she was flailing so he couldn't examine her. The porter scrambled from beneath him, bringing a hard knee up in his neck in the process. He pulled himself to his knees, looking for Cameron and seeing him stretched out across the path behind, quite still, his head lying back, sharp jaw skywards, hat knocked off; his rifle was a short distance away. As he felt the shock of loss, he saw a pulse beating in the Scot's neck exposed by the open collar of his shirt. Relief flooded him.

Cameron's eyelids flickered open and he stared for a moment, then groaned and reached a hand to the back of his head, wincing with pain. When he brought the hand away Guy saw the fingers dark with blood. There was a tin ration pack close by; probably he had struck his head in falling. With another part of his mind Guy heard Rosinante screaming; now he was sure it was pain.

The porters were raising a shrill chatter; some had already started running as he went and knelt by Cameron – cracked bare feet and pale toe nails, ulcerated, dry, mud-caked legs, leaping past towards the lower ground where the guns were. He wondered if they had seen the enemy or whether the shots were the cause of their panic. He knew that unless he could stop them 'B' Company must be swept back. There would be no stopping them once they debouched down the scrub slope ; the thorn bush either side of the track was impenetrable. If the enemy attacked it would be a massacre with no armed men to reply.

· The welter of impressions jostled for a moment; he made an effort to halt the merry-go-round, and the priority became clear. Unless the porters could be stopped and a way cleared for Aimes's and Stainton's companies to get back to them they were all dead men, Cameron and himself included. His first thought was for his revolver; it had fallen from his hand when he landed, but a quick glance failed to reveal it. The sight of Rosinante, half up on her hind legs gave him the idea that if she could be manoeuvred across the path it would form a barrier against the porters. He scrambled to her, calling her name. There was blood on her front legs, and in her withers just in front of the saddle he saw a small hole where a slug had entered. He tried to calm her frenzy and ease her round, finding Cameron beside him, his face pale beneath the dust, his eyes abnormally green and bright.

'We have to stop them!' Guy said. The mare fought, screaming and thrashing her head from side to side, catching him painfully on the knee. He knew they would not move her.

'The ration packs!' he called, moving away.

They bent to the nearest of the square tin loads dumped along the path, picked them up and lunged back through the jostling tide to place them in a line from Rosinante to the opposite side of the path. The porters jumped over them, some stumbled, picking themselves up in blind terror, knocking against each other. Guy and Cameron went back for more tins and placed them in a line behind the first, afterwards starting a row above. The porters swerved through the grass to the side, some trying to leap Rosinante, who scrabbled up on her hind legs again, driving them back. She fell, pinioning one man beneath her; his cries joined the unholy din from all sides.

"When they had the barrier two tins high, Guy picked up Cameron's rifle and laid it on top, aiming up the track into the advancing horde. It had as little effect as Cameron's out-thrust palms and shouted orders to stop; the porters continued to swerve past into the grass where already a narrow track had been beaten curving round back to the main path behind them, but the volume flooding past had been lessened slightly.

Cameron collapsed in a sitting position behind the tins, holding his head forward in his hands. Guy saw blood still oozing from matted dark hair to a stain spreading over the back of his shirt. His priorities changed. Pulling the handkerchief from his pocket he formed it into a pad and placed it over the wound, fastening Cameron's fingers over it to hold it in position; then he removed his helmet and tore off the stained puggaree bound round it, using it to bind the handkerchief in place, knotting it tightly against the Scot's forehead. Cameron smiled up shakdy as he finished.

Guy clasped his shoulder encouragingly and pulling his whistle up on the lanyard blew a loud 'B' three times, wondering if the barricade had eased the pressure sufficiently to allow the Dulcineas to fight their way through.

Rosinante was still screaming. He took Cameron's Express and moved to her. The formerly pinioned porter was sitting a short distance away nursing his leg and moaning piteously. Poor Rosinante! He felt an absurd grief as he placed his boot firmly on her neck and the double muzzles of the rifle below her ear, pressing her head to the ground. He pulled the right trigger. She jerked at the report and he felt the life struggle out of her beneath his foot. He offered a brief prayer for green pastures in the Valhalla of war horses. Before he had turned away a fat fly the size of a bluebottle had settled on the mess the rifle had made.

The porters were still scrambling past, but he wondered where the warriors had got to; there was an ominous silence from the flank. After the fusillade aimed at Cameron and himself he had heard nothing. At the rear Heighurst would have heard the firing; he would be leading the marines on the heels of the flying porters.

A shot rang out from behind, towards the marsh, followed by two more and then another three – a revolver and five modern rifles. They were closer than the sporadic volleys which could still be heard from the fighting at the van. Stainton was evidently shooting his way through the porters. He recalled the shocking glimpse of warriors close to his left as Rosinante fell, and a dozen ideas of retreating towards Stainton, slipping sideways into the long grass, making another attempt to halt the irresistible flood of porters, shooting them to form a human barricade, or building up more ration packs, setting fire to the dry grass flashed through his mind. He turned to Cameron. 'I suggest we build a redoubt!'

The Scot eased himself to his knees. 'I'm with ye!'

As Guy ran back for a ration tin he had a sudden image of the red and blue embroidered hassocks in his father's church at Godalming, and he knew he would worship there again.

He lifted a sixty-pound tin and carried it back, placing it by Rosinante's still rump to begin a left wall extending back from the barrier across the path. Cameron followed suit. Guy heard him talking Swahili and when he looked round found they had been joined by one of the headmen – Baba, Cameron called him. The man had a double-barrelled gun which he laid carefully behind the barricade before starting to collect a ration tin.

'*Jambo!*' Guy smiled as he passed. 'Good man!'

'*Jambo, bwana!*' Baba replied with a wide grin.

Guy wondered how he would react when the attack came. He heard shots from behind the porters, a crescendo of sound from their throats, and above it a high, blood-chilling cry rising, falling and rising again and again. His pulse seemed to stop momentarily, then raced. It was a sound such as he had never imagined, made more terrible since it came from throats he could not see behind the terrified Swahili stampede. Gunfire and the screams of wounded or dying punctuated the evil chant.

He saw Baba standing quite still with the ration tin he had collected, his expression frozen ; he pointed to the front wall of the redoubt they had formed, and the headman placed the tin without seeming to know what he was doing. Guy motioned him down, then held the Express rifle out towards Cameron. The Scot shook his head. 'Ye'll make better use of it today.' He unfastened his cartridge belt and handed it to Guy, then turned to Baba and held his hand out for the gun the man had reclaimed.

The headman stared at him, wide-eyed.

'Leave yer cartridge belt!' Cameron said briefly.

Comprehension dawned in the yellow-stained eyes, and he handed his gun to the Scot. Afterwards he stood with lowered head and raised his right palm to his chest.

'Peace be with you!' Cameron said.

Baba stood, evidently debating whether it was right to leave his master in such a predicament; the porters thudded and fell against the barricade, moving tins out of line, toppling the upper layer to the ground and leaping over. The sight seemed to settle his mind, for suddenly he unsheathed his sword and waved it dangerously round his head.

'Save yerself!' Cameron snapped, bending with Guy to repair the walls of the 'L'-shaped redoubt. Instead Baba leaned over, collared a porter who had fallen the other side, and heaved him bodily over to help. With his aid they soon had the tins in place again, and lay behind with their shoulders pressed against them, Baba with a dagger at the throat of the terrified porter to add his weight to hold the line.

The war cries and gunfire had given way now to an equally ghoulish agonized shrieking as if the porters were being massacred with spears or hand weapons at close range. Despite the strength he had drawn from the extraordinarily vivid image of his father's church, Guy felt his legs shivering uncontrollably as imagination supplied the scenes of carnage still hidden behind a curve in the track ahead. The ration tins against his shoulders shook as a few escaping men flung themselves on top and over. The air was filled with dust-stained white cottons and the acrid smell of fear. More rifle fire came from behind, rather closer now, he was glad to hear, but was it close enough – ?

'My mother lives in Mallaig,' Cameron said. 'Next door to the post office – a haberdashery.'

Guy turned in surprise. 'I know it,' he replied, thinking of Scottish holidays.

Cameron's face was ashen beneath his tan. 'Ye know I attended the university at Glasgow – ?'

An increase in the noise ahead riveted their attention for a moment and they aimed their guns up the track.

'I'd thank ye to speak with her,' the Scot went on. 'And concernin' this business at Witu –'

Guy held up his hand. The stampede had thinned; there were no more shocks against the barricade, no leaping limbs, the few stragglers appearing around the track were all swerving past the end of the redoubt on the path that had been beaten through the long grass. He guessed their pursuers would appear at any moment.

'Stand by to repel boarders!' he said quietly, and shifted his shoulder to the butt of the Express, aiming at a point where anyone running down the path would first come into view around the bend.

The porter whom Baba was holding gasped. Glancing towards him, Guy saw he was staring past the side of the redoubt, eyes wide with fear. He flung himself on his back in a rolling turn, bringing the Express up from the parapet in the same movement. Above him, practically against the wall of tins, a savage with white and yellow-painted mask was staring down, arm upraised with a flat-headed spear pointed at his chest. Guy fired on the roll. He heard a gulp as the mask jerked backwards and the man fell away, disappearing in the long grass. He saw a movement to the left and brought the rifle round to cover the spot – white paint on red grease between whiskered stems. He pulled the left trigger and heard a thin, high cry after the report. There were shadows of movement where the face had been.

Remembering a passage in the instructions enjoining the advance against natives 'who have a superstitious fear of the white man', he rolled forward to his knees and called to Cameron at the same time as he broke the gun and extracted the spent cartridges. 'Take the left! I'll take the right! Fire together on the order, then forward together! Don't lose touch!' He pushed fresh cartridges in the breech, and snapped the gun shut, seeing more movements in the grass way to their left. He swung and fired as a warrior appeared on the path. The man leaped back for cover without a sound.

Guy beckoned Baba to come with them and bring the porter. All four crouched at the edge of the grass by the still feet and legs of the first warrior he had dropped.

'Fire!'

The two reports rang out together, left and right, and they pressed forward into the grass either side of the painted corpse. Guy noticed that his shot had scored the man's neck and entered under the jaw, thrown grotesquely back in death; blood traced a thin path from the open mouth over the white stripes of the cheeks, glistening like an effigy. He stepped past, easing the stems of grass aside with the barrel of the Express, wondering how he would be able to swing the gun quickly if the enemy appeared. He heard Baba and the porter following. He signalled to Cameron and they knelt, listening. The heat and stillness were intense, the smell of vegetation and baked soil enclosed them. His pulse skipped as he heard a rustle of movement ahead to his right. The sounds continued stealthily. They were close, but it was impossible to judge how close. Visibility was no more than two or three feet. It was an eerie feeling, stalking or being stalked in bright sunlight, yet shut in by endless curtains from all perception of the enemy save the sounds he made. The brushing noises seemed to be closing from both sides.

He looked towards Cameron and whispered, 'Fire!'

The double report rang out again. He felt as if they were firing needles through a gigantic haystack, the chances of hitting a million to one against. The sounds ceased. He flicked the underlever to break the run and re-loaded, holding two extra cartridges between the fingers of his left hand as he snapped the breech closed. Summoning all his nerve, he pushed forward again; he could hear Cameron moving beside him, and Baba behind, but the silence outside their own little circle was almost audible, tingling on his eardrums and surrounding tissues. He forced himself on.

Rifle fire blazed up some distance to the right – modern guns. Heighurst! The marines were engaging the warriors on the path ahead of the redoubt. A second volley crashed out. There was no question, they were modern guns firing disciplined volleys. His spirits leaped. He called to Cameron for another round, and they knelt and fired. There was a cry of pain from very close in the direction his Express was pointing; he pulled the left trigger. A surge of movement followed the report as if the area just before them were alive with warriors. He broke the gun with feverish haste and re-loaded with the cartridges between his fingers, afterwards drawing the breech back to his waist to give himself better leverage for the swing he would need when the first savages broke into sight. He heard Baba suck his breath in sharply, and sounds of frantic movement behind as the porter broke and ran.

Gradually he realized that all the sounds were moving away. He looked at Cameron, and saw his teeth white between the grass stems.

'Ye'll never make a better shot in yer life!'

The sounds distanced rapidly.

'White man see in elephant grass,' Cameron hissed. 'Him call on him *mizuka* point'm gun!'

From behind they heard an English command to fire, and a volley crashed out. Cameron's grin dropped away.

'"B" Company!' Guy exclaimed, falling to the ground over a tangle of grass roots.

Another order sounded and a second volley; they heard the zip of the bullets parting the grass above, followed by a command to advance in close order.

Guy reached for his whistle and blew a long note, the signal to cease fire, then another. The sounds of the advance lessened. He shouted, 'It's us!'

'It's Greville!' an astonished voice said.

'We're coming back to you!' he called.

The relief was intense, and he found himself blundering through the coarse stems in all directions as if emerging from the sea unbalanced with weariness – indeed he was utterly done up now he had time to think about it. He heard the rattle of a machine gun above the rifle fire from the marine's action away to the left, and deep huzzas drowning the cries of the hit. The battle had turned. He felt a miraculous sense of escape. He had known he would come through, but he began to wonder how they had done it. He staggered in thinning grass to the open light of the track, and heard a roar from the Dulcineas, stained, brown-grey figures with British beards, solid as the main bitts, smiling broadly.

He waved his helmet at them.

Cameron emerged shortly twenty yards away and sank down on his knees, then keeled over. The nearest bluejackets hurried towards him.

Guy saw Aimes coming up ; he pointed back into the grass. 'A party of the beggars in there! Making off.'

Aimes pulled out his compass, steadied it a moment, then waved his men into the grass.

'Don't chase far!' Guy called. It was more important to reach Witu.

Cameron's face was gaunt in the light from the lantern hanging from the tent ridge. He lay still, a clean bandage around his brow accentuating the darkness of his sunken eyes. A surface scrape and bruising the surgeon had said, nothing to worry over; he had lost a quantity of blood, but would soon make it up.

It would take him longer to recover from the blow to his self-esteem; the Scot blamed himself for the near disaster to the porters. A closer supervision of Jumah and the man would have been discovered sooner, the water would not have been lost, the column would have been closed up, the sultan's men would not have found a gap in the defences. He had become obsessed with what he regarded as his failure, uttering terrible maledictions on Jumah, who with the luck of the drunk had come through the action unscathed, even staggering to his master with the dripping head of a Witu warrior in mute expiation; he had hacked it from the piles of dead left by Heighurst's Gardner guns. In fact only just over a hundred of the nine hundred odd porters and seedies acting as porters had been killed or wounded, the remarkably low total due chiefly to the narrow track through the grass becoming clogged with bodies and warriors indulging an orgy of decapitation; that had been the saving too of the little party in the extempore redoubt.

Guy heard the howl of a hyena; packs of them seemed to be circling the camp, crying each time from a different direction. There were sufficient carcasses hidden in the bush and swamp and elephant grass to keep them gorged for a month. The expedition itself had come off lightly – apart from the porters – but the enemy had suffered terribly. Trails of blood had been found where they had carried off the bodies, but in places the slaughter had been so great and the white advance so rapid they had been forced to leave their dead.

'He'll carry a load!' Cameron said grimly. 'I'll prepare it myself. A hundredweight! He'll not stop 'till we see the ocean again!'

'You're becoming a bore about Jumah.'

'I never asked for ye to sit there!' The Scot glared up at the tent ridge. 'He was drinkin' scent if ye wish to know – eau-de-Cologne to be exact.'

'He had a fragrance about him.'

'The banyans buy the poisonous stuff from German traders and sell it along the coast. I shoulda sniffed him out long before.'

A lion roared somewhere in the distance. It was an uncomfortable sound.

'Eau-de-Cologne, old clothes, potato gin, guns, gunpowder,' Cameron went on, 'it's all the Wa-Deutschi have brought to East Africa.' His eyes lowered to stare at Guy. 'Tak' yeself to the "Lion's" palace at Witu an' see the German manufactures there. I can guarantee a portrait of the Kaiser as principal decoration – a spike stickin' from his helmet and a marshal's baton – war lord o' the Prussians!'

Looking at the Scot's intense expression Guy wondered suddenly if his dislike of all things German had coloured his view of the Witu plot.

Cameron tried to raise himself on an elbow. Guy put out a restraining hand. 'I need you fit tomorrow. The Lion hunt! Remember!'

'Ach, not one of ye has the smallest idea of what's happening out here – *never* Mackenzie an' he's paid to find out! The Arabs know, so do the Germans. There's a great change coming over Africa. The Arabs see it. They know they havena power to resist and it's why they're kickin' over the traces. Some recognize the inevitable and they'll mebbe throw in their lot with the new power – whoever it is – but many will fight. They know they can never win but they'll fight for their pride and because it's all they know.'

'Like Fumo Akari?'

'He was mebbe in two minds – flattered by all the attentions the Germans paid him, an' yet resentful.'

'So he kicked over the traces!'

'Aye. But the Germans were ready for it.'

Guy gazed at him. 'Why should you care? The Arab empire hardly deserves to survive – not by your account. You yourself said there are whole areas where the native population has been wiped out in the interests of the slavers –' An image of the living skeletons on the decks of the *Dulcinea* came vividly to mind. 'Can the Germans do worse?'

'*We* should do better.' He went on quickly, 'When I came out here, a few years ago now, my head was stuffed full of notions as ye know – following in the master's footsteps –'

'Livingstone.'

'Aye, he was my pattern. I knew many of his works by heart. I had dedicated myself to his purposes – bodily as well as spiritually. I had undergone tortures to make my body able to withstand the rigours he described. I slept on boards in winter, and in the summer outside in the heather. I walked whole days over the hills with nothing but a compass and a pocket stuffed with biscuits. Fifty miles was nothing, and I could manage a reel at the end of it. By the time I got out here, the reality was somewhat different. Instead of Christianity spreading its blessings to the simple Africans I had pictured, I found morose savages defrauded of their land, groaning under the exactions of the white pioneers of European "civilization", who spread its benefits by means of their poisonous spirits and the sale of guns and powder.'

"Why should you wish to further its spread?'

The Scot gave him a withering glance. 'Our civilization has more to commend it than tradesmen.'

'Missionaries?'

'Perhaps. But it is the missionaries even more than the traders who are bringing about the great changes I spoke of. Not through conversions – their performance in that respect has been lamentable – their failure there is well nigh complete! It is their presence – the presence of different national missions that will surely lead to the changes. Every year they grow stronger. Already the London Missionary Society has a steamer on Lake Nyasa, did ye know that? Carried up in small pieces from the coast! They're opening up the interior side by side with the white trader and with as much dedication to their ideals. Fine, selfless men who have done much good. But each society has its own native adherents, as much for protection as any genuine conversions – and like all organizations, each feels a necessity to enlarge itself. So ye see – they are the seeds from which the struggle will grow. Each government, British, French, German, there's no difference, will be drawn in in support of its own nationals. Public opinion will not allow them to do otherwise. Look at our presence here after the murder of just one missionary and his family.'

'You believe that out of all the Europeans, we should be the ones?'

Cameron smiled briefly. 'I see a benign government of the natives by an elite of British planters and administrators – the "guardians" if ye like of the Platonic ideal – bringing the African up gradually to their own level, enlightening him with the best face of our civilization, not debauching him by contact with the wurrst, money-grubbing elements who view riches and success as the only measure of applause in this wurrld, or the next for all I know. For this a settled *government* policy is necessary, it cannot be left to the indiscriminate spread of trade, or before long the whole continent will be debauched and exploited and the African will have come rightly to despise and reject us.'

'Why should we be the ones?'

Cameron's brow crinkled beneath the bandage. 'I'm surprised to hear ye, of all people, askin' that question!'

'Perhaps because you will not answer it!'

'Ach, 'tis a simple difference. We do not wish to rule the African. As ye know our Liberals have not the slightest desire to do so. The German Government has that desire.'

Guy smiled. 'You do surprise a fellow! The philosophers shall become the rulers. My father would applaud you. But has it not always proved unworkable?'

The Scot looked slightly surprised at his knowledge of the Platonic ideal. 'The German empire under the Hohenzollern stands as Sparta to our Athens, would ye agree?'

'Indeed I would!'

'There's yer answer,' the Scot pronounced in the manner of a pedagogue. 'We are the holders of the torch. Ours is the banner with the strange device, signifying freedom, human dignity, moral progress. Which is more, we have the material resources Athens lacked, with which to transform the ideal into the reality. What better place to start than here in Africa amongst these simple savages?' He stared at Guy with burning eyes. 'There is little time left. The traders and missionaries have seen to that.' His fingers clenched and unclenched on the sheet.

They heard footsteps approach the front flap of the tent, which opened to reveal the surgeon. He lifted the mosquito veil and entered, nodding at Guy. 'Greville! Mental stimulation for the patient.' He beamed at Cameron. 'I've long held there is a peculiar affinity between the mind and the ailments of the physical body which is not explained by our science.'

'Indisputable!' Cameron snapped. The surgeon's brows rose.

'Either that or there are spirits which can be summoned by those who have the art,' Cameron went on.

The surgeon stepped to his side and took his wrist. 'You refer to the local witch doctors.'

Cameron bristled at his tone. 'I've seen sufficient proof of the power of the mind over the body since I've been out here to write a dozen articles for one of yer precious journals, doctor. I've seen men under a spell on the very point of death until informed that the spell was lifted – and up they jumped and walked away as if there was never anything the matter wi' them.' His eyes glowed in the lantern light from the ridge. 'I've witnessed a score of such incidents.'

The surgeon harrumphed. 'I have a sleeping draught here –'

'I have my own, thank ye.'

'I don't doubt it.' He looked around for the Scot's mess tins.

Guy bent and handed him a galvanized mug and spoon and a jug of boiled water. 'Much obliged, Greville.'

'I thought mebbe ye had come to relieve me of some more blood,' Cameron went on. 'Or what about a nice wee blister!'

The surgeon turned to Guy. 'I'd say he was improved!' He tipped the powder into the mug from the packets, one after the other, then mixed in water and handed the mug to Cameron, who propped himself on an elbow and stared suspiciously.

'You must cover yourself during the night,' the surgeon went on. 'There is no better prescription for catching the ague than coolth of skin during sleep in these latitudes. And hard by the swamp.' He turned to Guy. 'I mention the swamp on account of the miasmas and night exhalations arising and bringing typhus, malaria, numerous other fevers – as I'm certain Mr Cameron is well aware. A chill on top of the inhalation of such fever-laden air has proved fatal to many a fellow in the peak of condition.'

Cameron looked up darkly. 'Yer health, doctor!' He drained the mug in one. 'Ye an' yer cursed potions. I believe ye know little more of the cause of the maladies ye represent to treat than my old *mganga* in Zanzibar.'

The surgeon turned to Guy. 'Oblige me by ensuring the truculent fellow covers himself with a blanket tonight.'

The Scot looked straight up at the tent ridge. 'I believe the potion is working, doctor. Unless mebbe it's the talk makes me so tired.'

'You'll be as right as ever in the morning. Allow yourself to perspire freely under the blanket.' He made towards the mosquito veil, nodding to Guy before he ducked under. They heard his footsteps moving away.

'The sneaky hypocrite mixed in a dose of quinine!' Cameron grimaced. 'I've lost half my blood, so he wishes me to lose the salts from my epidermic layer.'

Guy picked up the woollen blanket from where it had been left rolled at the foot of the bed and was about to spread it when he saw a large golden-brown scorpion in its folds, barbed tail curving back over the armoured body. He shook it to the floor and brought his boot down on it, shivering as he felt it crack.

'It appears scorpions take the good doctor's advice!' He examined the rest of the blanket before spreading it over the bed.

'It hasna done that one a lot o' good,' Cameron said drily.

Guy turned the light down. 'Open up your pores now, like a good fellow!'

Cameron scowed, as he moved to the entrance and raised the mosquito veil. When he looked back briefly the Scot was staring straight up at the tent ridge again.

Outside he was attacked by swarms of mosquitoes, settling on all exposed skin, even biting through his socks above his boots. He cursed himself for taking off his gaiters. The more he slapped and capered, reducing his wrists, hands and face to a battleground of squashed corpses, the more the humming creatures attacked. He ran to the officers' camp fire, whirling his arms, jumping over the figures still huddled as close as they could get to the flames, and tried to immerse himself in smoke.

'I thought we was to be entertained to a reel,' Heighurst said. 'Aimes's bin tellin' us the most astoundin' yarns,' he went on.

A cloud of smoke blew into Guy's face, bringing tears to his eyes.

'Our modest hero preserves a discreet silence as feats of unsurpassed gallantry are related in hushed tones around the evenin' fire.'

The smoke dispersed. 'A lucky shot,' Guy said.

'He admits it! Single-handed he drove off savage hordes. One elephant gun and unflinching British pluck –'

Guy sought out Aimes among the glowing faces. 'If you continue to draw the longbow at my expense, I shall see to it you haunt the masthead for a long while on our return.'

Heighurst tut-tutted.

He strode away for a final round of the perimeter before retiring. He felt pleased with the tale Aimes was putting about. Probably the bluejackets of 'B' Company were spreading similar yarns around the men's camp fires. They would be putty in his hands for a while; there was nothing a British sailor respected more than unthinking courage.

Chapter Fifteen

*G*uy was with the German van when the native skir-mishers ahead ran into sniper fire. He was riding the little grey, formerly the surgeon's mount but released to him with evident relief. She was not in Rosinante's class, and had to be urged on with repeated heeling and sharp slaps. Mann was with him on his large bay, and as soon as the firing started he was off towards the sounds before Guy could stimulate his mount to action.

He dug his heels in unmercifully and persuaded her past the German sailors jogging along the track between high grass and thorn bush which curved gently to the right in a hollow between slopes rising either side. As the path straightened, he came on a view of dense forest right ahead, and less than half a mile away at the edge of the trees a gateway of thick palm trunks constructed in the shape of a box with a gabled roof. High thorn hedges extended either side of this massive structure, and beyond, between the trunks of the splendid trees he caught a glimpse of thatched roofs and a flagstaff flying a blood-red flag.

Witu! Very much sooner than they had expected.

Over the grass in which the skirmishers were hidden replying to the enemy sniping fire he saw a sweep of blackened stubble and twisted, scorched thickets where the defenders had burned a clearing round the town more than five hundred yards deep in front of the thorn hedge and pallisade.

Stopping for a moment to survey the approaches, a hill, scattered with palms and scrub to the right, more gently rising ground to the left, he reined the little grey round and kicked her into a semblance of speed back towards Saxmundham, meeting on the way the German first lieutenant. Seeing him, and Mann close on his heels, the German wheeled after them.

'Witu!' Mann said, '*Nur eine halb-Meile!*'

Saxmundham was wreathed in clouds of cigar smoke with Captain Herder beside him, surrounded by officers and aides as they rode up. Guy outlined the situation and the lie of the land.

'The hill to starboard commands the main gateway?' Saxmundham said.

'Ideally situated.'

'The road from Mkonumbi enters the town from that side,' the Old Man went on. 'D'you suppose the hill might command both gates?'

'It's possible.'

Saxmundham turned to Herder. 'I propose piacin' the main battery on the hill – if they can command both gates so much the better – and advancin' the right nankin' companies and the Kingfishers and a seven-pounder and two Gardners into position for an assault on the Mkonumbi road gate. Your force, captain, together with our marines and all the askaris to be deployed along a broad front at the edge of the clearin' ahead, ready to launch the assault into the town once the main gate has been destroyed.'

The German captain nodded. 'Your men on the side road will make the alarm.'

'A feint,' Saxmundham nodded. 'Suggestions?' He glanced round.

Herder shook his head, and turning to his first lieutenant, issued a string of orders, while Saxmundham told off midshipmen to inform the officers commanding the British companies of their place in the scheme. After all were scurrying away, he turned to Guy. 'See to the positionin' of the battery and coordinate the half-companies for the right feint, Greville.' There was no hint of yesterday's anger. Guy wondered if he had been forgiven.

'And Greville, have that fellow Cameron show the porters the whip. I have no desire for a repetition of yesterday's fiasco.' He sucked at his cigar. 'However much scope it might give you for showin' off. How is Mr Cameron?'

'Well, sir. The night's sleep has put the colour back in his cheeks.'

Saxmundham nodded. His eyes were keen with anticipation of the coming battle. Guy saluted and urged his unwilling mount back towards the guns.

As the allied columns deployed through the grass and the donkeys were harnessed to help the teams on the drag ropes, the sniping fire from the enemy who lay hidden in small groups in every fold of burnt clearing and behind many of the gaunt black bushes, was augmented by heavy fire from behind the thorn hedge itself. Cast-iron round shot, bullets, slugs, pellets, old iron, hummed from a variety of ancient cannon, muskets, carbines, even a few modern American Remingtons, by the sound of them, ripping through the scrub, and tearing the grey soil around them. High above the noise, 'Hearts of Oak' rose from Saxmundham's bandsmen, the notes throbbing incongruously amongst the still palms and tropic creepers, but extraordinarily reassuring.

As Guy sought for a track for the field pieces around the hill to the right, diverging from the main deployment, the missiles about their heads thinned away ; only occasional strays zipped through the undergrowth or thumped into branches nearby. Behind him the bluejackets had forgotten their former weariness and were hurling themselves bodily at the drag ropes as if their lives depended on it. Above, the sun blazed towards the zenith; the air was still, the sky over the motionless palm fronds a burnished bowl of heat.

As they reached higher ground the going became easier, and there were frequent level areas along which the guns were trundled at the run as on the drill ground at Whale Island. Guy spurred his pony ahead, and came upon a grassy spur above an outcrop of rock which commanded the main gate some seven hundred yards away below; it was an ideal position and he turned back to lead the teams to it. Within a short space they were wheeling the guns into position.

The Mkonumbi gateway was hidden by the forest surrounding the town, and the road itself was impossible to make out in the scrub stretching away beyond; after watching the bursts of several ranging shots creep up to the main gate, he left the battery in charge of the gunner with orders to keep up a steady bombardment, and started picking his way around the side of the hill to where he knew the road must be. He could make out the route of the Dulcineas' and Kingfishers' right flanking column by the sounds of the donkeys they had harnessed to their field gun, and occasional dust clouds as they crossed dry ground. There was no firing from this quarter; evidently the enemy was concentrating on the defence of the main gateway. He heard the British Gardner guns stutter into action from the rising ground opposite the battery he had positioned, and shortly afterwards the distinctive crack of the Hales war rockets going off; turning he saw their bright tails as they rose towards the town. Their explosions merged with those of the shells from the seven-pounder battery. He saw the flicker of flames through the trees and thought he heard the cries of the 'Lion's' men running to extinguish the blaze. Gradually the bombardment rose to a crescendo, the phizz of the rockets punctuating the whine and thunder of the shells. He wondered how long the defenders could hold out with their antique weaponry.

Descending through scrub, he caught sight of the flanking party as they began their deployment in grass flanking the Mkonumbi road gate, which he made out as the same solid construction as the main gate. As he approached, the King-fishers' commander strode towards him along the path they had come, a stocky, square, black-jawed man with a thrusting manner and black brows joined over his nose by a lighter ridge of hairs. He glowered at Guy as if to indicate that possession of a pony in no way overrode his own authority in the area.

'Feint be damned!' he said without preliminaries. 'We're going in!'

Guy saluted. 'A most effective feint!'

The commander's brows drew together.

Guy patted the rolled Union flag which he had transferred from Rosinante's saddle. 'Mind if I join you? I'm keen to beat our allies inside.'

'Great Jehosephat!' The commander's lower lip jutted dangerously, and he called over his shoulder. 'Pasco! Where's the bloody bunting?'

Guy felt his colour rising. 'Two chances are better than one,' he snapped.

The commander stared. 'Get down off Death or Glory there. By God, we'll have a fair race!' He turned away muttering and strode towards the seven-pounder, which was being hauled up a short incline to command the gate. Guy walked the grey to an acacia and swung himself out of the saddle. Unlashing the Union flag, he used the line to tether her to a branch. He patted her neck.

'So long, grey one!' He added in an undertone, 'I'll show the brute a clean pair of heels!'

He pulled out his revolver, which Figgy Duff had found for him after the skirmish and checked its action before pushing it back in the holster, then moved along the path towards a party of Dulcineas he had seen. They were kneeling when he reached them, firing volleys by order at snipers who had sortied from the gate in strength and spread across the burnt clearing, melting away in hollows behind rising ground.

He watched for a moment, hoping that the gunner was making good practice at the main gate; he ought really to be up there with him. Hanged if he was going to allow Mann to the flagpole first!

He heard the *Kingfishers* Gardner burst into action from his right, and a moment afterwards the seven-pounder cracked; the shell went over the gate and burst in a massive tree beyond. He heard an order to lower the sights. After a moment of strange quiet the bugle rang out for the advance. The bluejackets' roar almost drowned the ripple of orders from the half-company commanders, and the grass became alive with movement. As he went forward, the seven-pounder cracked out again. This time the shell ploughed up a shower of stones and earth before the gateway.

The grass thinned, and he was jogging across the clearing, revolver thrust ahead, eyes searching the ground for any sign of movement. The gate was some five hundred yards away. He reserved his energy, feeling the Dulcineas just behind, hearing a furious banging of guns and old field pieces from the thorn hedge, white smoke rising in clouds through the branches of the trees, hearing the throb and whistle of projectiles in the air. Glancing briefly to his right, he felt a surge of exhilaration as the whole British line swept on in unbroken order, rifles throwing blinding shafts of light, the men whooping and cheering. The seven-pounder went off again; the shell ploughed through the gable above the gateway, stripping off some of the

timbers, but failing to explode. Black forms rose from the
ground some distance ahead, moving fast and low towards
the sides. The Gardner gun rattled and a few fell. Others
appeared, firing on the rise before streaking away. A bugle
sounded the halt; half-company officers called for volleys.
The men knelt; rifles cracked in waves of sound down
the line. More of the running figures fell. The cannonade
from the hedge was fading; only a few reports and puffs of
smoke told of defenders still active.

Guy saw eight of the Kingfishers running for the
gate in the wake of an explosion from a seven-pounder
shell; they carried packages – the gun-cotton party. A few
shots sounded from the hedge as they sprinted up, but the
Gardner was brought to bear on the smoke, and the men
reached the gate unscathed and threw themselves to the
ground under the timbers, working for minutes it seemed
before they rose again and raced back for the British line;
a cheer rolled to greet them. One fell halfway back to his
division. A moment later the gateway exploded in a cloud
of smoke, small pieces of timber, splinters and dust rising
against the leaves behind. Another cheer rose from the
British line, and as the bugles sounded the advance again
the force moved forward at the run. Guy forgot his resolve
to husband his strength, and sprinted, using both flag and
gun arms as pistons to carry him forward; in short time he
was alone in front of the pack; two other officers were also
out ahead but some distance away; one was the belligerent commander. He forced himself on with lengthened
stride. He could hear guns but whether they were from the
enemy or their own lines was not clear.

Coming suddenly on the body of a warrior, half hidden behind a slope, he leaped it, racing down and almost stumbling over another who must have been dropped by the same volley. Climbing the other side his legs began to feel heavier. He tried to skirt a line of gnarled, burnt thorn but caught his ducks; he heard them tear as he plunged on. His lungs hurt, and he wondered if he had misjudged the distance. A patch of rougher ground forced him to bound rather than run, and he leaped from hummock to hummock, picking his course like a mountain goat. Suddenly the gap in the thorn hedge where the gateway had been was only a few yards ahead. Flinging a glance over his shoulder he saw that he had left the commander a good twenty yards behind, and other officers were gaining as the men became slowed by the rough ground. Behind, the bluejackets with rifles and fixed cutlasses were bunching in a thick wedge as they converged on the gate, yelping like huntsmen. He made a final burst towards the opening, leaping craters made by the seven-pounder shells and the guncotton. He was in Witu!

The road lay straight between rows of palm-thatched beehive huts arranged as neatly as a surburban street; he paused for a moment in his headlong flight, holding the revolver straight before him, glancing quickly to right and left. There was no sign of a human being – only hens fluttered away in the dust and two goats eyed him sideways. A mangy black dog ran at him, yapping furiously, but hesitated a few yards away, in two minds whether to attack. He jogged on, wondering if all the neat huts were as empty as they appeared to be, or if he were being watched by a hundred eyes from the shadows. Perhaps it was already too late to avoid pushing straight into an ambush. Was it the sun giving him these hallucinations? Surely he had no business to be here running alone on this strangely deserted road inhabited only by poultry and domestic animals! Another dog, braver than the first, rushed at him with slavering teeth. He aimed his revolver above its head and fired. The dog turned tail and bolted.

He reached a junction where the path he was on met a wide main street similarly lined with thatched huts, several blackened or burnt to charred posts. It led up to the Kipini road gate, and he saw and heard German bluejackets charging towards him from that direction. The first wave of relief turned to anger as he recognized a dusty figure in the lead: Mann was racing for the flagpole, and a good ten yards closer than himself. He lengthened his stride, and swerved towards him, summoning all the power he could muster in the final sprint.

Mann saw him coming and also put on a finishing burst. Guy knew he had no chance. His breath rasped up from tortured lungs as he forced himself on, watching the German through a mist of sweat.

His ears churned with the roar as Mann reached the flagstaff, clutched it for a moment to steady himself, then placed his rolled flag between his knees and began unfastening the halliard.

A moment later Guy reached him, choking with the anguish of the final burst and dizzy with the heat. He tried to control his features, arranging his lips in a smile as he held out his hand. 'My congratulations!' He felt his lips twitch with the effort.

Mann seized the hand heartily. 'My friend —!' His eyes widened with concern.

Guy felt his cheek muscles ache with the effort of holding the smile.

'It was so close,' Mann said.

'Close!' Guy gasped. 'It is an honour – to be cut out by a fine sportsman –'

Mann stared, then suddenly handed him the loosed halliards. 'You shall have the honour! My friend, you shall pull down the "Lion's" flag!'

Guy held the lines for a moment. Had it been anyone but Mann, he would have thrown them back in his face. He looked up at the blood-red cotton, and started hauling.

The Germans gathered around roared their approval. Dulcineas and Kingfishers running up the road joined in as the flag dropped. Guy handed the halliards back to Mann. 'I am much obliged.' He grinned and patted his rolled Union flag. 'I shall have to find a suitable pole for ours!'

Mann thrust an arm across his shoulder. 'My friend.'

By the time Saxmundham and Herder rode into the town, preceded by the band playing 'Loch Lomond', both British and German flags were flying side by side in the slight breeze.

Saxmundham waited until the notes from the perspiring bandsmen died away, then thrusting his cigar between his lips, reached for his gold hunter and held it up in an ostentatious gesture. The bluejackets and marines, British and German, clustered around, silent and expectant, eyes alive with satisfaction. Not a living soul had been found in the town.

Saxmundham raised his voice. 'My lads – *Deutscher und Engländer –*'

There was a roar of approval.

He waved the hunter. 'We have arrived in good time for dinner.'

There was a moment of silence, the men wondering if there was more to come; a few chuckles broke out.

'*Mitagessen!*' he bellowed suddenly, and a full-blooded roar of laughter greeted the perfect timing. He held his arms high and wide as if to indicate that all the goats, fowls, sheep, pigs and grain they might find were theirs for the taking. His beaming face was swathed in clouds of cigar smoke.

When the men had dispersed, he leant down to one of the midshipmen. 'Have my steward fetch the champagne, Dickinson! We shall be in the sultan's palace as I understand the rascal calls it.' He glanced at Herder, then at the other officers. 'Gentlemen, I fancy it will be cooler in His Highness's late quarters. At least,' he added, sucking at his cigar, 'until we make a bonfire from 'em!'

Herder laughed politely. 'It will not be necessary to collect wood, captain!' He gestured at the timber and thatch huts.

Saxmundham chuckled. 'I dare say they need fumigatin'!' He wrinkled his nose. 'The black scamps!'

As Guy walked with Cameron and Heighurst behind two native guides along the track leading to Katawa, where the Scot was certain Fumo Akari and his followers would have fled, his thoughts returned to the 'Lion's' palace.

It had been a disappointment. He had hoped for too much perhaps. He had expected it to reveal at least some clue to the arms intrigue and the murders. Yet a thorough search had turned up nothing. He hardly knew what he had expected to find – letters perhaps in that schoolboy French, arms manifests, articles that might have suggested the presence of Pierre Suleiman or the identity of his employers. There had been nothing of the kind. A few German rifles left in the hurried evacuation, probably stolen from the murdered planters, several German field pieces of ancient make abandoned near the approaches to the gateways, and, as Cameron had surmised, an enormous tinted photograph of Kaiser Wilhelm I as centrepiece of the audience chamber had borne mute testimony to the German interest, but that had been known in any case. Why had the 'Lion' turned on them? Did he see the eclipse of Arab power and resent the new order? Even so that would not explain the arms shipment. He seemed no nearer a solution than he had been in Zanzibar.

He wondered again how he was going to spirit Akari from out of the midst of his followers; two dozen picked marines, two native guides, who were undoubted rogues, four porters, two sickly donkeys bitten by the tsetse fly, with sullen owners, and Heighurst, Cameron and himself– a light flying column indeed in hostile country swarming with several thousand warriors smarting from defeat and the destruction of their homes. It was a tall order!

The two guides turned and stopped, waiting for them. As Cameron went up they started chattering excitedly and pointing off to the right of the track where the park-like grassland they were traversing sloped away into a dip; on the further slope Guy saw mangoes and other trees with denser foliage than the palms and acacias or clumps of mimosa they had become accustomed to. He looked towards the westering sun, estimating something over an hour to go before sunset. If the guides were indicating the water they had promised earlier they could hardly have reached it at a more convenient time.

Cameron turned to him. 'There's a swamp down there –generally flooded at this time of year. I'm inclined to think we'll find our water.' He searched the ground. 'The game tracks have been more numerous lately.'

'Capital!' Guy said with more energy than he felt. 'How far?'

Cameron imitated a grinning Swahili. '*Mbalikidogo, bwana!*'

Guy turned to Heighurst. 'There's little sense in us all going. I suggest Cameron and I scout towards the swamp while your fellows have a spell.'

Heighurst's face was pale with fatigue. 'Thank'ee, kind zir!'

'We'll whistle you up if we find anything.' He turned back to the leading donkey and slipped his Martini Henry and Cameron's Express and the cartridge belts from the top of the baggage, seeing Duff leave the waiting column of marines to join him. The sergeant glared but said nothing.

'Carry your gun, sir!'

He nodded at the marine's own rifle and blanket pack on his back.

'I'll manage, sir,' Duff said quickly. There was an anxious expression in his eyes, and Guy had a curious feeling he was being protective.

'Come on then!'

The guides had already started off along a trampled track at right angles to the Katawa path, and they swung after them.

'If you find the water hole,' Heighurst called, 'I'd just fancy some venison for tiffin.'

Guy waved his arm in reply.

They had not gone far when Cameron stopped suddenly and pointed down. There were pad marks in the trampled grey loam, large and rounded, the outlines extraordinarily sharp in places. 'Lion!' he said.

Guy felt the back of his neck tingle, and glanced round quickly to see where Duff was with his rifle.

There was an amused glint in Cameron's eye. 'We'll need to keep a good watch tonight.'

'I confess I have one eye lifting already.'

They started off again. 'A lion willna go for a man if he stands up to him – unless mebbe he's an auld fellow that finds difficulty catching his meat. They like to take their prey at a disadvantage. If you run from him now – or go to sleep –!'

'How d'you know this one's not an auld fellow?'

Cameron chuckled. 'If ye can shoot the Wa-Galla as ye did yesterday ye've no need to trouble yeself about an auld *simba*.'

He had scarcely finished speaking when they heard a yell of alarm from ahead. The two guides had turned and were running back towards them shrieking, '*Kifaru* –!' Beyond, past the outline of a stunted mimosa, Guy saw a flock of birds rising in equal alarm from a large grey rock. He wondered for an instant if the sun had affected him for the rock appeared to move.

Cameron was running up the track towards the natives. 'Yer gun!' he called back. 'Rhino!'

At the same moment the beast drew clear of the mimosa; Guy saw through an opening in the scrub the flash of white horns curving up from a lowered head, and a flurry of dust and stones as the monster charged, snorting and rasping, hooves pounding the earth like a drum, then more thorn bushes had shut out the view of all but its scored leather shoulders and gleaming facets of the barrel rump and back, the short tufted tail upraised like a banner. He heard himself calling, 'Figgy!' as he turned and beckoned for the gun. The marine was already beside him.

He heard a higher cry of terror from ahead, and looking up the path again saw flailing dark limbs and white cottons as one of the guides tossed in the air above the beast's back. Cameron had leaped into the grass off the track and was taking aim. The monster stopped in short space, at the same time flicking round on itself with extraordinary agility, and was about to charge its victim again when Cameron fired.

The shot stopped it for a moment, and apparently dazed or perhaps just annoyed, it began swinging its great head and trotting round as if to sniff out its new tormenter. Guy saw its evil eye peering low from a maze of wrinkles as Cameron pulled the trigger a second time; he heard the click of a misfire. Simultaneously the beast seemed to pick up his own scent; it lifted its head, shook it sideways as if checking on the range by eye, uttered a bellow of rage and gathered way straight down the path towards him.

He was already on one knee with the Martini Henry to his shoulder; he peered along the sights at the bulge around the small eye, but the beast was so close and jerking so rapidly that he shifted aim to the lower neck, wondering if he could get a shot past the grotesque head and through the folds of armour plating where he imagined its heart to be. He felt his own heart thudding, but after a moment of fear stiffening his every bone and sinew, an unnatural calm descended. As he squeezed the trigger he felt at one remove from the scene.

He heard Cameron yell, 'Jump!' as the gun recoiled. His shot seemed to have no effect. The monster bore down like an express, its huge bulk filling the path, twin horns gleaming wickedly, the foremost some three feet long, curving back above thick, flaring nostrils. He reached up for his helmet, pulling it off and throwing it in a gentle arc to the right-hand side of the path, at the same time flexing his knees and taking off in a standing dive sideways to the left.

He felt the wind of the beast and the warm smell of it and the shudder of the earth as it careered past. A sharp pain tore his left shoulder down his arm as he landed, jarring on stones. His heart was pounding again. He heard the beat of hooves slowing and imagined the monster performing another of those tight turns to come back and finish him off. He knew he would not be able to produce another such leap. He slid further into the grass, feeling for another cartridge.

The sounds stopped.

After a moment he heard Cameron calling his name, and Duff joined in. He raised his head slowly above the grass, gun at the ready. Their faces broke in relieved grins as they saw him, Cameron shaking his head.

Guy tried to keep his voice steady. 'Where is the brute?' As he spoke he saw it some twenty yards on down the path, massive folds of the dusty grey hide quite still. He glanced at Duff. The marine looked as shaken as he felt. He handed the gun back to him.

'The wind was behind ye,' Cameron said, glancing at his arm; he looked down and saw his tunic sleeve spreading with blood.

'It was be'ind that thing an' all!' Duff said, looking again at the gigantic mound blocking the path behind.

'Rhino,' Guy said. His legs were growing steadier, and as he surveyed the monster he began to feel a thrill of pleasure. 'D'you fancy Heighurst might enjoy the meat?' he asked Cameron.

'It's believed the horn has aphrodisiacal properties!'

He glanced at Duff, 'Don't let the sarn't hear of it! But what a brute!' he went on, now thoroughly elated at the kill.

'It's a fair size,' Cameron said cautiously. 'It'll be interesting to see which one of us it was that dropped him.'

Guy looked round sharply. 'He had a fair amount of life in him when I fired!'

'Ah, but it often takes a wee while —'

The sound of native voices reminded Guy of the wounded guide. He turned quickly. 'I clean forgot!' The two natives were making towards them, one limping and being supported by the other.

'The thorn bush he landed in did most of the damage,' Cameron said with a grin.

Guy strode towards the injured man, worried suddenly about the reduction in speed that must result if he were badly hurt. The guide adopted a pained attitude as he approached, then turned himself around in response to Guy's gestures. His kunzu was ripped in several places, his skin lacerated and bleeding. Cameron came up and addressed him, feeling his back and legs.

'It's my guess there's nothing more than bruising here,' he said straightening. 'He'd make more of it if he had a fracture.'

Guy was about to put his whistle to his mouth and blow for the marines, when he heard Heighurst's voice.

'Bless my soul!' It was a passable imitation of Saxmundham. 'I ordered venison, Greville!'

'We forgot to take glasses,' Guy replied penitently.

'But you must study the habits of these fellows. Venison don't charge, Greville!'

'I understood they was extremely *deer.*' Guy turned to indicate the guide. 'If you'ld care to minister to the wounded, we'll have another crack at the water.'

Heighurst looked at the Swahili, still supported by his companion.

'An over-enthusiastic member of the flying column!' Guy explained.

Duff's voice came from behind. 'You needs medicaments an' all, sir.'

He became aware of the pain in his arm; he flexed it —nothing broken. 'It can wait,' he said, and beckoning to Duff started up the path again. Cameron joined him.

After some forty minutes' walking the track began to fall away, and the bush on either side grew thicker and greener with large trees, mango, paw-paw, cashew nut amongst them; ahead they saw short grass of a lusher green than before, and shortly afterwards the magical gleam of water. As they approached they saw it was interspersed and fringed with reeds, and shoaled with black mud. They heard faint splashing sounds, plops and grunts.

'Hippos!' Cameron said quietly.

Duffs voice came from behind. 'Are they as big as rhinos, sir?'

'Bigger.'

'Do they come at you?'

'Not unless you annoy them.'

'Gawd help us!'

Guy heard sounds of movement from ahead and tensed, staring round the blossom of a mimosa; fifty yards away a pair of horns, graceful as a lyre, ascended high above the undergrowth, and an antelope with delicately marked eyes, slender neck and plump, deep red, white-spotted and streaked body hung for an instant before descending; scores more appeared about it, mostly without horns, their bodies arcing above the intervening thickets like a great school of red and white porpoise. Guy watched entranced.

'Water buck,' Cameron said. 'The wind again. We'll not bag anything this side.'

As they opened more of the swamp they saw before the far fringe of shining mud a line of flamingos, reflected like rose-pink mist in the ruffled water. One bulbous hippopotamus head was showing above the surface in the centre of the sheet of water, and there were other bumps of eyes and nostrils around it. Soon the head disappeared.

'They don't really show 'till sunset,' Cameron said.

Harsh calls and thrashing wings close to the right startled them, and a flock of guinea fowl with curiously naked necks and flashing blue plumage marked with sharp white and black whirled away. Cameron swung his rifle and fired; Guy turned and snatched his own from Duff, cursing himself for not taking it before. Cameron's second barrel cracked out as he slipped off the safety catch and raised his piece towards the nearest bird, now more than forty yards away. He fired on the swing; to his astonishment it plunged towards the water.

Cameron looked round with raised brows.

The sky above the swamp-lake was now alive with birds of all shapes and sizes and variety of calls. 'We'll need to lie low for a while.'

Guy examined the ruddy faces around the glow of the fire, reflecting on the curious way in which a group of men knit so quickly into a team. Without any real effort on his part, simply by virtue of their common purpose and isolation in strange and dangerous surroundings, they had gained a common identity and become members one of another. He knew that each would be prepared for almost any sacrifice so long as he felt it was for the group and the purpose to which the group was committed. It was a spirit which owed nothing to the drastic strictures of the Articles of War. It went far deeper – a memory carried in the blood from the primitive past when cooperation had been essential for survival.

He looked at the faces of the two guides, one with thick, flattened nose, heavy lips, flat receding forehead to a frizz of close black hair, another lighter in colour with a finer bone structure, more Arab than negro, and wondered where they fitted in the evolutionary chain, and how far there was between the separate points they had reached and his own position – how far between them and the sergeant of marines, sitting in a curiously ape-like posture holding a leg of duck with both hands as he gnawed, the ends of his moustaches shining and moving like metronomes. His eyes passed along the faces; he contrasted Duff's full, square forehead with the narrow temples of the more negroid porters and wondered about the difference in cranial capacity; what feelings, higher appreciations and abilities were denied the negroes? Duff, he knew, was sharply intelligent, and looked it. His face was full of power above and below the eyes. Called to a higher station in life, he would have made a man of distinction. If all the powerful fellows were gentlemen, where would the good marines come from?

Cameron had finished eating, and was staring into the flames. He was another who would have made his mark in a higher sphere, perhaps more of a mark than Duff, for his abilities were augmented by passion. But perhaps the passion was itself a result of his humble origins. He longed most of all for what he could never be, a gentleman – one of the select band he castigated at every opportunity. As a laird, perhaps all that ferocious energy would have been reserved for his estates and Africa would never have seen him. Africa would have been the poorer; so would he have been himself. He had learned much from the Scot.

And yet there was so much about him he didn't know. He hadn't known until the day before in imminent danger of their lives that he had attended Glasgow University. Reading what? More important areas lay buried. As a caravan leader through this dark, virtually unexplored country, Cameron had surely been in many tight corners with nothing to draw on but his own stock of courage and resource, but he never spoke of it. He described the tribes in fascinating detail, but of himself nothing – only his fervent opinions. Even there he was adept at drawing down the blinds. Until the previous evening in the tent Guy had not really plumbed the depth of his feelings about the British mission in East Africa; he had spoken of it, but never with such desperate fire and anxiety for time running out.

Guy studied the sharp profile and deep eyes beneath the bandage flickering orange in the firelight and remembered his determination to come on the expedition despite the head wound. His anxiety to prove his fitness had even smacked of desperation. At the time it had seemed all of a piece with his character, but thinking over it now, he began to wonder. Mackenzie suspected the Scot of ambition; yet they would scarcely penetrate far enough to make his name as an explorer. Besides it was a naval party, and he was in command; if anyone's name were made, surely it would be his own?

A tingle of alarm touched the back of his neck. Cameron was up to something. The vulturine way he was crouching staring into the fire seemed to emphasize the disturbing questions. . . .

The Scot turned and saw him staring. His brows raised; he looked surprised and normal. Guy wondered if he had allowed his imagination to run away with him.

'What plans have ye for tonight?'

'What d'you rate our chance of keeping to the path in the dark?'

Cameron whistled through his teeth. 'I'd not push yer luck too far.' He went on as Guy gazed at him, 'It could be done –if there are no clouds.' He sounded doubtful.

'A desperate fellow!' Heighurst said quietly. 'A night march on top of two days' scrapping, and a rhino to boot!'

'I intended an early morning start,' Guy said. 'Surprise will be our chief weapon. Speed is essential. if we can use the four hours before dawn while the "Lion's" asleep, we may surprise him before Katawa.'

'Unless the men are rested we shall be the ones surprised,' Heighurst said.

Guy looked at Cameron.

'I'd agree with the both of ye.'

'Exceedingly helpful,' Heighurst muttered.

'It helps,' Guy said. 'A straight-line graph. Take the midpoint – two hours' march before first light!'

'I won't argue with that,' Heighurst replied.

'Nor I,' Cameron said.

'I suggest we tell off three watches,' Guy went on. 'Two hours on, four off. I'll volunteer for the middle watch, so you two may get your sleep without interruption –'

'Very sportin'!'

Little time was taken in scouring out the mess tins and preparing for the night, and after the men had settled themselves under their blankets as near the fire as they could stretch, there was no talk; soon the sound of snoring overlaid the crackle of the dry branches in the flames.

Guy lay awake, thinking of Cameron. The night stretched above, spreading from the void and the lonely galaxies, its silence magnified by the myriad noises from outside the thorn *boma* the marines had constructed. Two lions were on the move, roaring responses to each other, now close and drawing brays of alarm from the tethered donkeys, now far away, always from a different quarter. From the swamp the grunts of hippos could be heard very clearly, and splashing as they sported; cicadas kept up continuous music, their strings pointed by the deep croaking of frogs and other cries he could not identify.

Had it not been for his recent misgivings about Cameron, he would have been vastly content. Something in him stirred in response to the country; he felt layers of European artificiality loosening ; if he stayed out here, perhaps they would drop away altogether, leaving him as God intended, a natural man, free from the tyranny of convention and the monstrous machine of society which, as Cameron had said, sought to grind a man down to its own pettifogging level. Viewed under the great African night it seemed scarcely conceivable that anyone could tolerate such a closed system as he had been born into. He had an image of civilization as a vast blanket thrown over people, shutting them off from what they were or could be, cutting them from their natural inclinations and all their past.

Even as the revelation came to him, the logical side of his mind subjected it to analysis. It hardly squared with his previous reflections on the path of evolution, still less with the realities of native life; the Masai, according to Cameron's account, had a far more rigid system of social convention. Natural and free they might appear in one sense, but how limited and constrained in others. Mrs Grundy was, after all, a small price to pay for the brilliant complex of Christian morality and intellectual and material progress evolved over so many centuries in Europe, and offering such unlimited hope for the future of mankind. To imitate the 'noble savage' – existing only in the minds of untravelled European romantics – would be a deliberate step backwards, denying the promise of man's further evolution into a higher, more comprehending, morally purer, more finely tuned instrument of the Creator's will –

He was woken by Heighurst a moment after falling asleep with the great bowl of the heavens imprinted in his mind. The fire crackled and spat, lighting the encircling thicket with orange, playing shadows under the tired faces of the marines being roused. He felt cold and stiff as he raised himself and pulled the blanket over his shoulders.

'Course nor'-nor'-east, lights burning,' Heighurst said brightly.

He rubbed his eyes. His thoughts returned to Cameron, wondering if he should tell Heighurst of his suspicions while the Scot slept. What could he tell him? That he had unnatural ambitions – a lean and hungry look?

'Any alarms?' he asked.

'Nothin' to speak of

He felt for his revolver and strapped it on.

Heavy clouds rolling over the stars and shutting out the light of the moon in the early hours put an end to the plan for marching before first light. Any doubts Guy may have had were ended by the torrential rain they brought, soaking the party to the skin and reducing the native guides to demoralized bundles of wet rag. The marines, stumbling and cursing in the dark, constructed a hasty shelter with ammunition boxes and the donkeys' small tarpaulins and blankets in the lee of the *boma* and huddled close beneath it while the fire sputtered and the beaten earth of the camp was turned into a marsh.

Sleep was impossible, and it was with relief that they rose from their cramped positions at the first hint of a lightening in the east, packed their bundles, loaded the shivering donkeys and set out behind the guides, who had been bullied by Cameron into a semblance of life.

They walked rapidly for two hours, their restored circulation and the coming of day raising their spirits despite continuous rain, and they covered a greater distance than in the whole of the previous afternoon's march. Resting under a baobab tree they made a breakfast of steaming cocoa, broken biscuits and a regulation dose of quinine, and started out again as the sun began to break through thinning layers of cloud, raising steam from the earth and their clinging clothes. The warmth was sensuous for a while but soon became oppressive. The rain continued. The sun climbed into more cloud and they pulled off their shirts and tunics to let the rain cool their skin. Ahead, the grassland rolled on endlessly, broken by palms and clumps of trees like a manorial park.

As the time approached for the next halt, Guy said, 'I feel we should go cautiously now.'

'We must be coming close,' Cameron agreed.

Guy turned to Heighurst. 'It may be dangerous to proceed further by day – at least until we've made a reconnaissance. If you'd care to search out a site for a zariba I'll take Cameron on.'

'I've bin thinkin' on the same lines,' Heighurst replied, and pointed towards a patch of scrub on gently rising ground with rock outcrops to the left of the track. 'It looks the very thing – thick as a pig and the ground slopes away charmingly on three sides. We'd hold it against an army.'

'Capital!' Guy moved back to the donkeys to take his Martini Henry and once again Duff came forward to carry it for him. With Cameron, they set out again after the guides, now a good half a mile ahead, while Heighurst led the marines and donkeys up towards the thorn thicket.

The rain thinned as they went, and after a while stopped altogether. The clouds began to disperse; soon the whole sky to the southward was clear and the blue area grew at such a rate it was evident they would soon be exposed to the direct rays of the sun. They pressed on as fast as they could in the expanding heat, the clothes stiffening on their limbs; odd thorn branches stretched out, detaining them and scratching, drawing blood on their hands and wrists as they freed themselves. Way ahead their guides plodded on, giving no indication of seeing a sign of life.

After another twenty minutes the sun burst through. The heat was suddenly a brand, burning their shoulders. Guy reached for the canvas cap with attached handkerchief to cover the back of his neck which Duff had stitched for him while waiting for supper the night before, and placed it on his head. He turned. 'How's that?'

'You looks a proper Arab, sir.'

He had a vision of the little Sambuk, and conflicting sharp desire and remorse struck him again. He tried to shut out the images by thinking about Cameron, and what it was he could be up to. The Scot was striding effort-lessly and silently beside him, apparently sunk in his own thoughts. He remembered Saxmundham saying there was something deuced odd about a fellow that kept as zestful as Cameron in this climate. He realized how hot and weary he was, and pulled out his pocket watch.

'Spell-oh?'

To his surprise the Scot replied, 'Thank the Lord! I thought ye were carryin' on for ever!'

They threw themselves in the grass by the side of the track, there was no shade in sight, and sipped water from their flasks.

'It's odd we haven't seen a soul,' Guy said.

'No, the 'Lion' will not be dawdling. He'll mebbe expect us to come after him, and he had a good start, remember.'

Duff said quietly from his left, 'Don't move quick, sir, but look over there.'

He turned slowly in the direction the marine was pointing. A large swallowtail butterfly was resting, wings outstretched on a damp depression in the soil. The markings were a brilliant yellow on black, the hind wings each with red and black eyes. Guy stared fascinated. It was a perfect specimen. He wondered which of the scores of swallowtail varieties it was. Two whites fluttered together as he watched, chasing each other up and down before settling near it, their wings opening and closing nervously.

'Oh, Figgy!' he said, 'I'd dearly like him.' He noticed the marine was removing his helmet. 'You'll never catch him with that!'

Duff did not reply, but turned the helmet over, extracting a length of spring wire coiled round inside. Next he pulled out a folded muslin net which had been tucked all round inside the brow band, and after replacing the helmet on his head, began threading the wire into the net.

Guy watched, amazed.

'A stick, sir,' Duff said at last. 'That's all that's wanted.'

'Lor! Figgy, and where've you hidden the killing jar?'

'The 'erbs is in me baccy tin, sir.'

He looked round for a stick, but there was nothing in sight, nor any tree that might provide one. If they waited much longer they might lose the precious creature in any case; he took the net from Duff and rose, stooping cautiously towards the swallowtail, but taking care that his short shadow did not pass over it as he closed. Then lowering himself gingerly to one knee and holding the ring of the net with poised wrist like a quoit, he aimed and threw. It swirled, dropping sweetly over the butterfly, which flew up, fluttering into the muslin as it tried to escape. Cameron and Duff cried their congratulations, the marine hurrying over with the herbs in his tobacco tin.

Guy waited until the beautiful creature had exhausted its first frantic efforts, then eased it patiently along the folds of muslin until he could urge it into the tin. He snapped the lid shut.

Cameron and Duff were very silent. He thought it was because they were watching, but he had a sudden premonition that there was some other reason as he raised his eyes.

Copper coloured bare legs, gleaming with oil, ringed with anklets of fine, black monkey hair, met his gaze; from behind the muscular calves staves, hung with white hair, stood out horizontally like the wings of mercury. His marrow froze.

The faces of the warriors frowning down at him shone with a reddish clay and were encircled from lower lip to crown by a stiff frieze of ostrich feathers, which gave their heads a massive appearance. One pigtail hung down over each brow. On their shoulders, piles of kite's feathers were bunched promiscuously, and flowing lengths of coloured cottons hung like scarves over their backs or their bare, clayed and oiled chests to a hide knotted like a belt around the waist; otherwise they were stark naked.

Cameron's descriptions rose vividly to mind; el moran –young warriors of the Masai. They stood with exactly the careless arrogance he had described, stooping over their spears, some two dozen of them, all magnificent specimens over six feet tall with lean muscle. In their right hands they held spears, the blades two and a half feet long and several inches broad, the shafts tapering at the bottom into spikes, in their left hands oval shields of buffalo hide painted with sinuous designs in red, white and black; a short sword was clasped at their right side; at their left, he knew a knob-kerry or skullsmasher would be tucked into the waistband, but these were hidden by the shields.

He looked round at Cameron and Duff; they were still as a *tableau vivant,* the Scot with a restraining hand on the marine's arm.

Chapter Sixteen

On no account go for yer gun!' Cameron said. 'Rise slow – calm as ye like –'

Guy did as he was bid, staring into the finely formed, rather slanted dark eyes of the nearest moran.

He had no sooner straightened than there was a shout of command and the warriors turned into file and broke into a jog past him, shields held in front, vertical spearheads reflecting darts of light. Another command and they turned from file into line, making off at right angles; another shout and the line became a square; soon afterwards alternate ranks of the square were travelling past each other in opposite directions like bandsmen countermarching, the spears revolving in the warriors' hands. It was an impressive display of military discipline; Guy watched with what he hoped was cold contempt, his hands holding the tobacco tin and butterfly net well away from his revolver holster. Suddenly the warriors broke ranks and charged through the grass with spears shaking wildly, pulling their faces into fiendish masks; Guy noticed as in a nightmare, that each man had the two lower middle incisors missing. There was a shout and the charge broke, the warriors scattering for cover. Another shout and they formed in single file again.

As the alarming display continued, Guy saw with lowering heart another party of el moran on the track ahead, forcing their own two native guides before them at the points of their spears; they were making sport of them, laughing and jeering and calling as if they were driven cattle; the guides were speechless with terror.

This second party arrived as the tactical evolutions of the first group concluded; all gathered in an ellipse around Cameron, Duff and himself, gazing at them insolently as they leaned on the shafts of their spears with that curiously effeminate, languid droop, one foot raised and resting on the other calf.

Cameron bent, plucked a handful of grass, spat on it and went up to the warrior who had been issuing orders, now standing in front of Guy. He offered the grass to him.

The warrior stared for a moment, then thrust the point of his spear shaft into the ground and rested his shield against it. It seemed to be a signal for the rest of the group to do the same; afterwards they sank down beside their weapons, drawing their knees up to their chins and watching intently.

'*Gusak!*' the leader said.

Cameron thrust out his hand and the leader grasped it. '*Sobai?*' he demanded.

'*Ebai?*' Cameron replied, then turned and pointed at Guy. '*Lybon!*

The leader looked at Guy, his eyes moving from his face down to the tobacco tin and muslin net he was holding, and he started talking rapidly. Cameron evidently did not understand everything for he called to one of the guides, thrown to the ground nearby, to act as interpreter.

After several three-sided exchanges, Cameron turned to Guy, 'I have informed our friend, ye are a great white *lybon* —a medicine man ye might say. He was not inclined to doubt it after witnessing yer performance wi' the butterfly!' His eyes gleamed. 'I believe that is our strongest card just now. He wishes to know for what purpose ye caught it.'

'What d'you suggest?'

'I believe we may turn this to our considerable advantage. Let us say the butterfly is in connection with a spell ye wish to place on Fumo Akari at Katawa. These,' he waved at the warriors, 'are scouts for a cattle-raiding party. If they attack Katawa on account of Akari havin' the evil eye placed on him – it may be we can creep in by the back door while the battle's in progress and take our man!' His keen face was alight.

'Incite them to make war on Akari!'

'If it's moral doubts yer havin', forget them! This is a Masai war party. They'll attack someone whatever we do. They'll take someone's cattle, of that there's no shadow of doubt. It will only be justice if we persuade them to attack our man, who fully desairves his punishment. Is that not so!'

Guy was repelled by a tactic reminiscent of the Arab slave raiders, but the alternatives he turned over rapidly all fell on the weakness of their own position, and their lack of trade goods or bargaining counter of any description. 'So be it,' he said.

Cameron turned to the interpreter. Guy looked at the moran leader, noticing under the scowl and grease and clay, rather fine features ; his nose was straight and well raised, his cheekbones pronounced, his eyes with that slight Mongolian slant reminiscent of an ancient Egyptian relief were bright without the yellow-stained cornea of the Swahili, the lips thin and well formed. He lounged with aristocratic hauteur as he listened to the guide. Guy glanced at the other warriors ; many had equally fine, intelligent faces beneath their frightful scowls. He guessed this was one of the purer-blooded clans that Cameron had told him of; the aristocracy of the plateau. They had come a long way for their cattle-raiding. But the Scot had told him they found the coastal peoples easy game.

Cameron turned to him. 'Fumo Akari is at Katawa. The moran have seen his flag flying over the village. His warriors have been constructing a higher *boma* since they arrived and he has many with him. Our friend has heard of the "Lion's" defeat by our forces. I think it likely he was planning an attack in any event. If that makes yer mind easier!'

Guy wondered if this were so. Since last night he had found himself scrutinizing Cameron's every word for hidden motives.

'I've informed him the great white *lybon* will paralyse the "Lion",' Cameron went on. 'He may go in and smite his followers hip and thigh! I believe he looks forward to the prospect. It will give him great kudos.' He smiled, 'I think he'd appreciate it if ye'd give yer blessing to the enterprise!'

Guy looked at the leader. Fixing him with the stare he reserved for recalcitrant bluejackets, he took a step towards him, holding the tobacco tin out before the man's eyes, which became suddenly apprehensive. He pulled the lid open with a flourish, exposing the swallowtail, motionless. The warrior uttered a grunt and stared at the creature. Guy saw out of the corner of his eye, other warriors rising and approaching. He lowered the tin, and spat in it, taking care not to hit the lovely wings, snapping the lid on again before many of the others had a chance to see the talisman. He knew that if he had reached for his revolver and fired, or even clapped his hands, they would have scattered to the four winds. He took another step towards the moran leader, and spat in his face. The look of fear was replaced by the nearest to a smile Guy guessed he could produce. At once he was surrounded by a pressing throng calling, '*Lybon!*' and straining to touch his stained and torn tunic. He raised his hands and they stopped. He beckoned the nearest forward, and spat full on his nose; the warrior gave an exultant bound, and another took his place; Guy spat on him with the same result, repeating the process again and again as they jostled, fighting for his favour. After treating a score or more his mouth was dry and he broke off to gulp some water from his flask. He noticed Duff's expression, and was hard put to hold his stern face.

When all had been anointed, it was his turn to receive the leader's blessing; he did so without flinching, praying the others would not wish to join in. Fortunately, they seemed content to wait by their shields, staring at him. He noticed that their faces had lost something of the ferocious scowl they had held.

He turned to Cameron. 'The seance is ended!'

Cameron approached the leader with a short piece of thorn twig. After both he and the moran had spat on it, he broke the twig and handing one half to the warrior, removed his felt hat and thrust the other half into the band. They uttered formal expressions of farewell and friendship, and Cameron stepped back. The other moran were on their feet by this time, their shields and spears in their hands. At a shout of command they formed in two files and with a flourish and twirl of their spears made off up the path, breaking into a chant in time with their marching bare feet. They looked less frightening from the rear; the wide sweep of ostrich feathers around their heads, flowing white and red scarves, the extraordinary wings of white monkey hair extending from their calves seemed merely grotesque pantomime accessories. Nothing could disguise their splendid physique, nor take away from their fearsome reputation.

Guy stared after them, arms folded across his chest.

When they had gone some fifty yards Duff broke the silence with an oath.

Cameron turned to Guy. 'An unexpected spot of good fortune!' His eyes were bright. Guy wondered how he could go through such a bone-chilling experience without a sign of reaction.

'I half expectorated it,' he replied.

Cameron doubled up with laughter. He was human after all.

'For a *lybon* ye've an exceeding low form of wit.'

Guy opened the tobacco tin and gazed at the lovely yellow and black wings of his swallowtail.

'Did you get anything from the fellow with regard to where this place is?'

'Katawa. The track leads straight here. Haif a day's march —that's a fair trek by Masai standards. We will come to some *shambas,* native plantations, and a fair stand of trees. The village lies just beyond.'

'Let's get back. See how Heighurst and his merry men are faring.'

They started walking back.

'What are yer plans?' Cameron asked.

'Luncheon.'

'The Masai will commence their operations before dawn.'

'We must be in position by then. A night march —' He looked at the Scot, brows raised.

'Pray there are no clouds!'

'Gawd help us!' Duff muttered from behind. 'When I sees you spit in 'is eye, sir —'

They walked on in silence. The glare pressed from all sides. The country which a few hours earlier had been soaked, shimmered in the heat like a desert; already dry cracks were appearing in the track. Nothing moved save themselves.

Guy was called as the sun set; he rose through deep violet and green depths with heavy head and limbs stiff, and levered himself up, dislodging a shelter of sticks and palm fronds Duff must have placed above his head in the heat of the afternoon, remembering with a sudden empty feeling the night march ahead. Sleep had only served to make him feel more tired. He noticed Cameron crouching beside a pile of grass and fern and gnarled branches that had been placed in the centre of the space inside the *boma* the marines had constructed. He was shielding a lighted match from the slight breeze. Soon flames were leaping up the dry grass; wisps of smoke blew across the red sky.

The duty cook had made a hash of bully beef, biscuit and dried peas which he started heating over the fire.

'Quite makes one's mouth water,' Heighurst said as they waited. 'Though I dare say that's difficult for some just now!'

Cameron grinned.

Heighurst glanced at Guy. 'Fire-pump jack! It's made a considerable impression on our lads. Figgy insisted you was hittin' the mark at ten feet.'

Guy smiled at the recollection of Duff's expression. 'Good manners are important.'

After eating, they washed the meal down with cocoa, leaving just sufficient of the tepid, yellowing marsh water to fill their flasks for the march. Guy would have liked to leave some water in the camp for their return, but none had been found in the vicinity.

The sergeant approached Heighurst. 'Arvey's took with a shiverin' fit, sir. I don't like the looks of Brown neither.'

'You've come to the right man, sarn't!' Heighurst gestured towards Guy. 'A regular first-class medicine man, don't you know!'

The sergeant turned a wooden face. 'I don't know as it'd do 'em a power of good, sir, that *lybon* treatment – not in their unhappy condition, sir!'

Heighurst's lips turned up. 'Very good, sarn't, you shall have me instead. Lead on!' He rose, and Guy followed the few paces to the men's side of the fire.

Harvey was a giant Yorkshireman with a high-boned face and quiet, pale eyes. As they leaned over him he was seized by a shivering fit, and his voice was shaky as he tried to answer Heighurst's inquiries through chattering teeth.

''Wenchin' again!' Heighurst said, patting him encouragingly on the top of his head. As he straightened he said, 'A strong dose of quinine'll set him to rights in no time, sarn't.'

'Sir!'

They passed on to Brown, a few paces away, a dark and thin-faced private with heavy black stubble over his lower face; his eyes were watery and he complained of pains in the guts and continuous visits to the head. Heighurst put a hand to his brow.

'Well, Brown – you don't look too hot!'

'I don't feel it, sir.'

'No, you don't.' He turned to Guy as they moved away. 'We shall have to leave those two poor fellows.'

Guy nodded. 'And two to look after them.' And the donkeys and their owners, he thought: six men to defend the camp in case of an attack; he didn't like to imagine the result. But to send the sick men back on the donkeys to the *boma* near the swamp would be an even more hazardous undertaking. They would have to take their chance here.

The odds were that the Masai parties and the 'Lion's' men would all be fully occupied around Katawa.

Heighurst must have been thinking on the same lines; he said, 'It would make precious little difference if we left four men,' and turned to the sergeant who had followed. 'What's your opinion, sarn't?'

"Ow many men will be required at Katawa?'

'An excellent question.' He looked at Guy, 'We leave two?'

Guy nodded. 'The least we can do for the poor fellows. And, sarn't – have everyone black their faces and hands from the embers before we proceed!'

They set off fifteen minutes later, one native guide in the lead so that the two could take turn and turn at the most nerve-racking position. They were followed closely by four marines – to be changed at hourly intervals – two at skirmishing distance beside the path. Guy, Heighurst and Cameron followed some thirty yards behind the advance guard with the main party of marines closed up in two files, the four porters in the centre carrying the Gardner gun, rockets, gun-cotton and ammunition.

Mosquitoes attacked, directly they left the smoke of the fire; they buttoned their shirts or tunics to their necks and slapped, hurrying on the pace, jigging and hopping when the bites became too much to bear. Later, as they passed the point where they had been surprised by the Masai, the mood changed; the bites became secondary to the possibility of warriors or ferocious animals hidden in the dark on either side. They walked in strained silence, every sense over-stretched; the deeper black of stunted

trees became el moran scouts approached by the skirmishers on bent knees with rifles at the ready, while the main
party halted and levelled their guns in support; darker
patches of grass or reed were crouching cats; the outrun-
ners of a herd of zebra circling hyenas until they heard the
high, whistling bark and the beat of hooves; large clumps
of bush became solitary rhinos, scenting before the charge.
Even the wheezing of a branch or palm frond stirring in
the breeze was charged with dangerous intent.

The Masai presence had not been envisaged in the
planning for the flying column and the more Guy thought
about it the more threatening it became; it would require
extraordinary good fortune to reach Katawa without alert-
ing their pickets, and he wondered what hope there would
be in the darkness of establishing their identity as the party
of the great white *lybon*. Did all the Masai even know
about the *lybon?* If skirmishing broke out they would be
at a disadvantage, picking targets by guesswork while the
warriors superior numbers allowed them to encircle them.

An owl hooted nearby; they froze; it was a favourite
Masai call. He looked at Cameron, and saw him trying to
peer through the night. There were no further sounds, nor
sign of movement, and after a while they walked on.

'It was mebbe a good sign,' Cameron whispered. 'It
might mean they're expecting us.'

'You told them we would be making a night march?'

'No, not exactly. I said we would be with them at
Katawa in the morning – whether in body or spirit I left
to their imagination!'

They halted at midnight and rested in a hollow square facing outwards with their rifles on their knees. From the distance they heard a weird barking which continued at intervals. After it the silence was even more intense.

Guy turned to Cameron. 'How far now, d'you suppose?'

'Two or three hours' march should suffice – if the Masai were correct.'

As they started out again, they heard some way ahead the low, reverberating growl of a lion; it was the first they had heard that night.

'His majesty!' Heighurst said.

It was answered by a roar from nearer to the right.

The guide ahead called out softly, '*Shimo!*'

'A hole in the path,' Cameron whispered, and turned to the sergeant behind, 'Pass it back!'

'Look out for an 'ole,' the sergeant said, and they heard the message repeated towards the rear.

Another owl hooted, or the same one perhaps, or a Masai picket; it came from ahead to the left. Guy had an unpleasant sensation of watching eyes as they advanced further towards where the moran would be camped.

He saw the advance guard freeze into patches of darkness, strangely small as they crouched, and put out a hand to halt the marines behind as he crouched too, bringing his gun to the ready. Way ahead something moved off quickly, rustling through the grass; he saw several shapes, more and more of them, bounding away, and the pale gleam of antlers. The advance guard was on the move again. He rose and followed.

They stopped at two o'clock some distance before the dark outline of a stand of trees, or a wood perhaps which stretched ahead. Cameron guessed they were the trees mentioned by the Masai as near Katawa; the distance fitted in with their estimate of the march. He questioned the guides, but as always they were vague.

'I'd give something to know where your friends are,' Heighurst said.

'I fancy they know exactly where we are.'

'I trust they know who we are.'

Guy looked at the massy dark of the trees. 'D'you suppose we should skirt around them?'

'If we are near Katawa,' Cameron replied, 'and if our friends are camped this side, I'd be inclined to agree with ye.' He spoke to the two guides, reporting afterwards that they were happy about staying in the open, but not about finding the way; the path led into the trees.

Guy pulled out his pocket compass. 'We'll navigate round.'

He stood, and the square dissolved into two files behind, while the new advance guard stepped out ahead in the direction he indicated. As a check to his compass course, he glanced up at the stars of the Southern Cross. Almost immediately the guide was in trouble up against barriers of thorn. He took the lead himself, turning and doubling to evade the barriers of undergrowth until he hardly knew in which direction they had come. After some twenty minutes of vain stumbling over roots and hummocks, caught and held by thorns, trousers torn, legs and arms lacerated, hearing the curses of the marines turn from occasional stifled mutters to audible oaths, he began to think they would still be doubling and twisting in the wilderness when the Masai attack began. Assailed by growing despair, he stopped and held a whispered conference; there was little discussion before it was decided they should attempt to get back on to the path. Casting around for a way, they at once stumbled on a game track that seemed to lead in the right direction and roughly parallel to the trees. Guy led along it thankfully.

After a while it became apparent that the trees were the beginnings of a forest which stretched on their right as far as they could see. Guy wondered how they were going to find the path again in the thick of it when the track they were on began to swing to the left around scattered palms and a low copse of heavier trees. Peering at the face of his watch he saw with a start that it was a quarter past three; they had lost more time than he had realized. There was precious little remaining before first light. He was about to suggest an immediate turn to try and regain the path when Cameron gave a low exclamation.

He was in the vegetation beside the track, bending over a plant whose leaves, spreading from a central stem, alternated with bell-shaped flowers, pale in the shadows. '*Sim-sim,*' he muttered, 'Sesame plants.' He straightened, pointing to the trees. 'Mangoes and coconut palms. We're in a plantation –overgrown and disused I suspect.' He straightened. 'Gentlemen, I believe we've arrived!'

'Where d'you suppose the village lies?'

'I'd guess, beyond the copse. At the edge of the forest, mebbe. I believe we should strike out through here.' He pointed off to the right.

'Open sesame!' Heighurst muttered.

The grass had grown thick where the plantation had been, but the thorn patches were neither so high, nor so dense as before, and they were able to take a more or less direct path towards the edge of the copse. When they reached its shelter, Guy halted the party and went on with Cameron and the more intelligent guide; they kept low in the dew-soaked vegetation, peering through the dark of the forest for any glimpse of the thorn *boma* around the village.

After a hundred yards they heard stealthy movements ahead, and stopped, ducking low. The movements continued. Guy raised his head until his eyes were just clear, staring towards the direction from which the faint rustlings came. At first he could see nothing, but as the sounds drew ahead across a clump of paler foliage he saw a figure silhouetted, then another and another moving slowly in file from right to left some two hundred yards away. The massy headgear of the moran was unmistakable.

'Masai!' he whispered.

The stealthy procession continued, silent figures crossing the pale area, one after another like a shadow show. He pulled out his watch. It was after four.

'They are deploying,' he hissed.

'They will attack with the furrst of the light.'

'Not long.'

'We must be close.'

'I suggest we make our way back.'

They turned and crept back towards the copse, keeping lower than before and examining the ground minutely before they ventured on it lest a sound give them away. It was a slow progress. By the time they reached Heighurst again Guy thought he detected a hint of lightening in the sky to the east. He described in low tones what they had seen.

'What d'you propose?' Heighurst asked.

'Wait until we can see. What do you propose?'

'Nothin' else for it. I've had me fill of blind man's buff.'

They tensed as a new sound broke the stillness, relaxing again as they recognized the lowing of cattle.

Cameron sucked in his breath. 'The "Lion" is awake.' He added, 'He's moving the herd to shelter.'

'Our friends will not have it all their own way.'

'By no means. I've a notion they will have cause to welcome our intervention.'

In addition to the lowing of the cattle, they heard cocks crowing and the first bird calls from the copse above. An owl hooted in the forest. It was answered by another with a double call, and another from far away. Guy shivered at the thought of the slaughter about to commence. He looked over his shoulder at the eastern sky; a hint of lightness was edging the deep black of the trees. A shriek sounded from ahead —animal or human? The bird calls stilled for a moment.

In the silence a terrible yell rose, piercing the marrow, gaining an inhuman pitch as it was taken up by hundreds of throats, falling, then borne up again to new heights of ferocity. The flesh of Guy's neck and arms crept. He strained his eyes towards the sounds, but could see nothing.

As the first waves abated, the note of a horn rose high, followed by the crack of firearms, desultory at first but growing in numbers. The flashes were visible through the trees ; they were concentrated from the direction he had seen the Masai take. He turned to Heighurst, 'A scratch breakfast? I fancy we shan't be overheard!'

'Sarn't!' Heighurst said, hardly troubling to keep his voice low. 'Break out the Huntley and Palmers!'

They cracked hard biscuit between their teeth, washing it down with miserly drafts of the evil marsh water, and tried without success to interpret the course of the fight from the fierce sounds. Details of their blackened faces began to emerge as the light spread overhead. They looked weary and gaunt. Those with beards came off best in a comparison ; two days' stubble and dark splodges of dried *l* lood from mosquitoes and thorn scratches had turned the others into hardened tramps; their grey and brown, shredded and blood-spattered clothes confirmed the impression. Heighurst was scarcely recognizable. Guy wondered if he looked such a desperate villain himself.

There was little to be seen from the battleground; the Masai were evidently using cover or re-grouping after the first assault, but the outline of the *boma* began to emerge as a solid grey line of bush beyond the undergrowth at the edge of the forest. Spasmodic flashes rippled from it, and bursts of white smoke thinned above.

Directly they had finished eating, Guy rose and led across the open grass between the copse and the forest, crawling, soaked by the dew and bent behind thickets. As they reached the trees, Heighurst gave the order to fix bayonets.

"Ow do we get on with the savages we chummed up with?' the sergeant asked amid the reassuring click of metal on metal.

'That's a poser, sarn't!'

'It's my guess they'll not prove hostile,' Cameron said. His eyes were sunk with tiredness, but were very green and clear.

'Trouble might arise if they mistake your intentions, sarn't,' Guy said.

Heighurst nodded. 'Let us give them no cause to do so.'

Guy turned to the marines, 'You'll recognize the Masai from their headdress of ostrich plumes.' He indicated an elliptical shape with his hands. 'And wings of white monkey hair on their legs, and anklets of black hair. Also a kidskin tied around their waist. If they have none of these marks they are the enemy.'

'Hear that lads,' the sergeant said, 'Haloes an' wings is angels. Correct, sir?'

'Well put, sarn't! Understand, our object is not to attract the particular attention of either party, simply to approach the village until we can observe the nature of the defences, then lay our plans to get inside to the "Lion".'

'Sir!'

'Discretion must be the better part –' he turned again to the men, 'although I have no doubts whatever of your courage as Britons should the necessity arise.' He looked along the intent, tired faces, and back to the sergeant. 'I never saw a body of men gave me more confidence, sarn't.'

'Sir! Picked men, sir, all of ' em.'

'Depend on it, we shall bag our lion!' He turned to Heighurst.

'You're aware,' Heighurst said, looking at the privates, Our object is strictly limited.' He pointed to the village. 'Simply to take the sultan in there. Alive. Nothing more. Directly we have cut him out we shall retire. Should any-one become separated, the rendezvous after shall be the copse –' he glanced at Guy, who nodded – 'where we made breakfast.

The marines growled their understanding.

Heighurst told off an advance guard of six men to pro-ceed in skirmishing order, and a machine-gun and rocket party of another six to stick close by the porters and guides, and with an admonition to the rest to stick close as glue, he signalled the advance. The skirmishers darted off in twos from thicket to thicket, dulled bayonets raised.

The sounds of fighting grew louder as they went, and another war yell rose from a different direction, as if the Masai had massed for the main assault on another sec-tion of the defences. They took advantage of the renewed clamour to break into a fast jog, not bothering to go qui-etly, nor entering the forest, but weaving by the edge of the trees. Soon they had a clearer view of the *boma* and saw the sultan's red flag inside.

In the open grass beyond a hand-to-hand encounter was taking place between the attackers and a party of warriors who had evidently sortied from the village. The thudding of spears on hide shields, grunts and high cries were interspersed with renewed outbreaks of yelling; clubs glistened briefly in the pre-dawn light, spearheads flew, painted bodies and painted shields writhed in confused snakes of movement, dark limbs upraised, shining like dew for an instant. Guy had a sudden insight into the nature of his trade – a glimpse of man of a piece with the animal kingdom, all pieces in the grand design, red as nature, blood the symbol. He had a revelation of his own nature, remembering his feelings as he had knocked over the two warriors with successive shots.

The vision faded. He searched among the trees where sounds of another conflict had broken out seeing for the first time above the line of the *boma* the stout palisade of the entrance gate. He ran forward to the skirmishers waiting for the rest of the party to close up and directed them towards the gate. They entered the trees.

It soon became evident from the sounds that the main struggle was taking place about the gate they were making for, and they circled it, almost over-running a large party of Masai crouching silently, fortunately wholly occupied with the fighting beyond them; evidently they were a waiting reserve. Guy signalled a cautious withdrawal, then set out on a larger circle back into the forest, crossing a path leading to the gate, but catching no more than a glimpse of the struggle as they darted over and pushed through burgeoning, thick-leaved vegetation and creepers beyond.

Having skirted the area, they pushed back towards the *boma* again, reaching it so quickly that it was evident it curved outwards. An attempt had been made to burn the vegetation immediately around it, but trees and thickets had prevented more than a token clearing being made. Guy could see no sign of life within or without; it seemed they had chanced on an unengaged sector. He examined the great thorn fence. It was too high to be scaled without ladders, too thick and loosely formed to be cleanly blown without several attempts, he guessed. He looked up into the trees, wondering if they might offer a chance of climbing along a branch and dropping over the other side; they were too far away, but as he looked an idea formed. He turned to Heighurst and pointed to a clump containing several high trees, thickly branched.

'Suppose we place charges in one or two of those trunks on the side away from the *boma?*'

Heighurst looked from the trees to the thorn hedge, and back to the trees. 'It's worth a shot.'

He formed the men into a defensive square with the Gardner gun party away to the side, while Guy seized the axe from the porter and running to the nearest of the large trees, started hacking at the trunk. He fashioned a deep cut slanting into the heart of the timber, then handed the axe to a native guide, indicating that he should do the same in the next trunk. Collecting one of the parcels of gun-cotton, pre-prepared with fuse extending, he thrust it into the wedge-shaped aperture. The guide had not succeeded in carving a deep enough bite by the time he finished, and he took the axe from him to complete the job, throwing it back afterwards and pointing to a third trunk.

When all three had been cut and charged with gun-cotton, Heighurst ordered the marines back into the forest to lie flat. Guy lit the fuses and ran back after them, counting. As he reached 'fifteen', the first charge went off, closely followed by the other two. They heard splinters of timber spattering through the undergrowth, and a great creaking and cracking of branches as the trees descended and settled in a cloud of smoke and dust. Guy rose, giving a shout of triumph as he saw that all three had fallen at varying angles over the *boma,* their branches and foliage interlocked.

Leaving the porters and guides in the care of the machine-gun party outside the *boma,* he and Heighurst beckoned the rest forward, each taking separate trunks at the leap with drawn revolvers, running up the slight incline to the lowest branches as Cameron ran up the third tree. They lost sight of one another as they threaded their way through the foliage, working down to the ground along what had been the higher branches beyond the line of the thorn barrier; calling to each other softly, they met again, still within the shelter of the leaves. They waited until all the marines had joined, then spread as far as possible in an even line before moving forward.

Emerging from the shelter of the foliage, they were confronted by a small group of warriors and elders advancing cautiously, one or two with levelled muskets or match-locks, several with bows drawn, the rest with spears poised. Their eyes widened at the unexpected sight of the uniforms, and they hesitated an instant.

'Front *rank, fire!*' Heighurst shouted.

The marines were already on the knee; as the volley rang out, Guy took a warrior with a long head crowned with a profusion of feathers as his point of aim. The man held a spear poised and a painted shield across his body; the thick lips were open, exposing dark gums and irregular, stained stumps of teeth. As he squeezed the trigger he saw a hole appear in the wavy white lines near the top of the shield; he held the man's gaze, seeing a look of surprise fixed for an instant before the arm dropped and he fell. Four others fell near him. Guy heard the bump of a musket firing, and felt the wind and phizz of an arrow close by his neck, a cry of surprise from a marine to the right.

'Rear rank, *fire!*'

The group before them broke before Heighurst's order was out; shouts of alarm sounded above the grunts and cries of those hit by the second point-blank volley.

'*Advance!*'

The marines rose with a deep roar, bayonets pointed. The warriors were already in full retreat. Guy fired to increase their panic, dashing after them, caught up once again in the fever of the chase, firing without aiming, catching a glimpse out of the corner of his eye of wide-eyed women staring from thatch-hung doorways, pendulous breasts, children, fowls scattering, a great round calabash breaking in small pieces as a child ran full tilt into it, its eyes over its shoulders white and round ; a heart-rending shriek of terror as it fell.

Ahead the fleeing group scattered in all directions between beehive-shaped huts. Chasing what seemed to be the largest number, he emerged on to a central dirt path similar to the main road traversing Witu. Heighurst was close behind him; they glanced at one another. Up and down the length of the avenue there was no sign of an imposing hut or building such as a chief might occupy. Guy looked around for Cameron. To his surprise he saw him down on one knee almost hidden between two huts, bringing his Express rifle to his shoulder; the flash of light from the moving barrel drew his attention, or he might not have seen him. Following the direction of aim, Guy saw two white-robed, bearded Arabs standing near the fallen trees they had just come from. They held rifles loosely, glancing about them as if unsure of the nature of the new threat. A few warriors were grouped behind them. Guy guessed one of the Arabs was the 'Lion'.

He looked back at Cameron and yelled, 'Don't shoot!'

He heard the report even as he shouted. Turning, he saw one of the white-robed figures fall.

He dashed towards the Scot, his initial surprise flaring into anger, 'You've killed him!'

Cameron stared up, a strange light in his eyes. Guy had an impulse to strike him, but swung away instead towards the fallen Arab, calling to Heighurst as he went.

The unhurt Arab was bending over his wounded companion, and the surrounding warriors made no show of resistance as he and Heighurst ran up, followed by most of the marines.

The breast of the fallen Arab's robe was spreading with blood, and the man was coughing weakly. His face was pale, his dark eyes blinking; he looked up at Guy, and seized with a fit of coughing moved a hand to his chest. Blood spotted the fingers and the neck and shoulders of his tunic. Guy saw his teeth mottled red, and the greying hairs of his beard at the corners of his mouth matted with blood.

'Fumo Akari!' he said urgently; there was little time.

The man's gaze shifted towards his companion, and Guy looked up, too. 'Fumo Akari?'

The standing Arab had a full, fleshy face and hard bright eyes, heavy lidded, narrowed and puckered as he returned the gaze. His lips were full and red between fine black hairs of moustache and beard; it was a sensuous, powerful face. His forehead, partly covered by the diagonal folds of a turban was broad and heavy. He stared at Guy without speaking, then looked beyond him. 'You aim for Lion, Mr Cameron?' His heavy lips drooped cynically.

Guy looked round. Before the Scot had a chance to reply, there was a shot from one of the marines who had formed a defensive square around them. An instant afterwards another fired from a different side. Guy saw warriors approaching them from every direction, grouping cautiously behind and between the huts. The shots halted them momentarily, but the numbers continued to swell; several had muskets aimed. Another rifle cracked, and a musket went off in the air as the warrior holding it spun, crying out briefly.

Guy turned to Heighurst. 'Time to retire!'

He wondered what to do about the wounded Arab. He was almost certain now that Akari was the one standing, but there was no time for further inquiry. Looking down, he saw the problem was resolved. The Arab on the ground stared sightlessly, his head to one side, lips parted.

Heighurst issued orders preparing his men for volleys followed by an advance diagonally right to cover their retreat. Guy swung his revolver on the standing Arab and motioned him with them towards the trees. The man glanced round at the warriors massing on all sides and stared back disdainfully. Guy shifted the gun quickly to his left hand and brought his right with all his weight behind it up beneath the Arab's breast bone. His breath was expelled in a shuddering cough. He struck him under the jaw. The fleshy head jerked back, and the man sprawled. Guy picked up his fallen rifle, fired it at one of the groups preparing to attack, then smashed it butt first to the ground. Bending quickly he pulled the Arab's jewelled dagger from its waistband sheath and hurled it in a high arc away over the *boma,* then seizing the limp right arm, dragged the man up in a fireman's lift, and turned for the trees.

Heighurst gave the order for the first volley as the warriors, raising a wild yell, came forward. Guy heard his voice steadying the men above the reports; then a second volley cracked out.

The Arab was a dead weight, but as he half ran, half stumbled for the cover of the branches, hearing Heighurst order the advance, he felt muscles stirring under his grip; he tensed for the attack. It came just as he reached the branches; he felt the man's hand on his cheek, fingers probing for his eyes. He heaved down on the right arm, ducking and launching his shoulder forward. The Arab sailed over, landing with a cry of surprise in the foliage, twigs and branches cracking under his weight. Guy leaped after him, and finding his head gave him a swinging blow with the inside of his fist; he felt the hairs at the side of the jaw rough against his knuckles. Scrambling up, he took both the man's arms and dragged him further into the foliage, draping him over a thicker branch. He paused, wondering how Heighurst was faring.

'Fumo Akari!' he said, gazing into the Arab's eyes.

The man stared back malevolently.

There was a rustle of leaves, and he saw Cameron pushing towards them; his gaze hardened.

'Help me up with him,' he said curtly.

The marines plunged in around them as they struggled to heave the Arab up into a thicker branch giving access to the trunk of the tree; the man seemed resigned to his fate, neither struggling nor assisting. The sergeant joined them and eased their task with brutal use of the bayonet, drawing a yelp as he plunged the point into his thigh.

'Ah!' he exclaimed throatily. "E moved too quick!'

'Sarn't!' Guy cautioned.

He pulled the Arab with him along the trunk; the man slipped, either by accident or design, nearly bringing Guy with him on top of the thorns.

'Sarn't,' Guy called, 'the bayonet!'

The Arab cried out as the sergeant moved towards them, a glint in his eye.

'Assist him to cooperate, sarn't!'

The Arab looked up wildly, struggling desperately to heave himself back to the trunk; Guy heaved.

'He's trying, sarn't.'

"E can try a little 'arder, sir.' He thrust the bayonet towards the Arab's left thigh as he swung on Guy's arm almost to his feet again on a main branch. There was a piercing yell as the flesh of his buttock drove on into the point of the bayonet. The sergeant grunted, jerking the weapon out, gleaming red. The Arab fell back again, moaning and writhing, nearly jerking Guy's arm from its socket.

'Get up!' he yelled. 'Sarn't!'

'No −!' the Arab's voice rose to a crescendo of despair, and he fought himself back to the trunk.

The sergeant plucked a handful of leaves and wiped his blade. 'That were a bloody shame, sir!'

'*Alive!*' Guy hissed.

"E looks lively enough, sir!'

Guy set off again down the trunk, the Arab keeping desperately close on his heels, the sergeant following, Cameron just behind. Heighurst and most of the marines had taken the other trees and were forming a defensive line in the burnt stubble outside the *boma* as Guy and the Arab scrambled down. They ran into the shelter of the undergrowth, and Heighurst retired his men after them.

'All your fellows back?' Guy asked, keeping a lock on the Arab's arm.

The sergeant started counting, then counted again. Before he had finished, one of the men said, 'Figgy copped it, sarn't.'

Guy started.

'Duff!' the sergeant said, repeating the name again more loudly. There was no response.

Guy s mind was numb; not Figgy! He glanced at the Arab, then at Heighurst. 'Look after the prisoner, will you!'

Heighurst regarded him coldly.

Guy returned the stare. 'I'll not lose Figgy.'

''We'll probably lose both of you.'

'If I'm not out in a quarter of an hour, make your way back.'

Heighurst's eyes were steady. 'I shall judge the case when the time arrives.'

Guy pushed the Arab towards him.

Heighurst seized the man and swung him round. 'Four volunteers!'

A chorus rose from the group. The sergeant pointed to the three nearest to him, "Aggis, Shorty, Downs – you'll do!'

Guy looked into their exhausted faces, and wondered if he had the right. . . .

'The rest of you, cover the rescue party,' Heighurst said crisply.

They ran forward, bent, using cover to the edge of the trees, hearing a low shout from a thicket to the left, where the Gardner gun and rocket parties lay hidden; a moment later they heard the rattle of the machine-gun. Almost immediately the marines on the left of the line opened with single shots. Guy caught a glimpse of muskets and spears, and saw a dark figure falling not more than thirty yards away through the trees. The firing stopped. The forest was quiet again. He beckoned to the sergeant, and for the second time sprinted across the semi-clearing for the fallen trees and took the nearest trunk in a flying leap, nearly slipping off the far side in his haste. He ran up the incline, hearing the heavy boots of the sergeant close behind; he realized with a sick shock that he hadn't re-loaded his revolver; he tried to think how many times he had fired.

Pulling himself through the narrow branches over the *boma,* he became aware of a flurry of activity, breaking twigs and rustling leaves just ahead, as if some heavy animal were trying to force a passage. The branches parted and he caught sight of a dark face with scarred cheeks and elongated earlobes hung with coiled brass; the eyes widened as they saw him. He lashed out with his boot. There was a cry of pain as he felt the nose squash, and the face had disappeared. He pointed the revolver and climbed forward cautiously, wondering if the scrabbling ahead meant advancing or retreating savages, thankful for the presence of the sergeant, breathing heavily behind his shoulder. As he pulled a branch aside, he saw the back of a warrior leaping from him; he went on with renewed confidence, soon able to work his way to the ground.

As the sergeant jumped down a little distance away, he heard a voice from the leaves behind. It sounded like Duff.

'Figgy! Where the devil are you?'

"Ere, sir!'

He turned and pulled himself through the branches towards the voice, suddenly anxious about what he would find.

The first thing he saw was the glinting edge of Duff's bayonet, then he saw the marine's eyes in the shadows.

'Are you hurt?' he asked, knowing the answer from the drawn expression. Duff was crouched like a wounded animal at bay under the shelter of a thick spread of branches.

'Me leg, sir.'

Guy saw the left leg of his trousers dyed red from mid-thigh to calf. An artery? He heard a dripping sound on the leaves beneath and saw that they too were dyed red and wet. He thrust his revolver in its holster and seized a flap of his own trousers, torn around the calves by thorns and branches, pulling upwards. The duck split straight up his leg to the waistband. He snatched for his pocket knife, opened it and cut the long strip off. He heard Duff slump into the leaves; he was half sideways, half crouching against a branch, his head lolling.

'Sarn't!' Guy called.

'Sir!' The voice was close above.

'Take his shoulders!'

He saw one of the other marines peering at him through the foliage; he wondered what had become of the warriors; the rustling sounds had ceased. Perhaps they were grouping, ready to surprise them directly they left the shelter of the foliage. 'Watch the front!' he called, and turned to help the sergeant, who had crept through under the thick branches above Duff. Between them they hauled the marine's head and upper body back until Guy could reach the leg. He cut the material away from the upper thigh above the thickly bloodied area and felt for the throb of the artery inside the leg. Pulling his handkerchief out, he rolled it into a hard pad, thrust it across the course of the artery and placed the duck he had cut from his own trousers over and around the leg, twisting at the same time, and tied a reef knot. Taking the knife up again, he sliced at one of the thinner branches above his head, working desperately until he had severed it, working again to cut it to a short length. He inserted it under the duck and twisted, seeing the crude tourniquet bite deep, and the depressed flesh go pale. Taking his whistle from around his neck, he used the lanyard to bind the stick in position.

'That'll do while we heave him out.'

'Shorty,' the sergeant called, 'Where's the niggers?'

There was a rustle of leaves and twigs, and after a moment the answer, 'Can't see, sarge –'

'Give us an 'and then. Shake it up!'

With one of the marines wedged in the fork of a thick branch above and Guy guiding the legs, they manoeuvred Duff upwards and dragged him slowly towards the trunk. The marine known as 'Aggis collected the rifles and backed after them. A trail of blood was scraped along the bark. Guy's mind filled with a mixture of relief that they had found Duff and concern about his condition; he wondered how they would get him back to the surgeon in Witu in time to save his life.

Haif a dozen marines were waiting under the tree the other side of the *boma* as they eased Duff's inert form along the trunk, and they lowered him into waiting, upraised arms.

Guy felt suddenly exhausted; he half jumped, half fell to the ground, hearing as if from a very long way off a new sound of exultant chanting from inside the village; he wondered vaguely what it was as he glanced right and left along the clearing. There was not a soul to be seen. Heighurst met them at the edge of the trees.

'Your spell seems to have worked for our friends,' he said.

He realized what the chanting signified, and shivered. Images of the victorious Masai running wild among the women and children and elders of the village overwhelmed him. 'The poor devils!'

Heighurst put out a hand to steady him. 'You look done up!'

Chapter Seventeen

Cameron slung his Express over his shoulder and set out with Heighurst after game for the evening pot. Guy watched them walk away. The spring had gone from the Scot's step. Since the affair at Katawa that morning he had been a shadow of his usual self. He had scarcely passed a word all day; his eyes had been withdrawn, his mouth clamped shut. For the first time in Guy's experience he had looked and walked like a tired man. Even his jaunty felt hat appeared to sag. By contrast Heighurst was straight and brisk despite the long day's march which had brought them back to within striking distance of Witu.

He wondered whether the Scot's listlessness was reaction to that idiot pot shot at the Arab and his own obvious anger, or whether there was another reason. He had been puzzling over the episode all day. Cameron could so easily have called out and given chase when he saw the Arabs, instead he had made off to the side and taken deliberate aim. At whom had he aimed? The one he had hit and killed or the 'Lion' beside him? Under normal circumstances at that range there was no question but that he would have hit

403

his target; he was an excellent shot. The circumstances had not been normal; he had been discovered and shouted at in the act of pulling the trigger. He thought of the strange look in the Scot's eyes as he had come running up; he had sensed anger and frustration, and guilt perhaps?

He strolled past a group of marines dragging branches to a pile of firewood, and came to where Duff had been made as comfortable as possible on heaped ferns beneath blankets. The marine s eyes were closed, but he seemed to sense Guy's approach, and he opened them, moving when he saw who it was as if he should not be lying flat out in the presence of his officer.

'Don't be an ass, Figgy!'

His eyes were sunk in dark hollows, his cheeks appeared yellow beneath the grime, the old bullet wound strangely shrivelled. Guy leant over him.

'How d'you feel?'

'Not too 'ot, sir.'

He stared up intensely. Guy had a feeling that he didn't expect to live. He sank down, by the man's shoulders.

'Chin up, Figgy!' On an impulse, he reached for the tobacco tin with the swallowtail inside, and opened it, removing the fine grass with which he had sought to protect the lovely wings from damage. 'Remember, I'm the *lybon!*'

Duff smiled dutifully.

'I dare say you distrust that mumbo-jumbo, Figgy. I don't. I fancy this fellow gave our Masai friends the victory this morning.'

The marine smiled again.

'I do indeed. It's a matter of belief, Figgy.' He thought of his own belief, wondering after that sickening victory chant and all it implied whether he could find it again. He reached out a hand to the blanket over Duff's shoulders. 'We shall be in Witu tomorrow – early. You'll be all right then.'

"Aggis told me 'Ow you would come back for me, sir –'

'Lor' –!' Guy gripped the shoulder, and went on quickly, 'You told me about a curious conversation you had once with this fellow, Cameron, d'you recall it?'

'Up the main top.'

'That's it.'

'I shan't forget that, sir.'

'Can you remember what was said?'

"Well –' Duff gazed up at the sky, his brow wrinkling. 'Afore I get up to 'im, 'e were beggin' forgiveness. It weren't 'is or'nary manner of speakin' –' His voice faltered.

'Don't worry, Figgy. Get some sleep!'

He was about to rise and leave, but the marine said, 'No, sir, I'm right enough now. Well, I'm about to shave off nice an' quiet when 'e ketches sight of me an' invites me up there with 'im an' makes out as 'ow 'e's jes' recitin'. Next thing we was avin' this yarn about relijin an' death an' 'ow diff'rent relijins 'ave diff'rent understandin's concernin' death. The Masai now, they don't Old with salvation, only annihilation, 'e says. Death is the end for them, an' to prove it they don't bury 'em – they 'eave 'em out to the edge of the village to be eaten by wild beasts –' His gaze shifted to Guy. 'I shouldn't like that, sir.'

'Figgy!' Guy said sharply. 'There won't be any hyenas within a thousand miles when your time comes.'

'Sir, you remember that rhino – ?' His voice was urgent.

'Shall I ever forget him'

'The monster with the two 'orns. I got it for you, sir. I told the sarge it were yours –'

'What on earth are you talking about?' Guy wondered if he were delirious.

'The 'orn, sir. I cut it off that big rhino.'

Guy stared at him. 'You haven't been carrying a rhino horn with you!'

'In me blanket pack.'

Guy didn't know what to say.

'Watch the sarge, sir. 'E got to 'ear what they do for you –in the way of a love potion. 'E wouldn't stop at nothing, the sarge wouldn't. I caught 'im a-sayin' 'e wouldn't mind a big 'orn like that. 'E'll carve it off. Directly I'm gone –'

'Nonsense!' He heard the anger in his voice. 'Belief, man, *belief!*'

Duff stared up at him. He heard two shots, then another and his thoughts returned to Cameron.

'So you had a yarn about death?'

Duff readjusted his thoughts. ''E was quite took with it.'

'Obsessed?'

''E asks me,' 'Ow many men 'ave you killed, my man, an' do you think it right a-killin' your fellow 'umans?''

Guy remembered the look on Cameron's face after he had shot the Arab and a connection flashed. 'Figgy,' he interrupted, 'That begging forgiveness you heard, might it have been for a death? That he brought about?'

Duff's eyes wandered up to the sky again, now darkening. "'E did say, "Duty washes clean all sins – even the takin' of a life," 'e says, an' 'e was carryin' on about duty an' faith, an' reason bein' no fit guide for a man as if 'e *would* believe it.'

As Duff was talking Guy had an image of Suleiman leaving his house that first night in Zanzibar while he was held prisoner, and walking back to the coffee house to see Cameron, *his master in the French intrigue* – Cameron inviting him perhaps to an upstairs room made available by Madame Orientale out of sight of his bodyguards, and killing him to prevent him revealing the plot and his own part in it. He thought back over the events of the night again. He remembered his own conversation with Cameron in the coffee house and the Scot's curiosity about his business with Suleiman, his surprising knowledge of the Arab. He remembered other facts revealed in conversations since – about Suleiman's wives – the little Sambuk out of favour – why hadn't he wondered about it before? He had been captivated by the new world the Scot had opened for him and so impressed by the man's esoteric knowledge of the area, he had conceded him knowledge of all that went on – even inside the walls of Suleiman's house.

The Scot had killed Suleiman and afterwards, struck by terrible remorse at his own treachery, and guilt at the murder, had poured out his soul to his God in the maintop, where he was surprised by Duff.

He went back again over that night in the coffee house; he remembered Cameron slipping into Swahili with Suleiman at one point after the introductions. He had thought it bad form at the time; they had all been speaking English. He had put it down to the Scot's lack of background. That was the point at which Cameron had warned Suleiman about him, and asked him to return afterwards! It would explain the sudden change that had come over the Arab as the gates of the house closed behind them, and his extraordinary lack of curiosity about the message he purported to carry from the 'Lion'. He had gone back to discuss the implications with Cameron. What had Cameron decided? Aware that Guy was British, had he killed Suleiman to prevent the British authorities questioning the Arab? He was struck by a hideous thought. Had he killed to save his, Guy's, life? Or had he, perhaps, just sent him away somewhere? In that case why had it been necessary to beg forgiveness? He remembered, after his night with the little Sambuk in Lamu, Cameron's certainty that she had no husband to accuse her of infidelity. He remembered the odd look in the Scot's eyes when he had tackled him about it.

Duff was looking up at him. 'I can't seem to recollect no more –'

'You've done famously, Figgy. Capital! You've helped a great deal.' He rose. 'I'll come round later. Chin up, Figgy!'

He passed on to look at Harvey, whose shivering fits had been replaced by feverish sweating and an insane restlessness amounting almost to delirium. It was his critical condition that prevented them risking another night march to get Duff to Witu earlier – that and sheer fatigue. The big man was still jerking, mouthing incoherently, his pale eyes staring from under a bandage that had been soaked and tied around his forehead to cool him. He didn't recognize Guy, but muttered, heaving his legs from side to side. Guy found the sergeant beside him.

"'E's 'ad 'is 'quinine, sir.'

'If he lasts this night – I fancy he'll pull through, sarn't. It would be as well to post a man to keep his blankets on.'

'Nobby's took now, sir. The shivers again.'

'Lor'!' He moved along to see Clark, huddled under a pile of blankets, and talked to him encouragingly of Witu as if it were naval hospital and Shangri-la rolled into one. It was neither, he thought as his mind returned to Duff.

'How's Brown getting along?' he asked as they moved away.

'On the mend, sir. 'E can't hold no solids, but 'e's better in 'isself

Guy looked at the sergeant's hard red face, the moustaches still recognizably upraised, the belligerent blue eyes, and thought of his promptness and resource and dependability under the intolerable conditions they had been through. He wanted to express his gratitude and respect.

'We've been very fortunate, sarn't,' he said.

'Sir!'

'A most successful lion hunt!'

The sergeant's eyes went briefly to where Fumo Akari was lying with hobbled legs and bound arms, his dark eyes smouldering, and his body twisted with the wounded buttock uppermost.

"'E didn't 'ave much of a roar did 'e!'

'He made a noise when you poked him!'

The sergeant's lips twitched. 'A touch of encouragement, sir!'

It occurred to Guy as he looked at the tethered 'Lion' that it would not be difficult for Cameron to kill him. He was lying apart from the rest of the marines' blankets, and at night the high *boma* they had erected would hide him from at least some of the sentries. If the Scot had killed Suleiman to cover his tracks, why should he not kill the 'Lion'? Wasn't that just what he had tried to do at Katawa?

The Arab had been in great pain during the march and had said nothing; Guy had not felt inclined to question him at the brief rests. Looking at the resentment in his eyes, he guessed he would get little from him if he did. But it was worth a try before Cameron got back.

He nodded to the sergeant and went across to squat down by the Arab.

'I must apologize for keeping you bound. Our orders are to bring you back to Witu.'

The Arab stared from under heavy lids.

'Had you come to Lamu, none of this would have been necessary.'

'This is your justice?'

'We have to inquire into the murders.'

'Inquire! You burn my town, you kill my people, what you inquire now? Inquire the murder of my vizier?'

'Murder!'

'Me, he try to kill.'

'You know Mr Cameron?'

The fleshly lips twisted up at the corners. 'Who does not know Mr Cameron?'

'Why should he wish to kill you?'

'He talk of justice, too.'

'You have talked much with Mr Cameron?'

The Arab's lids drooped, and a cunning look flitted across his face. 'You take me Lamu?'

Guy knew he would get nothing more from him. 'The decision is not mine.' He rose.

Akari called up to him, 'Your justice – Mr Cameron's justice – is give by gun. My justice is give by gun before your people come.' He raised his voice. 'I speak words of truth, Englishman! Is it not so! As Allah is great –' he yelled as if unable to contain his feelings. 'Your justice is stronger, that is all. I speak words of truth – you listen, Englishman –'

Guy left him. He, too, had thought Cameron meant to kill him.

It was difficult to think of the Scot as a murderer. Yet he would kill for conviction, of that there was no doubt. He tried to think why he should need to kill the 'Lion'.

Start from the beginning. Assume for the moment that he had been correct about Cameron as the mastermind behind the consignment of French arms; he might well have heard of the wrecked Frenchman and her cargo on one of his safaris – might even have chanced upon her himself. Assume that he had done so. He had sent the guns to Fumo Akari with a cock-and-bull letter purporting to be from the French authorities, and naming a courier, Pierre Suleiman, who would encourage the pretence. But why? Not to go against the lewali of Lamu, surely, for the lewali was loyal to the British. Yet that had been the implication in the letter. Was the Scot's whole, intensely British sentiment a masquerade then? He dismissed the idea at once. It was genuine if anything was. The man's desperate anxiety for a British East Africa before the Germans or creeping commercialism took hold of the country was his driving passion. Then why? It made no sense. His thoughts circled. He wondered if he were still on the wrong tack.

He threw himself down on the trampled earth and closed his eyes. He had a feeling that the answer lay just beyond the facts he had marshalled, frustratingly hidden behind his conscious mind. He had found it useful when confronted by similar problems to clear his brain by letting it wander over something entirely different.

He thought of the little Sambuk. Immediately he was back with Suleiman. He squeezed his lids tighter and expunged the man, repeating her name, seeing the lustre of her dark eyes again – 'My husban' call me his little Sambuk. For my marriage I come to him in *Sambuk* from Lamu –'

He sat up. Lamu was the key! He remembered Cameron's intense suspicion of von Pullitz's illness, and the anxiety with which he had greeted the news of the disaffection among the lewali's troops. Lamu was the key because the lewali was strongly in the British camp. It was from Lamu with the lewali's support and on the lewali's behalf – a mutual pact –that Cameron had intended bringing about the downfall of Witu. The 'Lion' was to be encouraged with French arms and worthless promises of French support to move against Lamu. The lewali would be prepared; he would be supported by the British who would never stand by to see him overthrown. A British-Lamu force would march to punish Witu. The 'Lion' would be overthrown; Witu brought within the Lamu influence either by adding the sultanate to the lewali's dominions or by putting one of the lewali's henchmen in place of the deposed sultan. The Germans would be pre-empted at the eleventh hour. Witu would become a British sphere of influence, in Cameron's view a vital staging post to the interior. He heard the Scot's accents, 'Witu will be the furrst rotten apple to fall!'

Unfortunately for him, the 'Lion' had got off before starter's orders and by killing the Germans brought in the very forces Cameron wished to exclude. He remembered the Scot's despair when he heard that Mackenzie had been instructed not to proceed against Witu without a German contingent. On top of that von Pullitz had been plotting to help the lewali's brother Selim to usurp his position. Perhaps with the help of Cameron's own co-plotter, Suleiman – opening up yet another possible motive for Suleiman's murder. In any event, the resulting disaffection amongst the lewali's troops had been yet another critical setback to his plans. Cameron had not only been foiled by ill luck, he had been outmanoeuvred by the Germans.

He had tried to kill the 'Lion' that morning to hide his tracks. He must try again before the Arab could be brought to trial and reveal the extent of the plot – perhaps even before he could be questioned by Saxmundham at Witu. In any case, it would be easier out here before they joined the main body. He would try again tonight – during his own watch while he and Heighurst were asleep.

He rose quickly and walked across to the sergeant.

Guy fought against rhythms of sleep pressing in to submerge him. The firelight was a red haze behind his lids. He had an image of Cameron creeping to the bound 'Lion' and placing a hand over his mouth before inserting a knife between his ribs. The Scot would need to create a diversion first or he was bound to be spotted by the sentries or by the sergeant, whom Guy had told off to watch the Arab. Probably he would wait until nearly the end of his watch in the small hours when sleep would be deepest and the sentries less alert.

Guy wondered how he would be able to keep awake that long. He pretended to stir in his sleep, opening his eyes cautiously as he did so. Cameron was pacing a short beat just inside the *boma*, the firelight tinting the floppy brim of his hat and the creases of his open shirt with flickering red.

He closed his eyes and rolled over on his other side. He heard the Scot's footsteps padding to and fro, the soft call of a sentry who thought he had glimpsed something. He listened. The stillness pressed in. He imagined Cameron and the other sentries peering in the direction indicated. There were no further sounds from the camp. Somewhere a long way off he heard the hideous cackle of hyenas. He wanted to turn and find a more comfortable position but he didn't want Cameron to know that he was still awake. He fought enveloping tides of sleep. . . .

He felt his shoulder being shaken roughly.

'Sir, Mr Greville, sir –' It was the sergeant.

'It's Mr Cameron,' the sergeant whispered.

He sat up.

E s gone.

'Gone!'

"E said 'e was goin' to the 'ead, sir. 'E wouldn't be no more 'n a minute or two, but 'e 'asn't come back.'

'How long ago?'

The sergeant paused. 'Ten minutes.'

Guy doubled it. 'Have you told Lieutenant Heighurst?'

'As you instructed me, sir, to keep an eye on 'im an' –'

'The "Lion" –!' Guy started to his feet.

"E's all right, sir.'

'Are you sure?'

The sergeant nodded.

'Give Lieutenant Heighurst a shake, sarn't. I'll need half a dozen men for a search party.'

The marine hurried off. Guy buckled on his ammunition belt, slipped on his boots and strapped his gaiters over them, by which time Heighurst had joined him with the sergeant.

'Which direction did he take?' Guy asked.

The sergeant pointed towards the outline of a thicket. Beyond it other patches of bush showed dark against the grass plain. If Cameron wished, he could have made clean away behind cover until lost to sight.

Heighurst said irritably, 'What's the fellow playin' at!'

Guy wondered if this was the diversion that had to be created before the attempt on the 'Lion's' life. If so, it was a remarkably clumsy one; practically the whole camp was alerted. It was difficult to think of other explanations; if the Scot were trying to escape before his intrigues were discovered, where could he be making for? It flashed across his mind that perhaps it was neither diversion nor escape, but a gesture to exculpate guilt and too many mistakes.

'Heaven knows!' he said. 'But if you'd care to stand the watch, I'll take a search party out. He can't be far.' A thought struck him. 'He might need help.'

'Why doesn't the goat call for it?'

'I can't explain now, but it's my belief he might make an attempt on the "Lion's" life. I suggest you post a man by him.'

Heighurst rubbed some sleep from his eyes, then stared at him.

Guy bent for his travelling compass. The six men that the sergeant had roused were waiting; after a quick glance along their tired faces, he beckoned them towards the zig-zag exit in the *boma*. They followed silently.

He knew it was hopeless directly they left the camp. Cameron might have gone in any direction and there would be no signs to pick up in the dark; simply finding their own way would present difficulties enough. Yet he had to make the gesture – for Cameron's sake.

His mind strayed back over their brief acquaintance – brief but sharp. And as he thought of his burning patriotism and contempt for the half-measures of the British Government and its servants, his anxiety that the sands were running out for the natives of East Africa and for Great Britain to shoulder her burden and squarely face her destiny out here, the more certain he became that he would not see the Scot again. Cameron was too proud to be brought back to stand trial for doing what he passionately believed was in the best interests of his country and the Africans, too proud to sit listening to counsel picking over the sorry tale of mistakes and misfortune that had marked his attempted intrigue. He thought of the Scot's buoyant mood on that night before they had set out from Zanzibar. 'I see my course clearly through the past as directed by an unseen agency – there is a purpose marked out for all of us –'

What happened to a man of purpose when the purpose failed?

They reached the thicket the sergeant had indicated and made a thorough search all round it and, as he expected, found nothing. From here the Scot might have made off in any direction. He placed half the party under the marine he recognized as 'Shorty' and sent him off westerly to rendezvous back at the thicket if they found nothing within the hour; he took the others easterly. He could tell by their manner they had little expectation of finding anything.

They pushed forward, calling Cameron's name softly at intervals, stumbling in holes, checked by thorns, diverted around seemingly endless lines of impenetrable undergrowth. In the distance the eerie howling of hyenas was broken by bouts of their obscene laughter.

Cameron could look after himself as well as anyone in the bush, but he would need good fortune and unwearying sharpness to survive alone; he would need the will, too. Guy wondered if he had it.

They came to a clearly defined game track running in a north-easterly direction and followed it, able to walk much faster, but neither seeing nor hearing any signs to make them think they were on the right track. After some fifty minutes they came to a solitary palm tree, its pale trunk curving outwards against the night and the stars, the fronds very dark above. Guy stopped and looked at the men. Words were unnecessary. He nodded and they turned and walked back.

Guy waited by himself for a few moments, feeling the hostility of the country around him. He tried to imagine what Cameron was feeling somewhere out there on his own. He should have realized the Scot would take this course; he had always been on his own. He looked up at the night, uttering a prayer for the Scot's lonely soul. In some unaccountable way his own faith was restored.

A breeze stirred the fronds above him. On impulse, he shouted out loud, 'Live I, so live I – to my Lord heartily – to my Prince faithfully.'

He made a half-turn, 'To my neighbour honestly –'

He turned again. 'Die I, so die I!'

The silence pressed in.

Postscript

at Lamu

Dearest Trojan,

We are back again after our march to Witu and I am in one piece tho' amazing tired despite I slept for the best part of a day when we reached the ship. There's so much to tell I hardly know where to start – you'll read some of it in the dispatches. You'll not recognize yours truly who 'sustained his previous character as a most capable and zealous officer!! working heart and soul for the success of the expedition', and who 'with Lieutenant Heighurst led a flying column of marines deep into the sultan's territory to take out the sultan to stand trial, a task which was carried through to success with exemplary skill and determination on the part of both officers in the face of the most severe and trying difficulties'!! Old Sax showed it me as I helped with the other parts!

In truth it's been the most beastly time. We have lost our Ist Lt, 'Jimmy' Smallpiece, he was

419

in command of base camp – he had a broken leg and ulcers all over but *would not* be left out. The camp was attacked by a party of the sultan's warriors and Smallpiece led the Sikhs in a sortie outside the *boma*. The enemy were soon driven off but he would not come back. There's any number of queer stories told by the Sikhs, apparently they couldn't count the number of spears and musket balls lodged in the brave fellow when they found him. This is the queerest part he left *me* his sextant and twelve-bore which Old Sax reckons the two things he valued most in this world. He wrote a note before he left the ship making them over to me. Nothing else. You see what that means, he had no one. The Service was his life and his family. You should have seen the faces of our Jacks when they heard the news, I'd give my ears to hear him damn my eyes just now. His type is the backbone of the Service, Trojan.

More sad news, there's little else – Duff, my dear old Figgy has been left ashore too sick to move. The poor fellow had a musket ball smash his leg in the fighting at Katawa where we went to fetch the 'Lion' back. The surgeon amputated it directly we came back to Witu. Old Sax gave him – Figgy that is – a bottle of his number one champers to help him through it and washed it down with brandy. The stout fellow didn't know where he was by the time we stretched him out on the table. I held his leg. I never wish to hear a butcher's saw again. At all events we burnt the town and took Figgy back to the coast on a donkey the same day. Pray for him, Trojan. You know he carried the horn of a rhinocerus I shot the whole way to Katawa in his blanket pack! And helped me catch a *swallowtail!*. He's somewhat battered – the swallowtail, that is – but I'll not part with him. I fancy he saved our bacon with a tribe of the most fearsome savages you ever saw called the Masai – notorious cattle stealers and skull smashers. They took my swallowtail for a spirit!!! and worshipped *me* for interceding with *Ngai,* that's their supreme God, they have many others of course.

I'm sad to say we've also lost Cameron, the Scot I wrote you of in my last. There's another stout fellow I shall sorely miss. It seems from inquiries Old Sax conducted that Cameron was encouraging the sultan of Witu to make bobbery with the lewali of Lamu so that the lewali would go against him and depose him. The lewali is one of our men, you see, and Witu was in danger of going over to the Germans. The consul out here believes the Germans are sure to take it in any case under the Berlin agreement. But we nipped another German plot in the bud, that is Old Sax did by leaving the *Egret* to look after the lewali while we went up to Witu so the German's favourite, a sneaky customer named Selim couldn't carry through his fratricidal intentions. First set drawn! It's only the first set believe me. Cameron was right when he said there are changes coming over East Africa. You can almost smell it. The Arabs know their time's up, but no one knows who will take their place. The Germans think it's *them*. I wonder! This fellow Mann, my German opposite number who's keen as mustard, I told him they could take the whole of East Africa if they wished but directly we required it we would take it from them and they wouldn't be able to lift a finger. They've no Navy you see. 'Ah,' he said, 'That will not be so easy my friend! *We* shall build a Navy.' 'Then we shall sink it!' I said in the friendliest possible way. 'You English!' he said. 'You think the world will *always* belong to you. But it cannot be. Everything comes up, everything goes down again. The nineteenth century we shall allow you but the twentieth century, my friend, shall belong to Germany!' He meant it too! I'm dead beat, Trojan, I've been propping my eyelids up to get this off by the steamer in the morning – so, good night now –

Guy signed his name, folded the letter and slipped it in an envelope. When he had addressed it and laid it down on the desk, he picked up the crumpled note he had found tucked in his blanket after returning from the fruitless search for Cameron ; he read it through for the hundredth time.

Greville – I conclude from my failure I was mistaken in my original direction – nevertheless I have a certainty there is a purpose for me here. I shall be given a sign. I have no regrets for the death of Suleiman. He was no friend of mine nor of the black people he enslaved but he will give you no further trouble. I placed him the morning after to his neck in the mud flats at low water whence so many of his victims took their last journey in this world. So he joined the majority. I have no remorse. It was you or him. From what I have seen since I have little doubt that I did right. So long – Alexander Cameron.

Guy thought of the repulsive images of the mud flats in his half dreams that morning in Suleiman's house; it would have been about the time the tide was flooding in over the Arab. An association of ideas after Fortescue's remarks – or a brief glimpse inside the Eternal mind? But Cameron had made the choice.

His head reeled. He rested his chin on his hands, wondering as he had so many times whether Cameron had survived the night. Impossible to imagine that fighting spirit laid low. He wished him God speed and purpose, and his mind wandered off to the little Sambuk; he wondered vaguely why he had omitted all mention of her in the letter, and whether Helen would think it odd after his previous silly enthusing. But what would become of her now that her 'husban'' was gone? It was something else he would never know.

Everything was most damnable.

PETER PADFIELD

There was a tap on the door, and in his weary state he looked up, expecting to see Duff. A bluejacket's head appeared around the curtain.

'Captain's compliments, sir, and would you go up to see him!'

9999337R00238

Printed in Great Britain
by Amazon.co.uk, Ltd.,
Marston Gate.